Dear Reader:

It is my pleasure to present *At the End of the Day*, the third and final installment in the *EX-Terminator* series, following *Nothing Stays the Same*.

Author Suzetta Perkins returns with her seventh novel with a cast of popular characters, consisting of couples and friends: the Richmonds, Thomases, Beasleys, Colemans and Broussards. From sexual harassment charges to stage 4 breast cancer to a grand wedding, the novel features all of the elements that make for interesting drama. And, as usual, there's plenty of that!

Thanks for supporting the work of Suzetta Perkins, popular among book clubs and one of my authors under Strebor Books. I appreciate you giving this book a chance, and if you enjoy it, I hope that you will read the author's previous titles: *Behind the Veil*, *A Love So Deep*, *EX-Terminator: Life After Marriage*, *Déjà Vu*, *Nothing Stays the Same* and *Betrayed*.

Peace and Many Blessings,

Zane
Publisher
Strebor Books
www.simonsays.com/streborbooks

ALSO BY SUZETTA PERKINS

Betrayed

Nothing Stays the Same

Déjà Vu

Ex-Terminator: Life After Marriage

A Love So Deep

Behind the Veil

ZANE PRESENTS

At The End Of The Day

Suzetta Perkins

STREBOR BOOKS

NEW YORK LONDON TORONTO SYDNEY

SBI

Strebor Books
P.O. Box 6505
Largo, MD 20792
http://www.streborbooks.com

ISBN 978-1-59309-409-6
ISBN 978-1-4516-6250-4 (e-book)
LCCN 2011938324

First Strebor Books trade paperback edition May 2012

Cover design: www.mariondesigns.com
Cover photograph: © Keith Saunders/Marion Designs

10 9 8 7 6 5 4 3 2 1

Manufactured in the United States of America

For information regarding special discounts for bulk purchases, please contact Simon & Schuster Special Sales at 1-866-506-1949 or business@simonandschuster.com

The Simon & Schuster Speakers Bureau can bring authors to your live event. For more information or to book an event, contact the Simon & Schuster Speakers Bureau at 1-866-248-3049 or visit our website at www.simonspeakers.com.

In dedication to all breast cancer survivors, especially,
Doris E. Rose, cousin
Carolyn M. Smith, co-worker
Robin Roberts, *Good Morning America* anchor

ACKNOWLEDGMENTS

I feel truly blessed to be able to introduce my seventh novel to my wonderful readers. You, the readers, have been a mainstay on this path that I've chosen—a journey that I love with a passion and has allowed me to continue to express myself creatively. Even as you've shared with me, I, too, see how my written work has evolved. And because of it, you've shown me the utmost love and respect as a writer.

I'm forever grateful to my publisher, Zane of Strebor Books International, who continually has been in my corner as I've evolved as a writer. Thank you, Zane, for believing in me. And to Charmaine Parker, publishing director at Strebor and who is now the author of her own literary work, thank you for your unwavering support. I'm also very grateful to Simon & Schuster, especially Yona Deshommes, publicist for Atria Books, for another wonderful year and your unending support. Yona, your support has meant the world to me.

Maxine Thompson, my agent, you've been a friend and a confidante. I can't say the word "success" without uttering your name because you've been such a vital part of it. Thanks a million.

What is a book without a slamming cover? Mine have been exceptional and I owe it to the creative genius of Keith Saunders of Marion Designs. Thanks, Keith, for making my covers hot. I get more compliments about them than I can count. Keep them coming.

I'd like to also give a special shoutout to my webmaster, Scott Murphy, who keeps my website looking awesome, informative, and user-friendly.

To my family, I owe a debt of gratitude for your continued support. You've been right with me every step of the way, and I thank you. To my daughter, Teliza, you've been a wonderful sounding board, helping me to keep things in perspective. To my son, Gerald, or better known to most as J.R., you've always got momma's back. Everyone raved over the trailer you made for my last novel, *Betrayed*. You've missed your calling. Although it didn't get a million hits on YouTube, it went viral in the settings it was meant to. And to my Dad, I appreciate our weekly telephonic book meetings about my novels. Although you might be disappointed about your girl, Peaches, who showed up in my novel, *Nothing Stays the Same* and reappears in *At the End of the Day* after you asked me a thousand times what happened to her, please don't hold it against me if her outcome isn't what you may have hoped it would be. I love you.

I would be remiss if I didn't say how extremely proud I am of my eldest granddaughter, Samayya, who has fallen in Grammy's footsteps, having won the Excellence in Writing Award two years in a row at her elementary school in Enterprise, Alabama. Your stories are wonderful and we're going to finish the book we're writing together, soon. I love you. And I love little Miss Maliah, too. She's my youngest granddaughter.

I'd like to give a great big literary hug to all of the book clubs, my Facebook friends and Fan Club, my Twitter friends, Linkedin friends, the winners of my contests, and all the readers who've supported me time and again. I have so many new friends that I don't know what to do. I appreciate your praise of my work, while some have even put me in the category of some of the great writers, of which I do hope to be like someday. A special shoutout and thank you to Sharon Evans, Mary Evans, LaSheera Lee, Candace Laughinghouse, Marny Marsh-Penix, Cornelia Floyd, Gabrielle Newsam, Cassandra Tripp, Sandy Dowd, Mary Bailey, Marsha McLean, Tanya Williams-Ortiz and Genevieve Knight who continue to support me year after year.

A special thank you goes to Charlotte Morris for the excellent article she wrote about me in Examiner.com entitled "Suzetta Perkins: Living a Literary Dream." A published author herself, Charlotte has been a part of my journey for a long time after meeting her years ago at the National Book Club Conference in Atlanta. She continues to support me in ways unimaginable, and I thank you, Charlotte. You are special to me. To Juanita Pilgrim, I say thank you for suggesting my opening scene in the first chapter of *At the End of the Day*. It worked.

In conclusion, give me a pen, a piece of paper, a computer—desktop, iPad, laptop and let me create. It's been so much fun sharing my thoughts with you, no matter how crazy some of them have been. I love hearing how you can't put the book down because I've got you all tangled up in the suspense—wondering what's going to happen next, who's going to get killed, or how that lying, cheating, no-good-for-nothing so and so is going to get out of a scandal. And in the words of my good friend and phraseologist, Marny Penix, there are probably more skeletal bones in the closet than in a catfish. Whatever your taste in a novel happens to be, thank you for allowing me to intrigue, entice, and keep you company along with your favorite glass of vino or cup of coffee.

PROLOGUE

Steam filled the interior of the off-white-colored bathroom as Denise exited the shower and crossed the length of it in bare feet on the black-and-white marble tiled floor to where she now stood in front of the elongated, textured mirror that occupied two walls. She stared at her image—hair wet and dripping and the one lonely breast protruding from her left shoulder. With her arm slightly raised, she examined her underarm but felt nothing.

Denise waddled to the side wall and flicked on the fan, allowing its coolness to reduce her body temperature. She stood in front of the mirror again, pressed firmly down on her hips, and looked at her breast to see if there were any changes in its size, shape, or if there was any scaliness on the nipple area. Her eyes became fixed and then she let out a large sigh.

She rushed to her oak sleigh bed that sat in the middle of her large master bedroom and lay down on the black and gold silk comforter, throwing her left arm behind her back. With the other hand, she used the finger pads of her three middle fingers and made circular motions across her breast. She stopped, and then felt again as she tried to reassure herself that what she felt wasn't what she thought it might be.

"God, please don't let this be. I'm getting married next week to the love of my life, and I can't offer him a semblance of myself. He's fine with my one breast, but if I take that away from him, he won't even have half a woman."

1

Rain threatened the New York sky. Rain or shine, there was going to be a wedding. It had been postponed six months because Denise Thomas wanted to share her special day close to her family and in the city of her birth rather than in Birmingham, Alabama, where she now lived with her fiancé, Harold, and their daughter, eight-year-old Danica. New York in December would not lend itself to the fabulous venue she'd chosen for her nuptials; however, on this June day that still held promise, she was going to marry her lover, the man she adored, and the cousin of her ex-husband.

Denise sat in the white Rolls-Royce limousine with its spacious, luxury interior flanked by her mother, grandmother, daughter, and two sisters. She watched as her guests arrived dressed in their finest, although it was the middle of the day, taking in the splendor of the crabapple trees, the beautiful violet flowers, and the rest of the floral extravagance that comprised Central Park in the Conservatory Garden. Conservatory Garden was said to be one of the hidden wonders of Central Park and a favorite place to have a wedding.

And then she saw them, Sylvia and Kenny Richmond—Sylvia dressed in an emerald green lightweight wool and silk skirt-suit with faux-jewel buttons; Rachel and Marvin Thomas—Rachel dressed in a stunning red Italian wool crepe suit that boasted a stand up-collar on her raglan-sleeve jacket over a matching classic

skirt; Claudette and Tyrone Beasley—Claudette dressed in a
Caroline Rose mushroom-colored long jacket of Italian polyester
with an oversized collar and a matching scoop-neck tank and
black silk slacks; Trina and Cecil Coleman—Trina in an ultra
conservative charcoal skirt-suit with a classic V-neck collar and
embroidered front panel; and the ever classy Mona and Michael
Broussard—Mona dressed in an Albert Nipon onyx polyester and
wool skirt-suit that looked absolutely fabulous on her. They were
her special family, and they strolled in the garden like they were
New York elitists, each lady's arm seductively looped in the arm
of her husband. They blended well with the movers and shakers
that were New York. It was Harold's family that brought the
'Bama with them, however, it didn't matter to Denise because
this was her day.

Everything was planned down to the minute. The ceremony
was to take no more than forty-five minutes, according to Denise's
wedding planner. Then it would be on to the Roosevelt Hotel for
the fabulous reception that would rival any platinum wedding
that was showcased on television.

It was time. At the direction of the wedding planner, the bridal
party was ushered from the limousine to the elaborate makeshift
staging area to await their cues. Denise could hear the beautiful
melodies of the string violinists floating in the air and could feel
the anticipation of the guests as they waited for her to come down
the aisle. Her mother and grandmother were escorted to their
seats. Her sisters, who served as maid of honor and bridesmaid,
respectively, glided down the aisle, each in knee-length, strapless
lavender satin dresses and diamond lily brooches that served as
hair accents placed in half-moon clusters in their upswept hair.
With long, Shirley Temple curls that hung past her shoulders,
Danica, dressed in a beautiful white satin cream dress with ruffles

at the bottom, waited to walk in before Denise so she could sprinkle lavender rose petals on the ground.

And then they were playing her music. All eyes were on Denise as she floated down the aisle as if walking on air, savoring every minute and in perfect time with the musicians. Her bronze-colored skin was radiant in a sleek satin organza strapless gown that conformed to her body, accentuating her curves like a fine piece of sculpture. The sweetheart neckline wrapped in a beaded overlay draped her shapely breast and her manufactured one like a freshwater mermaid, while the satin skirt was embellished with a beaded lace overlay accentuated with freshwater pearls, Swarovski crystals and rhinestones with sleek satin-covered buttons that ran the length of the entire back of the gown. A ten-carat diamond Eternity necklace decorated Denise's neck. Setting it all off was a bouquet of lavender roses mixed with sweet peas and parrot tulips that Denise clutched tightly in her hand.

Denise's thin lips stretched into an elongated smile when she finally looked ahead and saw Harold waiting for her and Danica standing beside her aunt holding the satin basket that was full of rose petals only moments before. Denise was the happiest she'd be in a long time.

"I pronounce you man and wife," the minister finally said, clad in his black and purple ministerial robe after a twenty-minute heartfelt ceremony that had guests dabbing at their eyes two or three times. "You may now kiss the bride."

Harold held his bride and kissed her passionately, Denise not shy in reciprocating. Loud claps erupted from the two-hundred guests who gave their approval of what they had witnessed. And when Harold and Denise finally parted their lips, the clapping intensified, sounding like thunder. The bride and groom turned to the audience, Denise waving her hand for all to see. They jumped the broom, the fairly new tradition in African-American wedding ceremonies, and walked up the aisle arm in arm, ready to start their brand-new life together. As if on cue, the sun peaked and immersed itself fully from behind the cloud that had threatened rain all morning, lighting up the New York sky in a blaze of glory.

"Denise is absolutely gorgeous," Sylvia said, as she and Kenny, along with the other four couples, filed out behind the wedding party to offer congratulations to the new bride and groom.

"Denise? Shoot, this place is fabulous," Mona said, still gazing at the floral splendor that made the Conservatory so popular among prospective brides. "Yeah, Denise looks pretty, too. Doesn't she, Marvin?"

"Okay, Mona, no need to press Marvin's buttons," Michael said, giving his wife a tiny jab in the ribs.

"It's okay," Marvin said. "Yes, Denise is beautiful and she looks happy, too. See, my boo," he winked at Rachel, "knows that I love her and only her."

"Mona, you did comprehend what my boo said?" Rachel countered, flicking her hand in Mona's direction. "Now shut up and let's get through this and enjoy the rest of the festivities. We know that Denise is going to show out because she wants us Southerners to know how they do it in the Big Apple. That's why she didn't want to get married in Birmingham."

"Hmmph, I think we look better than the rest of her guests," Claudette chimed in. "Maybe Denise doesn't realize that Atlanta is right next to New York when it comes to bourgeoisie."

Everyone laughed.

"You tell them, Claudette," Mona said, trying to quiet the laughter.

"Well, New York has a flare of its own that trumps Atlanta, L.A...." Trina began. Sylvia, Mona, Rachel, and Claudette threw their hands on their hips and twisted their bodies to look Trina in the eyes.

"Says who?" Mona huffed. "I'm from New Orleans, and I know we have a zest for the flare, but since I claim Atlanta as home, I'm here to tell you that it rivals all those big cities you named. Why else would everyone want to move there? You can't tell me that we don't entertain, that we don't live in fabulous houses, have as much disposable income, and can rock fashion right along with these wannabe New York socialites. Look at me. I catered an event for then Senator Barack Obama, who is now the forty-fourth president of the United States. What black socialite in New York can say they've done that?"

"All right, you've made your point," Trina said. "It's that…"

"It's that…nothing," Mona said, cutting Trina off. "I can compete with anybody, no matter where they come from…Los Angeles, Milan, Paris, and New York."

Trina rolled her eyes at Mona, while the others stifled a laugh.

"Okay, ladies, this is Denise and Harold's day," Sylvia said. "She wanted to have her wedding in New York so she would be close to her family. That's all."

"Yeah, right," Mona said, pulling her lipstick out of her purse and dabbing a little on her lips.

"I'm not in it," Kenny said, as Cecil glanced in his direction.

"Me either," Tyrone offered.

"You all know my wife," Michael uttered. "She can't keep her mouth closed and it's always going to flap a mile a minute. Mona didn't mean any harm, Trina."

Trina smirked but changed it to a smile as they approached the newlyweds.

Trina gave Denise an air kiss to each cheek. "You are so beautiful, Denise. God smiled on you today."

"Thanks, Trina. I feel wonderful—got my soul mate and our daughter standing next to me. Look at this rock?" Denise stuck her manicured hand out for Trina to see.

"It's beautiful."

"Five carats, Trina." Denise smiled. "I'm glad you and Cecil could come."

"We wouldn't have missed it for anything in the world."

"Move the line along," Mona called out.

"Wait your turn," Trina shot back.

"Girl, Mona isn't going to change," Denise said to Trina.

"Tell me about it."

Cecil kissed Denise, and he and Trina shook hands with Harold and the rest of the party.

"Look at my girls," Denise said as Mona, Rachel, Sylvia and Claudette surrounded her, leaving their husbands to stand behind them. "You all look fabulous…came to show these New Yorkers a thing or two."

"What did I say?" Mona put in, although Sylvia, Rachel, and Claudette ignored her.

"You are a beautiful bride," Sylvia said as she kissed Denise on the cheek.

"Ditto," Rachel said, taking her turn to give Denise a kiss.

"I've got to give it to you, Denise," Mona said. "You did it like I would have done it. I think both of us would've looked fabulous in that dress, and when you walked down the aisle, you worked it girl…wanted everyone to know that you were the exclusive…the headline news at eleven. I'm glad the rain decided to hold off."

"Well, thank you, Mona. I'll take that as a compliment from you. But I'm so glad you are all here to share in my day. I remember each of your weddings as if they happened yesterday. Why are you being so quiet, Claudette? Give me a hug."

"I wasn't being quiet, although no one can get anything in edgewise with Mrs. Mona Broussard flapping her chops," Claudette said. Everyone laughed. "But you look so beautiful today, Denise. I was thinking that maybe T and I will renew our vows one day and have a big shindig. I can afford it now."

"Yeah, I heard you have a world-class stylin' salon up in one of those fancy buildings in Atlanta with clientele that boasts many of Atlanta's rich and famous."

"She and T are also rocking in a brand new home that none of us have seen yet," Mona said, cutting in.

"So you've heard about me?" Claudette said with a smile on her face. She was surprised to know that Denise had knowledge of her success.

"Claudette, I would've had you do my hair if I was getting married in Birmingham. I love you all." Denise hesitated. "Are you going to give me a hug, Marvin?"

Marvin smiled as Rachel looked on. He placed a kiss on Denise's cheek and shook Harold's hand. "You both look wonderful and happy," Marvin said, not addressing his comment to only Denise.

Denise wondered how Marvin really felt seeing her and Harold together as husband and wife. She missed Marvin in many ways. He was so caring and loving. He'd do anything for her. Maybe if Marvin hadn't been so married to his job, they'd still be married, although it was her selfishness, if she was grown enough to admit it, which pulled her away from him. Then again and truth be told, it was her blatant indiscretion, her infidelity, her being caught with Marvin's cousin, the man who was now her husband, in a compromising position that broke the camel's back. The only thing Marvin was guilty of was planting the seed for what was now a giant Fortune 500 corporation for which Rachel now received the benefits. She wasn't mad because in the end, Denise knew that Harold was where her heart truly belonged.

2

Heads turned and eyes twinkled as the wedding reception attendees entered the ballroom of the Roosevelt Hotel. A giant ice sculpture carved in the shape of two turtle doves greeted the guests at the entrance. The ballroom was transformed into a fairy tale scene with a mixture of Old World intertwined with the glint and glamour of Hollywood. A gilded twenty-seven-foot ceiling magnified by a magnificent eighteen-tier chandelier, iron-laced balconies with arched windows, grabbed the guests' attention right away and left some breathless.

Ten-feet topiaries decorated with berries in hues of red, orange and purple were strategically placed around the perimeter of the room to give it a garden effect. Thirty-two round tables with service for eight were draped with egg-shelled-colored tablecloths with silk lavender overlays. Tall-fluted vases stood in the center of each table filled with a beautiful floral splendor of orchids, peonies, hydrangeas, calla lilies and roses. Fine bone china trimmed in silver sat on each table, and next to each place setting sat a menu that described the four-course meal and a miniature photo frame place card holder for each guest.

Everyone gawked at the splendor of the room. Sylvia and Kenny, Mona and Michael, Rachel and Marvin, Claudette and Tyrone, and Trina and Cecil, guided by a hostess, found their tables. Because only eight were able to sit at one table, Denise was smart enough to put Sylvia and Kenny, as well as Trina and

Cecil, at one table since they were related, and the others at an adjacent table. Their pride swelled when they saw their names on the silver placards.

A band played light jazz as people found their places. Ice sculptures that held large cocktail shrimp were located on either side of the ballroom. Bottles of champagne sat on each table and were quickly replaced when empty.

"Denise outdid herself, sisters," Mona said, still looking around and taking it all in.

"I would have expected nothing less," Rachel said, as she planted a kiss on Marvin's lips. "You're jealous because you didn't have anything to do with this shindig."

"You've got that wrong, Rachel. Every now and then I have to take time out for myself and let someone cater to me. No pun intended."

"Hmmph, if Denise had asked, your behind would have been right up in here orchestrating," Claudette said. Rachel and the guys laughed.

"What are you laughing at, honey?" Mona asked, giving Michael the *I know you aren't agreeing with Claudette* look.

"Because it's true, baby. And you know yourself that Claudette knows what she's talking about." Michael laughed some more.

"What are you all laughing at?" Sylvia asked from her table.

"Don't try and get in grown folks' business," Mona cackled. "It was nothing anyway."

"It must have been about you," Sylvia said, watching the others at the table trying to contain their laugher. "But I'll mind my own business."

"Mona is a trip," Trina whispered to Cecil, Sylvia, and Kenny as two other couples joined their table. "I wanted to pop her a good one this afternoon."

"You've got to ignore her," Sylvia said. "She's crazy, but she's good people."

"Would anyone like some champagne?" Kenny asked. "I'm pouring."

The whole table said yes, and he poured a round.

"May I have everyone's attention?" said the wedding coordinator. "Our wedding party has arrived. I will announce each person as they come in, and they will be escorted to their seats. Please stand when the bride and groom are announced."

Denise's mother and grandmother were escorted to a reserved table. Her sisters, Danica, and the groomsmen were seated at the head table. Harold's and Denise's families took up four or five more tables. Everyone stood as Harold and Denise were announced. They looked so happy, and Marvin was happy for them.

"I'm going to say hi to my sisters," Marvin told Rachel. "You can come if you want to. I'm sure everyone is wondering why I'm sitting away from the family; I think they understand why. I'm sure that's why Mom and Dad didn't come."

"You go on, baby," Rachel said. "I'll speak to them later." Marvin walked away.

"You think Marvin is thinking about the day he and Denise got married?" Mona asked.

"Why would you say that, Mona?" Rachel asked disgustedly.

"I'm sorry, boo. I didn't know that you were still bothered by Marvin and Denise..."

"Mona," Claudette began, "we don't want to hear it. Of course, it bothers Rachel. She went through a lot, and I don't care how long ago it was. My God, for an educated woman, you've got meal for brains sometimes. No pun intended."

"Hmmph. Michael, did you hear how Ms. Claudette shut me down?"

"Seriously, Mona, let's enjoy the evening without all of your commentary. Marvin is a good man. He is married to, and loves, Rachel. End of story."

"Pass the champagne. Maybe I should have sat with Sylvia and Trina. Can't have any fun."

"Mona, this is a happy occasion for Denise," Rachel said on the defense. "She is marrying the man she truly loves and Marvin knows that. Sometimes you need to keep your mouth shut and stop making something where there is nothing. Now pour me some champagne. I'm going to enjoy myself. I didn't get all dressed up to be sitting here talking about stuff that happened in the past. I'm ready to have fun."

"I'll do the honors," Tyrone said. "Hold your glass out, baby," he said to Claudette. "I'm ready to party, too." Claudette gave Tyrone a big, wet kiss.

"I'm ready to eat and get my party on, too," Claudette said.

Mona sat sulking until she took her first sip of champagne.

It was an animated crowd, each enjoying the meal and all the festivities that surrounded a fabulous wedding reception. Besides the meal, the guests were given champagne sorbet served in a lighted ice sculpture. Denise threw her bouquet and Harold shot the garter, both ending up in the hands of some of Harold and Marvin's relatives. And next was the cake.

The white cake with the embossed floral design had a garden theme. It had seven tiers with flowers in red and purple hues cascading around the cake. Denise and Harold cut the cake and daintily stuffed a piece in each other's mouth. And then there was a toast to the bride and groom by Harold's brother that made everyone weep.

"We'll now have the first dance by Mr. and Mrs. Harold Thomas," the wedding planner announced. Everyone clapped for Denise and Harold.

Harold and Denise glided across the room. They stopped and fell into a warm embrace as Peabo Bryson serenaded "Tonight, I Celebrate My Love." Sparks flew between them as Denise locked her eyes onto Harold's and he the same, each placing kisses on the other's lips, oblivious to the two hundred and something guests that looked on. They were in a world of their own, not to be separated by anything or anyone. They held each other tight and danced like it was their last dance. And then the music died, bringing them out of the world they had temporarily been transported to.

Danica stepped on the dance floor and asked to dance with her father and mother. Harold twirled Danica around and then held both of his girls as they danced to the band's rendition of "Fantastic Voyage" by Lakeside. Everyone clapped and soon the floor was flooded with old-school dancing.

Tyrone, Michael and Cecil made a trip to the men's room and then headed for the open bar, glad to be away from the women. As Michael sipped on his Bourbon while watching the dancers on the floor, he felt a nudge on his arm. He looked up in surprise.

"Dr. Michael Broussard, is that you?" the woman asked, holding a glass of champagne.

Michael leaned back to get a good look; her steel-gray eyes held his gaze. He combed over her flawless medium-brown face that was made up tastefully, although, Michael hadn't remembered her wearing that much makeup ever. The woman's hair was swept up on her head and trimmed with a diamond hair clip. She wore a black-and-white, sleeveless after-five dress with a bulging neckline that served a nice helping of breasts that one couldn't ignore. The rest of her body was pure delight, although Michael dared not stare too long. "Madeline...Dr. Madeline Brooks." He smiled, "Fancy meeting you here."

Madeline took a sip of her champagne. "Friend of the bride or the groom?"

"Both. How about you?"

"Denise is my cousin. I'm happy for her; she deserves it."

"It's a small world. And I agree that she does deserve it."

"So what have you been up to, doc?" Madeline asked, moving closer to Michael.

"Well, I'm practicing in Atlanta— Emory University Hospital. Doing well."

Madeline looked him up and down and smiled. "Michael, you are doing well, and I see you still have that smile and those dimples I remember. Now...I like your dome, although I couldn't have imagined you without hair, but it certainly looks good on you. You remind me a lot of the actor Morris Chestnut with a few years on you." Madeline puckered her lips and smiled. "You know what women say about a man who is bald."

"I'm not sure what they say, Madeline, but I do know that while some things haven't changed, nothing remains the same." Madeline looked at him with dreamy eyes and took a sip, which made Michael nervous. "So where are you practicing?"

"I'm still in New York. You won't believe this; I was thinking of moving to Atlanta."

"There's room enough for everyone," Michael said, shifting nervously from side to side.

"Since you're in New York, do you perhaps have time for a night cap and a little catch up...for old time's sake?"

Michael smiled again. "You're as beautiful as I remember, but I'm..."

"Hello, my name is Mrs. Mona Broussard, Michael's wife,"

Mona said with a severe frown on her face, cutting in on the conversation.

Madeline smiled and put out her hand that Mona refused to shake. "Madeline Brooks, Dr. Madeline Brooks. Michael and I were in medical school together at John Hopkins. I couldn't believe my eyes when I spotted him at the bar."

"I don't know what he's told you, but we are a happy family. We have one child, Michael Jr., and we're very happy."

"Okay, Mona," Michael said. "It was nice seeing you again, Madeline."

"You, too, Dr. Broussard...and Mrs. Broussard." And Madeline walked away, glancing back every now and then.

"Madeline? And what took you so long to tell her about us? You were over there yapping with her for more than five minutes. Who was that woman, Michael?" Mona demanded.

"Okay, Mona, that's enough. We were in med school together as she said. Nothing more, nothing less. Guess what?"

"What?"

"She's Denise's cousin."

Mona put her hands on her hip. "Denise's cousin?"

"Look, I didn't know that until tonight, Mona. I only went to the restroom and purchased a drink. I had no idea I was going to run into her. She's only a friend. Now get over it because she means nothing to me."

"So why are you acting like you're irritated?"

"Because I am. Woman, you know I only love you and Michael Jr. You've got that fine house back in Atlanta, shoot, you've got me, and you tell me all the time that I'm fine. Since I've met you, I've looked at no one else. I don't know why you acted out."

"I'm sorry, baby. I guess I look at too much reality TV and she is beautiful, young, and fresh."

"I'm your reality, and don't forget it."

"Kiss and make up, Dr. Broussard? I love you."

"I love you, too, Mona Broussard. Now give me a kiss."

"All right, the bride and groom are going to lead the *Soul Train* line," the announcer said. "If you want to get on board, it's time to get on."

The *Soul Train* line was one hundred persons deep. Harold and Denise led the way with Danica at their heels. Harold did some old school moves and Denise wiggled her hips in a sexy, sensual way that made the men howl. And then she collapsed to the floor.

Harold immediately dropped to the floor and picked up Denise's head. "Denise, what's wrong, baby? Denise!" he shouted.

The music stopped and the room became deathly quiet. Denise's mother nearly ran to where Denise was lying...where Harold was trying to get her to wake up, while Danica stood around crying.

"Call nine-one-one," Harold yelled. "Now!"

3

The reception came to an abrupt halt. The guests stood around gawking or holding their chests in fear. Upon realizing what happened, Michael and Madeline ran to where Harold was on the floor holding up Denise.

"Harold, let me look at her pupils," Michael began. After closer examination, he let out some air. "She's passed out. Madeline, do you have any smelling salt?"

"Yes, I have some in my clutch. I'll get it."

"Is she going to be all right?" a frightened Harold asked.

"From what I can see, yes," Michael replied. "Today has been an exceptionally overwhelming day for her. I'd chalk it up to too much excitement."

"Whew," Harold said, wiping his brow. "I don't know what I'd do without her."

"I've got the smelling salt," Madeline said, pushing through the crowd.

Michael took it and waved it under Denise's nose. She reacted, and then opened her eyes to a very thankful husband and guests.

"What happened?" Denise asked.

"Mommy, Mommy," Danica cried, embracing her mother.

"Baby, I'm all right. I guess too much excitement for one day."

"Oh, baby, you scared me," Harold said, kissing her all over the face. "I'm pulling your *Soul Train* card. We'll let the others dance the night away."

"Good idea, baby."

"Get the *Soul Train* line going," Harold shouted. "My wife only fainted."

The music started again and Denise followed Harold and her mother to the table where her relatives were sitting. "Sorry to frighten you," Denise said after a minute.

"Baby, we're glad you're all right and that there were doctors in the house," Harold said, stroking her face.

"Is Mommy going to be all right?" Danica asked, as if she hadn't heard what her father said.

"Yes, baby, Mommy is going to be all right." Denise held Danica to her heart. "Yes, Mommy's going to be all right." A tear fell from Denise's face.

"Did someone call an ambulance?" the rescue crew called out, rolling a stretcher behind them.

Harold got up and met them. "Yes, we did. My wife passed out, but thank God we had two doctors in the house. It appears she's going to be all right."

"Okay, then," the head rescuer said, "if you don't need us, we're going."

Harold shook the man's hand. "Thank you for coming. Glad we didn't need you." And the rescue squad was gone.

"Hey, cousin," Madeline said, coming over to where Denise was seated. "Glad you're all right."

Denise gave Madeline a big hug. "This is my day. I wanted it to be perfect because this is what Harold and I deserve. I love that man to death."

"I can tell," Madeline said, giving Harold a wink. "You've been holding on to him pretty tight. I didn't know you knew Michael Broussard."

"I knew his wife, Mona, first. She is a big-time caterer in Atlanta. She used to cater events for Marvin's company when I was married to him. Mona is crazy, but that girl knows her stuff, and she is an excellent cook. She recently catered a fundraiser for Barack Obama."

"Get out." Madeline let that roll around in her brain.

"Mona met Michael catering this huge fundraiser for a big philanthropist in Atlanta. I forget their names, but they own a television station or something in Atlanta."

"You must be talking about the Gordons. I know Kohara; she's a breast cancer survivor and a true champion of breast cancer awareness. She has fundraisers all the time."

"Yes, that's her," Denise said, wanting to change the subject. "So how do you know Michael Broussard?"

"We were in medical school together." Madeline looked into the crowd and saw him cuddling up with his wife. "He's as fine now as he was then."

"Well, he's happily married and you don't want to go up against the big, bad wolf. Mona will eat you alive."

"I've met her. Doesn't seem like his taste in women."

"Well, Michael Broussard loves him some Mona. They've been married for almost six years. And they have one child."

"Yeah, I was given the bio earlier this evening." Madeline sipped her champagne.

"As I said, they are happily married." Denise watched Madeline with interest. "I know you're not going to try and stir up anything."

"No, not intentionally. I've already hit that." Denise's mouth flew open. "Close your mouth, cuz. And it was very good."

"Look here, Madeline, don't you go meddlin'. Those are dear friends of mine. Mona's teeth are worse than any shark's bite. Ask anyone."

"I'm not scared of her," Madeline replied in a daze, still looking over at Michael. "She's not even competition," Madeline said under her breath.

"Here's some punch for my ladies," Harold said, handing a glass to Denise, Madeline, and Danica. "What are you ladies talking about? It must have been heavy from the look on Madeline's face."

"She's got a Jones for Michael Broussard."

"You need to leave that alone," Harold retorted.

"Remember, I saved your wife's life tonight."

Harold gave Madeline a look. "I'd expect nothing less." Harold dismissed Madeline and looked at Denise. "Are you all right, baby?"

Denise kissed Harold. "I'm fine, baby. Glad to have you by my side. Today is still perfect."

"It certainly is, Mrs. Harold Thomas. Let me go over and talk to Marvin. He's been a little standoffish tonight."

"You love him, don't you?" Denise asked.

"He's my cousin, my best friend. I can't imagine how he may have felt today seeing me marry his former wife. I thought we had moved on, but maybe the wound was too deep to forever forget. I'll be right back."

"So you don't think I can give Mona a run for her money?" Madeline asked Denise when Harold left the table.

"It's on you. I hate to see you end up in one of her Cajun concoctions because that woman will slice and dice you to your very core if you mess with her husband. I wouldn't play with that fire because I already know how that story is going to end."

"Denise, do you have to be so dramatic? I was only reminiscing. Michael made it perfectly clear to me in so many words that he was unavailable, and I'm not a home wrecker."

"That's better," Denise said, finally smiling.

"But make one wrong move Mona Broussard, and it's on," Madeline muttered under her breath. "I'm moving to Atlanta."

4

The plane ride back to Atlanta was uneventful, except for the ladies recounting over and over the excitement that Denise caused by passing out.

"She passed out because she realized she was a Thomas for the second time." Mona laughed and smacked Rachel's hand.

"No, she passed out," Sylvia began, "because it dawned on her what that bourgeoisie affair was really going to cost Harold and what she could've done with that money." Everyone laughed. "I'm not mad because I had the time of my life. It was definitely first-class all the way."

"Sylvia, I can't believe you're buying into this Denise back-stabbing mess," Claudette said. "But if you ask me, Denise wanted to show our Rachel what it was like to wed a real Thomas."

"Shut the hell up, Claudette," Rachel stammered. The ladies were in an uproar, including Rachel. Even other passengers on the plane glued their ears into the conversation.

"Well, I need a drink," Kenny said. "I can't believe you women can't go anywhere without causing any drama."

"Drama? And the Drama Queen Award goes to," Rachel began, "to...Mona Broussard!" Mona stood up and took a bow.

"She won that hands down," Claudette said.

"But you saw how I took care of Dr. Madeline Brooks, didn't y'all? Got all up in my man's face with that low-cut dress, showing those ancient titties. She might have been pretty and all, but she's got age on her. Anyway, Michael only has eyes for the Drama Queen."

"Got that right, baby," was all Michael would say.

"But I saw that Madeline woman stealing glances at you after the fact," Tyrone put in.

"Ohhh," Kenny said, slapping Michael with a high-five. "You're the man of the hour."

"Cut that crap out," Mona said. "And no one asked you anything, T."

"Cecil, Trina, are you sleep back there? I know you've got twenty cents to add," Kenny said.

"I'm not touching that with a ten-foot pole," Trina said. "I've had enough of Mona for one weekend."

"Okay, sistergirl," Mona said. "I was a little rough on you, but you know I love you, Trina."

"You promise to make me a big pot of gumbo and some jambalaya when we get back to the ATL?"

"Okay, Trina. I said I was sorry. You've lost your mind. Besides, what you want is expensive. Do you know what a pound of crab cost? But that sounds like a plan—girl's night out at Trina's house. I'll do it. Good idea, Trina."

"We best be invited," Marvin said. "I'll give you fifty dollars if you make enough for the men."

"I'll add another fifty," Cecil said. "We'll need enough to last the whole night." Everyone laughed.

"You're eating also Michael, Kenny, and Tyrone. How much are you all putting in the pot?" Mona hollered.

"Just our fingers, baby," Michael said, and the whole plane roared.

"But you have to remark on how beautiful Denise and Harold were on their wedding day," Rachel admonished. "They were so happy." She turned and looked at her husband. Marvin smiled. "I think this time, Denise did it right."

"I couldn't agree more," Mona said, with a faraway look as if recapturing the moment in her mind's eye. "I couldn't hold back the tears when they said I do."

"I didn't know Denise that well," Trina said, "but she looked radiant and sure as hell knew how to throw a wedding party."

"Amen to that," Cecil chimed in.

"She's come a long way," Claudette said.

"She sure has done that," Sylvia said, reflecting. "I laugh every time I think about the time she busted into our EX-Files meeting."

"Now that was hilarious," Mona put in.

"Not to everyone," Marvin interjected. He pulled Rachel toward him and kissed her. "My baby was about to beat Denise's ass, but she's a lady."

"What's that supposed to mean?" Mona called out.

"You won Drama Queen all by your damn self, Mona," Claudette laughed. Mona pointed a wicked finger at Claudette.

"Denise has endured a lot more than we'll ever know," Sylvia said. "And Marvin is a class act. Won't you agree, Rachel?"

"He is. When Denise announced that she had breast cancer, my Marvin was Johnny on the spot, ready to come to her rescue. Even though I was mad as hell, it was a turning point in mine and Marvin's relationship because, at that moment, there was no doubt in my mind what kind of man Marvin really was. I'll always love him for that."

"Yeah, and then the EX-Files rallied around Denise during her operation," Mona spoke up to make sure her point got across.

"But she fought a valiant fight," Sylvia said softly. "She beat breast cancer and Marvin and Harold were there to help her through. And fast-forward to yesterday. Denise deserved her day. It was beautiful in every way."

"You're right, Sylvia," Rachel quipped. "It was beautiful."

5

"Hey, baby, how are you feeling?" Harold asked as he unwrapped the towel that had draped his wet body, letting it fall to the floor, after which he plopped down on the bed next to Denise.

Denise looked up at Harold with hungry eyes and sat up on her knees. She placed her arms around his neck and kissed him gently, tasting his tongue and sopping up all the energy he cast her way. She gazed upon the man who was now her husband, his taunt body a true work of art, even for his forty-two years. His chest rose from his body like hills made for hiking, its thick terrain a treasure for anyone who wanted to make the climb.

Denise allowed her hands to climb across and down Harold's chest until she felt the bumps in the road which she squeezed, causing his manhood to swell at the bottom of the hill. Denise smiled.

"I guess you're feeling much better, Mrs. Thomas," Harold said, as he took in the swell of her one breast, not in the least bit disturbed by her missing one. Denise smiled again.

Harold pulled Denise to him, reducing the gap between them. Their bodies melded together like liquefied gold, each shouting the other's name as the heat between them intensified. They pawed and caressed each other like they were new discoveries—a new archeological find, leaving no road unturned.

As the beast in Harold roared within him, he mounted his prey and greedily stroked her fires. They'd been lovers for many years, but today was extraordinary. They had climbed some large mountains together and got over them intact. And yesterday was like bread from heaven when Denise finally became his wife and formed their perfect union. Harold filled Denise's cup until it overflowed, then lay limp as the sweat poured from his body.

With her eyes wide open, Denise ran her hand through Harold's silky and curly mane. Splashes of silver were sprinkled throughout his hair like new, baby sprouts after a seed has been planted. She could hear Harold's heavy breathing, which indicated he'd fallen asleep. Tears fell from her eyes as she fought back the urge to scream out loud.

How was she going to tell her husband that she'd found a lump in her good breast? Hadn't she gone through enough? Hadn't she paid the price for her sins? They were supposed to be enjoying the rest of their lives together with their daughter, Danica, and now...now when she had faith enough to believe that she and Harold had weathered the storm and found peace in the valley, it had come down to another test...possibly cancer. Even after being faithful in getting her mammograms each year—well, maybe that wasn't the total truth—but she didn't want to believe that this was her fate.

She wiped her face and resolved to fight the demon that possessed her body. She fought a valiant fight before and won, and with all of her sisterfriends to help her through, she was going to make it. But Denise wasn't sure she could tell them. And her poor daughter. Danica was the love of her life; there was no way God would take her away from her baby.

Harold stirred and rolled over. "Oooh, I fell asleep." Denise smiled at him. "Girl, you are so radiant today, and you sure put a hurting on me. Our lovemaking has never been so intense. Your body shook like a tree in a hurricane."

"And baby, you came like a super-active volcano, or was it an earthquake?" Denise laughed.

"How did it sound?" Harold teased.

"Rumble, rumble, rumble, rummmmmmmmmmmmmble!"

Harold laughed.

"Are you laughing at my interpretation of your climax? I really thought King Kong was in the room," Denise said as she broke out laughing.

"I'll say this one thing, you sapped all of my energy, girl. I mean it, Denise. We were acting as if this was going to be the last time we would make love to each other."

Denise shot up and flew from the bed with Harold right behind her. She went into the bathroom and closed the door before Harold was able to get a foot inside.

"Did I say something wrong, baby?" Harold asked from outside the door. "Let me in, Denise. Tell me what's wrong."

Silence. Harold put his ear to the door.

"Come on, honey. Tell me what's going on. I'm sorry if I said anything that offended you."

After a few minutes, Harold returned to the bed and sat on it with a puzzled look on his face. He was glad Danica was with Denise's sisters. He sighed. "Something isn't right," he muttered to himself. "I've got to find out what it is."

6

"Hey, Sylvia, this is your girl, Rachel."

"Girl, I know who this is. Your name is written all over my caller ID. Whatcha got cooking, sistergirl?"

"Since the kids are at pre-school, why don't we go shopping and have a little lunch somewhere?"

"That sounds good, unless you're going to act a fool. Don't have time for any of your mess today. I still haven't gotten over our shopping trip a year ago that ended up with the po-po sticking their guns and nightsticks up in your face. Could of gotten us both killed."

"If you had stayed your ass in the car, you wouldn't have ended up in my mess."

"Rachel, please. I was in it from the jump. If I had somewhere to dump your ass, I would have done so before we got to the bank that day."

"Girl, that was a crazy day. I cussed out Marvin and his secretary, Yvonne…"

"And don't forget the cashier at Macy's," Sylvia reminded her.

"That heifer deserved to be cussed out…acting like I was a common criminal because my card was declined and I made her try it again two or three more times." Rachel and Sylvia laughed.

"But that's behind us now," Rachel continued. "Marvin and the company are back on their feet, thanks to your man, Kenny."

"I would have never thought that Marvin and Kenny would have been a business match," Sylvia said. "But their partnership has survived because they believed and had faith in each other. They do have a good support staff."

"Watch and see if Harold doesn't come and join the group. I think he hinted to Marvin a couple of times during his and Denise's wedding reception that he'd like to rejoin the company."

"That would be great, I guess. Has Marvin told Kenny?"

"I'm sure he will. You're Kenny's wife. Why don't you ask him?"

"I will," Sylvia said. "Look, I was also thinking about you. If Harold and Denise should relocate to Atlanta, are you going to be okay with them being so close?"

"Sylvia, if you've noticed anything at the wedding, you should've been able to discern that Denise is now a happily married woman. She now has the man of her dreams. Somehow I feel that she and Harold were always a good fit; unfortunately, Marvin met her first, fell in love, and married her. And then as fate would have it, Marvin catches Denise with Harold. But God is good because now that good man Denise threw away is my man. I love Marvin so much, Sylvia."

Sylvia smiled. "I know you do, sistergirl, just like I love myself some Kenny Richmond. We all have been fortunate to find the man of our dreams. Mona—she made the catch of the day when she caught Michael. And then there's Claudette and T getting back together the way they did. There's something about love."

"Poor Ashley."

"Yeah, she's our sistergirl, too. Hopefully, something good will happen so that she'll get released from prison early. I wonder what Claudette would do if Ashley wanted her child back?"

"Tell her hell no." Rachel laughed.

"That's not funny, but you're right. Claudette nursed Reagan the day she left Ashley's womb. I'd say that Claudette is Reagan's momma."

"Amen to that."

"Okay, Rach, let's go. I'll pick you up in a few minutes. See if Mona wants to go. We know that Claudette is hooking up some hair in that high-rise building and Trina is laying down the law on somebody."

"You're right about that. It's been a couple of weeks since we've gotten back from New York, but I haven't forgotten that Mona said she was going to fix us some New Orleans cuisine. We've got to get Trina to commit to a date so we can have our dinner at her house. That's your husband's cousin. Handle it."

"Look, girl. I got that. Now get your rear in gear and let's go. And don't forget to call Mona."

"All right, Sylvia. Give me fifteen minutes. Honk the horn when you pull up."

"Okay. I'll see you in a few. Bye."

Code Blue, stat, room 313, the announcement came across the loudspeaker. Doctors and nurses alike moved feverishly through the corridor to help the patient in 313 who suffered a cardiac arrest. Dr. Michael Broussard rushed into the room to assess the situation, moving everyone out of the way, and finally deciding to intubate the patient.

One intern, two doctors, and several nurses moved back as Michael took charge and worked his magic. Tension was felt around the room, as the intern rubbed his knuckles against his lips and the nurses curled their lips up into tight knots. Watching the line of death caused a thin veil of sweat to cross the faces of these highly trained medical experts because their patient was no ordinary patient. She was the wife of Sterling Alexander, CEO of one of the largest banks in Atlanta. He was a powerhouse in the banking world and could make or break a nation. He'd also given millions to the hospital for research, and saving his wife's life would keep the gifts coming.

After the third assault on the patient, the straight line began to pulsate on the monitor, making beeping sounds that were music to everyone's ears. Cheers went up into the air. The intern ran out to see if Mr. Alexander had made it to the hospital, wanting to be the first person to give him the good news.

Michael made sure Mrs. Alexander was stable and doing okay. He waited for her husband to arrive so that he could get his approval to move forward with a multiple bypass. As he waited, one of his colleagues entered the room and motioned with his finger for him to come out. Michael was utterly stunned and taken aback when he walked out of the door into the face of Dr. Madeline Brooks.

"Dr. Michael Broussard, let me introduce you to our new doctor on staff, Dr. Madeline Brooks, although she tells me she needs no introduction," Dr. Kyle Bennett said. Dr. Bennett was one of Michael's good friends and a colleague. He looked forty, although he was forty-eight, with a head full of blond hair that he colored every other week. He was physically fit, and anytime he could get away from the hospital during the winter months, he could be found in Aspen on the ski slopes.

Madeline shook Michael's hand. Her hands were soft and she held his longer than he liked. Her hair was pulled back into a bun and accentuated the lean look of her oval face and thin lips that were painted with a clear lip gloss. He jumped ever so slight when she said his name. "Dr. Broussard, it's so good to see you again. I understand you saved a very important life today."

Trying to regain control, Michael spit his words out. "If I may correct your statement, all of my patients are very important to me. And how are you, Dr. Brooks?"

Madeline tried to hide the scold and decided to let it roll off of her shoulders. She smiled. "I'm doing well, Dr. Broussard."

7

"Hey, Rachel."

"Hey, Sylvia. Kiss, kiss. Mona is going to meet us for lunch."

"Good. Trina called and said she had time to meet us before she had to be in court."

"We haven't had a good sister girlfriend outing in awhile."

"I hope we nail down our gumbo night. We ought to be able to come up with a date between the four of us."

"I agree. Sylvia, I've been thinking a lot about Denise. Something's going on with her, but I can't put my finger on it."

"You say she may be coming to Atlanta. Do you think that may have something to do with it?"

"I'm not sure. Gauging from Marvin's conversation with Harold, they seem to be doing all right. I heard Marvin mention something about Denise not having a lot of energy."

"You didn't discuss it after he got off of the phone?"

"Girl, Marvin was onto another phone call, and I forgot. You better watch the road."

"Well, you need to sit back and be quiet for a minute. Your conversations always cause me to have to turn my head. Rachel, I'm so glad things have gotten better for our guys and the company, despite the recession."

"Yeah, thank God that these young kids will scrape three nickels together and buy some electronics no matter what."

"It's not only the young kids but grown folks, too—iPods, iPads, this, that, and the other—enough to boggle your brain."

"My man is focused and he and Kenny aren't going to let what happened to Thomas and Richmond Tecktronics, Inc. befall us again. To think the company my husband built from the ground up was almost taken over by those bullies."

"Thanks to Cecil for being the best damn corporate attorney in the world."

"Amen to that. God is good, Sylvia. Hey, you're going to miss your turn off."

"I don't know where my mind is today. I told you to stop talking, Rachel."

"My mouth is shut."

Sylvia drove on, as the ladies took a time out for private thoughts. It was a pretty day in Atlanta and all was well.

"May I say something, Sylvia?"

"What is it, missy?"

"I love you, Sylvia."

"I love you, too, Rachel."

"Look, there's Mona getting out of that big Suburban."

Sylvia found a park, and she and Rachel headed into the restaurant. They found Mona, who was already seated. Sister hugs were passed around.

"So good to see my girls," Mona said with a smile. "I need intelligent grown folk to talk to every once in awhile." The girls laughed.

"Oh, here comes Trina," Sylvia said. She waved her hand in the air until Trina finally saw her.

"Hey, sisters," Trina said, blowing air kisses. She sat down next to Mona. "You don't mind, do you, Mona?"

"Come on, Trina. You still hating on me for acting ugly at Denise's wedding?"

"Girl, I'm not mad at you, but I will be if you don't get my pot of gumbo and jambalaya cooking on the stove sometime soon." Everyone laughed.

"Give us a date that we can meet at your house and it will be a done deal," Mona said.

"How about two Saturdays from now?" Trina asked. "It'll be our summer garden party."

"That sounds good," Rachel said. "And make plenty of Hurricanes, Mona."

Mona was quiet. She looked down at her menu and tried to push back the tears.

"Oh, I'm sorry, Mona," Rachel said.

Mona waved her hand. "It's okay; I'm all right."

"What's wrong?" Trina asked, not understanding Mona's sudden mood.

"Next month will be the Katrina anniversary," Sylvia said. "Mona and Michael were down there when the hurricane hit and Mona lost her parents. August is always a hard month for her."

"I'm so sorry, Mona," Trina said, rubbing her back.

Mona laid her head on Trina's shoulders. "I miss them so much," Mona said. "I can't help but think about all the years I wasted not talking to my parents. And the moment we make amends, the hurricane ends their lives." The tears fell.

"You'll never know why it happened as it did, but thank God that you and your parents were able to make it right," Sylvia said.

Mona held her head up. "You're right, Sylvia. To think it was at Michael's suggestion that I went to New Orleans to meet his folks—but was able to make peace with my mother and father."

"Stop beating yourself up," Rachel chimed in. "As Sylvia said, you made it right."

"Thank you all for being here," Mona said, "although if Rachel hadn't mentioned Hurricanes, we'd most likely be talking about something else. But in two weeks, I'll be ready."

"If you need our help, let us know," Sylvia put in. "I'll write you a check before we leave. I want to eat good."

"Don't forget to tell your men folk, Rachel and Trina, about the fifty dollars they said they were going to give me for making extra." Mona laughed.

"I'll write a check now for Cecil," Trina said, pulling out her checkbook. "I may have a hard time getting it back, but it's all good."

"I know that's right," Rachel said. "Let me write you a check, too. Don't want you hunting us down."

"Is your check going to be good, Rachel?" Mona said with a straight face. "I haven't forgotten how you acted when your credit cards were on lockdown."

"You weren't even there, Mona. Sylvia had to endure my crisis at the bank. In fact, we were talking about that today."

"What are you all talking about?" Trina asked.

"Girl, you've got to catch up," Mona said. "Do you remember when Marvin almost lost the company? Well, he hadn't told anybody, including his spend-every-dime wife, Rachel."

"Please," Rachel said. "Let me tell my own story. Anyway, Sylvia and I were out shopping and my credit cards were declined everywhere we went. The killer was when I went to the ATM and tried to withdraw some money and the machine said there wasn't any. I beat that teller machine with my purse and acted as if the world had come to an end."

"Let me take the story from here," Sylvia interjected. "Trina, the police came and was about to take her sorry ass to jail. They had guns pointed at her. I tried to run interference, but they acted as if I was part of Rachel's mess and started to point their guns at me. But our girl, Rachel, acted so ugly and the rest of the day went downhill from there. I took her to lunch and she cut up in Steak and Ale. I don't even go there anymore."

Everyone laughed. "Rachel, you were a hot mess," Trina said.

"But that's how Cecil came on the scene. Marvin's world was crumbling all around us, and he hadn't let me in on it. He was too proud, but thank God we're doing all right. Now let's eat and talk about something else other than me."

"I agree," Sylvia said.

"One more thing," Trina interrupted. "Peaches' trial will be coming up soon. Guess who she has for an attorney?"

Rachel sat a moment and tried to think.

Sylvia looked at Trina. "Not Ashley's father?"

"Yep, Attorney Robert Jordan. If you remember, Peaches worked for his firm."

"I still can't imagine Jordan representing that witch," Mona said.

"It doesn't make sense," Sylvia cut in. "Jordan hated that Ashley married William because he was black. Why would he bend over and take Peaches' case?"

"That's a good question, Sylvia," Trina said with a sigh. "I've asked myself the same question once I learned that Jordan was going to represent Peaches. My gut feeling tells me there may be an underlying motive. What that is, we may never know."

"I'm glad they caught her behind after she escaped from that hospital," Rachel said. "Lord, the world wasn't safe with her out there in it. But what if Jordan gets her off?"

"We have to pray that he doesn't," Trina remarked. "Peaches has done some crazy stuff, to include killing her husband. I'm sure she's going to get time."

"If I wasn't a good person, I might have pointed that trigger at Peaches' heart and let her have it."

"No, you wouldn't have, Rachel," Sylvia said, giving her a harsh look. "You handled it the way you were supposed to. Okay, ladies let's eat and talk about something more pleasant, like gumbo in two weeks."

Trina licked her lips. "My mouth is watering."

8

Thomas and Richmond Tecktronics, Inc. had bounced back with a vengeance along with the confidence of its Board of Directors. The company's finance team and their internal audit system worked hard to ensure that the company's health and welfare were on sure footing. Transparency became the company's mantra. No more hidden secrets and all functions had a check and balance system.

Marvin Thomas stopped writing at the sound of the intercom. "Yes, Yvonne?"

"Mr. Richmond has arrived for his meeting."

"Thank you, Yvonne. Send him in."

Yvonne had been a faithful employee and executive assistant for more than eleven years. She was an asset to the company, and Marvin was grateful that through all of the company's woes, she didn't jump ship.

Marvin stood up and extended his hand to Kenny when he walked through the room. "Kenny, my man. What's up, partner?"

"You're up, partner." Kenny and Marvin slapped hands again and broke out in laughter.

"This feels so good, Kenny. The company is back on track and has received a clean bill of health."

"Marv, it's because you believed. Those were some shaky and scary days awhile back, but I'm so glad God saw fit to give us a second chance."

"I couldn't have done it without you, Kenny. I'm so fortunate to have a partner like you. That was God's blessing to me."

"I'm glad to be part of the team. So what is it you wanted to talk to me about?"

"Harold."

"Oh, yeah, I remember you mentioned something about him coming to work here."

"Yes, he wants to rejoin the firm."

Kenny's eyes lit up.

"Not as a partner," Marvin said, as if he could read Kenny's thoughts.

"The question is how do you feel about it? He was a great asset to us when we needed his help getting the company back on track, but at the end of the day, it boils down to how you feel about your cousin being in your face twenty-four-seven."

"To be honest, Kenny, I'm over all that stuff that was between me and Harold. The past is the past."

"Okay, Marvin, you're talking to me. Harold is now married to your ex-wife, the one he had an affair with while the two of you were business partners."

"You're right and I've thought about it. That's why it has taken me awhile to decide what to do. I've invited Harold here today to give him our decision. And besides, I have a wife now, and if you haven't noticed, she's the finest thing on this earth."

"Marv, my man, I'm going to leave that alone. I've known Rachel a long time, and she's my wife's best friend. Let's get back to business. It seems that you've made up your mind. What kind of salary do you propose to give him?"

"I think we can start him off with ninety thousand."

"Does he have any idea what you're thinking of paying him?"

"This is what he asked for, Kenny...at least to start."

"We've cleared it with finance?"

"Yes."

"Marvin, don't get me wrong. I know that you started the company, but now we're partners. I would have felt better if you would've come to me as soon as Harold made this proposal to you. To me, you've made all the decisions in advance and I'm only giving you its blessing. We've worked too hard to wind up in the mess we were in last year."

Marvin stared long and hard at Kenny without saying a word. Kenny didn't flinch. "You're right, Kenny. I owe you that."

"You owe the company and the Board of Directors who stood behind you. I like Harold. We had some one-on-one time, especially when we were trying to shake down Peaches."

"Don't mention that woman. I believe her trial should be coming up soon."

"Anyway, Marv, I concur with your decision to hire Harold. I think he'll do a good job for us."

"Thanks, Kenny. I appreciate you for being real." Kenny nodded his head.

"Hold on a minute; it's Yvonne." Marvin hit the intercom. "Yes, Yvonne?"

"Mr. Harold Thomas is here to see you."

"Thank you, Yvonne. Send him in."

Harold came through the door looking well rested in a two-piece Armani suit. He was a year or two older than Marvin, but the family resemblance was there. It appeared he had been eating well, a testament that married life agreed with him. Tinges of gray streaked his hair, but he looked good for his age.

"Come on in, Harold," Marvin said, coming around his desk to greet his cousin. Marvin shook his hand and gave him a big slap on the back. Kenny did likewise.

"Good to see you guys," Harold remarked, sitting down in a chair next to Kenny, while Marvin made it back to his seat.

"I see you've put on a couple of pounds since you said, *I do*," Marvin kidded, making the conversation light.

"Yeah, just a couple. I gained a few pounds before we got married, if you want to know the truth."

"So how is Denise?" Kenny asked.

"She's doing pretty well, although lately she doesn't seem to have a lot of energy. In fact, she had an appointment this morning with the doctor. I should be getting a call from her sometime soon."

"Harold, I've discussed your desire to rejoin the company with my partner." Marvin pointed at Kenny. "We are both in agreement that having you on our team would be an asset to the company. We appreciate all that you did to help us with our accounting situation and such when the company was going through the takeover crisis, and we're glad that you want to be of service to Thomas and Richmond Tecktronics. So, if you want to join the team, all you have to do is say yes."

Harold smiled and shook his head yes. "Marvin, Kenny, I want to thank you both for this opportunity. I've missed being a part of this firm, but I want you to know that I'm fully committed to doing the best job possible for the health and welfare of the company. I owe a lot to my cousin, Marvin," Harold said, slapping Kenny's arm, then looking back at Marvin.

"Your salary is as discussed," Marvin said, "and the only question remains is when do you think you can start?"

"I'd like to relocate as soon as possible. I've already folded my operation in Birmingham. It's only a matter of contacting the movers and loading up my household goods. Let's say I can be here a week from today."

"Sounds good," Kenny said.

"Harold, if you and Denise would like to stay with Rachel and me until you get a place, you're more than welcome to do so. I haven't checked with the keeper of the house, but I'm sure she won't mind."

"I really don't want to be a bother, Marvin. And I'm not sure that's a good idea."

"You're not a bother. You're family. Hold on, it's Rachel calling now on my private line. Good timing. Hey, baby, what's cooking?"

"Hey, baby," Rachel said. "Mark your calendar. We will be eating gumbo and jambalaya at Trina and Cecil's house two Saturdays from now."

"Got it, baby."

"And you owe me fifty dollars."

"Fifty dollars for what?" Harold and Kenny laughed in the background.

"What is all that laughing going on, Marvin?" Rachel wanted to know. "Are you in some bar on your lunch hour?"

"Girl, quit. No, Kenny and Harold are in my office. Now why do I owe you fifty dollars?"

"Didn't you tell Mona that you were going to give her fifty dollars for making some extra gumbo? And tell Kenny his cell phone is about to ring."

She's a brick house, she's mighty mighty... "My wife," Kenny explained. Marvin and Harold began to roar with laughter, catching their stomachs.

"Did you hear me, honey?" Rachel said, her voice raised and interrupting the laughter.

"Yes, I did. I'll have your fifty dollars waiting for you when I get home. In fact, I'm going to take you and Serena out to dinner tonight."

"I'm full."

"Eat a salad."

"Okay, baby. Love you. See you tonight. And you boys behave."

"Love you, too, Rachel."

"Tell Harold and Kenny I said hi."

"I will." Marvin hung up the phone and looked up at Harold and Kenny, who was on the phone.

"I think Kenny got the same message you did," Harold said to Marvin and doubled over again with laughter.

Kenny hung up his BlackBerry. "That was Sylvia telling me about our date with gumbo and jambalaya."

"You didn't have to pay your wife fifty dollars?"

"Did you hear me offer up fifty dollars?"

"Well, that isn't right," Marvin declared.

"Look, Sylvia paid our fifty dollars. You know that my dough is her dough. My baby knows she can get most anything out of me whenever," Kenny said.

"You all are making me hungry," Harold said. "How about I take you both to lunch? The Prime Meridian downtown sound okay?"

"Sounds good to me," Marvin said. "And by the way, you and Denise should be here in time to join us at Trina and Cecil's for some good food."

"I was waiting for you to ask." Harold laughed.

"Put it on your calendar—two Saturdays from now," Kenny said. "I'm ready for my gumbo."

"She's a brick house; she's mighty, mighty..." Marvin and Harold sang in unison before they broke out in laughter.

"Sylvia is my brick house," Kenny said. "And don't you forget it."

Laughter was all that could be heard.

9

H arold turned his Escalade into the parking garage across from the CNN Center. Tourists were everywhere, breathing in Atlanta as if it were the Mediterranean Sea or the Eiffel Tower in Paris. Once inside the CNN Center, light bulbs flashed as tourists clicked the shutters on their cameras.

The Prime Meridian was one of Harold's favorite places to dine when he lived in Atlanta. He'd taken Denise there on a couple of occasions and she fell in love with it. In the evening, they served dinner by candlelight and offered the most romantic setting.

The gentlemen breezed in and were seated right away. There were a group of professional sisters dressed in fashionable business suits sitting two tables away who didn't fail to notice the handsome trio. Kenny and Marvin wore designer sport jackets and tailor-made slacks that fitted them both to a tee. Harold tried his best not to take a second look.

The waitress smiled as she approached the table. "The ladies a couple of tables over said they would make room if you'd like to join them." The waitress looked over at the ladies and gave them a wink.

Marvin spoke up first. "Please let the ladies know that we are flattered by their offer, but we're married men and prefer to stay out of trouble."

"Speak for yourself," Kenny said.

"I'll let the ladies know," the waitress said. "I'll be right back."

"I want to see you walk your bad ass over there," Marvin cajoled. "After that exhibition Rachel put on at Steak and Ale the time I took Yvonne out to lunch when the company was falling down around me, I don't want to ever experience anything that humiliating again. Look at all the trouble I got into because of it."

"And you can't eat at Steak and Ale anymore," Kenny joked, after which he hit Harold on the shoulder. "You should hear Sylvia tell that story."

"That's why you need to keep your tail in that chair," Marvin said, anxious to move on to something else. "Hey," Marvin whispered.

"What?" Harold and Kenny whispered back.

"Kenny, ain't that the good doc, Michael Broussard, sitting over in the corner with that chick who was all up in his face at Harold and Denise's wedding?"

Kenny turned around slowly. "Where?"

"Be discreet. Way over in the corner."

"Oh, yeah, I see them. Damn, Michael Broussard, you are in trouble now. He's got some explaining to do. I remember at the wedding reception he said that the woman in question was an old schoolmate, but damn, they must have been more than schoolmates if she followed him all the way from New York."

"That looks like Denise's cousin," Harold cut in. "In fact, it is Madeline. I'm surprised you don't know her, Marvin."

"I don't ever remember meeting her before your wedding. She must have been away during the time I was...I was married to Denise."

"She's a piece of work."

"Lord, what would Mona say if she knew her one-woman man was holed up in a corner with another woman?" Marvin asked, being facetious.

"Does that make Michael a two-woman man?" Kenny said, trying to hold in his laughter.

"You can count, Kenny, my man," Marvin said, "one plus one makes two; right, Harold?"

"Marvin, don't drag me in yours and Kenny's conversation. I feel for Michael because the things I've heard about Dr. Madeline Brooks, he's going to be putty in her hands. She's not only a skilled doctor, but she has other skills as well."

"Umm, umm, umm," Kenny said, shaking his head.

"Well, Harold," Marvin began, "Michael doesn't appear to be too affected by Dr. Madeline at the moment, but I hope for his sake this is a leisurely lunch with an old friend that happened to fall out of the sky and land in Atlanta."

"I'll let Michael handle his business. He seems to know what he's doing."

"And here is our lovely waitress," Kenny said, trying to ignore the fact that his buddy was having a cozy lunch with someone other than his wife.

"And what would you gentlemen like to order today?"

"Oh my goodness," Marvin said, pulling his menu at eye level to hide his face. "Michael is looking this way."

"That's not on the menu," the waitress said, trying to be party to the mystery.

Harold ordered first. "Uhhh, I'll have the Peka'to Bay jumbo crabmeat salad with balsamic dressing."

"For me," Kenny proudly jumped in, "I'll have the hickory smoked turkey sandwich with French fries. Is he still looking, Marvin?"

"And for you, sir?" The waitress gave Marvin the biggest smile.

"I'll have the teriyaki seared salmon salad with dill vinaigrette."

"Thank you; I'll put your orders in."

"Thank you," Harold said with a smile. "No, Michael isn't looking. Oh, oh, he's getting up. Don't look back."

"What do we say to him if he should come to the table?" Kenny asked full of concern.

"Act natural," Harold offered. "The luncheon is probably a meaningless chitchat with an old friend."

"You can believe that if you want to," Marvin chimed in, "but I say it's more. Act natural; here he comes."

The table was silent. Marvin, Kenny, and Harold were like Golden Globe statues; they sat straight as an arrow with their hands crossed, except that they were sitting down.

"Gentlemen," Michael said as he passed the trio's table and walked out of the restaurant by himself.

"I say Michael is someone who's got something to hide," Marvin remarked.

"And God is not pleased," Kenny countered sarcastically. The trio laughed. "Where is Madeline now?" Kenny asked Marvin, not wanting to turn around and look.

"She's sitting at the table alone with a smirk on her face. I believe she thinks this is funny."

"Look, let me get up and say something to Madeline," Harold offered. "I'll see if I can get the four-one-one."

"Okay, by all means," Marvin said, as he watched Harold get up and walk toward Madeline's table.

"What's happening?" Kenny asked, wanting so badly to switch places with Marvin.

"Why don't you turn around and look? Harold is talking to Madeline. She's grinning like a Cheshire cat. Something about her I don't trust, Kenny. Michael better be careful."

"I know he doesn't want Mona to get a whiff of this, but we've got his back."

"Okay, Harold is coming this way with Ms. Madeline on his arms. Straighten up."

"Marvin, Kenny, this is Denise's cousin, Madeline," Harold said.

"Nice to see you again," Marvin and Kenny said in unison.

"Yes, I remember you both. I understand, Marvin, that you were once married to my cousin."

"That's correct," Marvin said with a stoic face.

"Sorry I didn't get to know you then."

"No problem."

"And Kenny, hope to be seeing more of you." Kenny's eyebrows went up. "What I mean is that I've relocated to Atlanta. I'm working in the same hospital as Dr. Broussard. We were in medical school together at John Hopkins. He has to be the most gracious person I know, giving me the ins and outs of the culture at Emory University Hospital."

"Good for Michael," Kenny said, trying to suppress a laugh. "Well, it was nice meeting you, Madeline."

"Nice meeting, you, too." Madeline gave Harold a peck on the cheek and waved goodbye to Marvin and Kenny.

"Michael is in trouble, guys," Harold said. "We're going to have to be on standby to save him from himself."

Marvin laughed. "And Mona, too."

10

"Hey, baby," Rachel said as Marvin entered the house, setting his keys down on the coffee table in the family room along with his briefcase.

"Hey, sweetie, how was your day with the ladies?" Marvin kissed Rachel, allowing his lips to linger longer than usual. "And where's my sweetheart, Serena?"

"As usual, we had a fabulous time gossiping and reflecting..."

"And planning that gumbo party we're supposed to have at Trina's?"

"Yes to your question. Do you have my fifty dollars?" Rachel stood with her hand open.

"My goodness, woman, you don't give a brother a break. I was getting ready to reach in my pocket and pull off a fifty before you had to go and ask for it." Marvin pulled out his wallet and pulled out a fifty-dollar bill. "Satisfied?"

Rachel smiled as she followed Marvin into the kitchen. "Thank you, Mr. Thomas. My wallet will feel full again."

"Where's my daughter?" Marvin asked, looking around for Serena. "Are you ready to go out to eat?"

"Baby, I ate too much at lunch. Sylvia picked up Serena and took her and Kenny Jr. to Dave and Buster's." Rachel rubbed Marvin's stomach. "It appears that your lunch hasn't digested either. That's why I made you a grilled chicken salad—something light so you won't be too full and sleepy when you're making love to me tonight."

"Umm, put it like that, you have no complaints from me. Sit down, baby. I need to run something by you."

"Okay, Marvin. Don't be messing up my groove. Serena is spending the night at Sylvia and Kenny's, which means we have the house to ourselves. I've got a hot tub waiting on us upstairs with some romantic music and your favorite drink—cream soda."

Marvin smiled. "Trying to make a brother holler. YES!"

"So if it's not important, save it."

"No, let me go ahead and share this with you because whether you're mad or not, we are going to make hot, torrid love tonight, and I'm going to take advantage of everything you've laid out."

"So what is it, Marvin, that you have to interrupt the pleasure in our leisure moment?"

"As you know, Harold was in the office today to discuss the job offer. Kenny and I offered him the job."

"Well, did he accept?"

"Yes, he did. Didn't even have to twist his arm, and we agreed to the dollar figure he asked for."

"So far so good. Remember your water is turning cold upstairs."

"I'm moving it along, Rachel. Anyway, he can begin work in one week. I made the offer for him and Denise...to...to stay with us until they find a place to live," Marvin rattled off so fast that Rachel wasn't sure what he said.

"You did what?"

"I told Harold that he and Denise could stay with us...but I'd have to clear it with the warden first."

Rachel began to groan. She went to the refrigerator and took out an apple, washed it, and took a bite out of it. She put it down on the cutting board that sat on the island butcher block, picked up a butcher knife and let it fall, splitting the apple in half. Then she looked at Marvin. "You did what? Marvin, please. I know you didn't say you invited your ex-wife and her husband, your cousin, who had an affair with her when you were married to her, to come and stay with us until they find lodging."

"I can set them up in a hotel if it will make you feel better. My water is getting cold."

"Marvin, I don't believe you. As much as I've embraced Denise and Harold, I'm not sure that I want them living under the same roof with me. Why can't we be normal like Michael and Mona?"

"Uhmm," Marvin groaned.

"And what's that supposed to mean? Mona and Michael are the only ones in our group of friends whose life is drama free."

"Uhmm."

"I know that uhmm isn't for Mona. Mona is who she is; she can't help herself. But she and Michael have it going on."

"Whatever you say, dear. Now can we go upstairs and get in that water you fixed for us? All of this talking has made me real needy. I'm ready to show you what I've got." Marvin grabbed Rachel from behind, took his hands and fondled her breasts, and squeezed his body against her buttocks.

"Back up," Rachel laughed. "I already know what you've got."

"Come on, Rachel. Harold and Denise will only be with us two weeks tops. It'll be nice to have some company in the house. Now, can we get on with the night you've planned?" Marvin squeezed Rachel and continued to rub his body up against hers.

"Jump back. Don't push me; you know I've got to have the last say."

"Fine with me, but I want you now, Rachel." Marvin puckered his lips and kissed Rachel all over her neck. "I need you, baby."

"You are no good, Marvin Thomas. Okay, let's go upstairs and see how naughty you can be. And I guess Harold and Denise can stay here. But I'm giving you fair warning, as soon as their two weeks are up, they are out of here. Now give it to me."

Rachel ran up the stairs with Marvin close on her heels.

11

Denise heard the motor of the Escalade as Harold pulled it into the garage. She had prepared a nice dinner of roasted chicken, collard greens, and yams for him. Quickly, Denise ran into the restroom near the kitchen to examine her face, to make sure that she looked good for her man. She inhaled and exhaled, awaiting the good news she was sure Harold would bring.

"Garage door open," called the pleasant female voice that alerted the owners of the dwelling that intruders had entered the house. "Garage door closed."

"Hey, baby," Harold greeted Denise with an extra smile.

"Hey, yourself. You've got a radiant look on your face. So did your cousin offer you the job?"

Harold kicked up his legs. "Yes! I'm in. We've got to get packing because I'm supposed to begin working a week from today."

"Oh my goodness, Harold. There are so many things to do. We've got to call the movers, box up our belongings, and find housing..."

"Hush, Denise." Harold gave her a big juicy kiss. "I've already taken care of it. All you need to do is take your pretty self around the house and tell me what you don't want to carry, and I'll get rid of it. The movers will take care of the rest. Marvin agreed to pay some of the moving expenses up to two-thousand dollars."

"That was mighty kind of him."

"It's not a lot, but it will help. I don't believe it will cost us over five-thousand dollars from the estimate I got. And it's not like they'll have to move us to the other side of the world...two hours up the road."

Denise smiled openly for the first time since Harold arrived home.

"Oh, ah, Marvin said that we could stay with them until we find a place to live."

Denise's smile faded. "I don't think that's a good idea, baby. We are at a good place with Marvin and Rachel. I don't want to change that."

"Look, baby, I say two weeks at the most, and we'll have a new place."

"Why don't we find a nice condo and move in? That way, we won't have to move twice, especially since you've got the movers to do everything."

"That's a thought."

"It is the best thing, Harold. Rachel and I have gotten very close, and I truly value our friendship. I don't want her to think for one moment I'm trying to make a play for Marvin, or vying for his attention."

Harold stopped and looked at Denise. "You still have feelings for my cousin?"

"Harold, you of all people ought to know better. Of course not, but Rachel may not think that with our past history. I'll agree I was a bitch back when she and Marvin were first dating. It wasn't so much that I wanted Marvin, it was the fact that he had moved on so quickly. That surprised me because I didn't think moving on was in his DNA."

"Give Marvin more credit than that. He's built an empire..."

"That you're now a part of...again."

"Marvin didn't say anything about us becoming partners. I think that's a long way off, considering how he kicked me out the first time."

"In due season, he'll offer you a spot on the big sign." Denise sighed and put on a fake smile. "I've fixed a nice dinner."

"Baby, forgive me, I forgot to ask you about your doctor's visit today. I was so engrossed in my good news, I forgot to ask you about yours. You were supposed to call me."

"I'm fine. My fatigue was probably due to all of the excitement leading up to the wedding is all. He gave me a clean bill of health."

"That's good news, baby." Harold kissed Denise again. "Where's Danica? I haven't heard a peep out of her."

"She's down the street at her friend Jana's house. She should be home in thirty minutes, but she knows to call before she comes so I can step out and make sure she gets home safely."

"We are so blessed to have Danica in our lives, Denise. Every now and then I wish she hadn't been the product of our lust, especially when you were still married to Marvin. Nevertheless, she's our daughter, and she's the best thing that has come into our lives."

Denise smiled. "You are so right, Harold. She's so smart—like me."

"Give me some credit. Her daddy has smart genes, too."

"I'll give you that, baby."

"Look who I married, Mrs. Thomas? Come here."

"Are you talking to me, Mr. Thomas?"

"Girl, do you see anyone else in the room?"

"No."

Harold pulled Denise to him, caressed her, and kissed her with all that he had.

"You went to the depths of your soul for that one," Denise said, smiling into her husband's eyes. "Always remember that I love you."

"Where's that coming from?"

"Just an expression of how I feel about you. Harold, it was a beautiful day when we got married. Everything I dreamed of. I've loved you for a long time, even before Danica was born. Even when we fought over who would raise Danica. You've been my everything, my soul mate, my lover, and most of all, my friend. Thank you for being in my life." A tear fled down Denise's face.

"Baby, you're all I've ever wanted. You complete me. You're my soul mate and friend... the mother of my child. Flesh of my flesh, and there will be no one but you. I love you, Denise."

They remained in each other's embrace for a long time. Harold kissed Denise again, and she laid her head on his chest, tears trickling from her eyes. Then she pulled up and wiped her face. "We better hurry up and have that romantic dinner because Danica will be here in twenty minutes."

"I'll wash up and get ready. Oh, you won't believe who we saw at lunch today."

"Who, baby? You need to hurry up."

"Madeline and Michael at the Prime Meridian," Harold said, his voice trailing off.

"Together?"

"Yep."

Harold walked into the kitchen, drying his hands. "They were having a very private conversation in the back of the restaurant. And guess what? Madeline has moved to Atlanta and is practicing medicine at the same hospital where Michael is on staff."

"Madeline asked me about Michael at our wedding. I warned her about Mona, but that cousin of mine is going to have to learn her own lesson. Did they see you?"

"Yep, they saw us." Harold sat down at the dining room table while Denise brought the food into the room. "And when they spotted us, Michael got up and left the restaurant. I'm sure he was uncomfortable, especially with Marvin and Kenny spying on them."

"Like you weren't doing your part." Denise tapped Harold lightly on the shoulder.

"Well, they kept encouraging me to look. What was I supposed to do? Not look?"

"Yes."

Denise and Harold laughed. Harold blessed the food and they ate. Twenty minutes later, Danica phoned home to let her parents know she was on the way. Denise stood guard at the front door as Danica made her way home.

"Hi, Daddy," Danica said upon seeing him sitting at the dining room table.

"How's my girl?"

"Fine. Jana and I had so much fun. We can't wait for school to start in a couple of weeks."

Harold and Denise looked at each other. It hadn't occurred to them how Danica was going to feel about their move. Denise made the first move.

"Danica, Daddy and I have some news to share with you."

"What is it, Mommy? I've got to call Jana to tell her what outfit I'm going to wear on the first day of school."

"You're only going into the second grade."

"Mommy, you're so behind the times. I've got to look fly."

Both Harold and Denise shot a *did I miss something* look at each other. Danica was growing up before their very eyes.

"Baby, what we have to tell you may hurt a little bit," Denise began.

"What, Mommy, what?"

"Daddy got a job today in Atlanta, so we will be moving in a few days. You'll make new friends and get to see Serena more often."

"I don't want to move," Danica shouted. "I want to go to school with my friends." Danica began to cry. Harold got up from his seat to console his daughter.

"Danica, sweetheart, it isn't that Daddy wants to uproot you. Daddy wants to give you a better life and to do that it means getting a better job. It won't be so bad once you leave. In fact, if it's all right with Jana's mother, she can come and visit you, and we'll bring you back to Birmingham to see her."

"It seems like everything bad is happening to us. We have to move and leave our friends and Mommy has cancer again." Danica continued to cry.

Harold's mouth flew open. He looked up at Denise, who had a paralyzed look on her face. "What are you talking about, Danica?"

"I heard Mommy crying while she was talking to Grandma on the phone today. I heard Mommy say she had cancer in her other breast."

Harold kissed Danica, stood up straight, and looked at his wife. "Is this true, Denise?"

Denise stood in place without saying a word, looking off into space. She hugged her body until it began to shake. Seconds later, her tear ducts broke like a collapsed dam.

Harold swallowed hard. "Denise?" Then Harold held his hand over his mouth and began to cry.

"I'm sorry, Harold. I'm so sorry, baby. I didn't know how to tell you."

Harold went to Denise and held her tight. "It's all right, baby. I do believe you tried the best you could to tell me this evening. You couldn't quite get it out." Harold continued to hold her. "It's all right, baby."

"I'm sorry, Daddy and Mommy," Danica said, sniffing. "I'll move."

"Oh, Danica," Denise said, pulling away from Harold to rush

to Danica's side with Harold at her heels. "Baby, it's not your fault. Daddy and I love you. Don't be upset. Maybe you can stay with your daddy's cousin, Janice, and that way you can go to school here until Christmas. That way you can see Jana every day. But after that, missy, you've got to come to Atlanta, although we'll come down and see you every weekend."

"That's all right, Mommy. I'll pack my things and go with you and Daddy. You might need me."

"You are too grown for your own self," Harold retorted and gave Danica a kiss.

"Daughter like father."

"Okay, Danica," Harold said, "that's enough. You're not too grown to get that booty spanked."

Denise looked at Harold and laughed. "I wasn't scared, Mommy," Danica said calmly. "Daddy knows I will call nine-one-one on him. I'm kidding, Daddy. Kiss?"

Harold watched his two girls. He had all he needed.

12

"Hey, everybody," Trina said, showcasing her fabulous legs in a pair of yellow shorts and a opaque-colored, lightweight silk napkin top with abstract yellow, orange and brown patterns swirling throughout. Trina was on her second Hurricane and enjoying herself. "Come on in."

"Hey, Trina," Sylvia said, followed by Kenny and Kenny Jr.

"Sylvia, you're working that halter top. I can't believe Kenny let you out of the house."

"My baby looks good," Kenny remarked. "There's no harm in showing a little cleavage and a little booty, especially since she's got the body to rock it."

"I'm not mad at you, Sylvia," Trina said, taking another sip of her drink. "Oh, here is the Thomas family. Hey Rachel, Marvin, Serena."

Kisses went all around. "Mona's outside in the cabana making sure everything is right for you all, and Cecil is doing what he does best when he's not defending a case—chilling."

"Thanks, Trina," everyone said in unison, following Trina through the house and outside.

An island setting met their eyes. "Look at this," Rachel said, waving her hand like it was a magic wand. "You really got it laid out, Trina."

"Cecil and Kenny worked on it last night. They did a good job, right, Sylvia?"

"Superb! I can't wait to chow down on this feast."

"Did you all bring your swimsuits?" Cecil asked when the group got close to the pool.

"I got mine," Mona hollered. "Hey, y'all. I hope you brought an appetite. There's going to be some good eating up in here. Where are Claudette and T?"

"I think that's them at the door," Trina said. "I'll be right back."

Following Trina was Claudette, Tyrone, and Reagan.

"Hey, everybody," Claudette and Tyrone called out, waving at everybody.

"Hey, you," Rachel said. "Look at Claudette sporting some short shorts to show off those skinny legs."

"The rest of my body may be heavy," Claudette said, pushing a braid out of her face, "but I can still strut my stuff."

"Mommy," Reagan called out.

"Did I embarrass you, baby?"

Reagan put her hands over her eyes.

Mona walked over to the group as they found their seats near the pool. Lawn chairs were scattered throughout, and four tables with umbrellas were placed in a cluster poolside, decorated with confetti and beads as if they were on an island resort. "You embarrassed Reagan," Mona said, strutting her stuff in a long peach-and-white strapless sundress. "But I've got to say you're working those Kenneth Cole shorts with the cuffs. Had the nerve to wear white."

"Well, Ms. Drama Queen, you aren't the only one who can sport a look when they get ready," Claudette said.

"Work it," Sylvia said.

"So, where is Michael?" Marvin asked. "I know he's not going to miss good food." Marvin stole a glance at Kenny.

"My baby is at the hospital," Mona began. "He's on call; he'll be here shortly."

"Cool," Kenny said, shooting a look at Marvin.

"Well, let's get this party started," Cecil said.

"Children, you can play in the kiddy pool over there," Trina said, pointing to the small rubber pool sitting off to the side.

"Yeah," Kenny Jr. said, running to the pool followed by Serena, Reagan, and Michael Jr.

"I want to get in the water before I eat," Rachel said. "My swimsuit is underneath my clothes."

"There's a small restroom off the cabana," Trina pointed. "Oh, look. Here comes Harold and Denise."

"Hello, everybody," Denise said as Harold waved. "We rang the doorbell and no one came, so we decided to come on in."

"Welcome," Cecil said. He stood up and gave Harold a brotherly slap on the arm and kissed Denise on the cheek.

"I can't believe we've been in Atlanta a week already," Harold said, getting himself a beer.

"We're glad to have you on board at the company," Marvin said, giving Harold a brotherly embrace. "Thomas and Richmond Tecktronics is on the move."

"Do the thing, baby," Rachel said, as she sported her two-piece, red bikini.

"Whoa, baby," Marvin said, stopping to check out his wife and give her a friendly tap on the behind. "Go on and jump in the water so these godless heathens will stop gawking at you. I'm right behind you."

"Give me five on that," Cecil said as he watched Rachel jump into the pool.

"Since no one is ready to eat, ladies, why don't the rest of us put on our swimsuits," Mona said, not to be outdone by Rachel.

Mona, Sylvia, Denise and Claudette followed Trina into the house and came out fifteen minutes later. They had on everything from a black, sexy one-piece that Sylvia wore; a hot, aquamarine-colored, skimpy two-piece number that Mona wore exposing her ample serving of breasts; a red, black, and white two-piece conservative swimsuit that Denise wore; a hot-pink, two-piece halter top that barely covered Trina; to a green-and-white, one-piece cover-up number that Claudette wore. They paraded out to the pool in front of their gawking husbands, looking like contestants at a Mrs. America Pageant. They strolled down the small incline, modeling as if they were on a runway before jumping in the water, all except Claudette who only wanted to put her feet in and Denise who sat down.

"Denise, aren't you going to jump in?" Mona called out. "The water feels good."

"No, I'm going to sit here with my husband and watch you guys."

"Girl, you better get in this pool and have some fun."

"Maybe later."

"Whew," Marvin said, now in his swim trunks after having watched the ladies walk past him. "That parade of women was like finding a bowl of Skittles."

"I don't know where you come up with that stuff, Marvin," Kenny said, "but you're crazy, man."

Sitting in his chaise, Cecil shook his head. "We got some fine women, and I don't know why I'm sitting up here with you guys. I'm getting ready to jump into the water."

"It's too bad Michael isn't here to see his wife parading in front of us in that skimpy number," Kenny said.

Harold and Marvin laughed.

"What's up with that?" Tyrone asked.

The guys huddled together, and Marvin became the spokesman. "A couple of weeks ago, Kenny, Harold, and I saw Dr. Michael Broussard holed up in the back of a restaurant with this chick who happens to be Denise's cousin. It looked intimate, and when Michael saw us, he got up and left the restaurant by himself."

"Did he say anything to you?" Tyrone asked.

"In that deep voice of his he said, *gentlemen.*" Marvin and Kenny howled.

"I'm sure it was business," Harold defended.

"Michael never misses one of our events. In fact, he was dead set on being here today," Kenny rushed to say.

Cecil rubbed his chin. "Mona said he was on call. Give him a break; he'll be here in a little while."

"Okay," Marvin interjected. "I'll give him the benefit of the doubt, but I'm saying, gumbo is the last thing on his mind."

"Don't forget it wasn't that long ago, Marvin, that you were in the hot seat. Miss Peaches had some incriminating photos on your ass," Cecil said. The others laughed.

"Yeah, yeah, let's get in the water."

"Now you want to get in the water." Cecil laughed. "Be careful how you judge."

"Good point," Marvin said and jumped into the water.

"I'm going to sit with my wife," Harold interjected. "She's so beautiful sitting over there by herself." Denise smiled.

The group played water games—the women against the men. Even the children joined them—Michael Jr., Serena, Reagan, and Kenny Jr. After playing in the pool, everyone enjoyed the savory taste of Mona's gumbo and jambalaya with all the trimmings. Everyone ate and ate until they had enough.

"Mona, girl, you outdid yourself," Trina said, lying on the chaise next to Cecil.

"Yes, you did," everyone else shouted out.

Around seven-thirty, the ladies helped Mona wash up the dishes and straighten things up.

"This was a fabulous day, Cecil," Kenny said, giving him a brotherly handshake.

"Thanks, Kenny, for making this a successful and fun day."

"Ready to go, Sylvia?" Kenny called out. "I know you and your girls can talk all night but this brother is tired. Too tired even for some rump cake."

The men laughed. "And you weren't going to get any anyway," Sylvia countered, giving Kenny a sultry, sexy look. The women laughed.

Rachel and Marvin, along with the others, said their words of thanks to the cook and the hosts.

"I really had a good time today," Denise said. "I'll remember it always." Harold gave Denise a passing look.

"Denise, there are going to be plenty more of these parties," Mona remarked. "This party will be a blur once the next one comes and goes. They get better and better."

Denise smiled and kept her thoughts to herself. "I look forward to them," she said.

"Calling all children," Sylvia shouted out.

"They're in the house playing video games; I don't think they want to go home," Trina said.

"Well, it's time," Kenny said, calling Kenny Jr. who reluctantly put the video game down and got ready to go.

After helping Mona with her things, everyone filed out to their cars after thanking Mona, Trina and Cecil again.

"Tell Michael we missed him," Kenny said to Mona. "He stayed away because he knew that I was going to give him a dominoes butt whipping."

"I'll tell him, Kenny. Goodnight, everybody. Thanks, Trina and Cecil, for having us over."

"Thanks, Mona. And the food was to die for."

13

"Hey, Kenny, what's the good word?" Marvin asked as Kenny marched into his office with a big smile on his face.

"What's the word? How about a contract with another school district for five-hundred computers with service contracts, maintenance clauses, future upgrades, and a possible switch-out in five years?"

"That is good news, Kenny. In fact, that's damn good news. We ought to celebrate."

"Lunch is on me. The ink should be dry on the contract as we speak."

"Thomas and Richmond Tecktronics, Inc. is a force to be reckoned with."

"Marvin, I believe we have truly come back from the brink. A year ago, I wasn't so sure, but today, I feel confident in saying that we have made it through the storm." Kenny looked around at Marvin's office. "You may want to think about upgrading your office, Marv. The one thing you don't have is your own restroom facility. You may want to jog around the building at lunch. With your own restroom, you can come in and take a shower right in your own office."

"And Rachel will think that I've got something to hide."

"Rachel needs to get a life. You've worked hard and deserve some perks."

"Speaking of something to hide, I can't believe Michael didn't show up at the gumbo feast."

"Yeah, I've thought about it, too. But I also thought about what Cecil said. Judge lest ye be judged. Michael is a big boy; if nothing's going on, there's nothing to talk about. It's his business anyway. And if Mona was suspicious of Michael, don't you know all of the girls would know by now?"

"You're right. From here on out, I'm minding my own business." Marvin picked up the phone at the buzzer. "Yes, Yvonne?"

"The other Mr. Thomas is here to see you."

"Send him in."

"Marvin, Kenny," Harold began as he walked into Marvin's office. "When are you going to upgrade your furniture, Marvin?"

"Damn. First Kenny; now you. What's wrong with my furniture?"

Harold laughed. "Nothing, Marvin. It's a little outdated. An executive who's excelling like you are needs to reward himself once in awhile. The same goes for Yvonne's area. It might help her look younger."

"Now that wasn't right, Harold," Marvin said, as he and Kenny broke out into laughter. "So what brings you by?"

"I'll let you talk in private," Kenny said, excusing himself.

Nerves were written all over Harold. "No need to go, Kenny. Please stay. I came by to tell Marvin that I may need to take some days off to take Denise to the doctor."

"Is she all right? How did her doctor's visit turn out?" Marvin asked.

"She has to get some tests and blood work to see what's causing her fatigue. Nothing to worry about," Harold lied. "I want to be with her when she goes so that I know first-hand what's going on."

"Take whatever time you need, Harold," Marvin said. "Family

is a priority. I think Rachel told me that Denise was stopping by the house today."

"She is and thanks, cuz. I appreciate your concern."

"Why don't you join me and Kenny for lunch?"

"Sounds like a plan, and I'm hungry. Let's not go to the Prime Meridian, though."

"Mrs. Thomas, the dining room is set up and lunch is in the fridge for when Mrs. Thomas arrives," Isabel said, picking up one of Serena's chapter books that had fallen to the floor in the family room.

"Thank you, Isabel. I can take it from here. Why don't you take an hour or two for yourself before you have to pick up Serena from school?"

"All right, Mrs. Thomas. Remember grilled chicken salad for lunch and key lime pie for dessert. Sweet tea is in the glass pitcher."

"Thanks, Isabel."

Rachel sighed and took one last look around the house. She couldn't believe that almost a year ago, she and Marvin stood to lose their home. She had so much to be grateful for and not a day went by that she didn't thank the Lord for restoring her husband's company and their marriage. And to think that all the worries she had about Denise trying to reclaim Marvin was small potatoes to the hell that ripped their lives apart last year. Rachel shook her head as she recalled Marvin lying in the hospital after his stomach had been pumped of the pills he'd taken that nearly ended his life.

Ding, dong. "I'll get it, Mrs. Thomas," Isabel said. "I'm on my way out."

"Okay." Rachel was blessed that Isabel decided to come back and work for them when their household returned to normal.

Serena loved Isabel, and Rachel couldn't think of anyone better to look after her daughter. Rachel turned around as Denise entered the house.

"Hi, Rachel," Denise said. She hugged Rachel and held onto her longer than usual.

"Well, hello, Mrs. Newlywed. Does it feel any different?"

"Because we have a contract as opposed to just shacking together?"

"I didn't say it to be offensive, Denise."

"Relax, Rachel. I know. I was thinking about the question to tell you the truth. And the answer is…yes, it feels different. It's made our family whole. Danica's mother and father are married to each other and are providing a perfect home for her."

"Wow, you were thinking about the question," Rachel quipped. "Come on in, girl, and let's have some lunch. It's so good to see you happy."

"I am happy, Rachel. Once Danica is here in Atlanta with me, I'll feel better."

"Why did you leave her in Birmingham?"

"She wanted to start school with her friends. She had her heart set on it, and I couldn't bear to uproot her at the time. Danica is staying with Janice until Christmas. Harold and I have been going to Birmingham on the weekends to see her."

"That's great. Ready for lunch?"

"That sounds good."

Denise followed Rachel into her oriental-themed dining room with the two large oriental vases that stood three feet tall in opposite corners. A large oriental watercolor hugged the far wall, while the heavy stained oak dining room set that included a table setting for eight, a large hutch and cabinet that contained their china filled up the other walls. Rachel was happy with her new dining room set that Marvin surprised her with for their anniversary.

"You sit here, and I'll sit here," Rachel said as she extended her hand out to indicate the chair Denise was to sit in. "I'll get lunch."

"I saw Isabel leave."

"Yeah, I gave her a few hours off. Sometimes, Isabel can be a little nosey. I wanted this to be our time."

"Thanks, Rachel. I feel special."

"Girl, you are special, but you're also family. I'm glad that we have come to this place in our lives that we can be good friends. I hope you like grilled chicken salad and key lime pie."

"My favorite."

Rachel and Denise chatted about the wedding, Harold and Denise's move to Atlanta, their kids and life in general as they ate their lunch. It was relaxing, and Rachel could tell that Denise was enjoying herself. After dessert, they went into the family room to relax.

Denise's mood seemed to change, Rachel noted. She was more somber—like something was on her mind. She sat down next to Denise.

"You all right, Denise?"

"Yes, no." Denise looked at Rachel and sighed. "I need to talk to someone."

"There's nothing wrong between you and Harold?" Rachel seemed anxious.

Denise patted Rachel's hand. "No, Harold and I are fine. We love each other more than life itself. I don't know how much longer I have to spend with him."

Rachel inched closer to Denise. "What are you talking about, Denise? You're scaring me."

"I don't mean to." Denise looked down in her lap with a forlorn look on her face. Then she looked up at Rachel. "I have stage-four cancer in my other breast. The prognosis isn't good. They've given me less than six months to live."

Rachel grabbed her chest, then moved over and hugged Denise. "Oh my God, Denise. No, this can't be true. Weren't you getting regular check-ups?"

"Yes, but for whatever reason, the mammogram didn't pick it up, although I will admit that I didn't go to my appointments as I should. A week before the wedding, I gave myself a breast examination, and I discovered the lump. I know this all sounds crazy, but it is what it is. This time I have no options but chemo and hope for the best...and the best is that I can last more than six months.

"It hurts because now that Harold and I have come full circle and made our lives complete, I have this death sentence hanging over me." Denise began to cry, with Rachel right along with her. "I won't get to see my baby grow up, get married, and have children." Denise broke down. "I don't know what to do, Rachel. I love Harold so much; I can't leave him like this."

Rachel wiped tears from her eyes. "Denise, listen to me. You have to pour meaning into each day and live it like it's your last. I think it's important that Danica spends this time with you, even if it means leaving her friends. Does she know?"

Denise nodded her head in the affirmative.

"Denise, Marvin and I will be there for you every step of the way. The doctors may have it all wrong, and anyway, God has the last say-so."

Denise took a Kleenex from her purse and wiped her face. "I don't want the ladies to know. Please promise me that you won't tell them, Rachel. I don't want anyone to feel sorry for me. I want to die with dignity."

"You won't be alone, and I promise I won't say anything. Why don't you try looking at this in a positive manner?"

"The test was positive, Rachel. I believe in God, but the tests don't lie. I do want to have a positive attitude, but the news is still too fresh. I faked it at Cecil and Trina's party, but I don't think I can do too many more of them."

"Now I understand what you meant when you said you'd always remember that day."

"Yes, I'm not sure if there will be another get together for me."

"There will be another. So is that why you fainted during your wedding reception?"

"Yes. I had been feeling weak for some time, but I overdid it that day."

Rachel hugged Denise again. "I love you, Denise. We have had our differences in the past, and that's what it is—in the past. I've seen you afraid; I've seen you grow. You really are a fabulous woman once one gets to know you." Rachel hugged her tight. "I love you."

"I love you, too, Rachel. I couldn't ask for a better friend."

14

Michael walked into the dark kitchen and fiddled around until he found a small pot to cook with. He tapped the palm of his hand with the pot—an indication that he was deep in thought or had forgotten something. He filled the pot halfway with water and stood there looking out of the small window over the sink, gazing out into the semi-darkness that was slowly giving way to the dawn.

Suddenly, the kitchen light flicked on. Startled, Michael turned around, almost spilling the water out of the pot. Mona stood at the entrance to the kitchen in her robe and gown with a perplexed look on her face.

"Why are you in the dark, Michael?"

"I'm not sure. Something about the dark has a calming effect."

"That's well and good, but there's nothing calm about stumbling around in the dark and making a bunch of noise when God said let there be light." Mona clicked the light switch on and off a couple of times for emphasis. "Why don't you sit down; I'll fix you some oatmeal."

"Do you trust me, Mona?"

Mona stopped what she was doing, turned on her heels, and took a good look at Michael. She raised her eyebrows and studied her husband like a research scientist who was on the threshold of making a new discovery. With her hands on her hips, she answered his question with a question. "Is there any reason for me not to trust you?"

"No, baby, not at all. I see I've got you worked up for nothing."

"Uhmm. That was a very serious question you posed, Michael, and one that deserves further explanation." Mona watched Michael with renewed interest.

"I'm not sure what it is, but lately I've been wondering if I've limited myself in my work. I want to do more...help more than the people who come to the hospital with a heart ailment. I've often thought about going into research to possibly help find a cure for cancer or Alzheimer's."

"Hmmph. I don't know what brought this on, but I'm glad that this is all that has you seemingly faraway lately. You are a first-class surgeon and you're already helping more people than you know."

"I want to do more, Mona. It's hard for me to express to you what I'm feeling, but there's a lot more that I can do."

"You can't cure everyone's ills. As it is, you spend most of your time at the hospital. Everyone missed you this weekend at the gumbo and jambalaya party. It was so much fun. I don't think you've had a break since you went to Denise and Harold's wedding."

"And I know my baby threw down because I tasted the fruits of your labor. You are a top-notch cook and the number one caterer in the world. I understand what you're saying, Mona, but you're missing my point. I've got to sort a few things out."

Mona smiled and went over to where Michael stood and gave him a big kiss. "Sit down, Dr. Broussard. Your baby's momma is going to fix you a real breakfast. And I didn't miss your point. I'll be your research project. You can find a cure for...whatever later."

Michael frowned without letting Mona see him. "Thanks, baby," he said without a lot of enthusiasm.

A Touch of Elegance was on the thirty-second floor. Dr. Madeline Brooks took in the décor and bunched up her face in a good sort of way to say that she was satisfied and that this was where she belonged. Michael had told her that one of his wife's friends was an excellent hairdresser, whose upscale beauty salon was located in the heart of downtown Atlanta, but you had to *pay the price to look nice*—a slogan that hung in Claudette's salon.

There were five hair stations in all—Madeline counted every one of them. Classy but not overdone. The décor was black and white with a touch of purple. Each stylist wore a black bib apron with the words "A Touch of Elegance" embroidered on it in purple with a comb and curling iron appliqué embroidered in purple, white, and red on the left bottom. Each stylist's name was also embroidered in white and purple at the top left.

"Good afternoon, welcome to A Touch of Elegance," Claudette said to the woman she thought she recognized.

"Good afternoon, I'm looking for the owner, Claudette Beasley. I have an appointment at one, and my name is Dr. Madeline Brooks."

"Hello, Dr. Brooks, I'm Claudette. Please come on back to my station where I promise to take very good care of you."

"Thank you. I've heard you can work miracles."

"Well, I do pride myself on my work and do keep up with the latest styles. All you have to do is let me know what it is you want."

"I'd like my hair swept up on my head with a cylindrical look in the back. I'd like to have small curls to fall next to my ears and at the nape of my neck on either side. I'm going to a very important dinner tonight given for the doctors at Emory."

"That can be achieved, and you're going to look fabulous."

"I'm very excited about this dinner. I haven't been in town very long, and this will give me a chance to get to mingle with other doctors away from the hospital. Dr. Michael Broussard, who I believe you know, has been very helpful in acclimating me to the hospital as well as to Atlanta." A frown passed over Claudette's face, but she remained quiet. "He's so talented; we were in med school together."

"Yes, Michael is very talented. He's saved many lives and has been featured on talk shows and at some very high-level medical symposiums."

"I told Michael he needs to go into research. That's where the money is. As I said and you concurred, he's very bright and talented. The world could use his expertise."

"Maybe he's happy doing what he does," Claudette said sarcastically.

"So, you know Michael very well."

"Yes, his wife is my best friend. Dr. Brooks, I believe I've met you before."

"I can't imagine where."

Claudette didn't necessarily like the tone of that statement, but she let it roll off her shoulder. "I know where it was...in New York." Claudette snapped her fingers, at which Madeline jerked back.

"I'm from New York, but I've never seen you before."

"Oh, yes, I remember now. It was at Harold and Denise Thomas' wedding."

"Oh," Madeline said, with her mouth open wide in surprise. "Yes, Denise is my cousin. We weren't very close, but she's family nevertheless."

"Denise and Harold are very dear friends."

"Well, I think they spent way too much money on that wedding. It's not like she hasn't been married before."

"I believe it meant a lot to Denise, and anyway, as bourgeoisie as she is, I didn't expect anything less."

"Well, Denise is Denise, but I'm going to be the belle of this ball. I wonder if Michael is bringing his wife, uhh…" Madeline snapped her fingers twice, "Mona, that's her name, to dinner? He didn't mention it when I spoke to him this morning."

"I'm sure if Michael is going to dinner, it will be with his wife… Mona."

Claudette went to work on Madeline, not sure if she liked her new client. She had a haughty air about her that didn't serve up well with Claudette. She washed her hair, rinsed, and conditioned it, but nothing extra. The more Claudette thought about her little chat with Madeline, the more she didn't care for her.

"Would you like to go under the dryer or have your hair blow-dried? It's better for the hair if you sit under the dryer. And because of the thickness and length of your hair, it's going to take a little while to dry. It's up to you."

Madeline sighed. "Dinner is at six and I have to stop by the hospital before I go home to change. Blow-dry and work your magic."

I'll work my magic on you, Claudette thought to herself. "Blow-dry it'll be."

Claudette blow-dried, curled and styled Madeline's hair in a beautiful up-sweep hairdo. After putting the final touches to her hair, Claudette handed Madeline a mirror.

Madeline swirled around in the chair, not wanting to miss any angle. "Well, you did a fine job, Ms. Beasley. I guess I didn't expect anything less since you came with a superb recommendation from Michael. He said you were one of the best. So, how much is this going to cost me today?"

"Eighty-five dollars plus tip," Claudette said, with a manufactured smile on her face.

Madeline looked at Claudette to make sure she had heard correctly. Since Claudette didn't flinch, Madeline scooped up her bag and pulled a hundred-dollar bill from her purse. "Keep the change."

"Thank you, and come again."

"I might. It'll depend upon how many men find me attractive tonight." With that, Madeline walked out the door while Claudette scowled behind her.

"Who in the hell was that?" asked Noel, one of Claudette's premier hair designers.

"Nobody you want to know."

15

Claudette hadn't been right since Dr. Madeline Brooks walked out of her salon. She appreciated the fact that Michael sent her clients every now and then, but there was something about this one that was shrouded in mystery. Was Michael sweet on Madeline?

She recalled that Madeline said Michael had been helping her to get acquainted with the hospital and Atlanta. To Claudette, that smelled like trouble. Why in the world was a married man taking time out with a single woman who was looking for an attractive man? For sure, Mona had no idea.

This was a hard call for Claudette. She didn't like meddling in other people's affairs. Michael would be mad at her if she said something to Mona about her conversation with the good Dr. Brooks, but Mona was her friend. The dinner was at six o'clock, and she had to put a plan into place without the help of Rachel and Sylvia.

Claudette went into her office and closed the door. Her office was full of exotic plants that sat against zebra-patterned wallpaper. Pictures of her family held in red frames hung on the walls. A large red file cabinet sat in one corner. An acrylic desk with a white flokati rug that sat on top of black shag carpet accentuated the rest of the room. To some, it would have been too much, but the room matched Claudette's personality and was tastefully done.

Picking up the desk phone, Claudette dialed Mona's number. It was three in the afternoon, and Mona should be home after picking Michael Jr. up from preschool. She heard the phone ring once, then twice, three times. On the fourth ring, Mona picked up.

"Hey, Claudette, how much money did you rob those bourgeoisie, cocktail-drinking broads of today?"

"Not enough, girl. I did have an interesting client, however."

"All of your clients are interesting. What's new? Hold on a sec; let me put in a movie for Michael Jr."

While Mona was away from the phone, Claudette wondered if this was the reprieve she needed to keep her nose out of Michael's business. This could be a mistake, but her adrenaline made her push on. Mona was back on the line.

"So where were we, Claudette?"

"We were talking about my interesting clients. Mona, I'm of a belief that money makes you a different person."

"That's the truth. In fact, my behind needs to get up and get ready for an event I'm catering this weekend."

"Aren't you going out to dinner tonight?"

"Dinner, tonight? Girl, please. Michael said he has to work late again at the hospital. He was acting strange this morning, talking about he wants to go into research. He needs to research his behind on to the house is what I told him."

"So, you're not going to dinner tonight?"

"Okay, Claudette, what in the hell are you talking about? You jumped from crazy clients to me going out to dinner. Didn't you hear me say Michael was working late?"

"Mona, guess who my client was today?"

"I don't feel like guessing. Tell me and put me out of my misery."

"It was Madeline Brooks, the woman at Denise's wedding that was trying to hit on your husband."

"You must be wrong. She lives in New York."

"How about she just moved to Atlanta and I did her hair so that she could attend a dinner tonight that's being held for the doctors at Emory?"

"Okay, Claudette, stop trying to push my buttons. You know how I get when you guys play pranks on me."

"Girlfriend said she was wondering if Michael was bringing you to the dinner."

Silence.

"Mona?"

"You started this, Claudette. Where is the dinner being held?"

"Well, that's the only piece of information Dr. Brooks withheld."

"I don't understand why you didn't get that vital piece of information since she didn't mind telling you about the dinner. And I believe that bitch did it on purpose because she knew you would tell me."

"That's precisely what I thought since I told her you were my best friend."

"Damn that bitch and Michael, too. I'm going to stomp both of their behinds into the ground when I see them. Do you know what Michael asked me this morning, Claudette?"

"No, what did..."

"He asked me if I trusted him. I thought it was a little strange because things have been good between us. Michael seems to be a little overworked. But he did say he was thinking about going into research."

"Guess what the good doctor told me? She said she suggested to Michael that he needs to go into research."

"Enough. I've heard enough, Claudette. Don't tell me another damn thing."

"Do you want me to call Rachel and Sylvia?"

"No, sweetie, this is something I'm going to have to take care of all by myself—Mona style. Dr. Michael Broussard has got some explaining to do. On-call, working late my ass. Sneaking behind my back like his damn cousin did when I was married to him. Well, Dr. Madeline Brown, Brooks or whatever your name is, you've messed with the wrong woman. And Dr. Michael Broussard will feel my wrath."

"Mona, don't do anything crazy. I toiled over whether I should tell you or not."

"Well, you told me. How else am I supposed to act? Anyway, if I found out that you were holding out on me with this time bomb, I would've been all up in A Touch of Elegance cussing your ass out."

"That's why I told you. Promise you won't do anything crazy."

"Good night, Claudette." And the line was dead.

16

The house was pitch-black when Michael drove his Lexus into the garage. Getting out of the car, he quickly exchanged his suit jacket for his white doctor's coat. He sniffed his body but felt confident that the residue from the night's event hadn't seeped into his clothes.

Michael opened the door that led from the garage into the hallway. He stopped in the kitchen to get a bottle of water before going up to bed. He placed his keys on the counter and opened the refrigerator, its interior light illuminating the kitchen for a moment. Before the door closed, he jumped and gasped out of fear at the figure that sat at the table in the dark.

"What are you doing sitting in the dark?" Michael asked as he moved to turn the light on in the kitchen.

"That seems to be the question of the day," Mona replied, with a severe frown on her face.

Michael looked at the table. It was set for two. Two metal steamers covered a plate each, while two glasses of wine sat untouched. Michael noticed that the plates weren't the good china nor were the glasses their good crystal.

"Why did you wait up for me, baby? You knew I was working late. We've been short staffed, and I've been doing a lot of fill-ins."

Mona turned around in her chair so she could get a good look at Michael. She was dressed in an old Michael Jackson T-shirt and her feet were bare, with her toes touching each other. "Do I look like a fool to you, Michael?"

"Mona, don't go there. I've worked hard today..."

"Hard my ass. The only thing hard on you was your penis from rubbing up on Madeline Brooks. How was dinner tonight?"

Michael's eyes were wide. "What...what are you talking about?"

Mona jumped up from her seat and got in Michael's face. "You know what I'm talking about, you lying bastard. Didn't have the decency to tell me the truth. Short staffed...but they hired Madeline Brooks. Got a whiff of you up her nose and she had to follow you to Atlanta. And don't play dumb and stupid with me. I know that you all had something going on before. You're smelling yourself; got that old ho's scent hanging around, which is making you get beside yourself. Well, I'm not having it. Is this why you asked me this morning if I trusted your sorry ass?"

"Are you finished?"

"I'll let you know when."

"Mona, you're being ridiculous. Where would you get a crazy idea about me and Madeline?"

"Where have you been, Michael? Do you know what time it is? It's a quarter to midnight and you stink. You smell like the bottom of a garbage can and stale cigarettes. I guess you thought you were going to tiptoe up to the room, jump in the shower, and lay next to me. Wrong."

"Why don't you shut up and let me explain?"

"Well, you've been home for ten minutes and I haven't heard you say anything that makes sense yet."

"That's because I can't get a word in edgewise. I'm going to bed. I've got a heavy work schedule tomorrow."

"Oh hell no, you aren't, Michael Broussard. If you can spend all night with that skank doctor ho, you're going to spend some time with me. I've been home all day with your son, who hasn't seen his daddy since when? Sunday?"

"Stop being dramatic, Mona. Sometimes you're too much, and I need a break from you."

Mona's eyes bulged.

"Cat finally got your tongue?" Michael asked. "Good, it's time for bed."

"Michael, I'm not playing with you." Mona's face was huffy and tears began to form in her eyes. "Timothy hurt me bad. He was my first love; please don't do this to me."

"I'm not my cousin, Mona. You are married to me. Get it through your thick skull that Madeline means nothing to me. Yes, I was at a dinner for the doctors on staff, but I wasn't with Madeline. Yes, she was there, but I wasn't with her."

"So why did you lie to me? Why did you say you were working late? Why wasn't I invited as I usually am? Huh? Can you answer that question?"

"Maybe because I knew how you would act when you saw that Madeline was there."

"Protecting her honor; what a damn shame."

"I love you, Mona." Michael went to Mona and tried to hold her.

"Don't touch me. You're filthy. You need to find somewhere else to sleep."

"I will." Michael picked up his keys from the counter, retraced his steps, pulled his car out of the garage, and sped away.

"Michael, please come back," Mona called out into the darkness. She stood at the door and looked longingly, but Michael Broussard was long gone.

17

Mona was livid. In her wildest dreams, she never thought that Michael would walk out on her—even if it was for some well-needed air. And so she waited all night until the wee hours of the morning for him to reappear so that she could make it right with him, explaining her paranoia about losing him to a woman who was his peer, who he had so much in common with. With all of Michael's protests about not having anything to do with Madeline and that she was only a friend, and that she, Mona, was the only woman in his life, she gave him his player card by being the ultimate bitch and paving the way straight to Madeline's bed.

The tears were still there as a new day dawned. Not even a phone call from Michael to say he was alive and well. Mona's bones ached from a restless night, tossing and turning, jumping up at every noise to see if Michael had returned. But he hadn't.

Mona sighed, her breath caught in her lungs. She knew she needed to get up to get Michael Jr. ready for school, but her body wouldn't move. The rumpled bed sheets told her story, not the one most would think, but nevertheless, it was a story.

Mona sat up on her arms as she heard the faint sound of water running. It was Michael Jr. His eternal alarm clock had kicked in and she had no choice but to get the ball rolling. She wanted to talk to someone about what she was going through, but as much as she was in everybody else's business, she didn't want her girl-friends to be party to her delicate situation. She'd have to woman-up and be her own one-woman support team today. It was because of her own doing, she was in this precarious predicament.

"Mommy, may I have some breakfast?" Michael Jr. called out.

"Yes, baby, Mommy has to get ready, but she'll get your breakfast in a moment. Do you have your clothes on?"

Michael Jr. walked into her bedroom. "See, Mommy, I put my clothes on all by myself."

Mona smiled. "Good for you, Michael Jr. You are Mommy's big boy. I'm so proud of you. Go get your sweater and go downstairs and read a book until Mommy comes down."

"Okay, Mommy. I want some pancakes."

Mona was not in the pancake making mood, but she smiled. "Okay, sweetie, pancakes coming up."

Mona fixed Michael Jr. pancakes, eggs, and a glass of orange juice. She fixed him a peanut butter and jelly sandwich, his favorite, for lunch, along with a red apple and a small bag of chips. Then she and Michael were off to preschool. Michael would be starting kindergarten soon.

After dropping Michael Jr. off, she returned to her car. Mona sat in it, not sure what she was going to do next. She pulled her iPhone from her Coach bag and checked for messages. Not a word from Michael. An idle mind was the devil's workshop. Mona started the car and headed straight for Emory University Hospital.

When she arrived, Mona parked in the visitor's parking lot. She sat a moment to regain her composure, hoping that Michael would understand that she had come in peace. She dressed simple in her mind—a simple black suit with a fuchsia blouse underneath. Exhaling, Mona got out of the car and proceeded to Michael's office.

"Hello, Mrs. Broussard," head nurse, Sandra Webb, said as Mona approached the nurse's station. "If you're looking for your husband, you just missed him. He's gone on rounds and will probably go directly to his eleven o'clock surgery."

Mona looked disappointed. "Do you think he'll come back here before going to surgery? I have something very important I need to share with him."

"If you want, I'll page him," Sandra said.

"No, that's okay. Those patients need every bit of his time as I do. I'll go to the hospital cafeteria and wait a bit. I'll come back up before his eleven o'clock."

Sandra smiled. "Okay, Mrs. Broussard. If I see him before then, I'll tell him you're here. Otherwise, you might find him in his office. I'll leave a message with his secretary, Michelle."

"No, don't do that, Sandra. I want to surprise him."

Sandra gave her a playful smile to say she understood, she had Mona's back, and that she was part of the conspirator's team. "Gotcha," Sandra said.

With that, Mona left the floor and headed to the hospital cafeteria, her life still on hold. How could she have been so foolish by accusing Michael of being secretive about his relationship with Madeline? She had no proof of anything, and there wasn't anything that Michael had done to lead her to believe there was any hanky-panky going on. But it was the fact that he lied to her... telling her that he was on call when he was not, that he went to a dinner without her, but Madeline was there. She couldn't believe that Dr. Madeline Brooks had moved to Atlanta and was now on staff at Emory.

But there was something about Madeline that Mona didn't like. How was it that she had come to Emory within a few months of them seeing her at Denise and Harold's wedding? Mona's mind raced a mile a minute. "Hmmph," Mona said under her breath. Madeline wants Michael, and she's determined to get him. *But not before I put a pitchfork through her heart*, Mona thought.

The hospital cafeteria was noisy. White coats were everywhere— doctors, nurses, and interns. Mona wasn't hungry, but she needed something in her stomach to combat her nerves. She picked up a bran muffin from the line and a bottle of apple juice and put it on her tray. After paying for her food, Mona picked up her tray and began to look for a seat.

As Mona looked for an empty space, she stopped and did a double take, shifting her head to the right to get a better look. She moved closer, and when she confirmed that it was Denise who was sitting with Madeline, she made a beeline for their table. It was apparent that Madeline had already seen Mona and was waiting with anticipation for her to approach.

Denise turned around. "Hi, Mona, this is a pleasant surprise."

"Oh, it is?" Mona said sarcastically, zeroing in on Madeline who sat back in her seat as cool as a cucumber in her new, starched white hospital jacket with Emory University Hospital embroidered on it and her hair pulled up in an elegant twist.

"What are you talking about, Mona?" Denise asked.

"Did you know that...whatever her name is was moving to Atlanta?"

"All right, Mona, I don't know what you're tripping about."

"I'm talking about the bitch who's sitting across from you, Denise. She wants my husband, and she moved here to be close to him."

"Mona, you're way off base. Madeline is my cousin who happens to be a doctor like Michael. She's always talked about moving away from New York because it's such a rat race. Don't come over her interrupting our lunch if you don't intend to be friendly. It doesn't become you."

Mona noticed that Madeline was rather enjoying their banter. "I don't intend to be friendly," Mona lashed out, her focus back on Denise. "It wasn't enough that you came running to Atlanta from New York to snatch Marvin from Rachel, but now you've got your cousin mimicking you. What did you do? Give her the manual on how to do it?"

"Let me handle this, Denise," Madeline said, standing up. She moved within inches of Mona. "Mona," she said with disgust, "this is my place of employment. I came to Atlanta to better my career. I can't help it if your husband happens to work at the same hospital I was given my opportunity. Now, you need to get over it and find somewhere else to eat."

Mona put her fingers in Madeline's face. "Don't think for one minute I'm afraid of you, Madeline. I will cut you down to the white meat with a quickness if I hear that you've been near my husband."

"A word of advice, Mrs. Broussard. Don't ever turn your back to me. I don't scare easily, and if a fight is what you want, I say bring it on. You've met your match with me."

Denise held up her hands. "That's enough, Madeline. Mona is harmless; she's more hot air than anything else."

"Denise, this is probably all your fault. You were probably sitting here plotting with your bitch-ass cousin about how to take Michael away from me."

Madeline sat down. She saw the look on Denise's face and she became worried. "I'm sorry, Denise; please don't let this upset you."

"It's too late. Mona, you were the last thing on my mind. Whatever feather is tickling your butt is not my issue or concern. I've got more important things on my plate at this moment. You see, I may not survive this round of cancer."

Mona covered her mouth with her hand, almost dropping her tray.

Denise didn't give Mona time to respond. "I've been diagnosed with stage-four carcinoma of the breast. That's why I passed out at the wedding. I'm in a fight for my life, and all you're worried about is whether or not Michael wants Madeline. News flash, darling; I don't give a damn." The tears began to fall from Denise's face. "I may only have a few months to be with my daughter and my husband. You'll have yours. Harold and Danica are my life and they are why I want to fight. Do you understand that, Mona?

"And for your information, I understand Rachel's outbursts and the way she acted when she first saw me with Marvin those many years ago. But you...you are nothing more than an old-ass Drama Queen performing to an empty audience. Rachel is a lady in every way. She's my true friend and since we've gotten to know each better, she understands what makes me tick."

"Look, Denise, I'm...I'm so sorry." Mona sighed. "I don't believe it...that you're going through this again. Sometimes I get so emotional and I act out, but that's no excuse. If there's anything I can do, please let me know." Tears fell from Mona's eyes. She gently put her tray down on the unoccupied table next to her and went to Denise to give her a hug.

"Mona, don't touch me. I don't want your fake-ass pity, your fake-ass tears, or your fake-ass hug. You detest me. You don't care about anyone but yourself. Anger management classes wouldn't help you. I will say this. When Madeline asked me about Michael when we were in New York, I told her to stay away from him because he was the husband of one of my dear friends. But you're no longer a friend of mine; get the hell away from me."

Leaving her tray on the table, Denise got up and left the cafeteria without a goodbye, with Madeline close behind.

"Now see what you've done?" Madeline said, leaving Mona standing by herself.

Mona picked up her tray and sat it on the discard table. She was disgusted at herself, but that didn't mean that Madeline Brooks was off the hook. Suddenly, Mona wasn't interested in speaking to Michael. He'd call when he was ready. Mona left the hospital feeling worse than when she'd arrived. She reached in her purse, pulled out her iPhone, and called Sylvia.

18

No one seemed to be in place today. Mona had called Sylvia's number six times and each time it had gone to voicemail. Mona sighed as she navigated her Suburban through the streets of Atlanta and its main arterials. As much as she fought against stopping at Rachel's house, she hopped on Interstate 85 and headed straight there.

Mona pulled up in Rachel's driveway, oblivious of the car parked next to her. With a heavy heart, she laid on Rachel's doorbell, hoping it would soon open so that she could bear her soul. After several minutes of non-response, Mona took to pounding on the door. "Rachel, I know you're in there; let me in."

Her heels clicked the cement on the front porch as she paced back and forth, her patience worn thin. She pounded the door again until it opened up to a less than hospitable Rachel.

"Are you crazy, Mona?" Rachel asked as she cracked the door open. "What is it?"

"What is it? Let me in; you won't believe the morning I've had."

Rachel blocked the entrance into the house. "What's up with you?"

"What's up with you? I know you aren't going to let me stand outside on the porch like somebody's stranger."

Rachel continued to block the doorway. Mona pushed Rachel's arm, but was outdone when Rachel stood her ground and denied Mona entrance. Mona tried to peek around her.

Mona huffed. "What are you hiding, Rachel? Is Michael in there?"

"Mona, please; I don't know what you're talking about."

"You know what, Rachel? Forget you. I came here because I thought I had a friend who loved me that I could share my burden with. How soon do we forget? It wasn't even a year ago that your devastated behind came running to my house after your husband's mistress showed up on your doorstep and delivered a photo of her and Marvin on top of each other naked."

Rachel pointed her finger in Mona's face. "You are the devil, Mona. You know good and well that Peaches was not Marvin's mistress and that photo was fabricated."

"Whether I do or not, this one fact I do know. You hightailed it over to my house for comfort. I gave you free room and board and counseling. But now that the table is turned, the best thing you can offer me is rejection."

"Come in," Rachel said, defeated. "Follow me."

An upset Mona followed behind Rachel. Two seconds into the family room, Mona's feet became glued to the floor.

"I was already in a counseling session, Mona," Rachel said with disgust. "Maybe you recognize my patient...the one you assaulted with your words this morning."

Mona didn't say anything. She blew air from her mouth and sat down. "Sorry," she said to Rachel. Then to Denise, "I really am sorry, Denise. I'm stressing because Michael didn't come home last night."

Shock registered on Rachel and Denise's face. Sometimes there was no understanding Mona, but now that they both somewhat knew what was eating at her, the acting out was somewhat justified because it was a part of Mona's DNA.

Denise got up from her seat and went and sat next to Mona.

"Your pouncing on us today in a public place was so foolish and ignorant. Whatever your personal vendetta is with Madeline, it has nothing to do with me. I was at the hospital to finish up some labs before I start my chemo when I ran into Madeline and decided to go to lunch. Mona, I can't do this...I can't fight for my life and fight you at the same time. I'm already weak. I want whatever time I have left on this earth to be quality. Please don't disturb that for me."

Mona looked into Denise's eyes. "I won't; I promise."

Mona reached out and hugged Denise for the longest time. Rachel came and stood over them, extending her hands on the shoulders of each person and whispered a prayer. When Rachel finished her prayer, she looked into the faces of Mona and Denise. "It's time to call the sisters."

19

S ylvia showed up on Rachel's doorstep within minutes after receiving the summons. The call came with extreme urgency attached to Rachel's voice. Sylvia's plans immediately became secondary to her new mission for the day. With it being a light day at A Touch of Elegance, Claudette rescheduled the few clients she had for the remainder of the day and placed them with her trusted stylist, Noel. It didn't take her long to navigate through downtown Atlanta traffic to Rachel's doorstep where her services were needed. Trina was in the middle of a high-profile murder case, and all calls requesting her help went straight to her voicemail.

The ladies—Rachel, Mona, Sylvia, and Claudette—were all assembled together to be an arm, shoulder, or whatever Denise needed from them. There weren't any crazy antics or amateur comedy routines displayed by virtue of the fact their eclectic group had come together. This was a serious moment, a time for consolation and prayer. Their friend, Denise, was dying and would need their support as she went through chemotherapy, even as the doctors said it wouldn't help because her cancer was too far along.

"Please don't stand around and mourn for me before I'm dead," Denise said, as she watched the stoic group who seemed unsure of what to say. "I'm still alive and what I need are hugs and kisses. Laughter…yes, your laughter is what I need."

Sylvia moved toward Denise and wedged her body in between

Denise and Rachel. She held Denise until Denise's head fell over onto Sylvia's shoulders. Tears cascaded down Denise's face. Claudette sat on the other side of Rachel while Mona stood over Denise massaging her shoulders.

Sylvia got up and asked everyone else to do so. Even in her weak state, Denise got up also.

"Hold hands," Sylvia said matter-of-factly. "We're going to pray for our sister." All was silent except Sylvia's voice. "Dear Lord, You are a God of second chances. You are a see all and know all God. We petition You this afternoon on behalf of our dear sister, Denise, who is in urgent need of Your help.

"We come asking for a miracle. You know all about her pain and the disease that has taken residence in her body. Lord, touch and heal her body. Make her whole. You said that we have not because we ask not, and today we're asking because we believe Your word and know that it doesn't come back void.

"Father, we ask You to give our sister strength and peace as she goes through her ordeal. I pray that my sisters who are assembled here today will surround Denise with love and understanding and exhibit the attitude of giving as we give of ourselves wherever and whenever Denise needs us. We thank You for Your blessings. Amen."

"That was a beautiful prayer, Sylvia," Denise said with a smile.

"It certainly was," Rachel agreed. "Know that we love you, Denise, and we'll be here for whatever you need."

"That's right," Mona interjected. "Not to take away from the moment but, Rachel, do you have some snacks up in here? A sister is getting a little hungry."

Everyone laughed.

"That's what I need," Denise said. "The experts say laughter is the best medicine...after prayer."

"I've got an idea," Claudette said, coming out of her somber mood. "Denise, what if I pick you up early on Saturday; wash, set, and curl you hair on the house; and then we meet up with the sisters and have brunch at the Prime Meridian?"

"Wow, you'd do that for me, Claudette?"

"Anything for you, Denise."

"It sounds wonderful, however, Harold and I are going to Birmingham this weekend to pick up Danica. I do appreciate the offer, though."

"What is everyone doing tomorrow?" Sylvia asked. "Maybe we can get together then."

"I may not be able to get away tomorrow," Claudette said. "I've got a couple of prima donnas coming to the shop, and they won't let anyone but yours truly do their hair. I can fit Denise in, if you all want to go ahead."

"No, Claudette should be there, too," Rachel interjected. "It was her idea."

"Let me think about it. Maybe I can rearrange my schedule. I'll make a few phone calls; everything should be okay. Do you think you can be ready by nine, Denise?" Claudette asked.

"Yes, I can." Denise smiled as she looked around at her special group of friends. "As I look at you all, I can't help but remember the night I came to know you."

"Don't go there." Rachel laughed.

"Rachel, I remember you walking the floor with your fists balled up, while I was up talking about Marvin and me kissing in Times Square. I swear you wanted to knock the taste out of my mouth. You had a whole lot of attitude going on." Everyone laughed.

"She did!" Sylvia interjected.

"You couldn't be talking about me, Denise," Rachel said. "Surely, I wasn't that bad."

Mona came from the kitchen. "You weren't that bad? If Denise hadn't taken her wig off, I bet all the money I have in my purse, you would've got up in Denise's face and put it to her."

"Come on, Mona. You're making me out to look like a she-devil."

"You were mad as hell," Sylvia said. "I was a little upset, too."

"And what did you think, Claudette?" Denise asked.

"Girl, I was praying that Rachel wasn't going to whip your ass." Everyone broke out in laughter.

Denise raised her hand. "May I say something?" The room was quiet again. "Believe it or not, that was a pivotal moment in my life. I was a drama queen, but I learned what friendship was all about. I'm sure if I hadn't seen Rachel with Marvin that night at the restaurant, I would have never entered your lives. You all are special to me…and I love you."

"Aw, Denise…" Rachel couldn't finish her words. She choked up and put her hands over her mouth and closed her eyes. Sylvia went to her side and rubbed her back. "Denise, I love you, too. Life is funny…crazy…with all of its twists and turns. But at the end of the day, I'm so glad we became friends."

"I love you, too, Denise," Mona said. "I'm going back in Rachel's kitchen to see what I can fix us to eat."

Rachel held up her hand. "Hold up a sec, Mona. Why did you ask if Michael was here when you first arrived? I know what you said about…"

Mona stopped in her tracks and held out her hand to stop. She cleared her throat and looked at Rachel, then at Denise. Claudette's eyes were bucked as if she was trying to hold on to Mona's secret. "No reason." Mona left the room.

Momentary silence enveloped the room. Strange stares were passed around the room. Claudette refused to participate and started to the kitchen to help Mona when the doorbell rang.

"I wonder who that could be?" Rachel asked, as she left the group and walked to the door to answer it. She peeked out of the peephole, let out a smile, and opened the door. "It's Trina," Rachel called out.

"Hi, Rachel. I rushed over as soon as I read my text," Trina said, out of breath. "You won't believe what happened today."

"Come in. The ladies are in the family room."

Trina seemed flustered. She followed Rachel to where everyone was still chatting.

"Hey, Trina," everyone called out.

"You missed the prayer," Mona said, trotting back in with a plate of cheese and crackers.

"Prayer?" Trina asked. "For what?"

Denise stood up. "They were praying for me. I have stage-four breast cancer." Denise lowered her head, then brought it back up. "It doesn't look good."

"Oh, Denise," Trina said as she gave Denise a big hug and held her, "I'm so sorry. Girl, I'm praying for you, too."

"Thank you."

Rachel pointed to a seat and Trina sat. "So what happened today that's got you all up in arms, Trina?"

"I just received word from my colleague that Peaches was murdered today."

Everyone gasped. "Murdered?" Rachel said, her eyes bulging from her face. "Are you sure?"

"Yes, I'm quite sure. A guard found her lying on the kitchen floor where she was on KP duty. They said that someone took a blunt object and hit her in the back of the head several times. She must've been hit hard because there were no signs of a struggle."

"Damn," Mona said.

"Of course there's going to be a big investigation," Trina went on. "The trial was due to take place in a month and Peaches had one of the best criminal lawyers in town. It doesn't add up. Who would want Peaches dead?"

20

M ona and Michael Jr. entered a very quiet house. Mona looked around to see if there was any evidence that her husband had been home while she was out. Nothing.

"Mommy, I want to be a Transformer for Halloween."

"Halloween is a little over two-and-a-half months away, Michael Jr. We've got plenty of time. Go and get washed up. Mommy will get you some snacks to hold you over until dinner."

"Okay, Mommy."

As Mona entered the kitchen, she noticed that the answering machine was lit up. Michael had left several messages. Mona wasn't certain that she wanted to hear what he had to say and ignored them until she got Michael Jr. settled in.

"Mona, we need to talk," Michael's voice said. "We can't continue like this. I love you. Call."

Mona clamped her hands over her mouth and suppressed tears that threatened to fall. She loved her husband with all of her heart and soul. Her life with Michael was the happiest her life had ever been. Jealousy had to take a backseat if she wanted her marriage to be whole. She had a good-looking man who was also a very good and loving husband. But more than that, Michael was a brilliant surgeon and well-renowned in medical circles. President Barack Obama had even considered Michael for the position of Surgeon General.

Slowly, Mona picked up the phone to dial Michael's number. Nerves wanted her to put the receiver down, but she dialed anyway. It rang and rang, and eventually the call went to voicemail. Disappointed, Mona hung up the phone without leaving a message. Before she turned away, the phone rang. Mona looked at the caller ID and smiled.

"Hey, baby," Michael said into the phone.

Mona paused and held her chest. "Hi, Michael."

"I guess you got my messages."

"Yes, all five of them."

There was a pause. Then Michael spoke again. "Mona, we need to talk. I hate this dissention between us. I want you to understand who I am—the man you married."

"I want that, too, Michael. It's been lonesome."

"I understand you had a run-in with Denise and Madeline today."

"So, does Dr. Madeline run and tell you everything? I don't know why I thought we could have a conversation without bringing her up."

"Mona, she is the root cause of why we're having this conversation at all."

"Michael, you may not see it, but as your wife sitting on the outside, it's very evident that Madeline came to Atlanta for one thing."

"And what is that?"

"You want me to spell it out for you? You want to hear me say that Madeline came to Atlanta to be near you so that your ego can be stroked?"

"Maybe my timing was all wrong. I had hoped we could talk and settle this Madeline thing once and for all."

"As long as she's in Atlanta, it'll never be settled."

"Well, she's on staff at Emory. You need to make up your mind as to what you want to do."

"Or else?"

"I didn't say that, Mona. You did. Good night." And the phone was dead.

Mona huffed. What had gone wrong? She knew. It was the moment Michael called out Madeline's name. She had to come up with a scheme to get rid of her.

"Were you talking to your wife?" Madeline asked, standing in the doorway to Michael's office.

Michael was annoyed at her sudden appearance. He ignored her and shuffled through some records that were on his desk.

"May I come in, Dr. Broussard?" Madeline asked politely.

"If it doesn't have to do with a patient, I'm not in the mood for conversation."

Madeline moved further into Michael's office and closed the door. She stood behind him as he wrote a note in a chart, bending over him and rubbing her cheek against his. He moved away, but she whispered in his ear. "You don't have to say a word; you can keep on working. I'll sit in a chair and wait until you're ready to talk."

Michael inhaled her scent but he would not be moved. "Not now," Michael said.

"I'll be quiet. You won't even know that I'm here."

Michael didn't turn around and continued to write in patients' charts. Ten, fifteen minutes passed without a word. Michael looked at the picture of his wife and child that sat on his desk without picking it up. He sulked. Ten more minutes went by when he decided to get up and leave.

Michael turned around in his chair and stopped cold. He thought Madeline was gone, but there she was lying on the patient examination table. Her hair was down and spread across the top of the table. Madeline's white coat was unbuttoned and laying off to the sides. Her body, fully clothed, was stretched out on the table, her legs propped up, and her healthy boobs sitting upright as if waiting for a doctor's thorough exam. The bottom of Madeline's skirt was hiked up to her waist, exposing all of her thighs, legs, and what lay in between. Thank God for the white stockings, although it didn't keep Michael's imagination from running wild or the bulge in his pants from growing.

"Get up, Madeline, and go home. I could report you right now, and that would be the end of your career."

"But I know you won't, Michael." Madeline sat up and smiled. "Look at you. Got a healthy hard-on. I always affected you that way."

"I'm a married man...happily married man," Michael reiterated. "Our time was long ago."

"So why did you sleep in your office last night? Didn't think I knew, did you?"

"I don't care what you know, but you need to get up out of here now, doc. This isn't a safe place for you."

"Why? Because you're afraid of yourself...afraid that you'll fall under my spell...afraid that you won't be able to resist what's before you?"

"Madeline..."

In an instant, Madeline scooted from the table and swooped down on Michael, encircling his lips with hers, straddling him while she sat in his lap. Her skirt was still hiked up to her waist and Michael felt her feminine part rub against his throbbing member and her breasts beat upon his chest, making it hard to ignore the rush of adrenaline that flowed through his body. The lustful part of him wanted to strip her naked and take her right there in his office, but the reasonable part of him knew that he had to resist no matter what the lustful part of his body desired. Michael pushed Madeline off of him.

"Michael, you're making a grave mistake. I want you, and I'm going to have you." She reached behind her and unhooked her bra.

Michael turned away at the sight of her breasts. He closed his eyes, sighed, and blew air from his mouth, remembering a time when he used to feast upon Madeline's luscious nipples and caress the whole of her breasts as he made love to her.

"Tempted, aren't you?" Madeline needled, as she held her breasts for him. "You used to make them feel so good, Michael. Helped me get through many tedious days of cramming for medical exams. Don't you remember? You would make love to me like it was a part of anatomy class. And you did it so well."

Madeline edged toward Michael and gently sat on his lap again, her breasts in his face. Michael stood up and Madeline grabbed the exam table to keep from falling.

"Your attempt to make me slip and fall into your trap is not going to work," Michael said. He pointed toward the door. "Get your clothes on and get out of my office. Don't ever darken my door again as long as you're on staff."

"You don't mean that, Dr. Broussard. I can always say that you sexually harassed me."

"You do that, and I promise you'll never work as a doctor again in any of the fifty states. Dr. Brooks, good day."

21

"Hey, baby," Rachel said, as she heard Marvin come through the door. "Serena and I are in the family room."

"Hi, sweeties," Marvin called back.

"Hi, Daddy," Serena said.

"Baby, come quick. A special news bulletin about Peaches' death is on."

Marvin hurried into the room. He stared at the television set. "Peaches is dead?"

"You didn't know? Shhh," Rachel said as the news reporter spoke about the incident.

"At three-thirteen this afternoon, Vera Franklin, an inmate in the Metro State Prison who went by the name of Peaches, was found by a prison guard lying in a pool of blood on the floor in the prison mess hall where she was on KP duty. Sources say she was hit several times with a blunt object to the back of the head. Ms. Franklin was due to come to trial in a matter of weeks for the kidnapping and assault of Rachel Thomas, wife of CEO Marvin Thomas of Thomas and Richmond Tecktronics, Inc. Ms. Franklin's death has been declared a homicide, and at this time, no one has been implicated in her death. This is Lindsey Shelton reporting live from Metro State Prison for WGCL-TV Atlanta."

"Thank you, Lindsey. In other news, Ashley Jordan Lewis, daughter of famed attorney Robert Jordan, may be released within the next week or so after a six-and-a-half-year stint behind bars for the arsenic poisoning of her husband, William Lewis, a Georgetown graduate."

"What?" Marvin shouted.

"Shhh," Rachel said, putting her finger to her lips.

"It has been determined that a series of errors by crime scene investigators and forensic lab specialists may have tainted the investigation in Mrs. Lewis' criminal trial, thus causing an overturn of the verdict that was rendered. There is still some red tape that Ashley Lewis must get through first, and WGCL-TV News will be first on hand to give you the latest update on this story. Again, Ashley Jordan Lewis will be a free woman in the coming days."

Rachel rubbed her hands together while walking in circles. "Can you believe that, Marvin? Just like that, Ashley's getting out of jail."

Marvin went and stood next to Rachel. "It's a miracle. I don't know what happened because Ashley all but admitted that she killed William. If she were black, no miracle under the sun would save her behind."

"Tell me about it. But I'm happy for Ashley. She was under a lot of pressure, although, I'd never condone killing William."

"Look at us, Rachel. We prayed for Ashley to be released. Even gave her the money she'd given to us for her release fund. We're acting as if she should stay in jail."

"Are we?"

"Sounds like it. Let's call Claudette to see if she's heard anything."

"Good idea. Marvin, what do you think Ashley is going to do about Reagan when she gets out? It would break Claudette's heart if Ashley wants her child back."

"Let's cross that bridge when we have to. The truth of the matter is that it will be for Claudette and Ashley to hash out. Where's your BlackBerry?"

22

Hugs were passed around as the ladies filled the lobby of the Prime Meridian. Extra special hugs were given to Denise, whose hair was sheared into a close-cropped bob that Claudette so beautifully styled.

"Denise, your hair is absolutely drop-dead gorgeous," Mona said, wanting to be the first to extend a compliment.

"Thanks, Mona. I have my stylist to thank for my fabulous do." Denise gave Claudette a wink.

"Ladies, this way," the hostess instructed.

The crew—Mona, Denise, Sylvia, Rachel, Claudette, and surprisingly, Trina, followed the hostess to their table. At one-thirty in the afternoon, the major lunch crowd had dwindled, and the girls were happy they didn't have long to wait.

"Someone will be here in a moment to take your drink orders," the hostess said.

"Thank you," Mona said. "I need a drink."

"How are you feeling, Denise?" Trina asked.

"Today, I feel pretty good. I start chemo on Monday."

"I'll be with you," Rachel offered, although her mind was already made up.

"Rachel and I are going to switch off," Sylvia interjected. "That way, someone will be available to pick the kids up from school."

Denise smiled. "You're all so thoughtful and I appreciate it. Now ladies, let's make this a lively luncheon before I regret having come here. I don't want you all to dwell on me. This is one of mine and Harold's favorite restaurants, and I'm going to live each day as if it were my last. And Sylvia, next week Harold, I, and Danica will be attending church with you."

Everyone looked at Denise. "You say that like the rest of us don't go to church...like we're straight-up heathens," Mona said, a smile erupting from the side of her mouth.

"Well, if the shoe fits," Denise said. Everyone laughed.

Rachel looked thoughtfully around the table. "You know, I have a lot to be thankful for."

"Yeah, you don't have to look over your shoulder every morning, noon, or night and wonder if Peaches has escaped out of prison again and is following you," Mona chimed in.

"That's right, although it's a shame that she was brutally murdered."

"Serves her right, Rachel," Claudette said. "She almost caused the breakup of your marriage—serving you with a fabricated copy of her and Marvin doing the nasty."

"Don't forget about the fifty-thousand dollars she tried to extort from Marvin," Mona plugged in."

"Yeah," Rachel said with a sigh. "I'm going to be in the pew next to you when you go to church next Sunday, Sylvia."

"My God, Rachel," Mona said nonchalantly, "did the earth shake and swallow you up whole?"

"Your butt needs to be somewhere getting some Godly wisdom because you sure need Jesus," Rachel retorted. "You're a long way from being a saint, Mona, and if you don't turn from your wicked ways..."

"Or what?" Mona wanted to know.

"Peaches will rise from the dead and come and take you to the depths of hell with her." There were chuckles all around.

"That is not funny, Rachel. If anybody's going to hell, it's Michael." Everyone stopped and looked at Mona who failed to elaborate on her statement.

"Oh my God," Claudette cut in. "I almost forgot. Ashley is going to be released from prison. I'm not sure when, but it's supposed to be within the next few weeks. Our prayers have been answered."

"That's great news, Claudette," Sylvia interjected, picking up her glass of water. "Where's the waitress? I'm hungry."

As if on cue, the waitress appeared at their table, took their lunch orders, and the ladies were back to chatting.

"So, what are you going to do about Reagan?" Sylvia asked.

"What do you mean, what am I going to do about Reagan?" Claudette countered with a perplexed look on her face.

"What if Ashley wants to raise her daughter herself?"

"Sylvia, I adopted Reagan as my own." Claudette tried to remain calm. "Ashley will always be able to visit Reagan whenever she likes, but I'm her momma now. Got that? Everyone else clear?" Claudette took a sip of her water. "I need something stronger."

There was a moment of silence. Denise hadn't participated in any of the dialogue, but listened to the banter passing back and forth.

"You all right, Denise?" Rachel asked, rubbing Denise's arm.

"Yeah. I'm enjoying your lively conversation. I have a question. Isn't it time for you all to be making some more babies?"

"Denise, you're crazy," Sylvia said.

"Well, I'm a one-hit wonder," Rachel interjected, taking a sip of her lemonade.

"You know Marvin's been hitting *it* every chance he gets," Mona chided.

"I'm pretty sure Michael hasn't missed a beat either," Rachel threw back. "You probably have welts all over your behind from where he's been hitting *it*." Everyone at the table roared, including Denise.

"We were talking about you, not me."

"I don't recall Denise implicating any particular person," Rachel said. "If you can't take it, Mona dear, don't dish it."

Mona was quiet and sat back in her chair.

"So," Sylvia spoke up, "how is the great Dr. Broussard? He didn't show up at our gumbo and jambalaya night, especially when his wife fixed the food."

"Yeah, we haven't seen him around," Trina said, speaking up for the first time in awhile.

"He's probably busy with all of his patients," Claudette chimed in.

Everyone's head turned and looked in Claudette's direction.

"You speak for Mona, now?" Sylvia inquired. "Ms. Motor Mouth can speak for herself. She has no trouble any other time."

All eyes were on Mona, who fidgeted in her seat. She rolled her eyes and raised her hand to get the waitress' attention.

"Don't ignore the question," Rachel pushed. "We'd like an answer."

"Kiss my ass, Rachel," were the four words that flew out of Mona's mouth.

"I wasn't the one who asked the question, dear," Rachel said, giving Mona one of her *don't even try* looks. Mona sighed.

"Well, since Mona's got lockjaw, we'll move on," Sylvia said.

"Trina is the only one without kids," Claudette interjected. "Maybe she's next to join the Mommy Fan Club."

"Not me," Trina said swiftly. "Can't have any."

"Sorry," Claudette mouthed.

"Here's lunch," Rachel called out. "I'm famished."

Everyone dug into their food as if it was truly their last supper.

The lively conversation continued, although Mona didn't contribute and picked at her food.

"Guess what Kenny Jr. asked his dad last night?" Sylvia announced, while chewing the last bit of her salad, her fork still in the air.

"Please tell us," Rachel said sarcastically but in a playful tone.

"He walked in the bathroom as big Kenny was taking a leak, and Kenny Jr. asked his dad if his penis was going to get as big as big Kenny's."

Clink. Rachel's fork dropped from her hand and hit her plate. "Too much information, but what did big Kenny say?"

Everyone waited on Sylvia's answer. Trina and Denise chewed their food in slow motion, anticipating the answer. Rachel had a grin on her face. Claudette wasn't amused but acted as if she was interested.

The countenance on Mona's face changed. All of a sudden she seemed uncomfortable, laying her fork on her plate. Mona looked up as Michael followed the hostess into the dining room and upon seeing her, stopped and walked over to the table where she and her girls sat.

"Ladies," Michael said with a smile but made it personal for Mona. "You all don't mind if Mona excuses herself to sit with her husband, do you?"

Heads shook in the affirmative followed by a "no" from Sylvia. Mona pursed her lips and pretended to smile, although it could've been real, and followed Michael to his table.

"So what's up with Mona?" Sylvia asked again. "We know you've got the four-one-one, Claudette…always babying Mona."

Claudette rolled her eyes but kept glancing over in Mona and Michael's direction. "Seems like they're doing fine." The ladies looked in Mona's direction.

"Mona told Denise and me that Michael didn't come home the other night. I tell you, it may have something to do with Denise's cousin," Rachel offered. "Seems that Dr. Madeline Brooks, you remember her from the wedding—she kept pawing on Michael—anyway, she's moved to Atlanta and is on staff at Emory. Marvin saw Michael and Madeline holed up in this very restaurant. I say that's got to be what's working Mona's nerve."

"You had that piece of information and didn't share?" Sylvia asked.

"Kenny was with Marvin. Surprised he didn't tell you." Rachel snickered.

Denise finally spoke up. "Madeline is my cousin, but I laid down the law to her. She knows that Michael Broussard is off-limits."

"So...your cousin does have ulterior motives for being here?" Sylvia asked.

"I'm not sure of her motives, Sylvia, but it's none of my business," Denise said, picking up her fork and diving into her salmon salad. "It's none of my business."

"I'm with Denise," Claudette agreed. "Anyway, this is supposed to be a fun lunch. We can tackle world issues later."

"I agree," Trina said. "What I want to know is what Kenny told Kenny Jr."

Everyone laughed.

Mona sat with her head slightly bowed, with fear in her heart, and very apprehensive as to what her husband was about to say. She looked back at her girlfriends, who took parting glances, trying in their minds to figure out what her drama was all about.

Michael looked gorgeous—like a piece of fruit, a juicy red apple to be exact, she'd been anxious to wrap her lips around all day. Boy, she missed him. When she got up enough nerve to look at him, Michael was staring back with love in his heart and a smile on his face. The warmth returned to her body, and Mona smiled when she realized there was nothing to fear.

"You look good, baby," she heard Michael say.

Mona's smile widened. "You look good, too. In fact, you are a sight for sore eyes."

"I want to come home, Mona. I want to come home today to be with my wife and son." Michael reached for Mona's hands that were sitting on the table. "You were right about Madeline, and I shouldn't have doubted you. What I want you to know, Mona, is that nothing and no one will ever come between us...ever. I love you with all of my heart."

Mona pushed back the tears and held Michael's hands tight. "That's all I want to hear, baby. I love you, too. And I'm sorry for my outbursts; I didn't have faith in us to believe that all I had to do was go to you in peace to work out my insecurities."

"It's not all your fault and I'm not going to sit here and let you take all the blame. Although I've never led Madeline on and was as surprised as you when I found out that she had moved to Atlanta and was on staff at Emory...actually 'shocked' is a better word to describe my knowledge of it, I knew that you would explode when you found out and accuse me of orchestrating her sudden arrival on the scene."

"But you lied to me, Michael. If you had been forthcoming...if you had told me from the jump, there would've been a different outcome."

"You're right, baby. Hindsight is twenty-twenty. But from here on out, there won't be any secrets between us. Trust and good communication are key to our survival."

"I want us...this marriage, and I'm willing to do whatever it takes to keep our family together."

"You don't know how sweet that sounds, Mrs. Mona Broussard."

Mona smiled. "My lunch is getting cold."

Michael motioned for the waitress to come to the table. When the waitress reached the table, Michael ordered two cocktails. "I'd also like to order whatever my wife was eating at the table where all those nosey ladies are looking our way…"

"That was the salmon salad, correct?" the waitress asked.

"Correct," Mona said as she smiled at her husband and let her hand slide up and down his arm. "And I'm sure my husband would like the same."

"That's correct," Michael agreed. The waitress walked away. Michael looked into Mona's eyes. "I'm going to cancel all my appointments for the rest of the day. I want to go home and make mad love to my wife before Michael Jr. comes home. Better yet, have Rachel or Sylvia pick him up from school and we'll pick him up later."

Mona stared at Michael. "Are you serious?"

"Do you have any objections?"

"We should have cancelled lunch and gone straight home. I would love to be made love to by my husband."

"You won't regret a minute of it."

"Welcome home, Dr. Broussard."

23

E mory University Hospital continued to be ranked amongst
the most prestigious hospitals in the United States. Its top
medical advances, top-of-the-line patient care as well as
education of health care professionals were the things that drew
Dr. Madeline Brooks to the hospital. Well, it was one of the
things because the major draw, if truth be told, was one of its top
cardiologists by the name of Dr. Michael Broussard.

Madeline couldn't get him off her mind. Day and night, her
thoughts were consumed with being with him forever—his wife
be damned. Her fantasies were wild and wicked, fueled by her
closeness to him as she sought him out daily to ask a question or
get an opinion on something she already had the answer to. She
wanted him bad and every time she was near him her sexual
stimulators would activate, opening the pores to her erogenous
zones and filling her heart with pure, unadulterated lust. And his
very presence made Madeline long for the days when they were
in medical school when she couldn't get enough of Michael
Broussard who satisfied all of her needs at the drop of a hat.

Clicking her pen and setting it down, Madeline closed the
patient chart she was working on. She checked her watch; it was
three in the afternoon. She hadn't seen Michael in awhile, and
she set out for his office before she had to make rounds. She
arrived at Michael's office and stopped at the receptionist's desk.
Her name plate identified her as Deborah.

"Is Dr. Broussard in?" Madeline inquired, staring at the closed door. It was only yesterday evening that she lay behind the closed door, trying to seduce Dr. Broussard with her body. Madeline hadn't missed the look he gave her full, braless breasts as he forced himself to resist her. If he had hesitated a second longer, she knew he would have given in. Madeline shook the thought from her mind.

"No," Deborah said. "He cleared his schedule and has gone home for the day. Would you like to leave a message for his secretary, Michelle?"

A frown formed on Madeline's face and she left without a response to the question. She walked at a fast pace, almost knocking down several doctors along the way. As soon as Madeline entered her office, she slammed the door. She found her BlackBerry and dialed Michael's number. Her call went straight to voicemail. She called several more times with the same result. She threw her phone across the room and balled her hands into fists. "I will have you, Michael, or else. I don't plan to lose. You belong to me."

Mona knew the girls were talking about her as soon as she walked away after announcing that she and Michael were going to spend the afternoon together and asked if Sylvia or Rachel would pick Michael Jr. up from school. They weren't even discrete about it. She saw their faces light up as if they knew what spending the afternoon together meant. It didn't take a rocket scientist to figure it out, and Mona was glad to be mending the broken fence that separated her and Michael.

"I almost feel like we're dating again," Michael said from the passenger seat as Mona navigated her way out of downtown to the interstate.

Mona smiled. "Nice, huh? I remember our romantic interludes."

"You are my queen, Mona, and I'm going to take out more time to do some of the stuff we used to."

"Baby, we enjoy being in the same room, sharing a movie together. It's not always about the sex, although you know your queen loves every bit of loving her king lays on her. And you are the best, Michael Broussard."

It was Michael's turn to smile. "So, I'm a good lover? Do I make you happy and satisfy all your wanton needs?"

"Yes to all. But I do want to add that you also satisfy all my needs and desires that are lustful, shameless, immoral, and those I will never tell a soul and will take to the grave with me." They both laughed.

"How about you telling me what those needs and desires are and I'll try and satisfy them for you."

"Can we wait until we get home?" Mona said seductively.

"How long will that take?"

"Michael Broussard, you are hot in the pants."

"No, I've got a ferocious hard-on, but I'm going to love you, Mona Broussard, like you've never been loved."

"Is that a promise?"

"A promise I will keep. Don't run that red light in front of you."

Mona slammed on the brakes. "Anxious."

At the end of the shift, Madeline hung up her white coat and headed for her car. She had been invited by some of the single, young interns to go with them for a drink after work. That wasn't her style, and for certain not with interns, but she was in a funk and maybe a couple of drinks would be harmless and help her to forget about Michael Broussard for the evening.

24

For several weeks, Michael ignored Madeline's phone calls and insisted he was busy when she happened to stop by his office. Home life couldn't be better now that he and Mona had recaptured the romance and magic back into their marriage. He picked up the photo of Mona and Michael Jr. that sat on his desk, looked at it and smiled. They were all he needed in his life.

He put the photo down as the phone began to ring. Michael's frown became a smile at the sound of his mother's familiar voice.

"Hey, Mommie, what's going on? Poppie's birthday celebration? Yes, I will tell Mona, and we will be there. So good to hear from you. Will talk to you later. Love you. Bye."

Before putting the receiver down, Michael dialed home. There wasn't an answer so he dialed Mona's cell phone. "Hey, baby, what you up to?"

"I'm in the elevator on my way to Claudette's to get my mane done for you, baby. What's up?"

"My mother called. Poppie is turning eighty-five years old next month. Mommie is planning a big celebration and has invited all of the family, which, of course, includes us. It's been a while since we've been to New Orleans."

"Yeah," Mona said, remembering her parents' death during Katrina. "We have to go to the celebration."

"By all means. I'm excited; it'll be good to get away from here for a few days."

"Okay, baby. We'll talk about it when you get home. I love you."

"Love you, too." Michael put down the receiver and grinned.

"Hello, Dr. Broussard."

Michael swung around at the sound of Madeline's voice. "What are you doing here?"

Madeline closed the door and locked it. "Your trusty guard dog was away from her desk. My timing must've been good as it seems that lately she guards your door like it was Fort Knox."

"So, do you have a medical situation you need clarity on?"

"Indeed I do." She moved forward.

"Stop right there." Michael watched Madeline with cautious eyes as she folded her arms over her chest, calculating her movements so as not to wind up in the predicament he was in the other night. "So what is it? I don't see any charts or a notepad."

"Don't need any. My medical problem is derived from the drought between my legs. I've determined that it is due to non-penile penetration."

"That's not my problem," Michael said with a stone face. "But maybe I can offer a suggestion."

"And what is that?" Madeline said with a flicker of hope in her eyes.

"There are a multitude of establishments here in Atlanta that sell the kind of things that may eliminate your drought as well as alleviate the need for the real thing. But if you prefer human flesh, you have a choice of ten appendages of your own that may help to assuage those needs. That's my medical opinion for today. Now I'm busy and you're excused."

Madeline scurried over her top teeth with her tongue. "Don't get flip with me, Michael. I'm quite aware what Atlanta offers in its sex shops. That's not what I crave at the moment." She didn't move and stared at Michael seductively. "I hope you will come to your senses." Madeline knocked her knees together. "I know you remember how good it was."

"I will have you removed if you don't get out now. I'm warning you, Madeline."

"Two can play the game, but I hope you'll see it my way. And by the way, Mona doesn't deserve you." Madeline dropped her arms to her sides, unlocked the door, turned around and stared at Michael again, and walked out of the door.

Michael breathed a sigh of relief, but in the back of his mind he was bothered by all of this. He didn't want to be the one to sabotage Madeline's career, but there was only so much he could take. Michael hit the intercom.

"Yes, Dr. Broussard?"

"Michelle, please come in and bring your steno pad."

Michelle came in, looked around, and sat in the empty chair next to Michael.

"What I'm about to dictate to you is confidential." Michelle shook her head to acknowledge she understood. "The contents of this letter are classified, and I must reiterate that you are not to divulge any parts of it to no one."

"Yes, sir."

"Date it with today's date. To Whom It May Concern: I am writing this letter to document several incidents of sexual harassment committed by a female colleague against my person." Michelle looked up at Michael and dropped her eyes quickly to her steno pad. "On the following dates, the described acts were committed by Dr. Madeline Brooks."

Michelle's eyes became wide as saucers. Even her nostrils flared. Michael noted that she seemed to have extreme difficulty writing the rest of his dictated words. "Sign it, Sincerely yours, Michael Broussard, M.D."

Michelle sat still for a moment without saying a word.

"That's all. Remember this must stay confidential. After I sign it, I want to lock it up in our confidential file until I give you further instructions. That's all."

"Are you all right?"

"I'm fine, Michelle, in fact, my wife and I and Michael Jr. will be going to New Orleans for a few days in a couple of weeks. My father will be eighty-five and my mother is planning a big celebration. I can't wait to put on my dancing shoes."

"Sounds like fun, Dr. B. I'm going to type up that letter and get ready for lunch."

"Okay. Remember, confidential."

Michelle nodded and walked out of Michael's office. He didn't put it past Madeline to turn tide on him because he was ignoring her advances. He needed to confide in someone. Marvin and Kenny were his most trusted friends. He'd call and meet them later for cocktails. There was no way he was going to let Madeline ruin everything he worked so hard for.

25

Earl's Tavern was the last place Michael would have thought Marvin would have chosen to meet because it was the place where Marvin met the destructive Peaches who nearly destroyed his life. Now that Peaches was dead, maybe the taint the place once had had now disappeared.

Michael adjusted his eyes to the dimness of the place as he entered. He moved his arm up and down like he was Moses parting the Red Sea, trying to divide or clear the smoke that clouded his vision. Once he made it past the cloud cover, he moved toward the bar.

Marvin and Kenny were already inside shooting the bull with Earl, the owner. Michael locked arms with Marvin and Kenny in turn and ended with the gentlemen's shake and the Obama fist. This was Michael's first time meeting Earl. Marvin introduced him and told Earl that Michael was Mona's husband.

"I remember Mona well," Earl said with a grin. "She was the beautiful and feisty one. She had me going for a minute. At the time, I didn't know that she was trying to get information out of me about Peaches, and I might have given her the four-one-one, too, because she was batting those long eyelashes and laying it on thick, if you don't mind me saying so."

"That's Mona," Michael replied. "She's a real actress when she wants to be. But so that we're clear, that feisty woman belongs to me." Michael laughed and Earl joined him.

"Yes, sir. Man, she's too much for me. What are you all having?" Earl asked, after which he turned toward Marvin. "Coke for you, Marvin." Earl and Marvin laughed.

"Earl, today I'm not drowning my sorrows, and as Paul in the Bible said, I've put away strong drink—forever. Coke it is. And I'm paying."

Michael shook his hand. "No, I got this, Marv. Let's go and sit at one of those round tables."

"They've got some good chicken wings," Kenny said, pretending to lick his fingers.

"How do you know?" Michael asked.

"When Harold and I came here on a stakeout looking for Peaches, we had to wait awhile. I'm telling you, if it weren't for the chicken wings, I might not have made it." The guys laughed.

"This must be serious since we couldn't invite Harold to come along," Marvin interjected.

"Something like that," Michael mumbled. "I can trust you guys with what I'm about to tell you. Marv, remember how your life was turned upside down last year with that Peaches mess?"

Marvin and Kenny passed glances between them but now gave Michael their rapt attention.

"What is it, Michael?" Kenny asked cautiously.

"It's Madeline."

"Oh," Marvin said, comprehending.

"The mistress you were dining with in the corner, in the back at the Prime Meridian," Kenny said, making his own assumptions.

"She's not my mistress and I wasn't trying to wine or dine her when you all saw me that day. It was a mere lunch between two colleagues."

"Okay, we got that," Marvin said facetiously.

"Look guys, I need to confide in you."

"Two beers and one Coke," Earl said, sneaking up on the trio. "Will there be anything else? I'm so glad you fellas gave me a chance and stopped by."

Marvin took his Coke and lifted it. "To you, Earl."

No one else said anything and Earl took off.

"This Madeline," Michael began, "has venom running through her soul. I'm not sure she would be in Atlanta now if she hadn't seen me at Harold and Denise's wedding. We have a history. Back in medical school, Madeline and I used to date. While I knew she would make a great doctor someday, she was also good in turning me out."

"Ouch," Kenny said, interrupting Michael's train of thought.

"Anyway, we used to have what people call mind-blowing sex— and it was that good. I couldn't get enough of her and she couldn't get enough of me. I'd be in class dissecting a cadaver, and all I could think about was how long it would be before I could tap into that ink well, or what we called it between ourselves…banana pudding."

"Lord, have mercy," Marvin exclaimed. "The pudding was that good."

"Yes, my friend, it was better than good."

"You better not let Mona hear you say that," Kenny chided.

"You got that right. One time, I thought I might have to wear a girdle to keep my banana pudding dipper from trying to push through my slacks. Her stuff was like a magnet and, and I swear, every time I was near her…well, you have an idea of how it was."

"Friend, she messed you up. How in the world did you get away from her?" Kenny asked.

"I graduated from medical school before she did. My parents were so proud of me: I graduated in the top ten percent of my class. I was so happy that I didn't let them down, especially behind some good-ass poontang." The guys laughed. "After graduation, I knew I had a new priority. I was going to be responsible for saving real lives, and so when I became an intern, I buckled down and turned all of my energies into being the best doctor that I could be. I'm not considered to be a world-renowned surgeon because of my good looks."

"What good looks?" Marvin joked. "Kenny, did he say he was good-looking? Thank God for your skillful hands."

"Anyway," Michael began again, "that's the background on Madeline that takes us to today. She is trying to pursue me. We had some openings at Emory, and she asked for a transfer to be near me, hoping to recapture what we once had. She knows I'm in love with my wife, but that means nothing to Madeline. She came into my office one evening last week, got up on the patient table and laid there with her legs propped open like she was a piece of Rothschild candy. Back in the day, I could easily say like that woman did in the commercial, *Not now, I'm in the middle of a Rothschild.*"

"I need another beer on that one," Kenny said, slapping both Michael's and Marvin's hands. "Brother, you ran your player card into the ground."

"Last year was a nightmare for me, but this, Brother Michael, is pure porn," Marvin interjected.

"Don't forget Peaches had a picture of your two nude bodies in a sling."

"Michael, I don't remember a damn thing."

"That's a shame, Marvin, because Peaches looked as if she was enjoying herself."

"That was some crazy night. Met her in this very bar; I was tore-down drunk. Although I've never admitted it to anyone, I believe Peaches did have sex with me. I could never scrape her sick, sickening scent from my body, no matter how many showers I took."

Kenny and Michael glanced at Marvin as he wallowed in the pain of that awful event.

"Your time has passed and you weathered the storm," Kenny heard himself say. "Let's get back to Michael's situation."

"To cut to the chase, Madeline has been very persistent in trying to gain my affection. She keeps calling me and shows up at my office making suggestive gestures, and when I've sent her packing or rebuke her for what she's doing, she keeps telling me that she's going to have me or else. She even took off her bra and put those double D's in my face."

"Hell! Did you tickle the black olive for old time's sake?" Kenny said, then laughed along with Marvin. "Lord, I don't know what I would've done if tempted with the same proposition."

"You'd run like hell," Marvin said, "because you know Sylvia would stomp your butt in the ground, pack Kenny Jr.'s clothes, and leave your ass before the clock struck twelve."

"You're right. I'm not leaving my good woman for no woman, I don't care how fine she is or what she throws my way. I had enough of that in my former life."

"Kenny, are you through?" Michael asked. "You are so comical to watch. You and Marvin both know that your wives have you on tight strings. Yes, Mona has me on one, too."

Earl brought the trio a round of drinks. "You sure you don't want any wings? They're cooking up a fresh batch," Earl said.

"Yes, I want a five-piece with potato salad on the side," Kenny said.

"Make that two," Marvin said, holding up two fingers. "You want anything, Michael?"

"No. I've got to go home and eat my wife's food. I'm not complaining. But guys, I'm afraid that Madeline might do something crazy."

"Crazy like what?" Kenny asked, taking a sip of his beer.

"Crazy like possibly bringing me up on sexual harassment charges."

"Damn," Marvin said. "I didn't even give that a thought."

"I haven't done anything to her or with her. And the more I reject her advances, the more I fear her. I threatened her today. Threatened to call security. Threatened her career. I wrote a letter today and addressed it to our EEOC Office explaining that I believe Madeline is sexually harassing me. I put the letter in a safe place, in the event I need to use it."

"You need to send the letter to the EEOC now before Madeline ends up sending them one first. Then you'll have hell to pay," Kenny said.

"I thought about doing that but it would be the end of her career. Maybe if I can appeal to her good senses, she'll stop pursuing me and find someone else who is worthy of her love."

"It's going to be the end of your career if she files first," Marvin said.

Michael sighed. "God help me."

A young waitress balancing two plates full of food stepped up to the men's table. "Your wings are up."

26

S ylvia armed herself with cool compresses for Denise and loads of paper towel to clean up the vomit from the floor where Denise lost it all. She was glad that Rachel hadn't made it back with the kids. Chemotherapy wasn't sitting well with Denise and her high spirits seemed to evaporate along with it. She was almost through week two, and Denise felt worse now than when she had started.

"I'm so sorry, Sylvia," Denise said, as Sylvia helped her to bed.

"Girl, that's what I'm here for…to make it easy on you."

"I'm sorry that I'm not very good company right now. I feel so drowsy."

Sylvia wiped Denise's face. "Go on to sleep. I'm going to clean up the bathroom. When you wake up, I'm going to have a scrumptious bowl of chicken soup for you."

There was a low mumble and Denise was asleep. Sylvia quickly cleaned up the mess and sanitized the bathroom. It had only been two weeks, but Sylvia was feeling the stress and strain of seeing her friend suffering and in pain. The journey before paled in comparison to how Denise reacted to the chemo this time. Sylvia was worried.

Sylvia sat down after she finished cooking the soup. The last time she checked in on Denise, she was still asleep. Before she could catch a good breath, Rachel and the children entered the house.

"Hi, Mommy," Kenny Jr. said. He kissed Sylvia and she kissed him on the forehead.

"How was school today?"

"I had so much fun, Mommy. I painted a dinosaur."

"That's a good boy."

"Hi, Serena and Danica," Sylvia said, not wanting to ignore them.

"Hi, Auntie Sylvia," the two girls said in unison and gave Sylvia a kiss.

"I fixed snacks for you all in the kitchen," Sylvia called as the children headed in the direction of the kitchen before she got it out of her mouth. "And wash your hands first."

As Rachel was about to open her mouth to say something, there stood Danica. "Auntie Sylvia, is my mommy all right?"

Danica's eyes searched Sylvia's and Rachel's. At eight years of age, she was a beauty and wise beyond her years. She looked so much like Denise with her thick head of hair that was pulled back into a ponytail. She had Harold's mouth and nose. Even at eight, it wasn't hard to notice that her body was shaping out nicely, and she loved the latest fashions.

"Your mom is very courageous, Danica," Sylvia said. "She's putting up a good fight. She's a little weak, but we're going to be right here to help her through whatever she needs."

"She's going to die," Danica said flatly, as if she already knew the answer. Danica lowered her head and headed for her room before either Sylvia or Rachel could wrap their arms around her.

"That's so sad," Rachel said, taking off her jacket and laying it on the back of the chair. "She loves her mother so much. That's all she talked about in the car. So how is she?"

"Today wasn't a good day. She's been sleep for almost three hours…puked all over the bathroom as soon as we got into the house."

"I'm scared, Sylvia. We're going to lose her this time, and Danica knows it."

"The nurses said that we ought to think about getting Hospice."

"Already? She just started chemo."

"Rachel, I think Denise's cancer was much farther along and she ignored it. I heard that the doctors said the chemo wasn't going to help."

"We need to pray, Sylvia. We need to pray right now." Tears began to roll down Rachel's face. "That's my friend lying in there. I'm really getting to know her and I love her so much."

Sylvia got up and hugged Rachel. "I love her, too. Let's pray."

The two ladies prayed for God to grant a miracle for Denise. Her life had only begun—a new husband and their family together as one. Denise's life couldn't end right now.

"Hey," said a weak voice. "You guys talking about me?" Denise asked.

"We'd be lying if we said no," Rachel said, going to Denise and giving her a hug and a kiss on the cheek. "But it was all good."

"That's all I need to hear. Sylvia, did you make that soup? I only want a tad bit; I'm not real hungry."

"Yes, a small bowl of soup coming up," Sylvia said excitedly as she prepared to leave the room.

"I'd like for you to eat a bowl of soup with me, if you don't mind," Denise said without asking. Both Rachel and Sylvia nodded. "Where are the kids? I don't hear any noise."

"Danica is in her room and Kenny Jr. and Serena are eating the snack I prepared for them. I'm going to go and set up the table and put the soup in the bowls. Denise, you and Rachel take your time."

"I'm hungry," Denise said, rubbing her stomach while trying not to close her eyes.

"Let's follow Sylvia. It won't take her long, Denise."

"Okay, Rachel, after you."

"Hi, Mommy," Danica said, startling Denise. Danica went to Denise and held her around the waist.

"How's my sweetheart? Are you getting adjusted to the new school?"

"It's all right. I'm worried about you, Mommy. I don't want you to be sick."

"Baby, Mommy's doing the best she can. Know that I'll always love you." Denise put her arms around Danica's neck as Danica continued to hold her tight.

27

"Another piece of turkey bacon, baby?" Mona asked Michael, as she stood over the stove making breakfast.

"No, sweetheart, I've had enough. I've got to get to the hospital shortly, even though I don't want to leave you."

"I'm enjoying our time in the morning. You're usually up and running."

"I told you, Mona, I was going to spend more quality time with you and Michael Jr. I'm looking forward to going to New Orleans next week. It's been awhile since we've seen the family."

Mona turned away from the stove and looked at Michael. "Even though Mommie and Papa are gone, I'm looking forward to going home, also. My sisters and brothers and their families will all be in New Orleans at the time, and I'd like to spend a day or two with them."

"That's sounds like a good idea, baby. If you want to stay some extra days, you should think about it."

"I would if Michael Jr. wasn't in school. I feel bad taking him out that Thursday and Friday."

"It won't hurt him."

"I know." Mona went to Michael and gave him a kiss. "I love you, Michael."

"I love you, too, Mona. Turn that stove off and come sit on my lap." Michael wrapped his arms around Mona's waist when she sat down. He kissed her again. "I'm blessed to have you as my wife." Mona smiled.

"So is Doctor Madeline behaving?"

"I think she's gotten the hint that I don't want anything to do with her. It's a good sign since I've not heard from or ran into her in the past couple of weeks."

"Sylvia and Rachel told me that she hasn't been to see Denise, and she's her flesh and blood."

"Madeline is all about herself...and to think she's a doctor who's taken an oath to save lives. I never saw it coming."

"Well, I hope she's out of our lives for good."

Both Michael and Mona stopped talking when they heard the phone ring. "I'll get it, baby. You need to get ready to get out of here."

Mona picked up the phone and answered. "Hey, Claudette. What's up, girl?"

"Mona, it's a great day. Ashley has been released from prison."

"What? Are you sure?"

Michael stopped and turned around with a question mark on his face.

Ashley is out of prison, Mona mouthed. Michael made a great big O with his mouth.

"Yes, and I'm planning an impromptu welcome home party for her at my house tonight. Are you guys busy?"

"Michael is still here; let me check to see what his schedule is like tonight." Mona covered the phone. "Claudette is throwing Ashley a small welcome home party tonight at her house. Are you free?"

"Baby, tell Claudette we'll be there. Ashley is going to need all the friends she can get. Tell Claudette I said hi. I'm out."

"Okay, baby. I love you. Be careful and have a good day."

"Love you, too. What time do I need to be home?"

"Hold on, sweetie. Claudette, what time do you want us to come over?"

"Is seven too late?"

"No, that's great. Let me tell Michael." Mona placed her hand over the receiver. "The party will start at seven, so you need to be home by six. Smooches."

"Okay. Give me a kiss. See you tonight."

"All right, Claudette, I'm back. Do you need me to do anything?"

"Yes, as soon as you take Michael Jr. to school, come to the house. I've got all you need to make up some chicken and turkey salad sandwiches. I'll run out and get whatever else you need."

"I hope you used fresh chicken and turkey."

"Yes, Mona. Hurry up; I'm so excited."

"What if Ashley doesn't come?"

"She'll be here. She's on her way over as we speak."

"Are Rachel and Sylvia coming?"

"They're next on my list to call."

"Don't forget to invite Trina and Cecil."

"I know what I'm doing, Mona. Talk to you later."

Mona hung up the phone, picked up a piece of turkey bacon, and put it in her mouth. A smile hung across her face as she reflected on how nice it was to share conversation and breakfast with Michael this morning. God had smiled down and given her a chance to make it right with her husband. Her family was her heart, and she loved both of her boys—big Michael and little Michael—with all that she had.

"Mommy, may I have breakfast?"

Mona smiled at Michael Jr. and gave him a great big kiss.

28

C laudette was tied up in knots. Her knot was in a knot. She had fervently prayed for Ashley's release from prison and now the day had come. Claudette wasn't sure why the excitement of Ashley's release affected her differently than the rest of her friend circle, but in her heart she knew why—she and Ashley were joined at the hip by a common denominator by the name of Reagan.

In her flurry of activities this morning, Claudette stopped in the middle of the floor as if an alarm had gone off in her head. It had to do with something that either Sylvia or Rachel, perhaps Mona had said about the possibility of Ashley wanting Reagan back. It hadn't really registered…no hit her until this very moment. Claudette exhaled and let the moment pass, not wanting to conjure up ideas in her head that were placed there by others.

She loved Ashley and, at Ashley's insistence, had adopted Reagan. Maybe it was because Ashley believed she would be in prison for the rest of her life. Whatever the reason, Claudette was more than willing to provide a comfortable place for Reagan to live. It wasn't because she didn't have kids of her own. Reebe was finishing her last year in college at Hampton and Kwame had a life of his own. He was attending the School of the Arts in Florida because he wanted to be a sound engineer for a recording company one day. Claudette's smile was a proud one when she thought of how her children had elevated themselves when she had once given up on them.

She jumped at the sound of the doorbell. Claudette ran her hands down the length of her clothes, stopped at the mirror in the foyer to get a last look, and breathed in. When she got to the door, she breathed a sigh of relief when she saw Mona standing there with her hands on her hips, decked out in a fuchsia satin long-sleeved blouse, black gauchos with a large leather belt with pink-ice stones running around the perimeter of the belt buckle, and black, calf-leather boots. Mona was a true diva.

"Hey, girl," Claudette said upon opening the door.

"Hey, yourself, girlfriend. Claudette, I love this Mediterranean look."

"This is the first time you've been to my new home."

Mona looked around, peeking in every nook and cranny, twirling around to take in the vaulted ceilings with eight skylights. She ran her eyes along the banister on the second floor that looked over into the mega-large family room with its white, plush carpet. Mona's eyes stopped when she saw the large hand-painted, original piece entitled "Reflections" by Charles Bibbs hanging on the wall.

"Claudette, that's from the Bibbs' Obama Collection. I know you paid a pretty penny."

"I won't even tell you how much, but I love it," Claudette said, enunciating each of the one syllable words in *I love it* with passion. "I could never treat myself to some of the things I truly liked, art being one of them; so every now and then, when I get in the mood, I appreciate myself with a little gift." Claudette smiled.

"Well, girl, you and T have arrived. Your house is drop-dead gorgeous—I mean, absolutely beautiful. We need to give you a house warming." Mona couldn't stop staring.

"We've come a long way from our other neighborhood, you reckon?"

Mona stopped and looked at Claudette. "You and T deserve it. You've worked hard all of your lives and the dividends have paid off."

"When God gave T and me a second chance, we didn't take it lightly. God is so good, Mona. You ought to try Him."

Mona stared at Claudette for a moment. She pointed her finger at her chest, then upward. "I want you to know that He and I have a connection, and it's between Him and me."

"Good, I don't have anything else to say about it."

"Are you losing weight?" Mona asked, conveniently changing the subject.

"Can you tell?"

"Yeah, I can tell. You're rocking that outfit. It's sassy, showing off your new curves—burnt orange and brown looks good on you."

"I hadn't told anyone this, but I've been working out at the gym. You know, my baby loves the way I look."

"Hmmph, T's working that behind, too."

"I won't tell."

"Well, let's get started. I don't think we need to do a whole lot. Your place is beautiful. Simple is more."

"I have a WELCOME HOME banner and balloons that I'm getting ready to pick up."

"That should be enough for decorations. I'll make the sandwiches and a potato and pasta salad. Do you have vegetables for a nice tossed salad? I like spinach greens with shredded carrots, radishes with small baby tomatoes. Do you have any walnut raspberry vinaigrette?"

"Mona, you're a trip. Look in the fridge; if it's not there, call me on my cell. I'm on my way out."

"Okay, Claudette. I hope I don't get lost in this big kitchen of yours."

"Please, you and the good Dr. Broussard aren't living in poverty. I'm now doing me. I'm out."

Mona watched as Claudette sashayed out of the kitchen and disappeared into the foyer that led to her garage. It made her smile to know that Claudette and T had come so far from where they were. The thing that Mona observed and made her want to take a self-evaluation was that Claudette and T weren't pretentious people. They were simple but enjoyed life. Mona never thought that Claudette loved art or some of the other finer things in life because she only looked at her one way—and that was as a hairdresser.

Claudette had a giving heart—a giving spirit. Ever since their support group, the EX-Files, was founded by Sylvia to help them move forward with their lives when they were divorced women, Claudette and Ashley established a bond, although not at first. But somewhere along the line, it happened, and after Ashley went to prison for killing her ex, Claudette was always in her corner rooting for her. Because of that friendship...that bond, it was Claudette who Ashley asked to take care of Reagan when she was born—in prison.

There was a sudden knock at the door followed by a doorbell. Mona pushed herself from her thoughts and whirled around, not sure in what direction she should go. Being unfamiliar with Claudette's house, she moved from one place to another until she found the front door. She hesitated. Claudette wasn't here, so there was no need for her to answer the door.

Curiosity made Mona peep through the peephole. Standing on the front porch was what appeared to be a frazzled white woman. Mona pushed her eye on top of the hole to get a better look and thought there was something familiar about her. Mona jumped back when the woman reached forward and hit the doorbell, the chimes piercing Mona's ear. Without another second thought, she opened the door. Mona's eyes got big as saucers.

"Mona?"

"Ashley, is that you?" Mona looked around and didn't see a car. "How did you get here?"

"Are you going to invite me in? I expected to see Claudette."

"Yeah, girl, come on in. It's so good to see you." Mona wrapped her arms around Ashley's neck and gave her a big hug.

"It's good to see you, too." Ashley walked into Claudette's house, her eyes observing and taking in everything. "Wow, Claudette's house is beautiful."

"It's absolutely gorgeous. This is my first time seeing it, too. Come on in and make yourself comfortable. How are you, Ashley?"

Ashley followed Mona into the kitchen and sat in a chair at the bar while Mona picked up a knife and began to peel potatoes. "It's good to be away from the dungeon. If not for my own experience, I wouldn't have imagined the life of a prisoner—being under lock and key in a tiny cell doing the same old thing Monday through Sunday for the past six years. If it wasn't for the liberty I had working in the prison library, my mind wouldn't be worth two cents—I would have gone to pieces."

Ashley looked up at Mona. "If I could go back to the day I put the arsenic in William's oatmeal, I would've gotten up early, picked up my things, and walked out of William's life for good. He didn't deserve to die like that."

"But you didn't deserve to be treated the way he treated you either. Poisoning him was wrong. If only you had enough courage to walk, the group would've had your back."

"Hindsight is twenty-twenty."

"I know, but you're home now and we're going to celebrate."

"I don't know if I deserve a celebration. If my father hadn't fought the system and found all of those discrepancies in the lab reports and the withholding of certain information, I'd probably still be in jail. Don't get me wrong, I'm celebrating life beyond bars, but I'm quite aware of what got me there in the first place. Where's Claudette?"

"She had to make a run…well, since it won't be a surprise, she's picking up a few things for the welcome home party we're having for you tonight. I'm supposed to be finishing the food prep."

There was a moment of silence before Ashley spoke again. "How's Reagan?"

Mona put the knife down and turned to look at Ashley. "Reagan is doing fine. She's beautiful; she looks like both you and William." Ashley smiled. "Claudette has done a fine job with her."

"Claudette told me she's playing the piano. One of William's sisters is a classical pianist."

"I didn't know that. But Reagan is good. I made one of her recitals."

"I've missed her. Claudette brought her to the prison a few times, but Reagan didn't like to go there, and Claudette stopped bringing her. I have lots and lots of pictures, though."

"So what are your plans for the future?"

"I don't know, Mona. That's a good question."

29

M ichael Broussard exhaled as he finished grafting the blood vessel to the last of the three diseased heart vessels in the tedious triple-bypass surgery. The patient's blockage was so severe that it was a miracle he had survived prior to coming to the Emergency Room.

"Good job, Dr. Broussard," one of the attending nurses said. "Mr. Swift certainly has you to thank for saving his life."

"God gave me the ability to help patients like Mr. Swift. I have to give Him the credit but I appreciate your vote of confidence."

"Broussard, you saved that man's life," Dr. Kyle Bennett said, as he walked up to Michael, who was taking off his gloves and preparing to wash his hands.

"That's what I went to school to do. Let's get some lunch, if your schedule permits."

"Good idea. I'll make my rounds after we eat."

"I'll meet you there in five minutes."

It felt good to have saved Mr. Swift's life today. It would have been sure death if he hadn't gotten to the hospital when he did. Michael thought about how fragile life was...how in the blink of an eye, a simple mishap, a medical malady, or being in the right place at the wrong time could turn one's life upside down. Pulling off his scrubs, he thought about Mona and Michael Jr. and how much he loved them. He was going to make some permanent changes in his life.

He headed toward the cafeteria and waved to a couple of colleagues along the way. Kyle had already claimed a table for them, chatting away with another colleague while waiting for Michael to join him. After paying for his food, Michael waded through the crowd of hungry folks to his seat. With his sandwich in the air, Michael stopped when he saw Kyle motion with his eyes.

"Ten o'clock," Kyle said, still nodding his head to the left.

"Ten o'clock?" Michael asked. He looked at his watch. "Did I miss something because it's close to being one?"

"No, man. Don't look now, but your devil in a white dress is behind you to your right at the ten o'clock position. If her eyes could burn a hole in your body, you would be scorched by now."

"I'm going to let her sit back there and stare. I don't have any time for Dr. Brooks, and that includes my free time. But I believe she's gotten the message because she hasn't come to my office or tried to call me in the last couple of weeks."

"I hope what you're saying is true, doc. Dr. Madeline Brooks looks like a time bomb ready to go off. Tick, tick, tick."

"She may be, but I've got something for her."

"I hope so, Broussard, because this could become a serious matter. From all that you told me, I'm like your buddies who said you need to let Human Resources know, just in case."

"I'm trying not to go there, if at all possible. Her reputation and mine are on the line. If I can resolve it amicably, that's what I'd like to do. I have faith in that our last talk settled things as far as where I stood and that Madeline's behavior was unacceptable and wouldn't be tolerated."

"Don't look, but she's getting up."

"Is she coming this way?"

"No, she's exiting the cafeteria. If you look now, you'll get a glimpse of her backside."

Michael turned in the direction Kyle indicated at the very moment Madeline turned around. There weren't any sultry looks or suggestive movements. Madeline rolled her eyes, turned around, and kept on course.

"Maybe you're right, Michael," Kyle said, having witnessed the cold shoulder Madeline gave Michael. "If that's the case, maybe you did the right thing by holding your peace."

"Look here, Dr. Kyle Bennett aka Dr. Lover Boy, you're single with no distractions. You can love them and leave them if you want to. I've got a wife and child that I love dearly, and I wouldn't dare sacrifice my marriage and the good loving Mona gives me for even one night of indiscretion with Madeline Brooks."

"I'd hit it, but she's not my type."

"Kyle, who are you fooling? Anything with two legs and boobs is your type."

"Did I ever tell you I have a fetish for women who wear white stockings?"

"You are sick, Lover Boy. All these white stockings running around here must have your hormones swimming."

"Broussard, you don't know the half. I have to shake temptation off of me every time I enter the OR. There's a new female intern on my beat who insists on wearing a dress every day, and when she comes into the OR, although in scrubs, I can't help but fantasize about her."

"Do you know what the cure for that is, Bennett? A sexual harassment suit. Just think sexual harassment or malpractice when you have a knife in your hand and your fantasy comes to life. I bet you'll change your tune."

"Boy, you know how to spoil lunch and a fantasy all at the same time."

"I deal in the real." Michael looked at his watch. "Got to get up and make rounds so I get out of here on time. I have a welcome home party for one of our friends tonight I must attend. I'll catch up with you later, Kyle."

"All right, Michael." Kyle's' head turned sharply as a cute nurse in white stockings passed by. "Sexual harassment." Michael Broussard laughed, picked up his tray, and walked out of the cafeteria.

Michael looked up at the sound of the buzzer. "Thank you, Deborah, for reminding me that it's time for me to get out of here. My wife will have a fit if I don't get to this party on time."

"That too…but you have a visitor…"

"Whoever it is, tell them I'm on my way out and they can either leave a message or make an appointment with Michelle."

Michael turned away from his desk when he heard the door creak and shut in almost one seamless move. Anger replaced his tranquil mood when he saw Madeline holding up the door. Michael jumped up and put his hand out to motion for Madeline to leave, but she pushed his hand out of the way, moved quickly past him to his desk where she grabbed his BlackBerry, shut it off, and threw it back on his desk.

"We're going to have a talk, you and I," Madeline said, capturing Michael in her cold, steel-gray eyes.

"I don't have time for your shenanigans, Madeline. I have a party to attend for a friend, and I don't want to be late."

Madeline picked up Michael's BlackBerry for a second time, but held it. "You need to make time for me because it will be to your detriment if you don't." She went to Michael and pulled on the collar of his white coat. "I saw how you and Bennett were looking at me today."

"Madeline, I only looked up because Bennett mentioned you were in the cafeteria and that you were leaving."

"That may be, but that's not what this discussion is about." Madeline sat on the edge of Michael's desk and toyed with the phone that was still in her hand.

"You have one minute."

"Why are you avoiding me?"

"You're wasting time."

"You're the one in a hurry. You haven't answered my question."

Michael stared at Madeline. He wasn't sure what her motive or intentions were, especially since she insisted on bursting into his office unannounced. Her bazaar behavior sent up a flag, and whatever it was, he wasn't going to be held hostage to it.

"I'm not avoiding you. Maybe you forgot our previous conversation about me being a happily married man and that I wasn't interested in your advances."

"Well, Michael, I'm going to be blunt and to the point. Beating around the bush has gotten me nowhere. I want you…all of you. My desire to have you is so strong that I can already taste the salt dripping from your wet body when we make love. You and I were so right; our bodies were made to be together."

"That was then; this is now, Madeline. My desire isn't the same as yours."

"Let me make my intentions clear for you, since you're making me spell it out. I want a baby…one with your intelligence. I believe our X and Y chromosomes will produce a highly intelligent child, who will rise to the occasion and make a name for his or herself because he or she will make breakthroughs in medical research."

"You say that as if you were getting ready to mass-produce a new breed of human-being, although it seems you've given this a great deal of thought. You're crazy."

"I hate to deflate your ego, Michael. I'm talking about one baby—one who will be a great surgeon one day like his or her mother and father."

"I already have an heir who possesses my genes. I'm afraid that I can't make your dream come true."

"You're going to give me what I want, Michael."

Abruptly, Madeline jumped away from Michael's desk and pounced on him, clawing at him while trying to put her mouth on his. Michael pushed her away, suddenly afraid of the demon that seemed to possess Madeline's body.

"Madeline, you need help…you need to see a psychiatrist. I don't understand your sudden interest in being with me, especially when it's not going to happen."

"Michael, I've been very lonely. Seeing you again, the man who was once my lover and friend, only provided the hope I so desperately sought these past few years. I've had many lovers since you, but none like you. You were my soul mate, Michael. I once entrusted my heart, soul, and body to you—I trusted you unequivocally. You were my universe—the stars, the moon…the sun." Madeline looked at Michael, tears now dripping from her eyes. "Michael, I need you."

"I'm in love with my wife; she's my sunrise and sunset. There are a lot of single professionals that might enjoy being in your company. Take Bennett, for example; he's been looking to settle down."

Madeline pulled off her white doctor's coat and began to unbutton her dress. "I want you."

Michael snatched his BlackBerry from Madeline's hand and prepared to leave. Madeline blocked the exit. "Step away from the door, Madeline."

"Move me," Madeline challenged, continuing to take off her

blouse. Now she stood in front of the door in a pink, lacy, push-up bra, her eyes all the while staring at Michael while he tried to avoid hers. Next she unbuttoned her skirt and let it fall to the floor, kicking it away. There was no slip to hide the pink thong that narrowly covered the orifice that led to the canal Madeline said could produce a highly intelligent child. "I'm yours."

Michael laughed, and Madeline slapped him hard in the face. Michael looked at this mad woman and shook his head. He restrained himself from hitting her back but gave Madeline a quick push so he could leave the room. The demon in her unfurled and Madeline slapped Michael again, digging her nails deep into his face.

With the backside of his hand, Michael swiped at his face. At the sight of blood on his hand, rage grew inside of him and he was no longer able to contain himself. Michael slapped Madeline hard, knocking her down. Madeline fell hard and lay on the floor. Michael looked after her, but offered no assistance. Saving lives was in his hands, but murdering Madeline was now in his heart. He walked out the door.

30

Claudette and T, Sylvia and Kenny, Rachel and Marvin, and Mona circled Ashley, giving her all the love she could soak up.

"Ashley, you're a sight for sore eyes," Marvin said, planting a kiss on Ashley's cheek. "Even though I didn't go to see you when you were incarcerated, my heart was there and I was praying for you."

"Thanks, Marvin. Thank you all for this wonderful celebration." Ashley stood in the middle of the group and tried her best to hold back the flood gates of emotions. She hadn't received the same kind of love from her own family. To them, she had been a disgrace—she defaced the family name in their way of thinking. A smile peeked from under her burdensome thoughts. "Group hug."

"God, Ashley, you remembered," Mona pointed out. "That was our famous phrase during the time we were all trying to find ourselves and find the man who would complete our lives."

"And when did you need a man to complete your life?" Claudette asked, with her hand on her hip and a smirk on her face.

"When..."

Claudette held up her hand. "Don't start lying now, Mona. You've never needed a man to complete you because you were busy getting what you wanted. And bam, you used them up and threw them away like last week's trash when you were done."

"Damn, Claudette. Knock a sister all the way to the ground. Love, that was a long time ago."

"So where is the man who now completes you?" Sylvia asked.

"He'll be here," Mona answered, as if the question irritated her. "Anyway, this party is all about Ashley. And I say it's time to eat." Mona looked at her watch. "We can't wait on Michael forever; he'll be along in a minute."

"I do want to go on record before we end this segment of conversation by saying I did find my good man," Rachel said. "Didn't I, honey?"

Marvin smiled at Rachel. "Yes, you did, baby. I was in the pool of rejects with the rest of you messed-up sisters." Everyone laughed.

"Speak for yourself, brother," Mona was quick to say. "As Claudette already pointed out, I didn't need a man...well, I wasn't sulking like the rest of you."

"It wasn't even like that, Mona," Sylvia interjected. "Some of our wounds were fresh, unlike yourself, and we needed help moving on—with or without a man. The support group that I established was to help heal wounds. Remember, Ashley had only been weeks from the divorce court." Ashley pinched her lips, and didn't say a word. "In fact," Sylvia went on, "you were like the rest of us—in denial, drifting along, that is until Dr. Michael Broussard happened to fall in your lap."

"And wasn't I the lucky girl? Seems to me that was also the same night Kenny was trying to put the moves on you."

Kenny leaned over and gave Sylvia a big kiss. "Mona, you got that right, although I also remember you were a real bitch that night."

"Ouch," Rachel said, covering her mouth to stifle a laugh.

"Girl, Kenny is telling the truth. I wanted to know why Sylvia had the nerve to bring Kenny, of all people, to this big, star-studded affair, after what he'd done to her a long time ago."

"All right, Mona," Sylvia interrupted. "As you said, that was a long time ago. I'm happy with my man." Sylvia pulled Kenny to her and kissed him passionately on the lips.

"You go, girl," Claudette shouted.

"I was hot after Sylvia that night," Kenny continued, "and I wasn't going to let her slip through my fingers." Everyone clapped. "But this night is about Ashley." Kenny gave her a big hug. "Sylvia and I are so happy this day has come."

Ashley hugged Kenny. "Thanks, Kenny. Your words mean a lot to me. All of you have been so important in my life, especially Claudette. If it wasn't for her, I don't know how I would've survived all those days in that jail cell. I love you, Claudette...T."

Claudette and T walked over and stood on either side of Ashley. They made a circle and hugged Ashley.

"Group hug," Rachel said. Everyone joined in.

"Okay, enough of this. Time to eat," Mona cut in. We have some wonderful chicken and turkey salad sandwiches, pasta salad, potato salad and whatever else is over there."

"Kenny, say grace," Marvin said.

After Kenny said grace, everyone dug in and piled their plates high with the delicious food Mona had fixed.

"There's wine, club soda, and a dazzling fruit punch with a kick," Mona said, enjoying the quiet as everyone munched on their food.

Ding, dong. Everyone jumped when they heard the bell.

"I'll get it," Mona said. "Michael has finally arrived. Mona flew to the door, but she masked her disappointment when she opened it. "It's Cecil and Trina Coleman, everybody."

"Hey, everybody," Trina said, as she and Cecil moved into the dining room where everyone had gathered. "Sorry we're late, but

I had to wait for Cecil to get home from the office. And you must be Ashley."

"Yes, I'm Ashley." She put down her sandwich to shake Trina's hand and then Cecil's. "You are the attorney who handled Marvin's case," Ashley said to Cecil.

"Yes, and we appreciate your kind gesture. I didn't learn that you were Robert Jordan's daughter until later. He was a tough opponent."

"That's Daddy. He hates to lose at anything."

"I understand where he comes from. I'm pretty much of the same mindset. Well, it's nice to finally meet you."

"You, too, Cecil."

"Do you have any plans for the future?"

Ashley stopped and watched the faces that looked back at her. Although she hadn't said anything to anyone, she'd given it a lot of thought, although she hadn't shared that with Mona earlier. Before she knew it, she blurted it out. "I would like to go to work for Marvin and Kenny, if they'll have me."

The room was deathly quiet. It was apparent that no one had any idea that Ashley had given her future any thought. No one believed she was even going to get out of jail anytime soon. And no one could believe that she wanted to go to work for Marvin and Kenny.

"What would you be interested in doing, given the nature of our business?" Kenny asked.

"I'm an event planner. I have a well-rounded background in marketing and promotions. I'll move mountains to brand Thomas and Richmond Tecktronics with the likes of Sony and Mattel. Have you thought of shortening your company name with something catchy?"

Kenny's eyebrows raised and he shot a glance in Marvin's

direction. Marvin stood with his hands folded as he appeared to grapple with the idea, letting it roll over in his mind.

"Hmmph," Marvin said. "I'd like to hear more. Stop by the office on Tuesday next week. In fact, I'll have Yvonne set up a meeting so we can discuss this some more."

Rachel looked at Marvin, but instead of looking back, Marvin picked up another sandwich. "Mona, you put your feet and toes in this. I haven't had a turkey sandwich that tasted this good in a long time. Where is Michael?"

"I'm going to call him. He must have gotten tied up." Mona left the dining room with her iPhone to her ear.

"Where is Reagan?" Ashley finally asked. "I had hoped to see her."

"She's with Reebe," Claudette answered. "They'll be here in a half-hour. Reebe's in town, and she took Reagan shopping and then to a movie. I wanted us to get settled in with you first before Reagan made her grand entrance. I hope you don't mind."

Ashley shook her head no, although Claudette saw the disappointment on her face.

"Why don't we make a toast to Ashley's coming home?" T said.

"Man, I didn't know you could talk," Marvin said, teasing T.

"Oh, I can talk, it's only because every time we get together you all dominate the conversation." Everyone laughed. When they calmed down, T picked up his glass of wine and began to speak. "This is a very happy occasion. Our sister, Ashley, has a chance at new life. Ashley made my wife a happy woman when she allowed Claudette to look after, then adopt little Reagan, who is a joy to this family. Ashley will always be a part of our lives. We love her and embrace her. As we move into the future, my wife and I wish Ashley nothing but happiness."

"That was beautiful, T," Claudette said.

"It was. Thank you, T," Ashley said, allowing the tears to finally fall from her eyes.

Rachel held her hand up. "I would like to have a moment of silence for Denise. As you all know, Denise is not doing well with this bout of cancer."

Ashley gasped. "I didn't know."

"She's in the late stages of breast cancer and didn't receive the same prognosis as when she went through this before. So if you would bow your heads, let's pray silently for her, Harold, and Danica—that Denise will be healed and that the family will have strength during this very trying time."

All was silent. After a minute or two had gone by, everyone took a sip of whatever they were drinking and savored the moment— good or solemn. All heads turned when Mona reentered the room, her head hung and her eyes red it appeared from crying. Everyone waited for a report.

"He's not answering his cell phone. In fact, his calls are going straight to voicemail."

31

T
he ladies pampered Mona until they made her laugh. "Eat up, everybody," Mona said, although no one needed her gentle nudge to get them going. Some were on their second helping.

All heads turned at the sound of the doorbell, Mona standing up straighter than the others. She didn't take a chance at getting her feelings hurt by running to the door, so she waited until Claudette left and returned, except that disappointment crept inside once again at the sight of Reebe and Reagan. Mona fled to the kitchen.

Ashley blushed as she looked at six-year-old Reagan, her daughter, mimicking the way Reebe dressed—tight-fitting blue jeans with a gold Phat Farm T-shirt. Ashley was amazed at how much Reagan had grown. Memories of when she was a baby still dominated her head.

"Hey, everybody," Reebe said, waving her hand. Reebe was a cross between Claudette and T, although the five-inch heeled boots she wore made her look much taller. She sported natural hair that had been braided and picked out. Her thin, medium chocolate frame, hugged by her tight-fitted jeans and T-shirt made her look like one of Tyra Banks' Top Models. She had turned out to be a beautiful young woman. Reebe went around the room and kissed everyone, and when she stopped in front of Ashley, she threw her arms around her.

"Reebe, you look so good," Sylvia said, admiring Claudette's oldest child. who looked like a successful young woman. "I can see that school is agreeing with you."

"Yes, I'll be graduating next semester. I've already got a job lined up in New York with ABC Television in their promotions department, but you know I'm looking at the bigger picture— producer of my own show one day."

Claudette beamed. Everyone knew she was proud of Reebe, especially after their blow-out about the beauty shop being burned down years ago.

"You all know that T and I had hoped Reebe would come back home. Everyone else is coming to Atlanta, but if she's going to be happy in New York, we're happy."

"Mom, I love New York," Reebe said to assure her. "I met so many wonderful people when I interned there this past summer, who were willing to show me the ropes and really get my feet on solid footing when I return as a full-time employee. As I said earlier, I'm looking at the bigger picture and maybe when I achieve that, get married and have a family, I may consider coming back home. Close your mouth, Mom. Yes, I said married, but that's way into the future."

"Ooooh," Claudette said, finally ending in a laugh. "Our oldest daughter has grown up, T."

"That she has," T replied.

"I'm going to be a producer like Reebe," Reagan said, cutting into her big sister's spotlight.

"Reagan, you are beautiful," Ashley said, brushing her hand over Reagan's hair that was fluffed out. "She looks so much like William," Ashley continued, as she fussed over Reagan. Ashley looked up, "You and T have done a wonderful job, Claudette."

"Mommy," Reagan said, looking at Claudette, "Reebe and I

saw *Toy Story 3*. Reebe was cracking up. I was a good girl and ate my popcorn."

"I'm glad you had a good time, Reagan," Claudette said.

"Reebe said we're going shopping again. Mommy, I saw these cute boots. They're not as high as Reebe's, though." Everyone laughed. "Do you want to go shopping with us, Miss Ashley?"

Ashley looked around the room, zeroed in on Claudette, and then back to Reagan before she smiled. "If you want me to go, I'd love to."

"You can go. Mommy is busy making ladies look beautiful so she can't go with us. I have fun when Reebe comes home."

There was a moment of silence while everyone in the room digested the conversation. It was obvious to everyone, including Ashley, that Reagan belonged to Claudette, although Ashley had brought her into the world.

Mona stayed in the kitchen while everyone fussed over the reunion between Ashley and Reagan. She wanted to join in the celebration, but her mind was somewhere else, somewhere it didn't want to go, and somewhere it didn't belong. Her mind was running rampant with thoughts of Michael being with Madeline after he had sworn his undying love for her. As if they were this happy couple living a fairy tale life, Michael had said so matter-of-factly that morning that they were a team and he was going to spend more time with her and Michael Jr. And without a doubt, he would be at the celebration tonight for Ashley—that they would be in solidarity with each other.

The noise in the other room irritated Mona. She shifted her thoughts from Michael's whereabouts to the knife that sat on the cutting board. She went to it, picked it up, and finally brought the knife down full force into the cutting board as a vision of Michael and Madeline together clouded her brain. The anger on her face and the knife in the board said it all, but it scared Rachel who had walked in from behind without Mona's knowledge.

"Mona?" Silence ensued. "Mona?" Rachel said again.

Mona slowly turned around, her eyes trimmed in mascara. She looked at Rachel as she held onto the knife without uttering a word. She sniffed.

"Mona, what's going on? Why the knife? Does this have anything to do with Michael?"

In a daze, Mona glared at Rachel. "You ask too many damn questions."

"What are you doing with the knife, Mona? I came in here to check on you since we haven't seen you in awhile."

Mona pulled the knife out of the cutting board and set it down. She went to Rachel, put her arms around her neck, laid her head on Rachel's shoulder, and cried. Moments later she lifted her head and dropped her hands, which Rachel grabbed and held on to. "What is it, sweetie?" Rachel asked again.

"Rachel…I think Michael is having an affair."

Rachel released Mona's hands and cupped her mouth as if in shock. "Not with Madeline. I thought things were better between you and Michael."

"They were…well, they seemed to be. Michael swore up and down that he had nothing to do with that woman. It's eight o'clock, and he should've been here. He swore up and down he was going to leave the hospital and be home no later than six."

"Maybe he's been in an accident or a patient went into cardiac arrest and Michael had to perform emergency surgery."

"If so, why haven't I heard from him?"

"Maybe he's not able to, Mona."

"Look, Rachel. I appreciate you looking out for me. I'm not

good company right now. In fact, I'm going to say good night and go home."

Before Rachel could respond, the doorbell rang. Mona grabbed Rachel's hand and clung to her as if it would make everything all right. Then she heard her name and stood still unable to move.

"Mona, Rachel, where are you?" they heard Claudette's voice say. "Michael is here."

Mona gasped, then wiped her face. "Okay, Rachel, maybe you were right. Help me get fixed up. Make sure my face looks okay."

As Rachel wiped Mona's face, Michael walked in, his face sullen and tight. "Hey, baby," he said to Mona, giving her a kiss on the lips. "Hey, Rachel. What are you two up to?"

Mona seemed lost for words, but now she took a good look at Michael. Ignoring his question, she threw out one of her own. "What's wrong with your face?"

"Rachel, do you mind if I have a word alone with my wife?"

Rachel looked from Michael to Mona. She wasn't sure if leaving them together was the right thing to do, considering Mona's state of mind.

"Please?" Michael asked. Rachel gave them a last look over and left the kitchen.

"What happened, Michael?"

"Baby, sorry I'm late. One word—Madeline. She and I had a terrible fight."

"Oh my God," Mona yelped. She took Michael's face in her hands and looked at it more closely. "Did she do this?"

Michael gently clasped his hands over Mona's and removed them. "Yes." Michael looked away, sighed, and then turned back to Mona. "She tried to come on to me again. She sang this sob story about wanting to have sex with me to make this highly intelligent baby."

"You already have one. Michael Jr. is smart as a whip."

"I told her so, but she wasn't hearing it."

"I tried calling your cell, but my calls kept going to voicemail."

"I can explain that, too. Madeline grabbed my phone from my desk and shut it off."

"You should've knocked that miserable woman into next week." Mona sighed.

"I may have done that."

"What do you mean?"

"She blocked the door to my office and began taking off her clothes. She lunged at me, begging me to make love to her. When I said I wouldn't, she slapped me in the face. Mona, I don't hit women, but after the second slap to the face, I matched her one for one, but I might have hit her a little too hard. She fell to floor and I left her there."

"What? Oh my God. What if she tries to bring assault charges against you?"

"Don't you think that crossed my mind?" Michael took a breath. "We'll worry about that when and if it happens; I'm praying that it won't. Right now I want to welcome Ashley home, snuggle up to my wife, and get on a plane this Thursday to see my family. Give me a hug."

Mona embraced Michael for the longest time. Her insecurities were getting the best of her. She knew it was a test…a test that she failed miserably. But this incident made her a believer, and from now on, she wasn't going to doubt her husband's love for her and their son.

32

She paid the fare and exited the cab without a single word. Ashley watched as the cab driver drove around the circular driveway and down the long cement path that led back to civilization. She walked the few feet to the brick steps that led to her parents' estate, thinking about the welcome home party Claudette had given in her honor but mostly about her daughter, Reagan.

Ashley wanted her child, but there wasn't a way she could convey it...not yet. Claudette had been Reagan's mother for six years, and she knew that if she made an attempt to reclaim Reagan now, all hell would burst loose, especially since Reagan now legally belonged to Claudette and Tyrone.

The door to the house opened. Ashley gazed up at her mother and offered a smile. "Come on in, Ashley," Clarice Jordan said. "It's nippy outside and you don't even have a coat on."

"Give me a minute, Mom; I'll be in soon." Clarice stared at Ashley and then closed the door.

Ashley sat on the brick steps, setting her purse in her lap, and let her mind wander. She couldn't believe how grown up Reagan was for her six years on earth. Reagan had so many of William's features. For a moment she thought about him—she could see his last moments before the poison had overtaken his body—William eating the oatmeal he enjoyed...that she had laced with poison and had placed in front of him to eat. Ashley thought about William's head as it slumped forward into the bowl, and her callous attitude, as she let him die while she got her things and walked out of the house for good. But her nightmare had begun as she was tried and sentenced for her husband's murder and then sent to jail to rot for her misdeed.

Her body shook and she grasped for air. The memory was so real. Ashley stood up and closed her eyes, trying to block the memories of that day—the day she had pried opened for review and now wanted to shut. She slung the strap to her purse over her shoulder and headed for the door. She prayed that her mother wasn't waiting inside for her because she wanted to be alone.

Once inside, Ashley dashed through the foyer, headed for the stairs when her mother called to her as she stepped from the library to where Ashley stood.

"Ashley, your father and I are here to help you, if you want it. Now that you're out of that awful prison, you have a chance to start a new life." Clarice hesitated, brought her hand to her mouth, sighed, looked up at Ashley and began to speak. "I hope this doesn't sound harsh, but I'm going to say it anyway."

A severe frown crossed Ashley's face as she waited for her mother's advice; she somehow knew it would eventually come.

"You need to separate yourself from your old friends. You're from a different world, and those people don't have the slightest idea what money, wealth, and power is."

"Mother, you are so out of touch. Those people you refer to are from the same world, the same human race that we're from. Those people are doctors, CEOs of a large corporation, and attorneys. They live in as fine a house as we do, so don't get on your high horse about your wealth and power when there are plenty of other people like 'those people' who you are sharing it with. Good night, Mother."

"You'll understand it by and by."

"You have a granddaughter who's six years old and very beautiful. You haven't once acknowledged her existence."

"The little girl you speak of now belongs to another woman who is now her mother. I hope it's not too late for you to produce a child by a fitting man so that I can be a grandmother."

Ashley looked at her mother with fire in her eyes. Her mother's old Southern ways were embedded deep inside. But even at that, Ashley had seen her parents treat black people with respect—on occasion, when her parents hosted a Christmas party, colleagues and staff persons came to the house, and some of them were black.

Ashley recalled one such girl who wore a short Afro and a tight-fitting dress who seemed enamored with her father. She hadn't thought about that in years. Maybe her mother noticed it, too. It may be the reason she acts the way she does, or says the things she says, about black people. It didn't matter; her friends were her friends—to have and to hold dearly. Ashley turned and walked up the stairs.

At the top of the stairs, Ashley headed for her room but before she could get there, a grinding noise made her stop. She followed the noise to her father's study, and there he was shredding documents while in his pajamas and smoking jacket.

"What are you doing?" Ashley asked. Her father stopped abruptly, looking from Ashley to the mounds of paper that sat on his desk awaiting their turn to be destroyed.

"Housecleaning. I've got too many old pieces of paper that have no more use or value that are taking up space and waiting for a match. Thought this was a good time to go through them and purge what I don't need."

As Ashley inched forward, Robert turned his back on the table he was working from and crossed his hands over his heart. "So how was your evening? Did you get to see your child?"

Ashley moved closer and smiled at her father. "I have some good friends. They welcomed me openly—gave me a nice welcome home party. And yes, I saw Reagan."

"They should've given you a great party. After all, you gave them a large portion of the trust fund your grandfather left you so they could restart their business—a deal I should have won."

"They used the money for my legal defense, if you want to know the truth. Dad, stop being bitter because you lost the case. I met Cecil Coleman tonight; he and his wife are very nice people."

"You need to stay away from them so you won't end up in the same situation that led you to murder your black husband."

Ashley stared at her father and shook her head. "I loved William. He was everything to me. I think he went crazy when he realized I was carrying his baby but it was too late because our divorce had been pronounced final. He wanted me back, even after his infidelity, and went crazy trying to make that happen. And I snapped."

"He got what he deserved."

Ashley came out of the fog and moved directly in front of her father, laying her purse on top of the papers on the table. "You are disgusting. William was a human being, for God's sake. What kind of person are you that you can have that much disdain for someone...someone who's not like you?"

"Ask yourself. You're the one who killed him."

Ashley huffed and grabbed her purse, knocking some of the papers to the floor.

"I'll get that," Robert Jordan said, although he nearly knocked Ashley out of the way as she reached down to pick the papers up.

"Vera Franklin," Ashley read, holding a document in her hand. "Isn't that the girl who used to work for you?"

"No, no, she's a case I worked on sometime ago." Jordan snatched the document from Ashley's hand.

"Yes, she is. I remember her vividly at one of the Christmas parties we had at the house. She wore a short ethnic hair cut—Afro, they call it—and she had on this tight, red dress with the faux-fur collar around it. I remember that she kept smiling at you."

"You're exaggerating, Ashley. That could have been a number of the girls in the office. Don't tell your Mom; several had crushes on me."

"And from what I heard, you slept with them all."

"I'm your father, and you don't get to talk to me like that. Remember, I can send you back to the gates of hell as easily as I got you out."

Ashley's nostrils flared. She picked up her purse and left the room.

33

It was a brisk October day in Atlanta. Clad in coats and hats, Mona and Michael Jr. walked out of the house when Michael announced that he'd put the last piece of luggage in Marvin's car and they needed to get a move-on. The airport was approximately a forty-five-minute ride from their house and they were grateful they were able to get a late-morning flight to New Orleans.

"We're here," Marvin said, pulling the car to the curb in front of the USAirways departure/ticketing terminal. Michael, Mona, and Michael Jr. jumped out, as well as Marvin, to help Michael with the luggage. "You look like you're going to stay through winter. I'm sure most of the luggage is Mona's."

"We'll return on Sunday evening," Michael assured him. "And don't forget. It sure feels great to get away from this place for a minute."

"Tell Rachel and the others that we need to talk about Thanksgiving," Mona called out, her back already turned toward the building, as she pulled her suitcase with one hand and held Michael Jr.'s hand with the other. Michael waved as Marvin drove off.

Check-in and passenger security check went smooth. Michael Jr. laughed when the security officer called Mona back because the metal detector screamed when she walked through. She'd forgotten that she had a large metal buckle on her belt. Once she took it off, laid it on the conveyor and walked back through the metal detector, they were on their way to their gate. Their flight didn't take off until ten-fifty-five a.m., which meant they had an hour before take-off.

As large as Atlanta's International Airport was, it never failed that Michael would see someone he knew—a former patient, a frat brother, a golf buddy, a colleague or someone who was a member of one of the several foundations he sat on. Today was no different, except the person was very well known to both he and Mona.

"Mona, Michael, where are you all headed? I'm sure if I took a guess, I'd be right."

Mona rolled her eyes as Michael answered. "Timothy, don't tell me you're going to New Orleans."

"Yeah, your daddy is my uncle and it's an opportunity to see my own parents. Mommie called and asked me to come home so that we could attend your father's celebration together. Fancy meeting you here. How are you doing, Mona?"

"As you can see, I'm doing well."

Timothy sat down next to Mona as Michael Jr. got up to bounce a small ball he'd brought with him. Mona cringed. "Look, Mona. Why don't we bury the hatchet and be friends? You and I were a long time ago." Timothy glanced at Michael, who was now monitoring the conversation. "You and Michael have a wonderful family, which means you've moved on with your life. I've not once interfered or come to your house, although Michael is my first cousin."

Mona held up her hand. "Timothy, I would never stop you from visiting your cousin. But you and I are different. We had a marriage that you dishonored. I went against my family to marry you, and I almost didn't get to tell them how much I loved them because I had become estranged from them. I can't help how I feel about you. Deception and infidelity are two words that I have a problem conquering when I've felt the brunt of it. Maybe one day, I'll forgive you."

"Why don't we talk about something else," Michael suggested.

Timothy sat back and watched the crowd of people as they moved in one direction or the other. Mona watched Timothy with interest as he scanned Michael Jr. who continued to bounce the ball.

"Wondering what our baby would've looked like?" Mona asked.

Timothy turned toward Mona with a surprise on his face, but also took in her beauty. "I'm sure he or she would've looked like their mom." Timothy held his head down, then looked in the opposite direction.

"Okay, you guys," Michael said, trying to defuse a potentially explosive situation. "We're going to a celebration. Please don't spoil this."

Mona rubbed Michael's hand. "We're not shouting and screaming, but Timothy is right." Timothy looked in Mona's direction as she began to speak. "I'm happily married and have a good life. It's time to let bygones be bygones. I've moved forward with my life, and what happened a long time ago, although I haven't totally forgotten, has to be buried." Mona looked at Timothy and pinched her lips together. She closed her eyes momentarily, then looked back at Timothy and let out a sigh. "I forgive you for what you did to me back then." There, she said it.

Timothy was taken aback. He looked at Mona while he ingested and processed her words. Then he forced his lips open. "I had hoped to hear that for the longest, Mona, but I want you to know how sorry I am for making you suffer. I was a coward and a sorry excuse for a husband. I've learned from that."

"What happened to your first wife?" Mona asked. "You know I met her, and she told me what you'd done to her."

Timothy looked away. "I've hurt a lot of people. I understand she's remarried."

"She was very nice...and she loved you, too."

"We will begin boarding flight 1710 to New Orleans in one minute," the airline attendant announced over the loud speaker.

"I guess that's us," Michael said, eager to interrupt the conversation between his wife and cousin. "Michael Jr., you're getting ready to see your grandma, grandpa, and a whole lot of aunties and uncles."

"Do they look like me?" Michael Jr. asked.

"Let's say you may favor a few of them since you have part of their genes running through your veins."

"Ewww," Michael Jr. said, turning up his nose.

"Boy, stop that," Michael admonished before letting out a little laugh. "Those genes made you as handsome as you are."

"We're now boarding all first-class passengers for flight 1710 to New Orleans," the airline attendant announced.

Timothy bunched up his mouth, and then smiled at Mona. "It's time for me to board. Thank you, Mona. Your words meant a lot." Timothy got up and patted her arm. "See you all in New Orleans."

Michael nodded, then looked at Mona. "You all right, baby?"

Mona held back tears. "Yeah, I'm fine now. For the first time in a long time, I feel vindicated. I can't explain it, but I feel free in my soul."

Michael put his arm around Mona and kissed her on the cheek. "That was brave what you did. You're growing up."

"Those in zone one may now board the plane."

"I guess that's us," Michael said. "Up, Michael Jr.; it's time to get on the plane and meet the rest of the family."

Mona held Michael Jr. by the hand. Tears she held back for something else forced their way down her cheeks for a totally different reason. Mona was thinking about her parents—the last time she had seen them and how Hurricane Katrina had brought their reunion to an end. Living in Atlanta made it easy to repress her feelings and the image of that fateful day. She didn't understand why she was supposed to live and her parents had to die, even though she and Michael were in the same house at the same time when her parents lost their lives.

She remembered being swallowed up in her childhood house by water as it climbed the stairs to the second floor behind her. She remembered crying for help and finally being captured by a helicopter crew as she and Michael made it to safety on top of the house. That was the New Orleans she remembered and imprinted in her head, that she couldn't let go of, and she wasn't looking forward to revisiting it.

34

The two-hour plane ride to New Orleans was uneventful. Michael Jr. fell asleep and now Mona was having a time waking him up. They embarked the plane and headed for baggage claim, hopeful that all of their luggage would be there.

The passengers from flight 1710 were gathered around the baggage turnstile, waiting for the first slew of luggage to appear. Mona casually looked around the room but resigned herself to waiting for her bags.

"Are you looking for Timothy?" Michael asked with a smirk on his face.

"Of course not," Mona replied, keeping her eyes straight ahead for fear that Michael would recognize her lie.

"Ummm."

"Michael, I don't know why you're tripping. Timothy is my distant, distant past."

"He's going to be at the party, which means you'll see him again. Are you going to be comfortable with that?"

Mona turned around and looked Michael straight on, the twist in her hips and the fire in her eyes that said she was in control. "I've purged all thoughts and feelings for my ex. The question is, have you? Dr. Madeline Brooks might have been your past, but somehow she's made it a point to be in your present. So if we intend to enjoy our time in New Orleans and celebrate your

father's birthday as you planned, you need to erase whatever unfounded thoughts you have in your head about me and Timothy.
He's old news—like worn leather on the bottom of my favorite
pair of shoes."

"Mona, all of that was unnecessary."

"I guess you won't ask me that silly question again."

For a fleeting moment, Michael saw Madeline's bare breasts
standing erect in front of him, tempting his manhood—his
weakness for her body. They had been passionate lovers once,
and the memory that was once dormant now sent chills down his
spine. Michael took a deep breath and shook his head like someone had stuck smelling salt under his noise. From the corner of
his eye, he saw Mona watching him, and it was at that moment
he knew it was going to take more than sheer will to exorcise
Madeline Brooks from his mind.

35

"Well, look who's gotten out of their office to stroll down to the lesser partner's office?" Kenny said, looking up as Marvin strolled into his office. "How did you get in here unannounced?"

"I hope you don't mind, but I bribed Candace with a free lunch at the cafeteria. And you're fifty percent of this company. Don't ever forget it."

"You mean until Harold decides to push for a third of the cut?"

Marvin looked thoughtfully at Kenny. "I don't think that'll happen. Harold and I have come a long way in mending our torn relationship, and now that my cousin and I have moved past that time in our lives, things are good the way they are. I keep wondering, though, what happened with his company. He seemed to be doing so well."

"Maybe it had something to do with Denise being ill, and they hadn't let on to anyone."

"No, Kenny. I don't think Harold knew that Denise had cancer. They may not have gone through with the wedding if he had."

"You don't think so? My thinking is that if he knew, it would have given their wedding even more purpose. But I agree with you, Marv. Harold didn't act like someone who had an inkling that his new bride was ill. It's such a sad state of affairs."

"Yeah, you're right. I came down to talk about Ashley."

"That was something, wasn't it?"

"Came out of left field. I didn't see it coming."

"Do you think Ashley has ulterior motives?"

"I don't know, Kenny. What ulterior motives could she have? She was never connected to us in any way, other than she stepped up to the plate when we couldn't see the first part of the rainbow."

"I say, we owe her."

"But, I don't believe she asked for that reason, Kenny. I think Ashley needs somewhere to belong. I'm sure it was only a thought that burst out when she was asked about her future."

"You know what, Marv? It would be good if she worked with Harold. He's taken on a lot of my work, and he's working hard toward bringing revenue into the company. Ashley talked about elevating the company, and with her background in pro-motion and marketing, she would be an asset to Harold."

"Let's call Harold and discuss this in some detail over lunch. I'm hungry."

"That sounds like a plan."

"Every time I think about lunch, I think about Michael. Wasn't it crazy how he turned up so late at T and Claudette's house, acting all strange?"

"Marv, I'm starting to think you're right. And I'm sure that Denise's cousin, Madeline, is the root of the problem. But damn, she's fine."

"I told you, Kenny. Don't allow that junk to take residence in your head. You'll wind up like me on last year, except there was nothing about Peaches I wanted. That's why it's not good to partake of strong drink."

Kenny laughed. "Yeah, it almost messed you up for life. Have you heard anything else about Peaches' murder? It had to be somebody in the prison she pissed off."

"I hate to see anyone get killed at the hands of another, but I would be lying if I said Rachel and I aren't breathing easier these days."

"Good for you guys. I'll have Candace call Harold and tell him to meet us out front."

"Good."

Kenny pushed his chair back and prepared to meet Marvin and Harold for lunch. Before he could move past his desk, Candace entered the room.

"What is it, Candace?"

"I was finally able to reach Mr. Harold Thomas on the line. He said that he won't be able to meet you and Mr. Marvin Thomas for lunch because he had to run home to meet the Hospice people."

"Jesus, Denise is in worse shape than we thought," Kenny said, bringing his hand to his mouth. "Thanks, Candace."

Kenny sat back down in his chair and digested the information. He hadn't given one thought to what he would do if something happened to Sylvia and Kenny Jr. The balance between life and death seemed to be separated by a thin line. His heart went out to Harold and Denise. A sudden knock on the door pulled him out of his trance.

"Come in," Kenny said, wondering where Candace was.

Surprise was written all over him. A smile enveloped Kenny's face when he saw his wife shadowing the doorway. He abruptly jumped up from his seat and went to meet her, planting a kiss on her lips. "Hey, baby, what brings you to Thomas and Richmond?"

"I wanted to spend a moment with my wonderful husband."

He kissed Sylvia again and showered her with a warm hug. "I love you, beautiful. You've made my day. We just heard a bit of bad news."

Sylvia looked up. Her eyes were red from holding back the

tears that had actually brought her to her husband's place of business.

"You already know, don't you?" Kenny asked.

"Yes, I was there when the Hospice people arrived. The woman," Sylvia sniffed, "the woman said…"

Kenny held Sylvia. "It's okay, baby. You don't have to say anything. We've got to pray for our sister…that she can beat this thing."

"They said maybe a week."

Kenny's heart dropped to the bottom of his stomach. He felt as if he'd been run over by a steamroller. "They could be mistaken."

"Kenny, Rachel and I have been with her over the past couple of months. I truly believe Denise gave up the will to fight a long time ago. She is rail thin and hasn't eaten in days. It was…ahh, ahh, ahh…" Sylvia lost it and cried on Kenny's shoulders. "She's going to die. It was so sad. And poor Harold…"

"Who's at the house with Harold?"

"Rachel's there. I couldn't take it, baby. I had to get out for a few minutes. And Danica is taking this in stride, being there for her mother as best she can."

"Knock, knock." Marvin walked in, but stopped when he saw Sylvia crying. "I was waiting…uhh, I'm sorry. Give me a call when…is everything all right?"

"They had to call Hospice for Denise. Harold is at the house now. Sylvia just left the house, and I'm afraid the news isn't good. Denise doesn't have long to live."

Marvin was quiet. He balled his hand into a fist and held it against his mouth.

"You okay, Marvin?" Sylvia asked, watching the countenance on Marvin's face change.

"I…I don't believe it. All that we've been through. And Denise finally found the peace she so wanted with Harold. This isn't fair. Life isn't fair." Marvin stood and shook his head. "You talk with Rachel today?" Marvin asked Sylvia.

"She's with Denise and Harold now."

"I'm on my way over there. I'll catch up with you later, Kenny."

"Okay, Marvin. Call us if you need us."

36

The weather was balmy when the Broussard family finally exited the terminal to wait for someone in Michael's family to pick them up.

"I'm hot, Mommy," Michael Jr. said, rubbing his arm as if the sun was burning him.

"It's not that bad, baby. We'll be getting in a car in a few minutes, I hope."

Michael had been quiet for the past fifteen minutes. Tension crept in between Michael's and Mona's good feeling like a roach that dared to walk across a kitchen floor in broad daylight in the middle of a tea party. Nasty.

It was another ten minutes before Michael's sister, Celia, finally showed up, baring her pearly whites with loads of hugs and kisses. Mona was not in a party mood, and she could tell by Celia's rambunctiousness that they were in for a long night.

"Hey, how's my nephew?" Celia asked Michael Jr., as she picked him up in her arms and soaked his cheeks with juicy kisses. "He's so cute." She put Michael down.

"What's up with you guys?" Celia asked, as she looked at the two adults who had frowns on their faces. "Michael, what did you do to Mona? You guys need to snap out of it," Celia said, popping her fingers. "We've been partying all week and we've got three or four more days to go."

"Hey, sis, we're tired out," Michael said. "Long nights at the hospital, but we're glad to be here. Can't wait to see everybody."

"Hey, Celia," Mona said without feeling, grabbing Michael Jr.'s hand.

"Everybody is going to be here, Michael. The house is already crowded. You all are staying with me. Forget the hotel; I've got plenty of room."

Mona sighed to herself and followed her family to Celia's Yukon. Celia and her husband, Roberto, were doing all right for themselves with a little help from Michael. The ride into New Orleans was uneventful save Celia's nonstop chatter about the last three days.

The gaiety in the house was worse than Mona had imagined. Orange, green, and yellow balloons and streamers ran from one corner of the house to the other. Caribbean music floated throughout the house and several people were up doing a calypso dance. Mounds of fresh fried plantains and pots of curried rice and chicken were being eaten. The celebration for Michael's father was well underway. Several of Michael's uncles and brothers as well as his brother-in-law, Roberto, were already inebriated, and Poppie was well on his way, too.

"Michael, Jacqueline, and little Mike, come here and let Mommie hold you," the elder Mrs. Broussard said. "Such a sight for old and sore eyes. Michael Jr., did your mommy tell you that you were supposed to be a girl?"

Michael Jr. frowned and looked at Michael Sr. and then his mother. "No ma'am."

"Well, the doctors read the test wrong and told them they were having a girl, and they were going to name her Katrina after that big storm we had a long time ago."

Mona dropped her head but didn't say a word.

"But I'm so happy that I have a grandson, and I'm also glad you could come, my children. Poppie is gonna be so happy, although he may not remember too much about what happened today because he's about partied out, and it isn't even the six o'clock hour yet."

"That's all right, Mommie," Michael said, embracing his mother and giving her a great big kiss. "We wouldn't have missed this for the world. Right, Mona?"

"Yes, Mrs. Broussard," Mona said politely, wishing she could find a large hole and hide in it. Michael's people were too wild and worldly for her. She gave Mrs. Broussard a hug and a kiss.

"Little Mike, you've grown so since Grandma Lucy saw you last. You're such a big boy."

Michael Jr. looked up at his parents and smiled. "Thank you."

"He's going to be a little shy for awhile since everyone is a stranger to him," Michael said, "but he'll warm up in a little bit. Let's go say hello to Grandpa." Michael held Mona's and Michael Jr.'s hand and led the way.

"What's wrong with them?" Grandma Lucy asked Celia as soon as Michael and Mona were out of earshot.

"I dunno, Mommie. Mona had on a funky attitude when I picked them up from the airport. I'll get to the bottom of it."

"See that they don't spoil Poppie's birthday celebration."

"Got it, Mommie." Celia kissed her mother.

The music was in high gear. Mona seemed to have relaxed, and after Michael Jr. was introduced to some of his young cousins, he was nowhere to be found, enjoying the lure of his father's side of the family.

"Michael, why don't you come and dance with your sister?" Celia asked with her arms outstretched, popping her fingers as the rhythm of the music enticed them to get a piece of the action.

"Okay, sis," Michael said, gyrating his hips to the sultry, Latin music. Michael was a very good dancer, and if he were to ever be approached about being on *Dancing with the Stars*, he was a shoo-in. But he wasn't famous in the entertainment circle. "Doris and Lucinda are cooking up a storm in the kitchen."

"You know how your sisters do. But let's not waste time talking about them. What's up with you and Mona? Mommie said she don't want nobody up in here spoiling the celebration for Poppie, and I agree with her."

"It's nothing, Celia. Well, we had a slight argument when we landed."

"About what, Michael? She don't want to be here? Tell her to go to her uppity people's house. Think they better than us anyway. She ain't got to stay here."

"Cool it, Celia. Mona was delighted to come." Michael twirled Celia after a spicy twist of the hips.

"So what is it then?"

"Well, looka here?" Grandma Lucy called out. "If it isn't Timothy Sosa, my sister Brenna's chile. Lord knows, the roof gonna cave in now."

Timothy walked in dressed down in a white-on-white jacket, silk shirt, and slacks. All heads turned in his direction. Timothy's smile was wide and infectious as he lifted his hands in one big hello to everyone.

Michael shifted his eyes to where Mona sat, chatting away with his brother, Reynaldo. He didn't miss Mona's stare as Timothy walked in, drinking in his good looks along with the others as everyone embraced him and said he was *muy bonito*—very handsome.

"Michael!" Celia called out.

Michael turned his head toward his sister, almost forgetting they had been the ones creating the live action with their spicy salsa on the dance floor. "What?"

"Brother, don't what me. I saw how you looked at Mona when Timothy walked in. What's up? Tell me."

Michael sighed and resigned himself to share with his sister, since she was being relentless in nagging him for information. "Timothy was Mona's first husband."

Celia gasped and almost choked on her own saliva. "What you saying? She still has the hots for him?"

"No, in fact, Mona hated him for years. She didn't know that Timothy and I were related until Timothy's first wife, Sadie, told her the first time Mona came to New Orleans with me. It was weird when Mona finally told me about it. Anyway, Timothy treated her badly, walked out on her, not even a year after they got married. Mona didn't know that he was already married to Sadie. Mona was also carrying Timothy's baby, and she lost it. So she's built up a lot of animosity and hatred toward him."

"So what does that have to do with her attitude today? Aw, she somehow found out Timothy was coming here."

"Celia, Timothy was on the same plane with us."

"Oh my God. I can understand her bad attitude now."

"Yeah, we ran into him at the airport in Atlanta. He literally begged Mona to forgive him."

"Well, did she?"

"That's the strange part. She did forgive him, but I think it was such a weight off her shoulders she wouldn't let it go. She seemed to be transfixed by him—had him on the brain."

"How do you know? Did she say anything to lead you to believe that?"

"No, she didn't. I assumed it. In fact, when we got off the plane,

I accused her of thinking about Timothy. Go ahead and say it... my jealous imagination. I'm the culprit in this mess."

"Well, I take back all those things I said about Mona, but you need to fix it, now. She's on her way over. And remember what Mommie said; don't ruin this celebration for Poppie."

"I won't. Thanks for talking this out with me, sis."

"Love you, Michael."

"Love you, Celia."

"What were you and Celia talking about?" Mona asked when she was finally in front of Michael.

"How much I love you."

Mona smiled. "You're telling a lie, Michael."

"Ask Celia. Anyway, I apologize for my ugly ways. It was un-becoming. I know I've got your heart."

"And you better remember that, Michael Broussard." Mona gave Michael a big kiss, and everyone began to clap.

"You got it, brother," Reynaldo hollered. "Give that foxy wife of yours all your sugar."

Michael smiled. "Brother, you better lay off that strong drink you keep throwing down your throat." Everyone laughed. When Michael turned to give Mona another kiss, he saw Timothy staring at them. Michael planted another sloppy, juicy kiss on Mona's lips, eliciting another round of applause. Timothy turned his head when Michael looked in his direction.

"Fast work, brother," Celia chided when the applause died down.

"I didn't earn a degree in medicine for nothing," Michael countered. "I'm the *heart* doctor. I may break them, but I can fix them back like new."

Celia and Michael slapped hands.

37

Marvin arrived at Harold and Denise's house and found Rachel waiting for him, her eyes bloodshot from all the tears she'd shed.

"Baby, you all right?" Marvin asked, Rachel being his first concern.

"Yeah," Rachel said weakly in a voice that was hardly audible. "Denise is lying there, almost unresponsive. Her eyes are open, but…" She wrapped her arms around Marvin's neck and held on to him for dear life. "Don't let go, baby. I'm so afraid."

"We've got to pray, Rachel."

They stood hooked together for almost fifteen minutes as they said their prayers for Denise individually and silently. The pain Marvin felt was more intense than he thought as he held onto Rachel as tight as she held onto him. All the anger he once had for his ex-wife had completely evaporated, praying to God to extend her life so that her daughter, Danica, would not have to grow up without her mother and her new husband, Harold, wouldn't be without his mate.

When Marvin finally removed himself from Rachel, his eyes were as red as hers. He pulled himself together and prepared to see Denise. He looked at Rachel, who took a seat in a chair in the living room. She watched Marvin with concern.

"Are those people still here?" he asked.

"You mean the Hospice people?"

"Yeah."

"They're gone. They brought in a hospital bed, an IV pole, and an oxygen machine."

Marvin was silent and wasn't certain he should intrude on Harold. Rachel noticed Marvin's hesitation. "I'll check on them. I'll let Harold know that you're here." Marvin shook his head.

Minutes later, Rachel returned. She shook her head in the affirmative and pointed her hand, like a good waitress would, in the direction he was to go. Marvin moved slowly toward the door of Denise's room and stood in front of it. He couldn't seem to go beyond it; his feet seemed to be welded to the floor. Then, with a stiff movement of his shoulders, he opened the door to her room and stood behind Harold, who was holding Denise's seemingly lifeless hand.

Marvin placed his hand on Harold's shoulder. Harold looked up and acknowledged. "She's sleeping."

In a matter of minutes, Denise opened her eyes and turned toward Harold. Marvin smiled and Denise smiled back. She tried raising her head, but was unable to do so.

"Hello, Denise," Marvin said.

Denise smiled again. "Hi," she finally managed to say.

"Rachel and I are praying for you. We love you...I love you." Marvin stepped forward and kissed Denise on the forehead. He looked back at Harold, who had tears in his eyes. Marvin got up and fled from the room, unable to bear the sight of Denise in that state.

Madeline sat at her desk, twisting left, then right in her seat, contemplating what she was going to do about Dr. Michael Broussard.

Someone must have fried his brains because, even if the good doctor had had amnesia, there was no way he could have possibly forgotten what they'd meant to each other once, how perfect they'd been as sexual partners, or the chemistry that had held them together like cement glue. Madeline hadn't known how much she'd missed him until she saw him at her cousin's wedding a few months ago.

For a fleeting moment, she thought about Denise. She picked up a pencil and wrote a note to herself, *I must call and check up on Denise.* As soon as she finished jotting down the note, her mind and thoughts were back to Michael. She flicked the pencil against the side of her head, but a revelation hadn't come to her yet.

I'll fix him, she thought. *I'll let everyone know what kind of man he really is. Why didn't I think about that before? He hit me, and then left me lying on the floor. I'm going to file a sexual harassment complaint against him. I'll say that he's been coming on to me since I arrived at Emory. After I ignored his constant advances, and he wouldn't take no for an answer, he attempted to rape me.*

Madeline smiled to herself as she let the thought simmer. Michael was away on his trip with his family, but when he returned Monday morning, he would have a rude awakening.

She jumped when she heard the door to her office open and close.

"Did I disturb you, Dr. Brooks?" Dr. Kyle Bennett asked.

Madeline looked up at Kyle with wandering eyes. He was a very attractive, single white male who seemed to be unattached, or at least not seeing anyone seriously, according to the gossip-mongers at the hospital. Some had questioned if he was gay, since he ignored half the population of single and desperate women on staff at Emory. If Madeline was in the mood to bet, she figured she'd have him entangled in her web in minutes flat. But her immediate craving for and obsession with wanting to be with Michael, overshadowed any desire to be with anyone else.

"No," she finally said. "Have a seat."

"I'll stand."

Madeline arched her eyebrows and crossed her legs. She made small circles with her foot as she explored Kyle's six-foot frame again with her eyes with renewed interest. She'd dated a white guy once, but he was all about trying to unravel and understand the mystery of the black woman's mystique, and Madeline didn't have the time or patience for his exploratory studies. She wanted a man who was ready to light her fire at the drop of a hat, like Michael had done on almost every occasion they were together. There was no time for a man who wasn't serious about what she had and could offer him.

Dr. Bennett was smart and intelligent. Madeline had even caught him giving her the once-over on more than one occasion. However at the moment, he was all business and pretended to ignore her sexual overtones.

"I have a film I'd like you to look at," Kyle said, handing an X-ray to Madeline. She brushed her hand up against his. "The patient," Kyle continued, moving his hand away, "has a pericardial disease, and I will need to operate, but I'd like a second opinion about how to proceed."

"I can see that, but why me?"

"Why not you? You're a cardio specialist on the team, and it makes sense to me that you'd have an opinion that I might find useful as I evaluate this surgery."

"Since I've been onboard at Emory, I've not once had a visit from you requesting my analysis of anything you've done. Why now? Is it because the almighty Dr. Michael Broussard is away and you can't navigate your way without him?" Madeline un-crossed her legs.

Kyle stopped to soak up Madeline's insult and assess her more carefully. He caught himself before he traveled too far up her hemline. "So, how are things going for you? Have you become acclimated to the climate here at Emory?"

"As you said, I'm a cardiologist, which means I came here with my specialty. I'm trained to help save lives by instructing patients on healthy living so the old ticker will last longer. And for those who find themselves in trouble, I'm here to help them out of a jam. Those are my priorities, and I can do that from anywhere."

"I find that refreshing. So, why did you come to Emory, Madeline...that is, since you can practice medicine and save a life from...anywhere?"

Madeline looked at Kyle Bennett differently. She wasn't sure what he was trying to imply, but she didn't like the tone of it. She felt as if he was trying to back her into a corner with a warning to stay her ass there or else. But why would he go to that length, unless Michael had shared something with him? Madeline studied Kyle with eyes that were much different from when he had first arrived in her office. She had a thought, but for the time being, she'd bank it until the time came to withdraw it. She decided to ignore his question.

"So does your ignoring the question mean you plead the Fifth?"

"So what are your suggestions about this patient's treatment, Dr. Bennett?"

38

The celebration party for Pierre Louis Broussard was well underway. Michael was well into his fifth glass of Bourbon and was dusting off the dance floor with his crazy and eclectic imitation of Caribbean dance moves. Everyone was hollering and egging him on, to include Mona, who clapped her hands as loud as the other family members. It was going well into the midnight hour with no thought of slowing down.

Mona was hitting the special punch that Celia had made pretty hard. The sweet nectar laced with tequila had her up on the floor doing a few dance moves of her own. She'd finally let her hair down and was having the time of her life.

The music moved into a slow, sultry Latin beat. Sweat poured from the dancers who hadn't relinquished their spots, moving from one rhythm to the other. With eyes closed, Mona was lost in a world of her own. She let the music rule her body as she swayed from side to side, gyrating her hips, begging anyone who dared to come with her.

"You've got beautiful rhythm," said the familiar voice as he whispered in her ear and moved in rhythm with her from behind.

Mona opened her eyes, scanning the room to see if her husband had observed what had transpired on the dance floor. She wasn't sure if she should keep on dancing or stop in the middle of the dance, but she didn't want to call attention to herself.

"You are so beautiful, Mona," Timothy whispered in her ear. "I was a fool to ever leave you."

Mona stopped and turned around to face Timothy. "But you did leave me, and now I'm married to Michael. Maybe it isn't such a good idea that we dance together."

"We're still family; only now our roles are reversed. When I was married to you, Michael was my cousin as well as yours. Now that you're married to Michael, I'm his cousin as well as yours."

"If you remember your role, then we'll be fine. I need something to drink."

"You've had four glasses of Celia's punch already."

Mona looked at Timothy again. "Michael isn't counting, which makes it none of your business."

"Feisty, Mona. That's what I loved about you."

"You didn't love me at all, Timothy. You used me."

"For what? I was already becoming a doctor. I had a family."

Mona's cheeks flared. "For what? For your own selfish, self-serving, egotistical reasons. You weren't a U.S. citizen, and when you ran into me, I became your pawn in getting your green card. You committed polygamy...you had another family tucked away, hoping to reap the benefits of what you were trying to do for them. And you would've had another child, if you cared."

"I know what I did, Mona, and I regret it to this day. I'm sorry I said anything, since we had made peace with each other."

Mona blew air from her mouth. She didn't want to talk about it any longer and walked away.

Michael wasn't so full of bourbon that he didn't see what he believed to be Timothy making a play for his wife. He put his temper in check and watched the scene play out before his eyes.

Timothy was breathing on his wife's neck—moving his body with hers, but it was Mona's abrupt halt on the dance floor, followed by an exchange of words with Mona walking away that made Michael smile. But he had to have a talk with his cousin. If Timothy thought that he was going to make a move on Mona, Michael was going to, short of breaking every bone in his body, make sure Timothy understood he didn't have a rat's ass chance in hell to do so.

The music was still going, although there were fewer dancers on the floor than there were a minute ago. Michael walked over to where Timothy stood nursing a glass of Celia's spiked punch and tapped him on the shoulder. Timothy turned around to see Michael staring in his face.

Timothy set his glass down on the nearest table. "So what's up, Michael?"

"What's up is you slithering up to my wife."

"My ex-wife."

"Timothy, I'm going to tell you this once, and I'm going to be decent about it, because you are family and I'm not going to do anything to spoil my father's celebration. So take this as fair warning: stay the hell away from Mona. You didn't mean her any good years ago, and you don't mean her any good now. She's my wife. We are soul mates—something you would know nothing about. If I see you look in her direction, you'll have to answer to me."

"Whoa, Michael, your threat is so full of venom and definitely unfounded. There's nothing you have I desire. As for Mona, she's my past. And for your information, if I was on the hunt and prowl, I'd be looking for a much younger woman. Remember, I had Mona first. Been there; done that. I'm nobody's clean-up man."

"You're disgusting, Timothy."

"It is what it is. I'm the least of your worries." Timothy looked at his watch and yawned. "It's time for me to be on my way. Great party. I've always admired Uncle Pierre. Good night."

Michael stood in place as Timothy walked away, kissed his mother on the cheek, and walked out of the door. He didn't care what Timothy said because he was going to watch him day and night. Michael didn't trust Timothy as far as he could see him, and he didn't care if he was his blood...his cousin. His gut instinct told him that Timothy was up to no good.

39

"Hey, baby, how are you?" Harold whispered, leaning over the hospital bed to give Denise a kiss. Light filtered into the spare bedroom of their condo that became an instant hospital room where Denise lay almost listless. Her eyes opened slightly upon hearing Harold's voice. She smiled, but nothing more. Harold held her hand, felt her gentle squeeze, and kissed her forehead again. He sat down in a chair that was positioned next to the bed and watched his wife.

When the hospice nurse stopped by yesterday, they prepared Harold for the worst. Their words felt like a serrated knife that had penetrated his heart—less than twenty-four hours to live. Harold cried like a baby.

Now he looked at her tired, worn body that fought a valiant fight. Harold wanted to blame Denise because she knew how important it was to be tested on the regular, especially since she had already had a radical mastectomy with her other breast. It was a moot point now; he was going to miss her dearly.

Harold jumped at the sound of his BlackBerry vibrating in his pants pocket. He dug in and pulled it out and saw Rachel's name sitting in his view screen.

"Hey, Rachel, what's up?"

"How's my girl?"

Harold got up from the chair and left the room and went into the kitchen. "She's weak." Harold began to tear up. "This may be her last day."

"What makes you say that, Harold?"

"The Hospice folks said that her organs were shutting down. She still hasn't said much of anything in the last day and a half."

"I'm on my way over now."

"I'd appreciate that. I could use a lift."

"I'll see if Sylvia's available to come with me. Mona is in New Orleans, but that's probably the best place for her."

"I'll see you when you get here, Rachel."

"Okay."

Mona woke up with a terrible headache. It had been a minute since she had partied like she had the previous night. Now an imaginary hammer pounded her head. She took both hands and squeezed her head, hoping the pain would subside.

"Mommy, I'm hungry," Michael Jr. whined, sitting up in the bed. Not this morning. She wasn't up to listening to Michael Jr. drone on and on, calling her name when the pain in her head said, *You had it coming.* She shook her husband, who cocked one eye open and closed it almost as fast.

"Mommy, I'm hungry and I've got to go pee," Michael Jr. said again, climbing over Mona to get out of the bed.

Mona pushed Michael Sr. with force until he lifted his head from the pillow. "What's wrong with you, Mona? It's nine in the morning, my head is throbbing, and I'm not ready to get up."

"Your son said he has to go pee. Since Michael Jr. is in a foreign place, his father needs to take him."

"Mona, please. The boy has been to the bathroom more than once since we arrived at Celia's."

"This is the first time that he's experienced quiet in the house, and he may have forgotten the landmark he used to navigate his way to the bathroom last night."

"Why am I having this conversation with you, Mona? You make a simple thing hard."

"Well, go on and take your son to the bathroom then. And while you're up, see if you can find something for him to eat. He says he's hungry, too. It's not his fault that you and I did all that drinking last night and are miserable now."

Michael looked at Mona and shook his head. "If your argument wasn't so convincing, I'd lie back down, pull the cover over my eyes, and pretend I didn't hear a word you said."

"Daddy, I've got to pee."

"Oh, hell, Michael Jr., give Daddy a minute. Now, I've got to go." Mona smiled and laid her throbbing head back on the pillow.

"I don't know why you're smirking. If we've got to get up, your tail is going to get up, too."

"Go, Michael, before your son has an accident. I need to deal with this headache I have in peace."

"Ohhhhh, too much tequila. That's worth a smirk of my own."

"Bye, Michael."

"Come on, son. I can tell this is going to be another long day."

Dr. Kyle Bennett peeled off his surgical gloves. A tough triple-bypass surgery was now over. He wanted to thank Dr. Madeline Brooks for her insight on a minor detail that was unique to his patient. It meant his calculations about the procedure would have good results. Yes, Madeline was definitely an asset at Emory, and he was going to be the first to tell Michael as much.

Kyle took the elevator down two floors and proceeded to

Madeline's office. He whistled a tune—his good mood evident. The receptionist was even the recipient of a great, big smile.

"Is Dr. Brooks in her office?" Kyle asked as he fumbled with the cute ceramic pilgrims that sat on the receptionist's desk.

"No, she went to EEOC," was the reply.

Kyle stood there and ingested what the receptionist said. "Did you say EEOC?"

"Yes, Dr. Bennett. Dr. Brooks said she needed to make some type of complaint. She didn't tell me what it was about."

"Okay. I'll call her," Kyle said, trying to hide his suspicions.

He turned away, and with haste, walked to his office. He needed to find out what Madeline was up to, although he wasn't sure how he was going to accomplish it. Kyle pushed the button on his dictation machine and began to dictate a couple of notes from an earlier consult, but he couldn't get what the receptionist said out of his head. Certainly, Madeline wasn't going to the EEOC about the things Michael told him, which according to Michael would be a lie if Madeline was filing the complaint. He needed to find out, and he didn't have to wait long. Ten minutes later, Madeline was knocking on his door.

"Come in," Kyle said, his good mood now totally evaporated.

"My receptionist said you came by to see me," Madeline said, pushing her way into Kyle's office. "So...was your visit work or play?" Madeline sat in the chair next to Kyle's desk and crossed her legs.

Kyle watched Madeline with interest. It was easy to see how a man could fall for Madeline without blinking once. She was in her late thirties, but she looked good...her pretty face, her fabulous legs, and her bountiful serving of breasts. Kyle was a breast man in every sense of the word, and he had to work hard to steer his eyes away from that part of her anatomy.

"No...I...I just finished with Mr. Porter's triple-bypass surgery and I wanted to compliment you on that bit of information you gave me after you looked at his charts. The information made all the difference and, of course, the outcome—a successful surgery."

Madeline smiled, although it appeared she might have been a tad disappointed. "Thank you, Dr. Bennett. It means a lot that you personally came to my office to thank me. Wonders never cease. I had hoped that it might have been on a more personal note, but since it wasn't, I won't take up any more of your time." Madeline batted her eyelashes.

"Oh, before you go, is everything all right?"

"Why wouldn't it be?"

"I guess when the receptionist said that you went to EEOC to file a complaint, I found that rather disturbing, since you've only been here a little over a month."

"Two months, to be exact. But it's nothing for you to worry about. I was in my sexist mood and needed some information."

"Okay. We want you to be all right because you're definitely an asset to this team, and we wouldn't want anything to interfere with that."

"No doubt, Dr. Bennett. Thank you for the vote of confidence. Good day." And Madeline was gone.

Something wasn't right and Kyle wasn't going to sit by and not get some answers.

40

Marvin shuffled through a pile of papers that had found themselves in the mile-high stack on his desk. Although he wasn't a true micro-manager, last year's fall from glory was a constant reminder that he and his partner, Kenny Richmond, had to always be on top of everything that went on at Thomas and Richmond Tecktronics, Inc. if they were to remain a viable company in the domestic and global markets. The partners had weekly meetings with all of their departments—from finance to development—because they were all integral parts of each other and one without the other meant a slow death.

The intercom buzzed, and Marvin stopped a moment to take the call. "Yes, Yvonne."

"Ms. Ashley Jordan Lewis is here for her one o'clock appointment."

"Send her in."

Marvin stood up as Ashley came through the door. Ashley was dressed in a lightweight wool, tangerine pantsuit set off by a cream-colored ruffled blouse. French tips accentuated her slender fingers—a white gold solitaire ring with a princess cut on her left hand and a simple gold band on her right hand. Her arms were in a ready embrace as she and Marvin hugged each other.

Pulling away, Marvin smiled. "You look good, Ashley. It's good to see you smiling."

"I feel good, Marvin. Second chances don't always come one's way, and I'm going to embrace mine and make it count. I'm glad to be here."

"Have a seat." Ashley fell into one of the chairs that sat in front of Marvin's desk. "I asked you to come today instead of next Tuesday because Kenny and I have decided to hire you, if you still want the job and are in agreement with the salary we're offering. As you are aware, you'll be working with Harold, however, he's had to take a leave of absence because Denise is very ill and, unfortunately, not expected to recover."

"Oh my God," Ashley exclaimed, covering her face with her hands. "Oh my God. I didn't get to know Denise well since I was carted off to jail about the time she had the mastectomy. Claudette told me that she and Harold recently got married."

Marvin sighed. "Yeah...it's terrible. I feel so bad for Harold."

"I forgot that you were married to Denise." Ashley felt Marvin's stare. "I'm sorry; maybe it wasn't such a good idea for me to say that out loud."

"It's all right. I won't say that I haven't thought about the time we were husband and wife, but so that the record is clear, I'm very happy with Rachel. My life with Denise was so full of promise at one time, but I've been over that. Harold and I are cousins who've come full circle in our relationship. I love him and will be there for him always. Now let's talk about getting you on board."

"That sounds good."

"How about Monday?"

"If the price is right," Ashley joked.

"Remember, I'm hiring a felon. I didn't say that to make you feel bad, but you know jobs are hard to come by in this economy and if you've got a record, the chances are slim to none that you can get a decent one."

"I'm sorry, Marvin. Please don't think I'm ungrateful."

"I don't, Ashley. After all, you've been awfully good to me. I can't thank you enough for your kind gesture on my behalf when I was in a sinkhole."

"I'd be glad to start on Monday."

"As I mentioned to you earlier this week, you'll be working in the Marketing Department. While Harold is out, Kenny will show you the ropes and share our expectations. In fact, if you have time before you go, I'll take you down to Kenny's office, and he'll be glad to give you the four-one-one. And," Marvin pushed a piece of paper across his desk to Ashley, "here's the salary we've come up with, should you decide to truly make the job yours."

Ashley smiled and took the piece of paper and turned it over. She looked down at the scribble on the piece of paper and almost choked. "Can I start today?"

"I figured you'd be happy."

"*Happy* isn't the word. Ecstatic is more like it. Thanks a million."

They both looked in the direction of the phone when Marvin's private line began to ring. He picked it up and started to say hello when all he could hear was sobbing.

"Baby, what's wrong. Rachel, talk to me."

"It's...it's...it's Denise. She's gone. She's gone, Marvin." Rachel's crying drowned out anything else she tried to say. "She's gone."

Tears welled up in Marvin's eyes. "I'm on my way."

41

The drive to Harold's house was met in silence. Marvin drove as fast as he could legally without getting a ticket to be at the side of his grieving cousin and wife. Ashley and Kenny sat stone-faced in their seats and stared out of their respective windows, each privately grieving and respectful of Marvin's grief. Upon arrival at their destination, Marvin, followed by Kenny and Ashley, climbed the few steps to Harold's front door.

A tearful Rachel opened the door and wrapped her arms around Marvin as he tried to enter. Red, swollen eyes expressed the depth of Rachel's grief. Ashley and Kenny scooted past Marvin into a room that was filled with sad faces and grieving hearts. Kenny spotted Sylvia as she came from the kitchen with a cup of hot tea for Harold.

Sylvia gave Harold the cup of tea, and afterward, nearly pounced on Kenny, holding him tight as if that would make things all right. Kenny hugged her back, being the support he knew his wife needed.

Marvin rushed to Harold as soon as Rachel released him. Harold stood as Marvin approached and they held each other in a silent embrace for more than ten minutes. Like a loving brother, Marvin wiped tears from Harold's face, making the others weep even more.

Kenny and Ashley offered their condolences and gave Harold a hug each. Harold sat back down in his easy chair and commenced to drinking the tea Sylvia had brought him.

"They...they took her moments before you arrived," Harold said out loud, although he was addressing Marvin. "I...I...I know she's in a better place because she suffered more than any of us know, but I don't know what I'm going to do."

Danica came from out of nowhere. "I'm going to be right by your side, Daddy. You still have me."

Tears drenched everyone's faces at the heartfelt statement Danica made to her father. After Harold put the cup of tea down on the table, Danica hopped on her daddy's lap and they cried together. Father and daughter held each other in an embrace for a long time while Sylvia, Rachel, Marvin, Kenny and Ashley held hands and prayed silently.

Suddenly, Harold stood up, Danica sliding off of him. "Denise wouldn't want us to sit around and mope. I think she'd want us to talk about the good times."

Danica took the lead. "I'm going to miss my mommy, but I know that she loved me this much." Danica held her arms out to the sides. "She had a good heart, and when she and Daddy finally got married, that was the best." Danica began to break down and Harold put his arms around her. "Mommy was my best friend," she continued. "I love her, and I'm going to miss her a lot."

Rachel went to Danica and held her on the other side. "We are all going to miss her, Danica. Your mother and my friendship got off on a rocky start, but when we became friends, I loved and treasured every moment I had with her. She was a true friend and I love her, too." Rachel brushed a tear from Danica's face.

"Thank you, Aunt Rachel."

At the moment when it felt like the house was going to cave in on everyone, Marvin jumped to his feet. "Why don't I take everyone out to eat?"

"You mean you're going to get up off of some money to feed all of us?" Harold asked with a smile.

"I'm not going to wait for him to change his mind," Kenny said.

"Me either," Rachel put in.

"I'm with the majority," Ashley added.

"Let's eat," Sylvia said.

"Thank you for being here for me. At the end of the day, it's about friends and family. You all continue to be supportive—Sylvia and Rachel always in place. Thanks for calling mine and Denise's family, too. I didn't have the strength."

"Well, after we eat, Sylvia and I are going to help you clean up before the folks start pouring in," Rachel said.

"I appreciate that, Rachel. Before we go, I want to let you, my family...extended family know again how much I love you. Uhmm...there will be two services—one in Atlanta and the other in New York. Denise wanted to be buried in her family's plot in New York. Her two sisters will come down, and Danica and I will go back with them to New York. I wanted you all to know before people start getting it twisted."

Everyone turned when Ashley spoke up. "If there's anything you need, please let me know."

"Sure, Ashley. I understand congratulations are in order." Harold looked at Marvin and Kenny, who nodded in the affirmative. "I look forward to working with you when I return to work."

"So do I. Take as long as you like; I've got your back."

"God keeps working things out for all of us." Harold had to stop to fight back tears that were trying to push through. "Thanks again, Ashley."

"All right folks, let's head to the Prime Meridian," Marvin called out.

"Has anyone called Claudette, Trina, or Mona?" Sylvia asked.

"Why don't you do that on our way to the restaurant, baby?" Kenny said, putting his arm around his wife's neck.

"Okay. I'm ready."

42

The group filed into the Prime Meridian and followed the waitress to their table. Light laughter now flowed from the once stoic group, reviving the healthy side of humanity that the sting of death had taken from them. Even at that, everyone was attentive to Harold and Danica's well-being, hoping that a meal among family would lift their spirits.

As soon as they were seated, in marched Cecil with Trina following behind by five minutes. They hugged Harold and Danica and threw air kisses at the others before being seated. Minutes later, Claudette and Tyrone found their way to the table, their eyes bloodshot from too much crying.

Before too long and after their orders had been placed, the group seemed to be themselves—talking about old times and telling funny jokes here and there. During an intense discussion about how Mona had cut up at Harold and Denise's wedding, Dr. Madeline Brooks walked in with her arm in the crook of an unknown white man who was twenty years her senior.

Madeline almost waltzed by but noticed Harold and Danica. As if on cue, she stopped while her eyes whizzed around the table, taking mental notes of who was there. She gave Ashley a second glance, not knowing who she was. Madeline cocked her head as Harold drew his head back as if to get a better look. Then Madeline smiled.

"This is my attorney," she said.

The men passed looks around the table. Everyone else remained quiet.

"Are you all right?" Madeline finally asked, her mouth on auto pilot. "And where is Denise? Is she still taking chemo?"

A severe frown crossed Harold's face. It was a look that seemed to scare Madeline as she drew the man closer to her.

"What's wrong with you, Harold?"

"Denise passed away today, but what do you care since you've only come by the house…what was it…once?"

Madeline's face went blank as she digested what Harold said. She slipped her arm from the gentleman and grabbed her chest as if she was overcome. "I'm so sorry, Harold."

"We'd best go to our seats since our hostess is still waiting for us to follow," Madeline's attorney said as he gave her a soft nudge.

"Yes, it would be best if you went to your seat," Harold said. "We're having a family discussion."

Madeline scowled at Harold before moving ahead to her seat.

"I don't know whose family she belongs to," Harold said, licking his fingers. "She and Denise were never close. I believe Madeline thought she was better than Denise because she was a medical doctor and went to medical school."

"It's a damn shame," Rachel began, "that this woman, who happens to be Denise's cousin and went to medical school so she could help heal the sick, didn't lift a toenail to help her own. I mean a DAMN shame. Look at her sitting over there, cozying up with some wrinkled old fart. Did any of you hear her ask what can I do to help…Harold and Danica…I'm so sorry for your loss? And what in the hell does she need with an attorney? She'll need one when I walk over there and jack that face up."

"Calm down, Rachel," Marvin said. He nodded to where Danica was sitting.

"I'm sorry, Danica. Forgive Auntie Rachel. I lost my head."

"It's okay, Auntie Rachel. I understand. I don't like Madeline anyway."

Everyone at the table was quiet. Each kept their private thoughts about Madeline to themselves, but here was eight-year-old Danica stating out loud what they felt. Out of the mouth of babes. Without scolding, Harold softly shook his head *no* to let Danica know that this wasn't the time to air her feelings. But truth be told, Harold wasn't very fond of Cousin Madeline either. Harold rubbed Danica's head and she smiled back.

"Did anyone call Mona and Michael?" Claudette asked. "I know they'd want to know."

"I called but left a message on Mona's voicemail to call me," Sylvia said. "I didn't want to leave a message about Denise on the phone."

"Speak of the devil," Trina said. "Michael is dialing me now. This is strange." Trina held up her hand. "Quiet." Trina answered her BlackBerry. "Hey, Michael, what do I owe the pleasure of your phone call? You and Mona acting all right down there in the Bayou?"

"Trina, I need your assistance," Michael said with some hesitation and a strained voice.

"What is it?"

"I need you to represent me?"

"Represent you for what?"

Everyone around the table sat stark still as they waited for Trina to continue her conversation. Inquiring minds wanted to know why Michael needed Trina's help.

"Trina, do you remember Denise's cousin?"

Trina jerked her head up. "You mean Madeline Brooks?"

Harold, Marvin, Kenny, T, and Cecil sat up straight and looked from one to the other and then to the corner where Madeline was having lunch with her attorney.

"Yes, one in the same. She's suing me for sexual harassment, but it really should be me suing her. I'll be back in Atlanta on Sunday evening. I need to sit down and talk with you as soon as possible. This has marred my father's birthday celebration, and I don't want to discuss it anymore until I see you."

"I'll be available when you come in on Sunday."

"Please don't share this with anyone. I'd like to keep this as private as possible."

"Okay. I'll do my best considering I'm sitting in the midst of all of our friends."

"Damn, double damn. Are Marvin and Kenny there?"

"The whole motley crew. But there's a reason. I've got some sad news. Denise passed away today."

"Oh hell no," Michael cried out. "My God, how's Harold holding up?"

"That's why we're here—to cheer him up as best as possible."

"Why didn't anyone call us?"

"Sylvia called Mona, but her call went to voicemail. She didn't want to leave the message on the phone. We were waiting for Mona to call back."

"Is Harold close by?"

"Yes."

"Let me speak with him."

"Harold, Michael wants to speak with you." Trina handed Harold her BlackBerry.

"Hey, man. I'm so sorry," Michael said. "Denise was family. My heart and prayers go out to you and little Danica."

"Thanks, Doc. I appreciate your kind words."

"Mona and I will be back on Sunday. Whatever you need us to do, we're there."

"Again, I appreciate it. I'm sure Rachel and Sylvia will have something for you to do."

"All right, Harold. I'll see you when I get back."

"Okay, man."

Harold ended the call and handed the phone back to Trina. Ten pairs of eyes focused their attention on Trina and waited with baited breath for her to usher out the four-one-one.

"Why are you all looking at me like that?" Trina asked.

"It doesn't take a rocket scientist to figure that one out, Trina," Marvin said. "Now spit it out, girl."

"Yes, we want all the juicy tidbits," Rachel added.

"You all are crazy!" Trina hollered, shaking her finger at each one of them. "Attorney-client confidentiality clause is in effect."

"Since we're all family," Sylvia chided, "that makes it our business. And what was the inference to Madeline about?"

"Kenny, you got a bold woman," Marvin said. "Likes getting to the heart of the matter. So what's up with that, Trina?"

"Desserts on me," Trina said. "End of discussion."

"Please allow me to change the subject for one moment," Harold said. "Again, I appreciate your support. It means the world."

"Well, Auntie Claudette has taken off a few days. Count me in. Danica, do you want to spend a couple of days with Reagan?" Ashley watched the exchange with interest, lost deeply in her own thoughts.

Danica looked up at Harold. "It's all right, baby," Harold said. "Spend the night tonight, and when Grandma Helen comes in, I'll come and get you."

"Thanks, Daddy." Danica kissed Harold on the cheek and he kissed her back.

43

Numb wasn't quite the word Michael felt at that moment. Delivering the sad news about Denise's death to Mona multiplied the impact of what bad news had done to his psyche. In fact, he felt like he'd been tied to a cement block and thrown overboard into a watery grave. Celebration was an understatement, but when he saw Poppie walk through the front door of his sister's house to start the birthday celebration all over again, he turned the dial from sad to happy.

"Hey, son," Poppie called out to Michael. "Ready for a real man's drink?"

"Poppie, it's only one in the afternoon."

"You nevah learned how to live, did ya, boy? You've got to take off your medical cap awhile, at least for the next coupla days, and get down and dirty with your poppie."

Michael smiled. He hadn't had one of these talks with his father in years. He saw Mona watching him, gauging his mental state, considering the battery of news he…they had received in the last five hours. He couldn't believe it when Kyle Bennett called and said that Madeline was filing a sexual harassment suit against him.

The bitch wants to play hard ball? He was going to play hard right along with her. He didn't know what kind of so-called evidence Madeline had contrived to support a claim of sexual harassment, but being nice was no longer part of his vernacular.

It was Madeline who came on to him, trying to recreate what they once had a long time ago. And now her attempt to flip the script and make it look as if he was the one coming on to her boiled the venom in him to the highest degree. The bitch had better pull out all the heavy hardware and artillery she had in her arsenal because he was going to blow her away. And he knew Trina would blow the wool right off of Madeline's lies and false accusations because all of Atlanta knew that Trina Coleman, prosecuting attorney, didn't play.

"Poppie, let's have that drink, but let me check on Mona first. We've just learned that a dear friend of ours passed away this morning. I've got to cheer her up."

"Tell Mona she can hang with the big boys awhile and have a drink, too. Might do her some good."

Michael smiled at his father. Poppie always had a way of making him smile. For the sake of his father and his mother, he was going to do his best to suppress the turmoil and stress his body was going through so he could enjoy Poppie's birthday. He crossed the room to where Mona sat motionless on the couch.

"Hey, baby, you all right?"

"Michael, I...I...can't believe all the bad news we received today. It seems like every time we come to New Orleans, something dreadful happens."

"It has nothing to do with the place, Mona. We can't ever predict the timing of things. Together, we will get through these trials."

Mona looked at Michael and smiled. "That's why I married you. You are a sensible man with intellect. Didn't hurt that you are the finest thing on this planet." Mona looked away and stared into space.

"What are you thinking?"

Tears streamed down Mona's face. She looked back at Michael.

"I was thinking about how nasty I was to Denise that day at the hospital. Even if I didn't know at the time how sick she was, she didn't deserve the punishment I gave her...all because she was Madeline's cousin. Although I apologized a thousand times, I don't think Denise really forgave me."

"I'm sure she forgave you, baby. Some of your doing was my fault..."

"No, Michael. You didn't make me lash out the way I did. I'm a grown woman with morals and scruples. I'm the wife of a prominent medical doctor in Atlanta, and surely I ought to know how to conduct myself in and out of public. This whole Denise thing has got me to thinking, Michael, about what kind of person I've become. Yeah, I'm going to always kick it with my girls, but I must be the woman I was born to be—proud, upstanding, real... like my parents brought me up to be. I've got a son who's growing up, and I don't want him to ever say somewhere down the line that his mama was this and that. I want my men to always be proud of me."

Michael smiled at Mona again and gave her a big kiss.

"Ooooh, weeee," Poppie said from the other side of the room. "Son, you brought that girl back to life."

"I did, Poppie."

"So, does that mean she don't need to join the mensfolk...that we can begin our party? Where is Celia? Celia!" Poppie shouted, "Get me a stiff drink 'fore your momma git here, girl."

"Yes, Poppie," Celia said from another room.

"I'm going to call Sylvia," Mona said, brushing Michael's arm. "I love you."

"I love you, too, Mona."

"We will get through all of this, baby. Know that I will be at your side through thick and thin."

"Thanks, Mona. I know why I married you. Now let me go and get in a few drinks with Poppie before he starts harassing me."

"Okay, baby. I'll see if Celia needs me for anything before I call Sylvia."

Michael and Mona kissed and held each other in a strong embrace. "We'll talk later." Michael got up and walked to where Poppie sat and gave him a big hug.

Mona walked outside for a breath of air. Although it was November, the air was balmy with overcast skies. Mona closed her eyes and tried to calm her nerves. The weight of the world seemed to be on her shoulders, and she pondered the predicament Michael found himself in. Was Madeline telling the truth, whatever it was? She was conflicted, but this was not the time to doubt Michael.

Lost in her thoughts, Mona was brought back to the present when she heard a car door slam. She stared down the long sidewalk as she waited to see who belonged to the footsteps that were hard and steady on the pavement around the side of the house she couldn't see. When the person came into view, Mona turned to go into the house.

"Hey...hey, Mona. Don't go in yet. I haven't had a decent conversation with you since you've been here."

"There's nothing to have a conversation about, Timothy. What brings you to the house so early? The festivities aren't supposed to start until five."

"You're here, aren't you? Anyway, Celia asked me to bring several bags of ice and some spice she needed that Mommie had on hand. I didn't mean to intrude."

"Sorry to have questioned you."

"Why can't we be friends, Mona? You seem to be very happy with Michael. I only want to talk. I can't forget what a good conversationalist you were."

Mona smiled a brief second, and then looked away, the smile gone. "There are a lot of things I've forgotten about you, Timothy, although the time you walked out on me and our unborn baby will never be forgotten. I trusted you implicitly, so much so that I left my family so that I could be with you. Now they're gone, and every time I think about New Orleans, my memory is of the day I was able to reconcile with them. So much time wasted."

"Surely, I'm not to blame for that."

"You don't even get it, do you, Timothy? Still the same man with the arrogant and smug way about himself. Don't worry about it. No, you're not to blame; I am. You better run along before your ice melts."

Timothy took another look at Mona, dropped his head and proceeded toward the door. Before he walked into the house, he turned around and looked at Mona. "I'm to blame; I made some terrible mistakes."

Mona stood without saying a word. She lowered her eyes so that she didn't have to look at Timothy.

"You're beautiful. And I hear you're the best caterer in Atlanta. Michael is lucky."

"No, I'm the one who was fortunate to have found Michael. He's everything a man, a husband, and a father should be. Maybe I do have you to thank, Timothy, because if I hadn't been single, Michael and I wouldn't be together."

A fake smile fixed itself on Timothy's face. In ten seconds flat he dropped it, turned, and walked into the house. Mona smiled.

44

M ona went back inside the house, her mind aired out for the moment. Even though it was early afternoon, Poppie's party was in full gear. The bad news of the morning would have to be set aside for the time being, since it would be difficult to stay sad in the environment inside of Celia's house. The good, bad, and the ugly would be waiting for them upon their return to Atlanta, but now it was party time, although Mona knew to lay off the tequila. She still had to meet with her sisters and brothers.

She checked on Michael Jr. and he was having fun hanging out with some of his older cousins. Mona ventured into the kitchen to see what her sister-in-law was doing.

"Have a sit-down, Mona," Celia said, popping a piece of crabmeat into her mouth. "You having a good time, girl?"

"Celia, you know I have a good time every time I come to your house. It's always a party here."

"You better know it. That's how us Caribbeans do it. We love to eat, drink and party. But we do have another side to life—the side where we love and take care of our kinfolk with all we got."

"I can easily see that. Michael has been good to me."

"Yeah, it's that kind of love," Celia went on before plopping another piece of crabmeat into her mouth. "Last night after all the fun ran its course, me and Roberto went to bed and girl... Mona he put some good luvin' on me."

"Too much information, Celia."

"Girl, you and Michael were probably too drunk to hear through them thin walls...I saw how much punch you drank, but Roberto made me wail into the early light."

"Celia, you're crazy."

"Mona, I mean that thing. That husband of mine knows how to please his woman. If Michael hadn't schooled me about getting my tubes tied, ya'll wouldn't be able to stay overnight because this house would be full up with children."

Mona smiled.

"Why you laughing with your eyes, girl? You like that, don't you? I know Mike be getting it on with you. I know my sister-in-law is feisty."

Mona laughed out loud. "I was smiling at how you change to your Caribbean dialect when you get comfortable. It is so cool."

"You from New Orleans and got a little Creo in ya. Don't ya'll talk French with an accent?"

"I've been away from home so long, Celia, and whatever I once had, is long gone. I guess it comes from hanging with those Georgia natives."

"I understand that's where you went when you married Timothy."

Mona's eyes became transfixed as she stared at Celia. "I don't want to talk about Timothy."

"Be careful of him, Mona. I have eyes. Doris and Lucinda have eyes, too. We all see how Timothy looks at you."

"Whoa," Mona said, going to the refrigerator and pouring herself a glass of the potent punch. "Look, my heart belongs to Michael. I have no interest whatsoever in Timothy. He is my past and will continue to be my past. Yeah, he's tried to be nice and respectful, but if you think for one moment I'm going to let that snake get up under my skin, you're barking up the wrong tree." Mona finished off her glass and poured another.

"That's all I wanted to hear. I saw the way he looked at you when he came in here a few minutes ago."

"As I said, Celia, there isn't anything I want from Timothy. His loss was my gain. I might not have met Michael."

"Okay, sister-in-law. And lay low on that punch." Mona and Celia laughed, "Oh, here are Doris, Lucinda, and Mommie. Poppie, Mommie's coming! Behave yourself."

"This my birthday party," Poppie shouted. The house roared with laughter.

The party was in full gear. Two of Poppie Pierre's younger siblings arrived, as well as Grandma Lucy's sister, Brenna; Timothy's mother. They all paid homage to the man who had worked hard for his family, bringing them from Trinidad to the United States in pursuit of a better way of life.

He started out farming but hard times caused him to leave it behind and become a fisherman. He'd done well in the fishing trade and raised four fine children, one of whom was a medical doctor in Atlanta, a daughter who was a social worker in a local hospital, a daughter who worked in local government, and another daughter who was a top chef in one of the finest restaurants in New Orleans. Although Poppie had begged Celia, Doris and Lucinda to open up their own seafood restaurant in the French Quarter, not one of the three were interested in being a slave to a business that had them smelling like fish twenty-four-seven, no matter how successful they might have been.

Well-wishers came and enjoyed the food—gumbo, jambalaya, rice, shrimp, and crayfish with seasoned corn. Even Mona helped in the kitchen. Michael smiled because Mona had become a part of his family, and he loved how she and Celia connected and became part of the sisterhood of the Broussard family. And like the caterer she was, Mona set about making everyone comfortable and happy.

Mona jumped at the sound of her name. "Hello, Mona."

Mona turned around and faced an older woman—her eyes of olive green and who looked a lot like Grandma Lucy but darker. Although Mona didn't know how old she was, she was beautiful with long, coal-black, wavy hair. Her smile was welcoming but alarming at the same time.

"Yes, I'm Mona, and you are?"

"I'm Brenna Sosa, Timothy's mother."

Mona forced a smile. "Nice to meet you after all of these years."

Brenna forced a smile of her own. "Yes, it is. I see why Timothy fell in love with you."

"Mrs. Sosa, this is probably not the time to talk about Timothy and me. I'm sure you know that Timothy was married to someone else at the time he married me and only used me to get a green card."

Brenna dropped her head for a moment and then brought it back up. "Any hurt that Timothy caused you, I apologize for him."

"It was not your doing, Mrs. Sosa."

"Call me Brenna."

"Brenna, that was a long time ago. I'm over it now. I...I've forgiven Timothy for walking out on me and our unborn baby."

"You were pregnant with Timothy's child?"

"Yes, but I lost it. And it was probably the best thing that happened at the time."

"Timothy still loves you."

Mona bucked her eyes. She was speechless and then she began to whisper. "Brenna, I'm happily married to your sister's son, Michael. Yesterday, when we boarded a plane to come here, was the first time I had seen Timothy in years. And he has feelings for me?"

"Mona, I don't think Timothy ever stopped loving you. He admitted to me that he'd made a mistake...a mistake that he can't erase, but he has a good heart. He's also a doctor making very good money."

"Brenna, I'm going to say this as gently as I can. My husband is the only man for me."

"I understand, Mona. It's been nice talking to ya."

"You, also." Mona stared at Brenna's back as she made her way back into the family room that served as the main dance floor. Mona turned around into Celia's smiling face.

"I don't know what Aunt Brenna's up to, but remember what I told you."

"Celia, I'm not going to fall for some fool talk about Timothy being in love with me, even if it's his mother doing the talking. Timothy doesn't even deserve the few minutes I've given him. Timothy is in my darkest past and will never be in my future."

"Just watch them. I love them, but don't trust them. Even Mommie wonders sometimes what her sister be up to. They don't mess with my house—and that includes my brother and his wife." Mona hugged Celia.

"Mona, I've got some bowls of gumbo that need to be served," Lucinda said.

"Coming!"

45

Harold walked down the hall to the room where he last saw the lifeless body of his wife. He stepped into the room; it seemed so different. The Hospice people had removed the hospital bed, the oxygen tank, and the IV pole. The room was empty and so was his heart.

Moving from room to room, Harold started picking up things, readying the house for the arrival of his sisters-in-law and mother-in-law. His sister was also on her way.

Harold felt lost, empty, like someone had ripped out his heart. He struggled with the idea that Denise was gone—that she wasn't coming back, wouldn't ever again lie next to him...make love to him. He was beyond pitiful, but he had to be strong for Danica.

Unable to move forward with his task, Harold flopped down in a convenient chair, and the tears spilled from his eyes. He looked like a shell of a man who had been battered and beaten, his empty and vacant eyes lost in another space and time. The phone's sudden ring brought him back to the present, and he reached down and picked up his BlackBerry from his belt holder.

He drew his face back and stared at the number—one he didn't recognize. Curiosity got the best of him and he hit the ON button to retrieve the call.

"Hello."

"Harold, this is Ashley. I called to see how you were doing."

Harold frowned, then put a smile on his face. "Thank you, Ashley. I appreciate you calling. It's so surreal. I can't fathom the idea of not seeing Denise again…you know…in the flesh…alive."

"It's going to be hard for awhile. You may need to find a grief support group. I hear there are some good ones out there that really help you through the grieving process."

"I might do that. I miss her so much. She was my heart, my life. I can't believe that after all that we've been through and then finally getting married, that our time together would be so short. I don't know if I can go on, Ashley."

"Harold, it's natural for you to feel that way, but know that you have a built-in support team in Sylvia, Kenny, Rachel, Marvin and me."

"You left off Mona and Michael."

"Didn't mean to, although I'd say Michael would be more help than Mona."

Harold laughed. "I know what you mean."

"Well, I'm going to hang up, but if you should need anything, please don't hesitate to call me."

"Thanks, Ashley. That was nice of you; I'll remember that." Harold ended the call and stared out into the room, as if he was waiting for Denise to come home any minute.

46

Poppie's birthday bash was in its second day and well underway by noon. Well-wishers were still coming in from across New Orleans, stopping by to bring birthday greetings to the man who was one of the biggest shrimpers in New Orleans.

Poppie loved a good Cuban cigar. All who brought gifts were well aware of Poppie's fondness for the Corona, and he received enough for his birthday, it seemed, to open up a small tobacco store. His wife, Lucy, tolerated the scent of her husband's habit in the early years. Now. after fifty-five years of marital bliss, she was happy she hadn't denied Poppie the one vice that made him happy, other than bringing in a boatload of shrimp. From across the room, she smiled at her husband as everyone made a fuss over him.

Michael sat with his wife while she spoke to Sylvia on the phone. "Funeral services for Denise are planned for Tuesday. We'll be there."

"Denise's family arrived from New York and assisted Harold with all the arrangements for Atlanta as well as New York."

"I'm sure that was a load off his mind."

"Harold and Danica are holding up best as could be expected."

"We're praying for them." Mona ended her call and folded her arms. Michael put his arm around Mona and consoled her. He had his own battle staring him in the face, and he hoped he could make it through Poppie's celebration without falling to pieces.

Looking up, Michael saw Timothy staring at him and Mona from across the room. He couldn't quite figure him out. Timothy had been acting rather strange the whole trip. He thought it rather odd that Timothy would take time off of work to attend his father's celebration, especially since he and Timothy had had very little contact in the past months. Although they were of the same profession and worked at the same hospital, something was up, and Michael wasn't sure that it had anything at all to do with Mona.

Before Michael could entertain his thoughts further, the doorbell rang. Michael noticed the puzzled look on his sister's face. After a few shakes of Celia's head, her arm stretched out—pointed in his and Mona's direction. They both stared as Mona's two sisters, her brother, and their spouses came through the door.

Mona gasped and drew her hands to her face as surprise overtook her. As her sister, Marcella, came toward her, Mona reached out and embraced her, tears running down her face. She held onto Marcella for more than a minute and repeated the same ritual again with her sister, Cicely, and her brother, Jean Claude II, and their spouses. Michael hugged them as well.

"How did you know we were here?" Mona asked.

Marcella smiled. "Michael invited us."

Mona looked back at Michael and grinned.

"Thought it would be a nice surprise for you," Michael said, giving Mona a big smile.

"It was," Mona replied.

Mona's family members followed her into the interior of Celia's house where the celebration was in full throttle. Poppie was feeling no pain and Mona held back from introducing her sisters and brother to him for fear of what they might think. But to Mona's surprise, her sister went up to Poppie and hugged him.

"Happy birthday, Mr. Broussard. I'm Mona's sister, Marcella. All the talk in New Orleans is about the great shrimper who turned eighty-five and is still on the job doing what he loves. I was happy to receive an invitation."

Poppie got up from his chair and hugged Marcella. "Thank you, my dear, for your kind words. And who else do we have here?"

Marcella introduced her husband, James; her sister, Cicely, and her husband; and her brother, Jean Claude II, and his wife. Mona was in awe because her sisters and brothers always had their noses stuck in the air and always thought highly of themselves. They were normally too good to socialize with what they called "little people" or "those people." She noted that her brother, John, hadn't come with the group, though.

"We have plenty to eat and drink," Poppie said, lifting his drink to his lips that he'd momentarily set on a table. "We love to have fun and today, we are celebrating another year God has kept me on earth. There's eatin', drinkin', and dancin'; take your pick. Welcome."

Mona's crew smiled politely and nodded their heads in acknowledgment. Marcella and Cicely hemmed Mona up against a wall, while their husbands, brother, and sister-in-laws followed Michael to get something to eat and drink.

"Mona, is that Timothy, your ex, standing over in the corner?" Marcella asked.

"I noticed him, too," Cicely said. "He's been staring at us since we arrived."

"I barely got a hug and you're starting in on me. Yeah, that's him." Mona sighed.

"We've got your best interest at heart. So what's he doing here, little sister?" Marcella asked, looking between Timothy and Mona. "Does he know Michael's Poppa?"

"He's Michael's cousin."

"What?" Marcella and Cicely said in unison.

"How did that happen?" It was Cicely's turn to do the interrogating. "You hop from one family member to the next available?"

Mona stared Cicely square in the face. "If you all had the decency to check up on your little sister more often," Mona said, sticking her finger in Cicely's chest, "then you'd know how it went down. I didn't even know Timothy was Michael's cousin until I came to New Orleans just before Mommie and Poppa died. That's when I found out. I forgot to say anything to you all because Katrina hit, and need I say more?"

"Okay, we'll let you off the hook," Marcella said, "but why is he looking at you like he wants to devour you? I don't care what Mommie said back then, I always thought he was cute, Mona."

"Marcella, I don't believe you, and as far as Timothy wanting me, you're imagining things. He can't get over the fact that I told him I forgave him for what he did to me."

"You did what?" Cecily chimed in. "Are you crazy, sister? That boy had you disconnect yourself from your family, all because he wanted a green card."

Surprise was written on Mona's face. "How in the hell..."

"Mommie told us. Serves you right."

"Shut up, Cicely," Mona said. "You don't have any idea. Anyway, it doesn't matter because I have a damn good man now who loves me unconditionally."

"He's good-looking, too," Marcella noted.

"I'm going to tell James that you are putting your eyes on my husband."

"Cicely, tell Mona that James knows I've got a roving eye."

"She's right, Mona," Cecily said, collaborating Marcella's statement. "And James isn't going to say anything either. He put his corporate dick where it didn't belong and now sister dear is making his ass pay. Your sister was going to do a Malena...Mirah...."

"You mean Lorena Bobbitt?" Mona asked laughing.

"Yeah, that's the one," Marcella said. "I can't say that my marriage has been as pristine as I've led on. So what's good for the goose was good the gander. And sisters, I've had a couple flings that I'm not going to apologize for."

"But what about James?" Mona asked mystified.

"I can't believe you're asking that question Miss Don't-Take-No-Prisoners," Marcella said.

"Let me tell your story," Cicely jumped in, now whispering. "Oh, did James find out about Marcella's last fling? You know Mommie and Poppa probably screamed at Marcella from heaven. Your sister had the nerve to be seen at one of the swankiest restaurants in New Orleans; I don't want to call the name in the event should someone overhear. Marcella was all up on the man, passing kisses back and forth in broad daylight. Mona, your sister knows that James' business associates take clients there to eat, and when they saw her, it didn't take an hour for the news to travel."

"Marcella," Mona said, "I don't believe what I'm hearing. Not the upstanding Miss Marcella Baptiste...a lady in every way, Mommie used to say about you."

"Well, now you know, little sister. Your big sister is no prude."

"Hmmph. And all this time I hated you because of your haughty attitude."

"Get over it, Mona," Marcella said. "I know you're sassy and tameless." The sisters laughed.

"So what did James do?" Mona asked.

"Straightened his tail right up," Marcella said. "I told him, if he was bad enough to wave his mistress around, then how could he condemn me?"

"What she really told him," Cicely said, jumping in again was, *'Nigger, if you don't straighten up, I'm going to divorce your ass. This is a warning to you because I don't need you. I'm still attractive and can get any man I want.'* And Marcella dropped her plaything on the side like a hot pepper she accidently bit into."

Mona looked from Marcella to Cicely. "Haughty!!" The sisters laughed. "Lawd, you are my sisters. All this time, I thought you stuck-up and phony bitches were trying to live like those white folks you all talk about."

"Now you know," Marcella said. "Lead us to all this good food and drink Michael's Poppa was talking about."

"Okay, but you need to stay away from the punch. It's laced with tequila, but umph, it's some kind of good. Let me introduce you to Michael's sisters properly."

Mona smiled as she led her sisters to the food. She felt a kindred spirit with them for the first time in her life. Their spouses and brother had already whet their palates and before long, James pulled Marcella on the dance floor and they were shaking it down. Mona smiled again, but the smile faded as she felt a hand on her shoulder and the smell of bourbon on the back of her neck. She jerked around. "What do you want, Timothy?"

"I want you, Mona."

"You can't have me."

"Even if he's been stepping out on you with Madeline Brooks?"

Mona turned on her heels and stared at Timothy. "I don't know what you're up to or trying to insinuate, but you've got it all wrong. Now get the hell out of my face."

47

M ona lay awake, internalizing Timothy's last words to her… *'Even if he's been stepping out on you with Madeline Brooks?'* What did he mean, what was he up to, how did he know Madeline, and why was he telling her those things? Mona believed in her husband, and she wasn't going to let Timothy's murmurings deter her thinking. What was Timothy, anyway, but a low-down, dirty, fake-ass semblance of a man who took her love for him and abused it—all because he wanted a damn green card so he could stay in the United States. And to think, he already had a wife and children who believed he was leaving them in New Orleans to go to Atlanta to make things better for them. That was almost twenty years ago now, but seeing his face brought it all back to the surface.

Michael was awake. Today, they would make their way back to Atlanta. He had tossed and turned all night, no doubt with the stress of what he was getting ready to face eating at him like poison. She hadn't thanked him for inviting her family to the house, but she would. Mona smiled as she recalled how for the first time she had had a real conversation with her sisters and now a new bond was formed.

The sheet shifted across her body as Michael sat up in bed.

"Mona, are you awake?"

She wanted to pretend to still be asleep. She knew that he had wanted to make love to her last night because it was the first time since they'd been at Celia's, he wore nothing to bed. Suddenly, Timothy's face appeared and disappeared, and she sat up. "I'm awake."

"Are you all right? You hardly said anything after everyone left. I thought we'd take advantage of the fact that Michael Jr. was sleeping in the living room with his cousins."

"Just tired. Thank you for inviting my siblings."

"They seemed to have a good time. We have to invite them to come and spend time with us in Atlanta."

Mona hesitated, then spoke. "Yeah, we should."

"Look, I'm going to call Trina to see if she'll meet me as soon as we arrive in Atlanta, after I get you all settled at home."

"Why don't Michael Jr. and I go with you? I'd like to hear what Trina has to say."

"Remember, Marvin is picking us up from the airport."

"Yeah, I forgot about that."

"I hope we can resolve this sexual harassment issue without it getting nasty."

"If you're innocent, as you say you are, the burden of proof will be on Madeline."

Michael looked at Mona. "If I'm innocent, Mona?" A frown formed on Michael's face. "Don't you believe me?"

"I want to, Michael. I can't help but wonder why Madeline is doing this? Did you do something to her when you were in medical school?"

Michael sighed. He seemed to contemplate the question Mona posed. He looked Mona in the eyes. "Hear me good: I've never done anything to Madeline. My God, I've been out of medical school for ten years or more and have been practicing ever since. Surely, if I had done something to Madeline, why would she wait until now to do something? It was a shock to the system when I saw her at Denise and Harold's wedding."

"I'm sure it was."

"And what is that supposed to mean, and where is this coming from, Mona? I thought you were on my side. I've been upfront with you."

"I'm sorry, Michael. Maybe I'm feeling the weight of this, too."

"I'm the one charges have been filed against and who stands to lose it all."

Mona sighed. "I'm sorry, baby. For real. I forget we don't live in a perfect world. I learned things about one of my sisters yesterday that all but destroyed this perfect image I had of her. You have this picture of someone (good or bad) and then out of the blue, something happens to distort, and sometimes corrode, the image you had. Suddenly, you can't trust your own instincts."

"Baby, I don't know how many times I've apologized about not telling you about Madeline, but you have to believe me when I say I have not touched that woman."

Mona looked in Michael's eyes. She knew he was telling the truth, but still something gnawed at her inner core. She'd let it be for now. "I believe you, baby. You go and call Trina and I'll get Michael Jr. up, so we can get ready to head to the airport."

"I love you, Mona."

"I love you, Michael."

The flight was uneventful. Michael was surprised that Timothy wasn't on the same plane headed to Atlanta. He wasn't sure what Timothy was up to, but he was going to watch him.

Marvin picked them up and gave them the low-down on how things were going for Denise's homegoing services. Harold was holding his own but would need somebody when it was all over. Neither Michael nor Mona said anything about the sexual harassment suit.

Settled in, Michael kissed Mona and Michael Jr. and said he'd be back soon. He was anxious to get to Trina's house, hoping his talk with her would set his mind at ease.

"Hey, Michael," Cecil said, clasping Michael's hand as he entered their house. "How was New Orleans?"

"My father deserved all the love he got. We had a good time, but it would have been better, if I didn't have this thing hanging over my head."

"Well, you've got a damn good attorney, and if you're clean, Trina will make it right for you."

Michael reached in his pocket. "Here's a carton of Havana's finest. I don't smoke, so I want you to have it."

"Coronas. Nice. Smooth. I do like a good cigar every now and then. Thanks, man. Here comes Trina."

"Hey, Trina," Michael said, giving her a hug.

Dressed in an orange and purple caftan and in bare feet with orange polish on her toes, Trina reached up and embraced Michael. "Hey, yourself. Where's Mona?"

"I left her and Michael Jr. to unpack. I thought it would be best if only you and I could talk first."

"No problem. We'll go into the library. Cecil knows the deal—attorney-client privilege."

Cecil shook Michael's hand. "Talk with you later, man. Thanks for the Coronas."

Michael followed Trina into the place she called her library. He hadn't been in this part of her house before. Books were everywhere. There were a ton of them—law books of every kind—Georgia Statutes, business law, criminal law, WestLaw, entertainment law, law and legal history, and legal theory. There were marketing books. There were books about the psychology of man. They all sat on white oak built-in shelves that took up three sides of the octagonal shaped room, separated by floor-to-ceiling windows that met at the crease in each wall. A large oak desk sat directly in front of the long wall. Facing the desk was a forty-inch flat television screen mounted on the wall that sat over a beautiful oak credenza that was adorned with expensive trinkets from Africa. On Trina's desk was the latest *Essence* magazine—probably the only book of pleasure inside of the room.

"Have a seat, Michael," Trina said. "Do you want something to drink?"

"No, I'm good."

"Okay, it's a little awkward doing things this way, since you haven't been formally charged with anything. Is your source reliable?"

"Yes, he is. You won't mind if I don't mention his name. He's on staff at Emory and I don't want him dragged into this."

"So we really don't have a case and this is all speculation at the moment."

"Yes."

Trina looked at Michael thoughtfully. "So what makes you think that what your friend has shared with you has any merit?"

"Madeline has tried to seduce me with a vengeance and I have ignored her advances. Trina, I'm going to be up front with you."

"You need to be, if you want me to go to bat for you and win. You do know that I'm a prosecuting attorney, but I will do this for you."

Michael sat back in his seat. "Oh. I owe you a debt of gratitude." He sighed and rubbed his hands together, then ran one over his head. "I'm not sure where to begin."

"Why don't you begin at the beginning?"

"Yeah. The nightmare began at Harold and Denise's wedding... that's when I saw Madeline for the first time in ten or more years."

"So she was someone you knew. How well did you know her?"

"Yes, I knew her; we attended medical school together at Johns Hopkins."

"Nothing obscene about that. But I take it that Madeline seeing you at Denise and Harold's wedding triggered some memories."

"What do you mean?"

"Memories—an old classmate she hadn't seen in years...maybe you worked on projects together, went out for a bite to eat...you know."

Michael stumbled. "Uhh, yeah, we did...uhh, work on projects."

"What kind of projects?"

"We were study partners and collaborated on several studies and research papers."

"Did you study anything else besides your medical books?"

"What do you mean, Trina?"

"Look, Michael. I'm trained to watch for certain traits in suspects/defendants that can make or break a case, as you are trained to understand how the heart works. And if something is out of kilter, you're able to recognize the defect and fix it. Your nervousness tells me a lot. You're holding back information that may be relevant to your case. Let me say further, if you want to prove your innocence, should this turn out to be a case at all, you have to shoot a straight arrow and be confident in the information you release or don't release.

"So what happened in med school that might be a trigger for Dr. Madeline Brooks to desire you in such a fashion?"

Michael slumped his shoulders and let out a deep breath. Trina folded her hands and waited. She was no longer the friend but his attorney.

Michael intertwined his fingers and pushed them together. He looked up at Trina, who was studying him, then looked away.

"I'm not trying to snare you in a trap, Michael. I need to know the basis for all of this, if there is one, so I can prepare a good case. I'm not trying to pry, but I have a need to know. Forget Trina, the friend. I'm your attorney, who's defending you for your career... your livelihood. Remember that everything you tell me is said in confidence. Although Cecil knows why I'm meeting with you, I will not discuss anything that is shared in this room."

"What I'm about to say, I haven't even told Mona. She knows that Madeline and I attended medical school together, but she doesn't know that we were lovers."

"Did you have feelings for Madeline or was it purely sexual?"

"Wow, you don't mince words."

"I can't if we're going to win. *Win* is the operative word. That's all I'm thinking about. You say you're innocent; I'm pulling out all of my guns. Got it?"

"Yes, counselor."

"You need to relax, Michael. Answer that last question for me, and we'll call it a night. I call this my prelim fact-finding mission or discovery. Once you've been charged, and I pray you aren't, but if you are, the questions will get tougher. And I'll need full disclosure."

Michael twiddled his fingers. "We were really into each other. I enjoyed the sex, and so did she...we were, I guess you would say, addicted to each other. In between the studies, in the car, in the bathroom of one of our favorite hole-in-the walls, we would sex each other."

"Did you love her?"

Michael pursed his lips, but nothing came out. He was silent for more than three minutes but twitched around in his seat.

"You okay, Michael?"

"Yeah. Maybe I thought it was love. I think in my mind that if I thought it was love, satisfying my huge sexual appetite didn't seem whorish, if you will. I will say that Madeline had an insatiable appetite that I was more than eager to satisfy."

"So you would agree that the sex was good?"

"I'm ashamed to say, but yes, it was beyond good."

Trina seemed to analyze Michael. The way she looked at him, Michael thought she might be having her own fantasy, but that would be conceited of him to think that way.

"Well, Michael, I think we've identified the trigger. Our dear Dr. Brooks, it appears, wants to recapture something she once had—a good memory that she probably fantasizes about all the time. Stay out of her way."

"Oh, I forgot. I shared with the guys my fear that Madeline was trying to seduce me."

Trina wrinkled her nose. "Uhm, funny, Cecil never mentioned it to me."

"He wasn't there. What I also was going to say is that I dictated a letter to my secretary a few weeks ago that Madeline was harassing me. I was going to mail it to the EEOC, if she chose not to leave me alone."

"That letter would be helpful, and if it should come to that, we'll need to subpoena your secretary to testify to this. You sure you didn't tell Cecil?"

"Do you share everything?" Michael asked, curious.

"Most things, but not everything. Many of my thoughts and dreams are in my head. Many times loved ones aren't as receptive to our thoughts and dreams and sometimes sabotage your desire to act on them. Those are the kinds of things that I don't share until I'm ready and feel confident about executing them."

"You always seem confident."

"Thank you, but this conversation isn't about me. I want you to stay as far away from Madeline Brooks as possible. No doubt you'll see her at Denise's funeral, if she comes at all. Rachel told me that Madeline stopped by Harold's once and stayed for only thirty minutes to say hello to Denise's mother. What a shame."

"So counselor, what do you think?"

"If you're innocent, we'll prove it."

48

Trina shut the door behind Michael as he left to go home. She stood at the door a moment, her head bent down with a hand on her hip, thinking about what Michael had told her. For his sake, she hoped he was telling her the truth. If he wasn't, she wouldn't be able to keep his dignity from being stripped from his soul. It might happen anyway, even if he told the truth, but in the end, he'd still have his license to practice medicine.

Footsteps. Trina looked up when she saw Cecil staring at her with a drink in his hand. She had a good man. Cecil took pride in the way he looked, even if he was slumming at home. Her eyes shot him a smile, then assessed the chocolate man in his starched jeans and soft yellow, Ralph Lauren polo shirt.

"Tough one, huh?" Cecil asked, as Trina walked toward him.

She sighed. "Possibly...depends." Trina stopped in front of Cecil and put her arms around him. "Do you love me?"

"What kind of question is that, Trina?"

"A real question. Relationships are tedious in this day and age. We've been together how long?"

"A long time to be with one woman."

Trina pushed back and gave Cecil a hard stare.

"Kidding, baby. You were reaching for something, and I threw in some bait to see if you'd fall for it."

Trina swatted his shoulder. "I was serious, Cecil. You get

married, say I do, but do you truly know the person? Before God and a hundred of witnesses, you said you'd love and cherish this person as long as you both shall live, but do you really know them? You're living this wonderful life, then some event throws you a curve ball and before you know it, a mountain of secrets are revealed that may have devastating effects on a marriage—things one partner might have thought would never come to light. Or another scenario...along comes some woman or man who is attractive and catches your attention, gets your hormones to buzzing, and some crazy bell rings in your head and says you've got to test the waters. And when you decide to test the waters, and realize after it's too late you've done a terrible thing, the first thing you want to do is run home like nothing has happened, and pick up where you put your real life on hold without consequences."

"Okay, Trina, what are you talking about? Did Mona find out about Dr. Madeline Brooks?"

"Oh, so what do you know other than what I told you? Had this tidbit and didn't tell me?"

"See, you want to gossip. I thought you knew anyway. The guys were talking about seeing Michael at the Prime Meridian sitting back in a corner having lunch with the lady doctor one day. That's all. Said to keep it under wraps. I haven't heard anything else."

"You keep a good secret. But you never answered my question."

"Trina, if I have to answer the question, then what we've been living all this time has been a lie. Why would I still be with you after all these years if I didn't love you? Eighteen good ones. I love everything about you—your brains, your wit, that fine body of yours that you've covered up with that oversize knapsack." Trina laughed. "Come here and let me feel you."

"See, it's all about the sex to you."

"Look, don't let Michael's issue affect what we've got at this residence. Sure, if I see a fine sister on the street, I may twist my head a little and give her a parting glance, but you're the one I married and come home to every night. Does that answer your question?"

"Very well done, counselor."

"Well, how about letting me feel that booty?"

49

Everyone was piled into Harold's condo. Three black limousines lined the street. Harold peeked from behind the curtain in his living room at the limos waiting to take him to the final curtain call for his dear wife. The last time a limo waited for him, it was barely four-and–a-half months earlier. A white Rolls-Royce stood glistening in Central Park waiting to whisk him and Denise off to their wedding reception. What a memory; a lone tear fell from his eye.

Harold turned when he felt a hand on his shoulder. "I'm here for whatever you need, Harold. I can't believe I'm saying this; we both loved her."

"Thanks, Marvin." Harold hugged him. "I can't thank you enough for all of your support. And Rachel has been a godsend." Harold turned away to keep Marvin from seeing his tears.

"I love you; we love you."

"Harold, it's time to go," Denise's mother said as she strolled over and patted Harold on the back. She smiled at Marvin. She and her daughters were all dressed in black satin suits with pillbox hats on their heads. Danica wore a black velveteen dress with an off-white satin collar and a large black satin ribbon that served as a belt.

"I'll lock up," Kenny said.

The limos were filled with Harold's and Denise's family members to include Marvin, Rachel, and their daughter, Serena. Kenny,

Sylvia, and Kenny Jr. rode with Cecil and Trina, and Michael, Mona, and Michael Jr. rode with Tyrone, Claudette and Reagan. Just as the line-up began to move out onto the street, a lone cobalt-colored Jaguar rolled into Harold's driveway. The driver got out—a woman who seemed miffed that the train of cars didn't stop. The woman hopped back into her car and pulled up behind Tyrone's BMW and followed the caravan to the church. It wasn't until Mona and Michael arrived at the church did they recognize the late arrival as Dr. Madeline Brooks.

Michael stayed in the car until Madeline passed. She was dressed in a lightweight, wool, chocolate designer suit with a mink stole wrapped around her shoulders. A large angular hat—the skull of the hat made of wool that matched the fabric on her suit surrounded by thick netting—sat on her head. She clicked her high-heels and walked as if she was someone of importance, looking into the first limousine for familiar faces.

"Who does she think she is?" Claudette asked, opening the door to get out. "Ever since that heifer came to my beauty salon, she put a bad taste in my mouth. I told my assistant if she called for another appointment to say I was not available." Mona and Michael remained silent.

The family lined up in the vestibule of Mt. Calvary Baptist Church, the church Sylvia and Kenny attended, and upon her arrival to Atlanta, so did Denise. Pastor Goodwin stood at the front of the line, waiting for the family to assemble so they could march into the sanctuary.

At the end of the family procession were all of Denise and Harold's good friends. Michael stayed tucked out of sight for fear Madeline would pull one of her Academy Award-winning performances in spite of the fact that she wasn't the star of the show. So far, so good.

"I feel so for Harold," Sylvia said. "He loved himself some Denise. It's a shame that it took them so long to decide to get married, considering all of their history. She really was a good person."

"She had issues like most of us," Claudette said. "I remember the day we met her at our support group meeting."

"Yeah. Remember how many of us were divorced at the time?" Sylvia asked.

"I remember the meeting when I received the news about my shop burning to the ground and how those circumstances brought me and T back together."

"I remember it as if it was yesterday," Tyrone said.

"But I catered the meeting that Miss Denise came roaring into and said she would press charges if we denied her access to our group," Mona said. "That was the meeting of all meetings. I thought Denise and Rachel were going to duke it out."

"But it also happened to be the meeting that we saw Denise as this vulnerable woman who needed a friend," Sylvia quickly interjected. "Who would've thought that her announcing she had breast cancer would bring us all together?"

"And then to know that she had conquered it...and now this?" Claudette said, shaking her head.

"We're moving ahead," Trina said. "I'm so glad we went to the wake last night. It'll help to make the day not so painful."

Cecil put his arms around Trina. "I love you."

Pastor Goodwin led the procession and the family was ushered to their seats. The program was beautiful, from the songs sung to Pastor Goodwin's message about letting God come into your heart so that you can make Heaven your eternal home. A group of breast cancer survivors that Denise had become associated with after her first bout with breast cancer sat together wearing their pink breast cancer symbol pins. At the appropriate time, they presented Harold and Danica a plaque in remembrance of Denise. But it was Rachel's words for a dear friend that made the congregation weep.

"Denise had a zest for life and she wanted to live it to the fullest. And she wanted to live it with the people who meant the most to her—her adoring husband, Harold, and beautiful daughter, Danica. If it meant giving up a breast, so be it. That's what she did the first time she faced the dreaded disease, driven by her desire to see her little girl grow up. This time she wasn't as fortunate, but she left a legacy for a lifetime—a legacy of love and friendship that her family and dear friends will forever carry in their hearts."

Poor, poor Danica. Her eyes were swollen from crying. There seemed to be no amount of consoling her. Flanked by her father and maternal grandmother, she barely got through the service. One more to go as Denise's body would be flown to New York for her final resting place.

At the end of the service, the church secretary announced that the repast would be held in the fellowship hall. Michael wanted to get away from the church as fast as his legs would take him but forgot that he didn't drive his own vehicle. As much as he wanted to go and speak to Harold, he stayed back among the mourners who fellowshipped on the way out of the sanctuary, hoping to avoid Madeline at all costs. Mona and the rest of the gang rushed to be with Harold, Marvin, Rachel and the rest of Harold's family to offer a shoulder to lean on or a kind word to ease their pain.

"So, you had the audacity to show yourself in public. I hear you didn't show up for work yesterday."

Michael turned around, slowly flexing his hands, and tried to show some level of control. "That's my business, Madeline. And today I'm here because we loved Denise like most of the people in this building, present company excluded."

"Uhm, seems I recall an incident when your wife ripped Denise apart in the cafeteria you and I frequent. Nasty attitude, that woman of yours. I don't know what you see in her."

"That's not up for debate. Excuse me; my wife is waiting on me." Michael started to walk away.

"Michael. Michael," Madeline said as he continued to move straight ahead. "Michael, I'm talking to you," she shouted.

Michael turned around, as did others who were standing near. "I have a present for you when you return to work. You're making this harder than I thought. I've repeatedly given you more chances than you deserve to make things right."

A thin veil of sweat covered Michael's face and head. If he could have knocked the smirk off of Madeline's face, he would have. "We are in a church...at the end of a celebration of the life of your cousin. How disrespectful can you be? You don't care about anyone but yourself. And whatever present you have for me, you can shove it up your behind."

Slap. "You sorry son-of-a-bitch."

Slap. Madeline swung her head around and looked into Mona's face. "That's for my husband who wouldn't dare hit a lady, although you don't qualify as one. I don't have a problem though, and if you want some more, we can step right outside and I'll do you the honors."

"You ugly-ass bitch," Madeline retorted.

"I got your bitch, ho. You are a sorry excuse for a human being."

"Let's go, Mona," Michael said, grabbing her arm. "She's not worth the time of day."

Madeline threw up her hands and adjusted the fur around her shoulders. She huffed. "You will pay for this."

Before they could exit the church, Pastor Goodwin was upon the trio, followed by a couple of his deacons. "Ladies and gentlemen, this is the Lord's house, not the devil's playground. You must leave right now. If you truly heard the message today, I wouldn't harden my heart to it. God loves you." Madeline walked away.

Michael raised his hand to shake that of Pastor Goodwin's. "Pastor, my name is Dr. Michael Broussard, and my wife and I apologize for disrespecting God's house." Michael put his arm around Mona. "Sister Denise was a very dear friend of ours and we wouldn't do anything intentional to ruin her day. The devil slithered in and unfortunately, you were privy to that ungodly display. Please pray for me...for us. I'd like to come again for worship."

The hardness rolled from Pastor Goodwin's face. He shook Michael's hand and grasped it. "You are always welcome in God's house. I don't know what went on a few moments ago, but I pray that we won't see that kind of behavior again."

"I, too, apologize," Mona said. "I don't know if you remember me, but I've come a few times with Sylvia Richmond. We're long-time friends. In fact, your sister, Margo Myles, came to our support group a long time ago and spoke with us about her husband's infidelity and her forgiving him."

"Yes, I remember that. Hmmm, that was a long time ago."

"How is Margo doing?"

Pastor Goodwin hesitated. "She's doing fine, and she's having a baby."

"Having a baby? I thought she said she had adult children."

"She does, but those things do happen. I hope I see you and Dr. Broussard in church in the near future." He shook Mona's hand and walked away.

"I must have touched on a touchy subject," Mona said. "He was anxious to get away when I started asking questions about his sister."

"Yeah." Michael kissed Mona on the forehead. "You are my shero. I was two minutes from knocking Madeline's brains out. I was going to ask God for forgiveness later. Thank you, Mona, for saving my ass."

"But I looked bad in the Reverend's eyes."

"You looked bad in the Lord's eyes. But when you batted those eyes of yours and started talking about Rev's sister, I'm sure he forgot why he stopped to talk to us in the first place."

"You're crazy, Michael. Let's catch up with the rest of the group. Did you see Ashley?"

"No, I didn't see her."

"She was sitting on the other side. She must have driven straight to the church. I kinda feel for her. You can see it in her eyes that she wants her daughter, but don't say anything to Claudette about Reagan and Ashley. As clear as a bell, Claudette said that Reagan is her child and she has the adoption papers to prove it. She might as well have said that Ashley's got to conceive a new baby if she wants one of her own."

"Well, that's their crisis," Michael said. "I'm not ready to face mine yet. I've got a meeting with the Chief first thing tomorrow."

Mona grabbed Michael's hand and threaded her fingers with his. "I'm with you all the way, baby. I'm ready to fight."

"Today was a sad occasion, but you've made me smile. Thanks, Mona."

"You're welcome, baby."

50

Michael stumbled around in the kitchen until he found the pot to make his oatmeal. His head was pounding and stress was getting the best of him. It seemed to take him forever to put the water in the pot and turn on the stove. The weight of Madeline Brooks' accusation was on his shoulders.

"Good morning, baby. You all right?" Mona asked.

"Yeah, I'm not anxious to go to the hospital this morning. Facing Chief is one thing, but facing my staff will be another."

"Maybe they don't have any idea what's going on. Maybe Kyle got it wrong."

"Kyle wouldn't have called me all the way in New Orleans when he knew I was celebrating my father's birthday to give me some news like that. Kyle Bennett is my best friend on staff, and I trust him implicitly."

"Grasping at straws, baby. Truth be told, I didn't sleep very well either. I've been thinking about this whole incident and praying that it's all a dream."

"That would be nice. Have some oatmeal with me?"

"Yeah, I'll have some oatmeal with my honey." Mona rubbed Michael's back. "It's gonna be all right."

"I hope so."

Michael felt like his neck was trapped in a hangman's noose, being dragged through the hallways for all to see as he made the short trek to the Chief's office. He stood outside for a minute or more before he was able to push the door open and enter. Chief's secretary, a large, burly black woman in her late fifties with large hoop earrings in her ears and sporting a sharp, close-cut hairdo, looked up as Michael entered and gave him a gracious smile.

"Morning, Dr. Broussard," Melissa said.

"Good morning, Melissa. I'm here to see Chief."

"Yes, he's waiting for you. Hold on a moment. Let me tell him you're here."

Michael stood back near the door and moved toward Chief's door when Melissa gave him the go-ahead. Chief was sifting through several stacks of paper but looked up over his bifocals when Michael entered.

Chief Calloway was in his early sixties, knew how to run a hospital, and was the best neurosurgeon in the world. For an African-American man, he'd done well and earned the title of Chief on his own merits and fortitude. Everyone at Emory liked him because he wasn't only a doctor's doctor, he was honest, rewarding, and a down-to-earth human being. If he had been a single man, the female doctors and staff might have eaten him alive. He was distinguished-looking with gray at the temples—and on a running scale, his looks were between medium and fine. He'd been married twice, but had found true happiness in the second. They had two children, ages twenty-five and twenty-three.

"Broussard, come in and shut the door. Damn, boy, what in the hell is going on?"

"What do you mean, Chief?" Michael didn't want to make any assumptions until the Chief made it known why he called him to his office.

"This sexual harassment complaint. Broussard, you've been here for ten years and your record is squeaky clean. Why now?"

"Chief, who filed a complaint of sexual harassment against me?"

Chief sat up, slipped off his glasses and looked Michael directly in the eyes. "Broussard, please don't treat me like I was ejected from the womb yesterday. I don't look that dumb to you. You know very well who filed this complaint, but if I have to spell it out, Dr. Madeline Brooks, the new doctor on board."

"She's evil."

"I've done a little background check myself. I see that you both went to Johns Hopkins for medical school at about the same time. Did you know her then?"

Michael didn't like this line of questioning and certainly his attending medical school with Madeline had nothing to do with his qualifications as a heart surgeon. "Yes, Chief. We were both preparing ourselves to be heart surgeons, and we shared many classes together."

"Did you have a thing for her? She is very attractive, and she's got that uhmm, nice ass."

Where was Chief going with this line of questioning? Surely, these weren't questions he had to debate with him. "Yes, she was as attractive then as she is now. We were good friends."

"So what is it, Broussard? Are you having an 'I've got a second chance to tap that ass' moment?"

"Chief, I don't believe you'd insult my intelligence in this manner. To think that I'd have a fling outside of my marriage is preposterous."

"Look at the ex-senator from North Carolina who might have been our next President. Been married a couple of decades and right in the middle of his campaign decides he wants to hump a beautiful campaign worker, although I didn't think she was that pretty. And look what happened to him. He had an affair, got the woman pregnant, and had the nerve to deny it. That could have been the President of the United States, except we knew that Obama was going to kick his ass, if they were up against each other in the primaries. But the worst part of the story is that Edwards' wife had terminal breast cancer, and he had the audacity to leave her for the other woman."

"You know Elizabeth Edwards died."

"Yes, God rest her soul, especially for putting up with that fool. So I'm saying Broussard, this is messy. You are one of my top surgeons and I can't have this kind of attention brought on the hospital."

"You forgot to ask me if I was guilty."

Chief Calloway looked at Michael thoughtfully. "Are you?"

"Hell no. In fact, I should file a harassment suit against her."

"Why?"

"You've got an hour?"

"Sit down."

Michael spoke candidly with Calloway, sharing things he hadn't intended to tell. Calloway was a captive audience, shaking his head and splattering the word damn out of his mouth every ten minutes as Michael gave him the uncensored version of the story.

"Damn, Broussard, this could get uglier than I first thought." And as if he had given it some thought, he said, "And I always thought the male species could out manipulate the woman. I say file your complaint, although an EEOC complaint isn't cause for disciplinary action. I've talked to you and got your version. You may need to get a damn good attorney, though."

"I've already retained one."

"Okay, our meeting is over. Report to duty. I have to remain neutral since both of you are on staff; I've listened to both sides. That's it for now."

"Thanks, Chief."

51

Everyone was in a somber mood around Thomas and Richmond Tecktronics, Inc. Marvin's mind wouldn't let go of the picture of Denise lying in her coffin. He had truly loved her once. He would have given her the world, but she didn't want him. It was his cousin, Harold, who she wanted.

He wiped the tears that dripped on his desk. Visions rolled back: the day he and Denise had gotten married; the time they had kissed in Times Square; the moment he'd found Harold naked with her; and Denise had come out of the bathroom naked and calling Harold's name. Marvin sat up straight at the last vision—one he thought he'd buried once and for all. But it was still there.

Marvin picked up the phone and called Kenny. "Hey Kenny, are you busy?"

"Hey, Marv. I'm training Ashley at the moment. She's going to make Harold a darn good assistant. She's got plenty of good ideas."

Marvin simmered on that for a moment then let it go. "Okay. How about joining me for lunch in an hour?"

"All right. I may bring Ashley with me."

Marvin frowned. "Okay." Marvin wanted to talk to Kenny alone...hash out his feelings. Harold and he had found each other again, and he didn't want the old memories to cloud their relationship when they'd made so much progress. Why, he'd even given

Harold a job. No, Harold shouldn't pay for the past because he already had. Marvin needed Kenny's crazy jokes and antics to put him in a better mood.

Rachel, like her husband, moped around. She went from room to room, but couldn't seem to concentrate on anything.

"Is there anything I can get you, Mrs. Thomas?" Isabel asked. "Your nerves seem out of sorts today."

"I'm going to call Mrs. Richmond and Mrs. Broussard to see if they'd like to come over for lunch. How about warming up some of that beef stew you made yesterday? And some cornbread?"

"Okay, Mrs. Thomas. Having your friends around will make you feel better."

"I believe you're right. Hand me the phone, Isabel."

Isabel chased after Rachel and told her to sit down in the family room. "I'll bring the phone to you in a second. Relax. You've done all you could for the other, Mrs. Thomas. It's time for you to grieve."

"I miss her, Isabel. I really, really miss her."

"I know, love. Let me go and get the phone."

Isabel brought the phone to Rachel. She dialed Sylvia's number and waited. "Hey, girl, this is Rachel. Why don't you come by and have some lunch with me?"

"I was getting ready to run to the store. I haven't done much of anything at home since...in the last couple of weeks."

"What about Marla? Isn't she keeping up the house?"

"Marla comes only three days a week. Sometimes I like doing my own things, Rachel. It makes me feel useful. I may hire her full-time if I decide to open up my own PR agency."

"You can shop later. I need you."

"Okay, sweetie. I'll be there in a minute. Who else are you inviting?"

"Mona. I haven't had a chance to talk with her since she's been back from New Orleans. Want to see how everything went."

"Okay. Do you need me to bring anything?"

"Only you."

Rachel ended the call and phoned Mona. Mona seemed more than eager to come over. It would take her about thirty minutes to get there. Rachel got up and went to the front of the house and looked out of the window. The neighborhood was quiet. It was at that moment, she thought about Peaches and the night she was kidnapped. She closed her eyes and returned to the family room.

Before Rachel could relax, there was a knock at the door. "I'll get it, Isabel; it's Sylvia."

Rachel raced to the door and opened it. She grabbed Sylvia before she was able to get in the door good. Sylvia held her, too, because truth of the matter, she missed Denise also.

Sylvia pulled back and came inside. "You've got it smelling good in here, Rachel. What are we having?"

"Isabel cooked some of her famous stew yesterday. It'll warm us up inside. Look at you all dressed up like you were going to see somebody special."

"Rachel, you know I like to get cute when I go out. Anyway, these are those new skinny jeans Oprah keeps ranting and raving about. Makes me look thinner."

"It does."

"I told Kenny that I was going to get serious about losing some weight and get a personal trainer to work with me."

"A personal trainer only works if they're male and fine. When you work out, you want him to know that you're doing everything he told you to do."

"Rachel, you are crazy."

"Tell me if I'm wrong. Go on, sister; say I'm telling the truth."

"I don't know what I'm going to do with you. Did Mona say she was coming?"

"Yeah, she's on her way."

"Something happened between her and Denise's cousin at the church yesterday. Do you know what it was?"

"No, but I hear that someone slapped somebody."

"Oh, I'm glad you called Mona. Now we have something to gossip about. I've been out of the loop."

"Me, too, Sylvia. Guess who I thought about a minute ago?"

"I don't know. Who?"

"Peaches."

"Peaches? For God's sake, Rachel, what could make you possibly think about Peaches?"

"I don't know, Sylvia. I went to the window and looked out, and all of a sudden the memory of Peaches kidnapping me that night came to me. The memory was crystal clear."

"Thank God, she's dead. Not that I'd wish death on anyone."

"I'm glad that crazy woman is out of commission. Have they found her killer? We've been so consumed with Denise that I haven't paid much attention to what's going on otherwise."

"We'll have to ask Trina the next time we talk to her. By the way, Thanksgiving will be here in two weeks. We need to make plans if we're eating together."

"Yeah, yeah. I think I hear Mona now. Isabel, would you get the front door, please?"

"Yes, Mrs. Thomas."

"Isabel is the sweetest," Sylvia said.

"Hey, hey, hey, ladies," Mona said, passing air kisses to both Rachel and Sylvia. "I'm so glad you called, Rach; I needed to be around my sistahs."

"We all need each other," Rachel said. "Denise's death has taken the life out of me. She suffered so much, but I'm glad she's in a better place."

"I didn't give the kind of time that you and Sylvia did, but my heart was there."

"She knew, Mona," Sylvia said. "If it would make you feel better, she asked about you a few days before she passed."

"Oh my God," Mona said, closing her eyes and putting her hand to her mouth. "I felt so bad after I went off on her at the hospital. I should've been venting my feelings toward Madeline."

"What happened with you and her at the church yesterday, Mona?" Sylvia glanced at Rachel.

"I really don't want to talk about Madeline, but here it is in living color. She was hollering Michael's name in the church, albeit after the service. She was all up in his face, and I went over to see what was going on. Then all of a sudden, that bitch hauled off and slapped Michael in the face. She didn't even see me and before she knew it, my handprint was on her cheek."

"What?" Rachel and Sylvia screamed.

"But why?" Sylvia asked.

"I guess you know she's been trying to come on to Michael. Since the day she saw him at Denise and Harold's wedding, she's made it her mission to get next to him. I understand the part about them being in medical school together, but please, that was over ten years ago. That bitch is crazy. She found out where Michael worked and got a transfer to Atlanta so she could be near him."

"That's so absurd," Sylvia said. "I've seen guys from my past, but it certainly doesn't make me want to drop everything I'm doing and run after them."

"The difference between you and Madeline," Rachel said, "is that you've got some sense. Even Denise said she was crazy. She didn't even come around at all when Denise was sick and she calls herself a doctor. And yesterday, all she wanted was to be seen. Denise's momma and sisters ignored her."

"Guess who I saw from my past?" Mona asked her eyes wide and with a smirk on her face. "It was eerie."

"Who?" Sylvia yelled. "You have so many exes." Both Sylvia and Rachel laughed.

"Laugh at my expense, but I'll tell you since you have no idea. It was my ex-husband, Timothy."

"What?" Rachel and Sylvia said in unison.

"Y'all are going to have to stop saying whattttttttttt. He was on the same flight we took to New Orleans. Said he was going down there for Michael's daddy's birthday celebration. The strange thing about it all is that he and Michael never talk. Michael had no idea he was going."

"Well, that was nice of him," Sylvia said.

"It was weird. At the airport, we talked and I told him I forgave him. When we got to New Orleans, he watched me the whole time we were there. Michael had to get him straight. The weird thing was he kept saying that he wanted me."

"Shut your mouth," Rachel said.

"Yes, even though I told him time and time again that I was happily married to his cousin, Michael."

"You told him," Sylvia said.

"But that didn't deter him. He kept watching me. Even sent his mother over to talk to me, I believe. He was saying some negative things about Michael. Celia, Michael's sister, said the family doesn't trust them. Timothy's mother is Michael's mother's sister."

"Damn, girl. You got all the gossip."

"I wished it was just that. Michael is being sued for sexual harassment."

Sylvia looked at Rachel and back to Mona. Rachel did the same.

"Who's suing him for sexual harassment?" Rachel asked as if she was afraid to hear the answer.

Mona wished she hadn't been so needy. "That bitch, Madeline."

"Say what!" Sylvia said. "We all have seen how brazen that woman is."

"Well, now he has the burden of proving it. Ladies, this could be Michael's career—all that he has gone to school and worked hard for. I can't believe this opportunist has come into our lives on a humbug and is threatening to destroy it."

Rachel began to speak with caution in her voice. "Do you believe Michael is innocent?"

"Of course he's innocent. My husband said that he's done nothing to that woman and I believe him—quite unlike your willingness to believe that Marvin wasn't having an affair with Peaches."

"I had something that made it hard not to believe, but I walked into that one," Rachel said. "It's funny you mentioned Peaches. I was telling Sylvia right before you got here that I had a vision of her."

"You're kidding."

"No. It's not like she can come back and haunt me again, but the night she kidnapped me came back with a vengeance. Don't ask me why."

"A lot of things are going through your head right now," Sylvia said. "With Denise's death still so with us, it causes us to take a look at ourselves and thank God for the blessings we have."

"You got that right, Sylvia," Mona said. "I didn't sleep all night, but I prayed that this situation with Michael will be all right. In fact, I'm going to church with you Sunday. You know Pastor Goodwin jumped on us about disrespecting God's house."

"Oh my God!" Sylvia shouted. "Pastor Goodwin saw what happened?"

"Girl, he rolled up on us and gave us some words and told us to leave. Of course, my wonderful husband apologized for us and shook the pastor's hand and told him that we'd like to come back to worship."

"Michael said that?" Sylvia turned to Rachel. "We might as well make it a family outing—church and a nice dinner somewhere."

"I'm game," Rachel said quietly. "I do need to go to church more often. Marvin used to go all the time before he and I got married. He'll be happy."

"Mrs. Thomas, lunch is ready."

"Thank you, Isabel. Okay, girls, let's do lunch and have a good time before our children come home."

"Sounds like a winner," Sylvia said.

"Thanks for the invitation," Mona interjected. "I really did need this."

"So did I," Rachel chimed in, rounding out the chorus.

52

The warmth of the day and the color of the fall leaves made a splendid backdrop for the turkey feast. For the first time since the Richmonds, Thomases, Broussards, Beasleys, and Colemans had been getting together for big holiday dinners, Claudette and Tyrone were the hosts for this perfect Thanksgiving. This year, Ashley would be joining them.

Claudette had called in some of her interior decorator friends to make the place look festive, and it did indeed. Brown and gold pillows and Thanksgiving motifs added spice to the living and dining rooms. A large cornucopia made of tightly woven straw with apples, bananas, pineapple, grapes and other fruit fashioned out of cloth and made to resemble the real thing pouring from its mouth, dressed up the buffet. However, the best part of the Thanksgiving preparations was that Claudette had put her foot in the almond and giblet dressing and the twenty-five-pound turkey she had roasted in her new industrial, state-of-the-art stove.

Tyrone finished slicing the hickory-smoked spiral ham that now sat in the chafing dish, and Reebe and Reagan placed neatly sliced cans of cranberry sauce in crystal dishes. The rest of the gang would complete the meal with macaroni and cheese, sweet potato soufflé, Waldorf salad, broccoli casserole and whatever else they chose to bring. Mona's specialty dessert was pecan pie and there would be several, and Claudette had her back with four tasty sweet potato pies.

Claudette, Reebe and Reagan were dressed like triplets in burnt-orange silk blouses with ruffles at the base of the sleeves and matching brown-tweed slacks, while Tyrone and Kwame, who had come home for Thanksgiving, were dressed in cinnamon-colored Ralph Lauren polo shirts and brown slacks. It was impossible to disguise that this was a family unit.

"Reebe, get the doorbell," Claudette called out, putting a pan of rolls into the oven so they'd be ready to cook when everyone arrived.

"It's Aunt Mona and her family with their hands full," Reebe called back. Reebe opened the door and let them in. She left the door cracked as she saw Sylvia, Kenny, and Kenny Jr. getting out of their car.

"Hey, Reebe," Mona said, going straight to the kitchen, followed by Michael and Michael Jr. "And look at Reagan. Y'all get out of here, matching from head to the floor."

"Hi, Aunt Mona, Uncle Michael, and Michael Jr.," Reebe and Reagan said together.

"It smells some kind of good in here," Michael Sr. said. "The others better hurry because I'm ready to start without them. Where's T?"

"Daddy and Kwame are upstairs in the men's room," Reebe said. "You all are going to watch football all day."

"Kwame is here? I haven't seen that boy in a long time. Point the way," Michael said.

"Hey, Mona, Michael, and Michael Jr.," Claudette said, flicking a long single braid out of her eyes. "Come on in. Put your stuff down at the end on the counter."

"Hey, Claudette," the Broussards shouted back.

"I'm going to find T," Michael said.

"Look, we're going to eat in a few minutes, so don't go up to the men's room and get comfortable. Here are the Richmonds."

"Happy Thanksgiving," Sylvia crowed, stopping to pass air kisses all around.

"Hey, Sylvia, Kenny, and Kenny Jr.," Claudette said. There was gaiety in the house. "I have a special table for the children to eat at so they can have their own special conversation."

"Kenny and Michael…come with me," Reagan said, grabbing her two best friends by both hands. "I'm going to show you where we're going to be sitting."

Sylvia put her hand over her mouth. "That is too cute. And why do you all have on the same outfit? Afraid you'd get lost in your own house?"

"Auntie Sylvia, that was wrong," Reebe said.

"Just messing with your momma. She acts like she's at Disney World or something."

"Keep that up and I'm going to send your behind packing to Disney World," Claudette said. "Leave me and my girls alone. You ought to see T and Kwame."

"Kwame is here?" Kenny Sr. asked. "Where are the men folk anyway?"

"In the men's room," Mona said butting into the conversation.

"Men's room?" Kenny asked dumbfounded.

"The football room…TV room, Uncle Kenny," Reebe said laughing.

"Show me the way." Everyone laughed.

"I told T not to keep you guys up there long because when it's time to eat, we're going to move without you, if you can't break away from the television," Claudette said. "What did you bring, Sylvia?"

"I brought a pot of collard greens, macaroni and cheese just the way my baby likes it."

"Well, I hope the rest of us like it, too," Mona cut in again, "because he's not the only one eating at this table."

"That's the bell again, Reebe."

"I got it, Momma. It's Aunt Rachel, Uncle Marvin, Uncle Harold, Serena and Danica."

"Ohh," Claudette said. "I haven't seen Harold since the funeral. I hope he's doing better."

"It looks like everybody's here," Rachel shouted, the men following behind with pots and pans. "Reebe and Reagan, you both look so cute in your matching outfits."

"Wait until you see Momma."

"Don't tell me Claudette is wearing the same thing."

Reebe shook her head yes.

"The Thomases are here," Marvin said, kissing the ladies and laying the pots and pans on the granite countertop in the kitchen.

"It's about time," Mona said. "We are starving. How are you doing, Harold?" Mona stopped to give him a hug before she kissed Danica and Serena.

"I'm making it, Mona. Work has helped to keep my mind occupied. Rachel and Sylvia keep Danica and me fed, but I'm sure their husbands are going to put a halt to that after awhile. Until then, I'm going to milk it up while I can."

"Good to see you," Claudette said. "The guys are upstairs in the men's room."

"Good," Marvin said. "Some good football is going down today. We're out."

"Well, don't get comfortable because we're going to eat as soon as these rolls get done. If Ashley isn't here by then, oh well."

"We need to wait for her, Claudette," Mona said. That remark elicited a frown from Claudette. Sylvia and Rachel passed looks between them.

"So why are you on Ashley's bandwagon all of a sudden?" Claudette asked.

"Didn't you invite her, Claudette? You're acting as if you may have some reservations about her being your best friend."

"That was uncalled for, Mona, and I don't know where you get off trying to judge somebody. There is nothing wrong between Ashley and me."

Sylvia cleared her throat when Reagan entered the kitchen, and all conversation ceased.

"Hi, Serena and Danica," Reagan said, with the boys standing behind her. "Do you want to see where we're going to be eating dinner?"

"Why not?" Danica said. "The discussion is getting pretty hot in here."

Rachel pulled back as well as the others.

"Out of the mouth of babes," Sylvia said. "Now don't you two feel shamed?"

"Saved by the bell," Mona said. "It must be Ashley; I'll get it." Mona winked at Claudette upon leaving the room.

"What's up with that, Claudette?" Rachel asked.

"It's nothing."

"Yes, it is," Rachel countered. "The air was thick with some bad vibes. You and Ashley on the outs?"

"No, it's that Mona put some idea into my head that Ashley might try to take Reagan from me. I denounced Mona's attempt to get me riled up, but here lately, I've entertained the thought on more than one occasion."

"Is that why you all are dressed alike today?" Sylvia asked. "Anyway, you know how Mona is. She loves to keep things going."

"Maybe I had ulterior motives, but Ashley is my...our sister-friend and I've got to empty those thoughts in the dumpster."

"Yes, you do," Sylvia said. "Ashley has supported this group even from her jail cell, and her friendship is worth more than a few of Mona's crazy ideas."

"But what if she wants Reagan back?"

"The idea really isn't farfetched. She is Reagan's biological mother and Reagan knows that," Rachel said. "But it was you, Claudette, who Ashley picked to raise her child. She wouldn't have agreed to the adoption if she wasn't sincere and at peace with her decision."

"I know, but all the same, I know how I would feel."

"Even if she does," Sylvia interjected, "you'll have to deal with it. I believe that you can come to some understanding about it. It's not the end of the world. My suggestion is that you, Ashley and Reagan go out sometimes...like to the movies or lunch. That may make Ashley feel as if she's a part of Reagan's life."

"Look who I found?" Mona said, entering the kitchen. "Ashley, Trina and Cecil. They are loaded down with goodies."

"Hi, everybody," Trina called out.

Ashley gave kisses all around as did Trina. "Where are the men?" Cecil asked.

"In the men's room," Claudette, Sylvia, Rachel, and Mona said in chorus.

"But they are about to come down because we're getting ready to get our eat on," Claudette said. "You all put your food down and we'll arrange it. You have five minutes to run to the men's room, Cecil, and then it's on."

"Gotcha, Claudette. I'm ready to get my grub on, too. You don't have to worry about me."

"Good."

Ashley turned to Claudette. "Girl, your house is so beautiful. I was so overcome the first time I was here and didn't get to see it real good."

Reagan and the other children walked into the kitchen. All eyes were on Ashley, who seemed paralyzed as she took in the beauty that was her daughter. She put her hand over her mouth, transfixed at how much Reagan had grown up—had erupted into a flower that had blossomed before her very eyes.

"Hello, Reagan. You are so beautiful."

"Thank you, Ashley."

"May I have a hug?"

Reagan looked from Ashley to Claudette, who nodded her head yes. In a deliberate and slow gait, Reagan walked toward Ashley's outstretched arms. Ashley latched on and hugged Reagan as if her life depended on it, but suddenly let go when she realized the world around her was deathly silent. Trying to recover, Ashley looked up as if she noticed the other children for the first time.

"And whose children are these?" Ashley asked.

"Raise your hand, Kenny Jr.," Sylvia instructed. "That one is mine and Kenny's." Sylvia smiled.

"He's so handsome."

And to not be outdone, Mona cut in. "Michael Jr., raise your hand. The one with the cute curls is mine and Michael's."

"Wow, you all have handsome children. And who do these cute little girls belong to?"

"The one in the white ruffled shirt and leather vest with the faux fur collar is Serena and she belongs to Marvin and me. And I'm not sure you remember Danica, but she's Harold and...and Denise's daughter," Rachel said.

"Yes, I remember Danica. You are so pretty. You look a lot like your dad."

"And my mother," Danica said without looking at anyone in particular.

"You sure do," Ashley said. "And I love your stylish boots and your top, or is it a dress?"

"It's a top, Miss Ashley. I'm wearing the new trendy tights underneath. My grandmother in New York said I was getting older and needed to wear some hip stuff."

Rachel, Sylvia, Claudette, Mona, and Trina's eyes twitched as they glanced from one to the other. Danica was fast becoming Denise incarnate.

"Well, you look beautiful."

"Thank you, Miss Ashley."

"Hi, Ashley," Reebe said, giving Ashley a gracious hug. "You are wearing that jumpsuit."

"It was the only thing I had in my closet that felt like a fall day."

"Reebe," Claudette cut in, "go seat the children. We'll be ready to eat in a minute."

Ashley turned to Claudette. "You and T have done a wonderful job. And thank you for being a mother to Reagan."

Everyone heard it. Everyone but Trina stood in a trance. Smiles evaporated the stone faced looks that appeared on their faces as they saw the tears well up in Claudette's eyes.

"You picked me, and I was going to do the best job I could raising your child. She's my heart."

"I know," Ashley said. "Okay, I'm ready to eat. I brought pumpkin pies since I knew there wasn't going to be any, if I waited on one of you guys to bake them."

Everybody broke up in laughter. "That was a good one, Ashley," Mona crooned. "And you hit the nail on the head."

"The rolls are ready," Claudette said, taking them out of the oven. "Dinner is served."

53

E veryone stood next to their spouse and headed for the dining room. They were paired together—like salt and pepper, cream and sugar—except for Ashley and Harold, who came alone, but by default, ended up sitting together.

The adults sat down to a table that glistened with Claudette's finest porcelain china—her latest expensive purchase. There was a gleam in her eyes as the ladies fawned over her beautiful table setting. Even T cracked a sly smile and sent Claudette a wink. It was a proud moment and she thanked God for the blessings he'd bestowed on her family.

The children—Reagan, Serena, Danica, Michael Jr. and Kenny Jr.—were in a world of their own at the table they shared with Kwami and Reebe, their overseers. They laughed and shared stories until they heard Claudette ring her little crystal bell and asked Marvin to say grace. They all stood and linked their hands together, including the children as Marvin took them to the throne of grace.

There was a collective sigh and the entire room exhaled after an exhaustive grace by Marvin. He thanked God for everything... the food that was on the table, the new house Claudette and T now lived in, Harold's return from the brink of a near nervous breakdown, that Michael win his battle of good vs. evil over the she-devil Madeline Brooks, Ashley coming to work for them, and his lovely family and those of his friends.

"And we thank God that Marvin has retired his mouth and pray that the food is still hot," Kenny said, still shaking his head. The room roared with laughter, although the children rolled their eyes while they bounced from one foot to the other.

"Everything is buffet style," Claudette began. "The children will go first. Mothers, if you need to assist your children, please do so now."

Mona looked at Claudette and laughed. "You are enjoying playing hostess with the mostess."

"If Michael Jr. needs assistance, and it looks like he does, you need to get up off your duff and help him. Don't want no mess on my carpet." Everyone laughed.

"Momma, I'll get it," Reebe offered. "You all enjoy."

"Thank you, Reebe," Sylvia said. "The teenager is completely gone."

"Yes, I'm all grown up now, and very soon I will be working in the world of television entertainment. I hope you all will come to my graduation."

"Of course, they're coming," Claudette said with a big smile on her face. "I'm so glad you all are here, if I didn't say it before, enjoy."

Clinging plates, chatter, and laughter filled the dining room. Everyone was having a good time. Every now and then Ashley would slap Harold's hand as they joked about something that happened on the job or what someone had said. Harold had even volunteered to spoon macaroni and cheese and more slices of turkey on Ashley's plate so that she wouldn't have to get up. And it didn't go unnoticed.

"So, Ashley," Rachel interrupted what seemed to be a pleasant conversation between Ashley and Harold, "Marvin says you seem to be enjoying your job."

"I am, Rachel. Everyone has been so helpful. Thanks to Marvin and Kenny, I've been given the latitude to implement some of my marketing ideas. And, thanks to Harold," Ashley said as she looked at him with fondness in her eyes, "we're making some remarkable strides that are going to take Thomas and Richmond to the top."

"Oh, is that so?"

Marvin turned his neck to look at his wife. "I don't know why you've got that condescending tone in your voice, Rachel." Everyone stopped eating and looked from Rachel to Marvin. "Ashley is doing a wonderful job. Don't you think so, Harold?"

"Yeah," Harold said, soaking up the amusement of the moment. "Ashley has some great ideas, and with the bosses' blessings, we're going to go places. I want to thank Ashley openly for pitching in while I was out." Harold lowered his head and brought it back up. "This is my first Thanksgiving without Denise. I miss her very much. Ashley has been right there to lift up my spirits."

"So how much lifting of the spirits have you been doing?" Sylvia cut in, feeding off of Rachel's vibes.

"I don't know what you mean, Sylvia."

"I mean, Denise hasn't been gone that long…"

"Hold it, Sylvia," Harold cut in. "Please don't misconstrue my words. Ashley has been nothing but a friend, just as you and Rachel have been. No more, no less. Let's not get this twisted."

Tears ran down Ashley's face. "Excuse me." Ashley got up and headed for the bathroom with Claudette right behind her. Ashley tried to close the door, but Claudette scooted in, locked the door behind her, and put her arm around Ashley's waist as she let it all go.

"I don't know why everyone hates me."

"Nobody hates you, Ashley. Sylvia and Rachel are protective of Harold, especially since they spent so much time at his house when Denise was ill. They became very close to Denise, and their aggression is due to the fact that it hasn't been that long since Denise passed away. I, too, noticed how you and Harold were being a little playful at the table and attentive to each other."

Ashley stood up straight and faced Claudette. "It means absolutely nothing. Truth is…everyone is here with someone. You, Sylvia, Rachel, Mona and Trina all have your husbands. Harold and I were the leftovers and were sort of given the last two seats at the table. All I'm doing is being cordial. I chose to come here for Thanksgiving instead of staying at my parents' stuffy house. Something is going on with my father. He's been in a weird kind of mood lately."

"I've got your back, Ash," Claudette said. Claudette hesitated and then proceeded. "Thanks for what you said about my being a mother to Reagan."

Ashley searched Claudette's face. "I meant what I said, although I find it hard to discuss Reagan with you, Claudette. I feel that you have this strong hold on her, and if I approach the subject or even try to embrace her, you put up this wall."

Claudette bunched her lips together. "Truth is, Ashley, you're right. I have no right to keep her from you because she's your biological child. You entrusted her to me. But I'm her momma now, and I can't let go of that."

"I can feel it. I'm not blind or numb to the fact."

"Do you want Reagan back?" Claudette asked with a pleading look in her eyes.

"You know the answer to that, Claudette, but you are her legal guardian. I want to spend time with her. I've been thinking about it a lot. I don't want to miss motherhood altogether." Ashley laughed. "I'd even thought about finding a sperm donor. While I have the ability to have a child and take care of one, I'd like to have that experience."

"You haven't been thinking of Harold as your donor?"

"Of course not!" Ashley shouted. "I don't believe this."

"Shhhhhhhhh," Claudette said. "I didn't mean to upset you. Look, why don't you, me and Reagan go to a movie and lunch one weekend?"

Ashley stared at Claudette. "Do you mean it?"

There was a heavy knock on the door. "What's going on in there?" they heard Mona ask. "Those heifers were wrong, Ashley. I told them they need to apologize to you. For God's sake, this is Thanksgiving Day…a day we're supposed to be thankful. Forget those skanks and come on out of there."

Claudette and Ashley laughed. After Mona knocked on the door a few more times, they finally emerged with tears in their eyes and laughter on their faces.

"What's so funny?" Mona asked with hands on hips that were pronounced and ready to do battle.

"You are," Claudette said. "Let's go back to the dining room before the others think there's a conspiracy."

"Serves them right," Mona said. "Serves them hussies right."

All was quiet when the three musketeers returned to the dining room. Ashley looked briefly in Rachel and Sylvia's direction but bowed her head when they stared in hers.

Ashley took her seat and placed enough space between her and Harold so they wouldn't touch. She barely looked in his direction.

"We're sorry, Ashley," Sylvia spoke up, being the bigger person of the two. "Rachel and I…"

Ashley held her hand up and stopped them. "It's okay. I'm past it now. I'd like to finish my dinner and have a piece of pumpkin pie."

Cecil cleared his throat. "A good football game is on now. MEN'S ROOM!"

"Let's go," Tyrone said, as he wiped his mouth with the linen napkin. "I'm ready to see Michael Vick stomp some booty on the field." The men laughed.

"You are a traitor, T," Michael said.

"I was all the way with Vick when he was a Falcon. I can't help it if he's now in the City of Brotherly Love. He's still my boy."

"That's a weak response, T," Marvin said. "Your behind don't live in Philly." The guys laughed.

"Why don't you men take that noise to *your* room," Claudette said.

"We're going," T said. "Men, get your helmets on and let's proceed to the ROOM!"

"To the ROOM!" Marvin, Kenny, Michael, and Cecil echoed T.

"You coming, Harold?" Marvin asked as he watched Harold with renewed interest.

"Yes, I'm coming, Marvin. I'd like to speak to Ashley before I join you."

There was nothing but utter silence as all eyes darted around the room. Ashley sat looking straight ahead, picking at her pumpkin pie to avoid the stares she knew were there.

"Ashley?" Harold prodded.

She finally looked up and around the table at the group who waited patiently for her to make a move. "Why are you all looking at me like that? Have I done something wrong?"

"No," Cecil said, waving and pointing his hand and finger for the men to retreat upstairs. As if on cue, all the men except Harold pushed their chairs back, got up, and headed for the men's room.

"Ladies," Claudette called, "I need your assistance clearing the table. I'm going to leave the food out on the buffet so that you can go back at your leisure."

Sylvia, Rachel, Trina, and Claudette got up from the table,

picked up the empty plates, and walked slowly away from the dining room. Rachel popped Mona on the shoulder.

"Ouch."

"Claudette meant you, too, Mona. Why are you still sitting down?"

"I have a front-row seat to the best and free Thanksgiving matinee in town."

Ashley closed her eyes then stood—she was a half-foot shorter than Harold. He escorted Ashley out to the front of the house and held her by the shoulders.

"Ashley, I'm sorry about what happened in there today. I'm not sure why you've been targeted."

"Yes, it was a right hostile environment. I feel disconnected from the ladies, although, I thought I was close. Maybe it's because I've been in prison or that I'm white. Sylvia and Rachel seem different somehow. I didn't know Trina."

"Don't let them get you down." Harold took Ashley's hands in his. "What I wanted to say was thank you for being supportive. It's been hard since Denise...since she passed away. Your wit and knowledge have kept me on balance, because many days, I felt that I was going to lose it and topple over somewhere."

Ashley eased her hands out of Harold's and folded them in front of her. "I'm glad that I could be there. The ladies may be right, however."

"What do you mean?"

Ashley couldn't look Harold in the face. "I...I may have felt something that was more than...well, you know. I'm sure it's because I've been alone for awhile and...and, I'm missing my baby. Reagan is growing up fast, but I haven't been there as a mother. Claudette has attached herself to Reagan, and since she is now her adopted parent, there's little I can do. And truth be told, I don't have the heart to do it. Claudette has been my friend when no one else was there for me."

"It's nothing wrong with being friends and co-workers. Denise is embedded in my soul, and I don't think I have room for anyone else, except Danica. She's the extension of Denise and me. I want to apologize if I did anything to make you uncomfortable, was out of line, or led you on in any way."

"You did no such thing; it was me who got caught up in the moment. I'm going to go inside, get my jacket and go home. Thanks for lifting my spirits." Ashley smiled. Harold patted her on the shoulder as he followed her into the house.

"What did you all talk about?" Mona asked in a hushed whisper as she ambushed Ashley and followed her into the dining room.

"Mona, leave Ashley alone," Claudette said, coming around the corner. "It's none of your business. Why don't you get us something to drink?" Mona gave Claudette the evil eye.

"If you must know, Mona, Harold apologized for your behavior."

"Ouch."

"He's in love with Denise, and surely you all should know that." Ashley picked up her jacket. "I'm going to leave because I thought my friends were here."

Claudette rushed around the corner, followed by Rachel, Sylvia and Trina. "You're not going anywhere, Ashley," Claudette said. "We are your friends and value your friendship."

"I, of all people, have you to thank…coming forward to help Marvin as you did," Rachel interjected. "If something is going on between Harold and you, it's your business. All I'm saying, it's too soon."

"Nothing is going on, Rachel. I work with Harold; that's all. Like I told Claudette, you all were paired with your husbands, which left me to talk with Harold. No big deal."

Rachel and Sylvia went to Ashley and gave her a big hug. "Look, we're about to get our drink on," Sylvia said. "Put your jacket down and hold out your hand so you can grab your glass."

Ashley placed her jacket on the back of the seat, then smiled. She turned to Sylvia and gave her another hug...then Rachel.

"All right, enough," Mona said, coming through the dining room with six large wine glasses filled to the brim. "Let's get our Thanksgiving party on. Party over here; party over there."

"This feels like a *Waiting to Exhale* moment," Trina said, ready to let the liquid push her mood up a notch. "To Ashley!"

"To Ashley," everyone said in unison.

Ashley swallowed the vintage liquid and thought about what had transpired tonight. She wasn't sure a seed had been planted or she had felt something all along, but Harold was a tasty morsel that she'd like to revisit. Rachel was right; it was too soon to push up on Harold. He was in a vulnerable state, and if he was to entertain her advances, it would be rebound sex—something to take away the sting of missing the woman he truly loved. And she'd still be lonely because Harold wouldn't truly be hers. She'd wait it out. In the meantime, she would enjoy the party and let nature take its course.

54

"Michael has some serious allegations levied against him," Cecil said, sitting up in the bed and patting the pillow next to his.

Trina tied up her hair and eased into bed next to Cecil with a book in her hand. "They were discussing Michael's situation? I didn't think he wanted everyone to know about it, but I did hear Marvin mention it in that sermon he called grace. Anyway, I thought you all were supposed to be watching football."

"We were, but some men gossip more than you women. Mona probably told the girls about Michael's lawsuit, and they can't keep anything from their spouses, especially Sylvia and Rachel. I love them, but they'd put the *Enquirer* to shame."

"They aren't like that at all, Cecil. Since I've come to know them, they are down-to-earth and sensible women. We have our sistergirl moments when we let our hair down and act a little crazy."

"You mean to tell me you act crazy with them?"

"Cecil, I'm in a court of law all day long, and when I'm not defending the State of Georgia, I'm doing research so that I can prosecute the scum of the earth who have the unmitigated gall to take another life, rob a bank, embezzle funds, and all the other evils of the world that I don't feel like recounting."

"How about we make a baby?"

Trina's mouth went to mute. She lay still on her pillow like raisins on a peanut butter and celery log—stiff without any movement.

"Did I say something wrong, Trina?"

"No. Uhm...I didn't see it coming."

"You know I want children."

"We aren't spring chickens, Cecil. Damn, we've been married since forever, and if I haven't had children in all this time, it must mean I can't conceive."

"Why don't we think about going to a fertility clinic?"

Trina got up out of bed, her book falling to the floor. "Damn, Cecil, we are in our early forties. What eggs I might have had are probably powder by now. I'm too old to have a child. Who's going to play ball with a five-year-old child when your arthritis has got you on a regimen of pills? Who's going to want to play dress up or have tea time with a five-year-old when, at the end of the day, all you want to do is get home, take your shoes off, and crawl in the bed?"

Cecil looked up at Trina. "What are you afraid of? What are you hiding? You act as if I told you to jump off the top of the CNN building. All I wanted was a little sexing."

Trina's nostrils began to flare. She stared at Cecil as if she couldn't believe what he'd just said. She knew he wanted a child more than anything else because he had harped on it for years. The truth of the matter was she couldn't have any because she had her tubes tied—something she'd never told Cecil and a secret she intended on taking to the grave. Yes, she'd lied about having a baby one day, and she'd figured Cecil wouldn't give it another thought as he seemed to be all into his career when they first got married. "A little sexing? You have a funny way of getting someone in the mood."

"Forget it, Trina. I'll fantasize about Beyoncé shaking her hair and those fine hips of hers. I can catch her on any TV station doing those commercials about luscious lips..."

"Whatever, Cecil. I don't care if you watch Beyoncé, Halle, Wendy, or Tia shaking their asses. Know this; I don't want to have a baby." Trina got back in the bed, turned the light out on the nightstand, turned her back to Cecil, and pulled the covers up over her shoulders.

It was Cecil's turn to be quiet. Maybe it was being around everyone's children that made him so desirous of a child. "I don't care about those women, Trina."

"Too late; you ain't getting none. Now I've got to get some rest. I'm working on mediating Michael's case so we can keep it out of the courts."

They both lay in the darkness with their eyes open, staring at the wall.

55

M onday blues were all over Ashley. Even after a four-day weekend that was anything but peaceful, Ashley couldn't shake the events that reshaped her mood, her thinking, and her resolve to settle the volcano that was active in her body. Seeing Reagan intensified the rumble in her stomach, and without saying it out loud, the hunger to have a child to raise as her own was paramount to her survival.

This morning, she and Harold had barely spoken two words to each other, instead opting to keep a safe distance from each other—at least for the time being.

Ashley buried herself in the proposal she was to present to Marvin and Kenny about the new marketing campaign. It was for a new line of revolutionary computers that would make the likes of the iPad accessible to all who weren't able to afford the other. She had even sketched out a plan to make it affordable for rural school districts.

Ashley jumped as Harold's voice boomed in her ear. "Are you going to avoid me all day?"

Slowly, Ashley put her pen down and turned around in her chair until she faced him. Harold was handsome but he was also a grieving husband. Remembering the stares from the ladies on Thanksgiving Day made her push her lustful thoughts to the back of her mind. "No, but I'm making sure I don't cross any lines that I might regret."

"We have a job to do and must work together in order for that to happen. Yes, you're an attractive woman but…I'm not interested, Ashley."

"Ouch."

"Didn't mean to be so forthright but figured I'd nip the frost in the air, so we can be business as usual."

Ashley turned her head so that Harold wouldn't see the deep wound he caused. She fought back tears. There was no way she'd let him know his words had pierced her heart, especially when her night dreams told her something else.

"Business as usual," Ashley finally said. She picked up the proposal she was working on and handed it to Harold without looking at him. "If you have time this morning, please review my draft proposal and let me know if you have any suggestions or changes."

"Ashley…"

"Yes?" she said, turning around to look at him.

"Are you all right?"

"No, I'm not. I regret that I shared my feelings with you the other night." A tear escaped and streamed down her face.

"No harm done. I do like you…"

"As a friend."

"Yes, as a friend."

"Would it be different if I hadn't just gotten out of jail?"

Harold scanned Ashley's face. He dropped his eyes, then looked up at her again. "Ashley, you're an intelligent woman. Your getting out of prison has nothing to do with anything. Marvin had enough faith and trust to hire you." Harold paused and brought his hands together to form a ball, then dropped them to his side. "I loved my wife dearly, and I'm not looking to replace the empty hole in my soul that Denise left. And there's Danica; I don't want to complicate her life. I will be honest and tell you, however, that when you mentioned your feelings, the thought of you killing your black husband did come to mind."

Ashley was embarrassed. "I asked and you told me."

"Okay, let's move on," Harold said, moving back to his work-space.

Ashley was silent for the rest of the day.

Trina sat in Michael's office, waiting for him to return from surgery. She got up and walked to his desk, picking up and looking at the few photos Michael had of his family. Putting them down, she paced the small area, browsing the awards and commendations that were hung on the wall as well as his credentials that certified he was licensed to practice medicine.

The minor squeak as the door was pushed open caused Trina to look up. Michael and another doctor came into the room.

"Hello, Attorney Trina Coleman," Michael said, shaking Trina's hand and motioning for her to sit in the chair opposite his desk. "This is Dr. Kyle Bennett, my associate and good friend."

"Hello," Kyle said. Trina nodded her head and shook his hand.

"Trina, Kyle is the person who told me about Madeline filing the suit. If it's all right with you, I'd like for him to stay."

Trina pushed back in her chair, her feet crossed at the ankles. "Michael, I may be asking you some very personal questions, and it's probably in your best interest as we seek to vindicate you that this interview is between you and me."

"I don't have any secrets…" Trina held up her hand.

Kyle nodded his head and jumped up. "No problem. I'm here when you need me." Kyle left the room.

Trina looked thoughtfully at Michael. "Although Dr. Bennett

is a good friend, we don't need anyone to compromise our case by being privy to what we're saying in this room. I'd rather that you had come to my office, but I understand how busy you are, so I'm here. Michael, some of the questions I ask are going to require you to give me specific answers, the nature of which might be very graphic. You tiptoed around the delicate stuff before, but now I need full disclosure so that I can properly represent you, if and when Dr. Brooks decides to take this to court. I understand that you have been reprimanded by the hospital but without repercussions."

"That's right. Chief Calloway called me in and shared the information he had and asked me to explain myself. I assume he'll share it with EEOC."

"Why don't you start from the beginning…I mean, when you were in medical school?"

"What do you mean?"

"You keep asking me that, but I'm sure you know what I mean—your real relationship with Madeline Brooks."

Michael looked at Trina as if trying to decide if she knew all about Madeline and him. Trina looked at him without blinking. She understood why women were drawn and attracted to this man. From his bald head to his well-toned abs that were covered by a white medical jacket today, he was delicious. She was in love with Cecil, though, and she removed her eyes from the distraction.

Michael forged ahead, leaving the real graphic memories of his time with Madeline in his "For My Eyes Only" memory box. As he spoke, Trina wrote feverishly, only looking up when Michael seemed to stall, separating tidbits of information to share from the ones he kept on lockdown.

Michael spoke about his love for Mona and their son, who was his everything. He moved through one phase of his life until he reached the last three months in which Michael's world had been turned upside down. He seemed exhausted. Then with one swift motion, he jumped up from his seat and turned the tide on Trina as if he'd been contemplating the question for a while.

"So Trina, do you and Cecil want children?"

Trina put her pen down on the pad she was writing on. She wasn't ready for the question that was thrown at her like a lightning rod. It had appeared so suddenly that it caught her totally off-guard. She collected her thoughts while she squirmed in her seat. Then she sat up and looked into Michael's eyes, which awaited her answer.

"We were all about our careers...Cecil and me. At the beginning of our marriage, I worked for a law firm where competition was stiff, and besides being the only African-American woman, I was only one of two women attorneys in the firm. I had to work extra hard to get where I am today. Cecil worked just as hard and there wasn't any time for a baby in our lives. Do I regret it? Maybe. We tried later but haven't been able to conceive. I guess my eggs were tired of waiting on a donor."

"Uhmm." Drumming the top of his desk with his fingers, Michael paused before he spoke. "My family means everything to me, Trina. This whole ordeal has been devastating and if Madeline goes forward with this trumped-up sexual harassment suit, it's going to tear my family apart. I've worked too hard to have my reputation tainted by an onslaught of malicious untruths because I won't give in to Madeline."

Without warning, Trina held up her hand as she pulled her vibrating BlackBerry from her purse as if it was the next scene in a perfectly orchestrated television production. She read the script in the caller-ID box and proceeded to take the call. "Excuse me, Michael, I need to take this."

Michael sat back, thankful for the small break from Trina's

interrogation. He hated that his life…his past life had to be such an open book, one that he had closed the lid on many years ago with no thought to ever reopen it.

"What?" Trina asked the caller. "My God, you've got to be kidding." She looked up over her phone at Michael.

Michael sat up straight, wondering what this new revelation was that Trina seemed to be excited over. He watched her facial expressions and her purposely chosen words for clues. No hint.

"I'm almost finished here. I'll be back in the office within an hour." She hung up the phone.

Michael looked at Trina with inquisitive eyes. "Everything all right?"

Trina sat with a faraway look in her eyes. And, as if coming down to earth, she looked at Michael. "You wouldn't believe what I heard."

"Try me."

"My colleague said that Robert Jordan, Ashley's father, has been implicated in the death of Peaches."

It was Michael's turn to say, "What did you say?"

"I don't believe it. He was Peaches' attorney of record. Why would he want to have her killed?"

"You know she worked at his law firm."

"Yeah, I remember Cecil giving us that news. I don't know what to make of it."

"I wonder if Ashley knows anything. She and her father were a bit estranged."

"Look, Michael, I hate to interrupt our session. I'm glad that you were forthcoming with the information."

There was a worried look on his face. "Will this information become public knowledge?"

Trina smiled. "As long as this case doesn't go to trial, it will be our secret. I have a relationship with your wife and the others, but

I take my oath seriously. Everything we discussed is confidential unless exposed during a trial. In order to mount up a good defense, we need to get something on Madeline—some-thing that will support your claim that she came on to you."

"I was thinking the same thing. I might have an answer." Michael stood up and shook Trina's hand, and she was gone.

Michael sat a moment and evaluated the last hour. He tried to reassure himself that full disclosure was for the good of the order… that in the long run, it was going to save his behind. He skipped around Trina's questions as best and as long as he could, but that's why she was the most sought-out attorney in Atlanta. She knew how to break you down, because in the end, you weren't going to make a fool out of her. And she was very proud of her record of sixty wins to two losses.

Turning around in his chair, Michael picked up the office phone and dialed. There was an answer on the first ring. "Chief, I need your help."

"Broussard, you need to straighten this mess out. We really don't need a big sexual harassment suit hanging over the hospital."

"Chief, I'm well aware. This is my thought."

Chief Calloway listened with interest to what Michael was proposing. Michael imagined Chief shaking his head in concurrence.

"Sounds like a good plan, Broussard. You have been authorized to move ahead. I don't want to hear anything except that this mess has been squashed."

"Thanks, Chief."

"Don't thank me yet. I want results."

"Gotcha."

"Carry on, and I hope this doesn't conflict with your duty as a doctor. Our first obligation is to our patients. Hear me, Broussard?"

"Loud and clear, Chief." The line was dead.

56

Trina sat up straight in the tall, black Italian leather chair in her office. She swiveled from side to side with pencil in hand, Trina's mind wandering as she rolled around in her head the question Michael posed to her.

"Don't Cry" by Roland Gresham was playing in the CD player. It was soothing but it didn't stop her from rehashing the moment long ago when she was raped by her male uncle. What she didn't tell her mother was that she became pregnant when the vile act was committed. Trina's mother didn't believe her when she said Uncle Woody, her mother's brother, had attacked her and put his nasty thing where it didn't belong, so there was a strain in their relationship. Even the scratches Trina inflicted on Uncle Woody's arms didn't convince her mother. So she went to a butcher all by herself and let the woman, who was known for cleaning unwanted babies from the womb like she was cleaning a pot of chitlins, clean her out, too. Trina cried for days.

It was years before Trina would let a man touch her. Cecil was the first, but he paid the price to earn the key that unlocked the path to her secret garden. Trina twisted in her chair and propped her face on her hands. The pain of eradicating the fetus, her unborn child, many years ago still haunted her. Trina had snuffed out a life that was half her creation, and the trauma of it sterilized Trina's brain to the point she wouldn't allow another fetus into her womb.

Tears slipped from her eyes. Her selfish demons had kept her from giving Cecil the child he always wanted, although it never totally exonerated her from wondering what kind of mother she would've been.

A knock at the door startled Trina. She picked up a tissue and wiped her eyes.

"Come in," Trina said.

A tall gentleman in a navy Brooks Brothers suit with a ruddy complexion, his black hair tossed about his head as if he had come through a blizzard, walked through the door. His cobalt blue eyes caught Trina's as he set his briefcase on the end of her desk.

"Counselor…"

"Counselor," Trina responded. Trina respected Attorney Robin Early because he was a no-nonsense kind of guy, and when on a case, his dedication meter went off the charts. Robin Early served as Trina's second chair and he was dependable, but more than that, he was a darn good attorney. Early could sniff out a lead and nine out of ten times, he'd be on the money. Everyone needed a Robin Early on their team. He was the reason Trina had won the cases she had. "What is it, Robin?"

"We have been asked to be the prosecuting team for Robert Jordan."

"It hasn't been an hour since I heard that he's been arrested in the Peaches case. My God, I'm sure it hasn't gone before the magistrate's office yet."

"Trina, somebody wants Jordan real bad. I don't know who he's double-crossed, but somebody wants him to fry in hell."

"Gosh, I've taken on a special case for a friend of mine. I didn't know I would be undertaking a high-profile case as this...being that Jordan is a well-known commodity in the ATL."

"Who is this Peaches person? I heard she was a common hooker."

"No, Robin, she wasn't. In fact, she was on Jordan's payroll... worked in his law office."

"So what was she doing in jail?"

"That is another matter that had to do with a friend of mine. Peaches' case was getting ready to come up, and I doubt if she would've gotten fifteen years."

"Well, there's something funky about this case. I can't wait to delve in."

"I can't either. Thanks for passing that urgent news on to me, Robin. Now, if you'd shut the door behind you, I'd appreciate it."

"Ashley, I've gone over your proposal, and I must say it looks pretty good," Harold said, scanning through it one last time before getting up from his seat to deposit it at Ashley's desk. "There are a few minor technical rewrites and some jargon changes that are industry standard."

"Thank you," Ashley said without looking up.

Harold stood at her desk, excited about the prospect of the proposal moving forward. "It's time to pass it on to Kenny so he can tweak it before Marvin takes a look at it. Kenny is the real technical whiz kid in this industry. If he sees a little rust on something, and he does have supertech capabilities, he'll iron it out right away."

Ashley tapped her hand on her desk. Harold dropped the proposal without another word, but when he returned to his seat, he slapped his hand on his desk. "Okay, enough, Ashley. I like you; we can be good together."

Ashley looked up and pretended to hear, although something Harold said must've sparked her interest. Her lips were pinched, but Harold's next few words brought her out of the catatonic state she was in.

"Why don't I take you to lunch in a few minutes and we can have a nice conversation about something other than work?"

"I'd like that," she finally said.

Harold turned back to the stack of papers on his desk. How he wished it was his wife that he was going to share lunch with. He'd have to remember not to talk about Denise too much because it seemed that Ashley needed this lunch as much as he did. He hoped that Ashley didn't read any more into their luncheon date.

"Harold, thanks for your feedback on my proposal. It means a lot that you thought it was worth submitting."

"Well, it is, Ashley. I wouldn't have stated the facts as I see them if I thought it wasn't ready for further review. The design team will be happy to know that their hard work is going to pay off; it certainly will be good for the company. Are you ready?"

"Yes."

Ashley shuffled some papers into a neat stack and picked up her purse in preparation for lunch. Just as she walked toward Harold's desk, the door to their office flew open. Marvin looked flustered as he walked through the door, looking from Harold to Ashley.

"What's up?" Harold asked his eyebrows arched high on his head. Before Marvin could answer, Ashley's cell phone rang.

"It's my mother," Ashley said, raising a finger. "Let me get this."

Ashley hit the TALK button and her mother's voice was hysterical, her words coming at Ashley a mile a minute. "Slow down, Mother. Now what did you say?" Ashley's eyes wandered back and forth as her mother continued to spit out the news that had her in despair.

"Your father has been arrested for murder."

"What are you talking about, Mother? Murder? Why would Daddy kill anybody?"

"I don't know, Ashley. You've got to come home right away."

Ashley clicked the phone shut without giving her mother an answer. Then she looked up and saw Marvin and Harold staring at her. "My mother said that Daddy was arrested…for murder? It doesn't make any sense."

"It doesn't," Marvin said, walking over to where Ashley stood and hugged her. "This is why I came to see you."

"What do you…how do you know, Marvin?" Ashley asked peeling herself away from him.

"Your dad is being accused of killing Peaches."

"Peaches? Who is Peaches?"

"Peaches is a woman he was defending, who also happened to be one of his employees. She was in jail for extorting money from me, kidnapping Rachel, and threatening to kill her."

"Peaches, yes, I remember Peaches."

"How do you know Peaches?" Marvin asked with a puzzled look on his face.

"She used to come to the house for the Christmas parties my parents would give every year for the staff. I believe…my mother believes Daddy was having an affair with her."

Marvin and Harold's eyes popped from their heads. "Are you sure, Ashley?" Harold asked. "I've met this Peaches woman, and she's not your father's type at all."

"Because she's African American?"

"Well," Harold began, "that's one reason. But she's a little hard-core…from the streets, if you know what I mean."

"It's probably why he liked her."

"She isn't as cultured as the women I think your father would take a fancy to." Ashley gave Harold a nasty look. "Please excuse me for my insensitiveness. I meant to say, she's not as cultured as your mother."

"Let me jump in," Marvin said. "You know your father is prejudiced. He hated your husband."

"That's why Mother didn't like William. She claims I'm like my daddy...crossing the forbidden line. She accused us of forgetting that African-Americans, or black people, as she called them, were once slaves that her forefathers worked on their plantations, and here we were cavorting with them like her father used to do her mother. Mother has some black brothers and sisters that she'd like to stay hidden from sight."

Marvin and Harold looked at each other and smirked. "Have your mother's black brothers and sisters tried to contact her?" Harold asked.

"Oh, yeah, they've tried, but my mother, a true white woman of the Old South, refuses to acknowledge any of them. Daddy, on the other hand, pretends to be prejudiced. They have issues."

"Well, I believe we all have some degree of prejudice in us," Marvin said.

Ashley jerked her head back as if she couldn't fathom what Marvin said. "Anyway, Daddy had a longstanding affair with this Peaches woman until mother threatened him with exposure and divorce, if he didn't stop running to Peaches' bed. I didn't like her; she used my daddy."

"Peaches won't be bothering anyone anymore. She was beaten to death while she was on duty in the kitchen at the jail. Trina called and told me she was appointed to be the prosecuting attorney in this case."

"Do you think Daddy killed Peaches?" Ashley asked no one in particular.

"You are innocent until proven guilty," Harold said. "Keep hope alive."

"Why would he kill Peaches?" Ashley asked.

"Maybe she was talking too much and threatened to expose your father. That's my theory," Marvin said. "I'm sure there's got to be more to it."

"Thanks for the lunch invitation, Harold, but I've got to go and see about my mother."

"Another time," Harold said, feeling Marvin's eyes on him. "Call if you need me. In the meantime, I'll send this proposal on to Kenny."

"Thanks, Harold." Ashley left the two men staring after her.

57

M ichael looked at his watch. It was four-thirty. He rubbed his head and shuffled a few more papers around until his desk looked tidy. He was about to turn the motion-sensor camera off when a light tap on the door made him stop and jerk his head toward the door. Without waiting for a response, the door flew open, and there stood Madeline with a wicked grin on her face.

Jumping up from his seat, Michael picked up his briefcase and proceeded to move past Madeline. She took her hand and gently pushed him in the chest until he fell back on his desk, his briefcase falling to the floor. With her legs, she intertwined hers with his and put his in a vise grip, grabbed his chin and kissed him on the mouth. Michael tried to push her away, but she was fast and furious and on top of him, and the way he fell on the desk put him at a disadvantage.

"Don't try and resist. You know how I make you feel when I touch you." Madeline waved her hand in the air. "You can make all of this go away, Michael." Madeline snapped her fingers. "I don't want to pursue this lawsuit, but it's your call. I've been very patient, but I can't wait forever."

"What do you want from me, Madeline?"

"Do I have to spell it out every time you ask me the same dumb question?"

"I don't understand any of this. You suddenly materialize after not seeing you for over ten or more years, and now you want to destroy my life."

"You destroyed mine, Michael." Madeline squeezed her legs tight against his, pulling up her skirt so that her panties lay on his pant legs. Michael tried to push her away, but she pushed him down, knocking his elbows flat on the desk. Madeline proceeded to unbutton the cotton shirt she wore under her white medical coat until her pink lacey push-up bra exposed her ample helping of breasts.

"Don't do this, Madeline. You could lose your license to practice."

"No…you'll lose yours after I tell the authorities you attacked me again. This time I'll put bruises on my body before I report it to the police."

"Let's talk about us," Michael begged.

Madeline pulled down the straps of her bra and let her breasts fall like a tidal wave with perky tips at the end. Michael closed his eyes, but not before he got an eyeful and remembered how he used to take her warm breasts in his hands, squeeze them and then take the erect nipples in his mouth and love up on them until it sent Madeline into a freaky frenzy.

Michael opened his eyes and stared at Madeline as she held her breasts, offering them up as a peace offering to her king. "I know you want them…you want me."

"No! Put your clothes on and get out of my office."

Madeline moved forward and let her erect nipples touch Michael's lips while the moisture between her legs begged her to ignite the flame. Michael moved back as far as he could, now on his elbows again. "You are a lunatic, Madeline, and I'll never give in to you. I love my wife; she's the only woman I want."

Slap, slap. Madeline pushed Michael full force on his desk and slapped him again. This time, Michael reached up and grabbed her wrists and squeezed them tight. "Go on and fight me, you piece of… but sure as my name is Madeline, you're going to pay. Oh, and I have another surprise for you. Now take your grubby hands off of me. My body is reserved for a real man who knows how to treat a real woman."

Michael released her but hadn't anticipated what was coming next. Madeline took her fist and hit him in the groin.

"Ouuuuuch," Michael yelled, as he controlled his voice so that no one would hear him outside of his office. He bunched up into a fetal position, protecting his manhood from further harm. "Bitch, you're going to pay."

"Bring it," Madeline said with a scowl as she buttoned the last button on her blouse. "Who are they going to believe? You or me? Get ready because your ass is getting ready to go before the firing squad."

"I wouldn't be so quick to judge. Every dog has his day and every cat his night, and at the end of the day, you're going to see that I'm right. Bring it."

Madeline huffed, sighed, and walked out of the door. Michael smiled. He had to fight the urge to wave to the camera.

58

I n record speed, Ashley drove to the outskirts of Atlanta to the plush neighborhood where her parents resided. She couldn't recall ever in life when her mother needed her…had called with such urgency that Ashley felt it was her obligatory duty to be there for her, and lickity split she went. Time and events in their lives that at the time were non-negotiable had worn their relationship down, but at the end of the day, it was Mother, whom Ashley did love, who needed her support.

Pulling onto the final stretch of road that led up to the Jordan's five-acre estate and then into the circular driveway, Ashley was astonished to see her mother standing on the brick walkway in front of the house as if she had anticipated Ashley's arrival at that very moment. She pulled her shades away from her eyes to get a better glimpse. Mrs. Clarice Jordan didn't wait for Ashley to get out of her new red, sporty Lexus that Robert Jordan had bought his daughter as a truce for "not being there" when Ashley was married to William. Clad in an old, worn-out, pink terrycloth robe and in bare feet, Clarice ran to meet Ashley.

Clarice pulled Ashley to her and hugged with all of her might. She pulled back and looked at Ashley with bloodshot eyes. "Ashley, we've got to do something. The police came and whisked your father away like he was a common criminal. After all the years he's given to the State of Georgia, I can't believe they had the audacity to say he killed someone. Your father wouldn't kill a soul. He's tried cases and got convictions, but never on God's green earth would he kill anyone."

"Mother, let's go inside and talk. Did the police say who Daddy was supposed to have killed?"

"If they did, I didn't hear them. I was too busy looking at the hurt in your daddy's eyes as they took him away. Ashley, he didn't say a word; those vultures handcuffed him like a common criminal."

Inside the house, Clarice dropped into the first chair she came to. She rarely even ventured into the formal living room. Today was different. None of the material stuff mattered. Her heart bled for Robert, her man, her husband, her provider for the forty-something years they'd been together.

"What are we going to do, Ashley?"

"First, we need to find out where Daddy is being held and get some answers. I'm sure Daddy has already dispatched his attorneys. Knowing him, he's already on top of things."

Tears ran down Clarice's face. "I don't understand it, Ashley. Who in their right mind would accuse your father of such malicious behavior?"

"Do you have any idea who Daddy is supposed to have killed, Mother?"

Clarice's eyes were wide. "No, do you?"

Ashley inhaled and exhaled, not quite sure she wanted to divulge the information she'd been fed by Marvin. Marvin could've heard incorrectly or Trina might not have known what she was talking about. Against her better judgment, she blurted it out anyway.

"Daddy is supposed to have killed one of his employees by the name of Peaches."

Clarice's chin jutted out, her ears seemed to vibrate as the word

"Peaches" sailed down her eardrums. Then Clarice took a good look at Ashley, a look that was disturbing and accusing at the same time.

"What did you say?"

"He's supposed to have killed a woman named Peaches."

"Where in the bloody hell did you hear such a thing? Why in the world would he want to kill the likes of that black baboon?"

Ashley looked at her mother. In that instant, she felt sorry for her. It was no secret that she didn't like Peaches either, but to call her out of her name was so unnecessary. Ashley chose her words carefully. "Maybe she was going to expose Daddy...for what, I don't know."

"Ashley, that's enough. I don't want to hear any blasphemy in this house. First of all, I understand that hussy was in jail. If your daddy has done such a thing as kill her, it would be good riddance."

"Mother, out of your very own mouth, and I can quote the scripture, too. You've said it is written in the Bible that *thou shall not kill.*"

Clarice glared at Ashley. "It was a mistake calling you. I thought after all that your father has done for you—fighting for our good name when you killed that...that no-good husband of yours, surely, you'd be first in line to help him."

"Maybe that's the problem, Mother. Daddy was fighting for *his* good name instead of giving me a good defense during my trial. Did a lousy job of it. Why else would I now be free?"

Ashley didn't know what hit her. *Slap, slap, slap.* Ashley threw her hands up to try and protect her face as Clarice lashed out. Clarice's complexion was a deep red when she finished assaulting Ashley. "Get your things, you ungrateful child, and get out of my house, now. I don't want to see you anymore. I don't know who you are, Ashley. Marrying that black man turned your brain inside out. Just like your whoring daddy. Yes, he likes black meat, too. In fact, he likes all kinds, according to his Facebook page he doesn't know I've been screening. Good riddance to both of you and may you rot in hell!" Clarice screamed.

"Please, Mother, don't be so dramatic. That display added ten years to your life. I'll find out what I can about Daddy. Consider it a favor; I'm curious, too."

"Get out of my house, now."

Clarice balled up her fits and shook them in the air. She screamed and shouted words that were incomprehensible to Ashley. Ashley wanted to go over and give her mother a hug, knowing that she had put up with a lot of stuff during her marriage to her father. There were things she knew about her father that she'd never tell a soul, and the rest, everyone knew it anyway. You'd have had to been blind or in a deep sleep to miss all the rumblings about the misdeeds of Atlanta's elite. It was dirty, sexy and all about the money.

Ashley climbed the stairs to her temporary quarters. It was time to leave Mother and Daddy's house. She'd been there longer than she had intended, and this was a perfect time to get a jumpstart on her new life.

Ashley drove away from her parents' estate with a few clothes and possessions and traveled toward the heart of Atlanta in search of her father. She called Marvin to get Trina's number, so she could minimize her search. After a battery of calls, she learned that her father was being held at the DeKalb County Jail.

Upon arrival, Ashley fought her way through the red tape, trying to get to her father, only to look up and see him walk in her direction, surrounded by several of his attorney friends and two others she didn't know. Robert Jordan stopped and held up his hand for quiet when he saw his daughter standing before him.

"Ashley, what are you doing here?" Jordan asked, perplexed.

"Looking for you, Daddy. Mother is worried about you, and I came to see what I could do to help. I see that I'm too late."

"I've been released on bail. They know it was a false arrest, and those pigs are going to pay for this."

Ashley looked at her father thoughtfully. "Daddy, did you kill that woman?"

Robert Jordan took Ashley by the arm and led her to the side of the lobby, out of earshot of the others. "Look at me," he said. "What kind of person do you think I am? For God's sake, Ashley, I'm an attorney and a law-abiding citizen. Whatever gave these idiots the idea that I was behind this hideous thing is beyond me. But my main man is going to prove I had nothing to do with the murder. Yes, Ms. Franklin was once in my employ, but for the love of God, I'd never take another life."

"Okay, I believe you…at least I want to."

"Ashley, go back to your friends and your job they neatly provided for you. To be my daughter, you amaze me. I thought we came from the same stock, but you keep proving me wrong. I thought you were a fool to marry William and then turn around and kill him, but giving that other black guy fifty-thousand dollars to fight that merger, when you knew I was the opposing counsel, was the last straw. You have never been on my side. I give; you take. You're riding around now in a brand-new automobile I purchased for you, but you *want* to believe that I didn't kill Peaches? Spare me your sympathy. I've got to go."

Before she got cold feet, Ashley reached up and placed her arms around her father's neck and gave him a peck on the cheek. Robert Jordan flinched, then looked around to see if anyone was watching. He turned back to Ashley and stared at her. "What did you do that for?"

"I love you, Daddy, and I believe you. You've always been so distant, and all I've ever wanted was your love. I'll call Mother and let her know that you're all right."

Ashley slid her arms from around her father's neck. "Thank you, Ashley. That's the kindest thing you've said to me in a long time. Believe it or not, I love you, too. I also love your mother, even though I haven't been the best husband to her. I'd say, let's go to lunch, but my partners are anxious to plot my strategy so that we can get in and out on these trumped-up charges. In the meantime, I hope they catch the real killer."

Ashley smiled at her father. "You're going to win, Daddy. Now go and plot your strategy so you can get back to life."

"I am. You know, Ashley, this is my teachable moment. I had no way of knowing how you felt when you were picked up for killing William. Now I know. I guess you can say we're kindred spirits."

"But you didn't kill Peaches. I killed William."

"Yes, that's the truth of the matter," Jordan rushed to say. He kissed Ashley on the cheek and took both hands and held her shoulders before sliding them down her arms. "I've got to go; the guys are waiting patiently over there. Thanks for coming to check on your old man. It meant a lot."

"You're welcome, Daddy." Ashley watched as her father rejoined his friends and moved out of sight.

59

"It's war," Michael declared, throwing his fist in the air. "That bitch wants to play hardball; well, she asked for it. I'm going to rip her lying ass to shreds, and by the time I'm finished with her, she'll beg to be on the first thing flying to New York."

Michael pulled out a chair and sat down at the kitchen table, drumming his fingers on the tabletop. He released a sigh while thoughts of Madeline trying to seduce him rolled around in his head. Mona would die if she got a glimpse of the tape that captured Madeline in action. However, Michael convinced himself that the spectacle Madeline made yesterday was for the good of the order and was going to save his behind.

He sat up when he heard Mona's slippers slide over the tiled floor, making a swishing noise that irritated him.

"Not going to the hospital today, baby?" Mona asked as she leaned down to meet Michael's lips. "It's awfully late."

A huge sigh rolled from Michael's mouth. "No…I've taken the day off. Kyle has my patients. I've got a lot on my mind."

"Work or the bulldog?"

"Bulldog as in Madeline?"

"One in the same.

"Sit down, Mona."

"Oh, this sounds serious. Let me put a piece of bread in the toaster and get a cup of coffee. I'll probably need it to take the edge off of my nerves. Want anything?"

"No," Michael said, as he watched Mona plop a piece of bread into the toaster and fill a cup of coffee, leaving just enough room for two teaspoons of sugar and a third cup of flavored coffee creamer. He loved watching Mona. Everything she did was so sensual, even when she wasn't trying. Her backside had a certain rhythm when she walked that woke up his soul and made his body tingle inside. None of the Victoria's Secret angels were a match for his baby's walk.

"Okay, baby, I'm back. So what has that egoistical bitch done to my husband now?" Mona took a sip of her coffee.

"She tried to seduce me in my office."

Mona put the cup down on the table and folded her arms. "And what did you do?"

"She barged into my office, pushed me back on the desk, and then clamped her legs around mine."

Mona stared at Michael. "Let me understand this because I'm a little confused as to how you allowed that to happen. You mean to tell me that petite Ms. Madeline manhandled a big old Mandingo such as yourself?"

"Now you didn't have to go and call me a Mandingo, Mona."

"You got the picture, right?"

"Mona, it happened so fast I hardly had time to react. The door opened and bam, she was there. That woman came in with a plan, but what she didn't know was I had a secret weapon."

"Secret weapon? What in the hell are you talking about, Michael?"

"A video camera that we installed in my office in the event the good Dr. Brooks decided to give me another chance to fall under her spell."

Mona relaxed and picked up her cup and took a sip of coffee. "Damn genius, if I say so myself, Dr. Broussard."

"My momma didn't raise no fool. I've got to protect myself, and if Dr. Brooks wants to sue me, then let her do it."

"My man," Mona crowed. "Let the bitch sue you; we've got something for her."

For the first time since yesterday, Michael allowed himself the luxury of a smile. Mona made him feel confident and he was glad that yesterday's incident was out in the open...that he didn't have any explaining to do should Trina have to roll the tape.

He wondered if Trina had viewed the tape, and if she had, what she thought. The camera lens didn't lie, and it would be obvious to a judge, or anyone else reviewing the video, that Madeline was an evil temptress. Whatever evidence she held was a fabricated lie.

"I'll have a cup of coffee with you."

"Sit down," Mona said to Michael, jumping to her feet and sloshing her way over to the stove. "I'm enjoying this, Dr. Broussard— my man and I having a morning cup of coffee together."

"I hope to have many more of them with you, my love."

"It must've been divine intervention that Sylvia picked up Michael Jr. yesterday to spend the night with Kenny Jr."

"Michael Jr. didn't go to school today?"

"No, it was a teacher work day, and the kids got a day off. Sylvia and Rachel are taking the kids to the aquarium."

"Talk about timing. Maybe I can get a little lovin' this morning, Mrs. Broussard."

"I think I can accommodate." Mona brought Michael's coffee to the table. "Sip on that and think about what the rest of our morning is going to be like."

They stopped when the doorbell rang. "Now who in the world could that be?" Mona said, shuffling to the front door. She looked out the window and saw a middle-aged, balding white man standing on the porch with some type of package in his hand. She opened the door slowly. "Yes, may I help you?"

"I have a package for a Dr. Michael Broussard. Is this his residence?"

"Yes, he…"

The bald-headed man thrust the package into Mona's hand, turned around, walked away and jumped into a car that sat idling in the driveway without further explanation. Mona finally took a good look at the package. It was from an attorney's office. She slammed the door and headed back to the kitchen.

"Who was that at the door?" Michael inquired.

"Here." She handed Michael the package. "Some scrawny little white man asked if you lived here, pushed the package in my hand, and disappeared."

Michael sighed. Nerves replaced the confidence he'd felt moments ago. He tore open the envelope and as he feared, it was a civil summons. Madeline had slapped him with the lawsuit for sexual harassment. Merry Christmas.

60

The forecast was for snow and it hit Atlanta like it had been a bad child deserving of the punishment. Blinding snow fell from the heavens and within an hour, Atlanta was buried under two feet of it with the weatherman predicting an additional four feet by nightfall.

Ashley watched the snow fall from the bedroom window of her new condo. It was relentless as it fell and covered the ground like a large white blanket. It appeared that Atlanta might have a white Christmas this year.

Ashley moved away from the window and started for her cell phone. She was sure no one was going into the office today, but she needed to call Harold to alert him that she wouldn't be there and that they needed to get an extension on the grant they'd worked on to fund the marketing proposal. Inadvertently, she'd forgotten to sign it and there was no way she could possibly make the trip into the office, even if she took the Metro.

Before she was able to push the TALK button, the phone rang. The caller ID said it was the office, and immediately she clicked on.

"Ashley, this is Harold."

"Hey, Harold. I was getting ready to call you. I won't be able to make it in today because of the weather, but I need you to see if we can get an extension on the grant proposal."

"That's why I'm calling. I realized the grant had to be in Washington today. I called, but we weren't able to get the extension. Since I've got a four-wheel-drive vehicle, I'm willing to brave it and come to your house to obtain your signature, if that's all right with you."

Ashley hesitated but not for long. "Of course."

"This is such an important document, and I want to insure that it gets to Washington today. As soon as I get your signature, I'm going to copy it into a PDF file and send it electronically. There's no way I'm going to let all of our hard work go down the drain."

"I agree, Harold. Let me give you my address. Got pen and paper?"

"Yeah. Shoot."

Ashley rattled off her address as if she was in a race...in a hurry.

"Slow down," Harold said. "I'm not sure I wrote it correctly."

This time Ashley took her time, enunciating each number and letter in her address with instructions to Harold to repeat it back to her. "Be careful out there," she admonished. "I'll see you when you get here. And...and thanks, Harold, for doing this."

"I'm doing this for the company. As I said, we've worked hard on this project and it would be a disservice to Thomas and Richmond Tecktronics if they lost this opportunity. See you in a little bit."

"Okay." Ashley hit the END button and held the phone to her chest. "He's coming to my house," she muttered under her breath.

Ashley put the phone down and flew down the stairs, stopping to pick up shoes and the purse she'd left in the middle of the living room floor. She fluffed the pillows on the couch, then ran to the kitchen and rearranged the flowers that sat in a vase in the middle of the breakfast table. Still on auto-pilot, she crossed the room and pulled out new Air Wick oil fresheners from her odds-and-ends drawer and put them into the wall sockets.

As an afterthought, Ashley took a bottle of wine from her small wine rack that sat on the black-and-brown marbleized kitchen counter and put it in the refrigerator. She ran her hands down the side of her body and then looked down.

"I've got to change into something decent—not too sporty... loungy but cute." Ashley ran up the stairs to her bedroom and put on a cute brown-and-turquoise running suit, splashed on a dash of Donna Karan Cashmere Mist, combed her hair and headed back downstairs. She allowed a small smile to grace her face and waited for Harold to come.

More than an hour had passed since Ashley spoke to Harold. Her eyes were glued to the television screen as the newscasters droned on and on about Atlanta being under siege and held hostage by a snow blizzard that wasn't the norm for this Southern city. In fact, all over the country, record snow and Arctic chill made flying from one city to another almost impossible, and normal city transportation was on lockdown.

Ashley rubbed her hands together as if a sudden chill steam-rolled over her. She sat up, then back down at the sound of any movement coming from outside. Moments later, she hopped up from her seat and paced the living room floor, looking through the blinds every few minutes to see if Harold had arrived. After fifteen minutes of pacing and checking, she sat back down and continued to listen to weather updates until she nodded off to sleep.

There was a knock at the door. Ashley shot up on her feet, took a deep breath, and crossed the room to the front door. She peeked through the peephole and added a smile when she saw Harold standing on the opposite side. He was dressed in a heavy winter coat with a thick brown-and-black tweed scarf that blanketed his neck and a brown gentlemen's hat covered his head. It took less than three seconds to open the door and invite her visitor in.

"It's treacherous out there," Harold said, pointing to the snow that had yet to let up. He took off his top coat after entering the condo and breathed a sigh of relief. "I wasn't sure I was going to make it."

"I was hoping you were all right after some time passed. As much as I didn't want to miss the opportunity to get the grant sent out, I almost called to tell you not to risk life and limb to get here," Ashley lied. "I'm glad you made it in one piece."

"You and me both. Danica is in New York with her grandmother, and I'm glad we got her out of here before the snow hit us."

"Will you go to New York for Christmas?"

"No, I'm going to stay here. I don't think I'm up to being around Denise's family during the holidays—the memories would be too vivid. I miss her so much, Ashley. If only I could have played God and made her well."

"Have a seat," Ashley said, directing him to the green, plush chair, while opting to sit on the love seat. "I can't say I understand how you feel but I can imagine how painful your loss is."

Harold sat in the chair, and placed a package on his knee. "You can't begin to know, Ashley. Denise was my everything—my sunshine and rain…the love of my life. She meant the world to me, and some days I don't know how I've been able to cope. God designed that woman for me—perfect in every way."

Ashley crossed and uncrossed her legs. She wasn't up to hearing him rant and rave about Denise, although she wasn't completely insensitive to his feelings. "It's all right to grieve," Ashley said with a semi-smile on her face. "God won't put more on you than you can bear. And, he's given you good friends to be there for you, if and when you need them."

Harold looked up at Ashley and smiled. "Thank you. I needed to hear that. Well, I better get you to sign this document so I can trudge back across town and get this out."

"Let's go to the dining room table."

Harold got up from his seat and followed Ashley into the dining room. "Your place is nice," he said, as his eyes roamed around the room. "So, you're an artsy person. I like art deco myself."

Smiling Ashley wrapped her arms around her chest and admired Harold for admiring her taste. "I love the stuff. I'm a little eclectic and I love bold colors. That's why the dining room is burnt orange. If I had to give a summarization of myself, I'd say that I'm like the earth; I come from the soil. I love anything earth-toned. I love fall colors."

Harold shook his head in agreement, pulled the document out of the envelope, and pushed it in front of Ashley. "There it is, my dear. Please sign at the appropriate places."

Ashley signed the document, got up, stood over Harold and handed the document back to him. He glanced her way for only a second, dropped his head and shook it in approval.

"Okay, that should do it. Come hell or high water, I'm going to get this back to the office and send it off."

Harold tried to stand, but Ashley was still hovering over him. He made an attempt to push back his chair, and Ashley took a few steps backwards. When Harold rose, Ashley was in his face. "Nice perfume," he said. "The fragrance is familiar."

"Cashmere Mist by Donna Karan." Ashley reached out and brushed Harold's chest with her hand. "Harold, I would apologize for my forwardness, but…but I can't help myself. I'm needy; you're needy."

"I can't be there for you, Ashley. My heart belongs to Denise."

"I know that, Harold, but hear me out." She tried to place her hands on his chest, but he moved back. Ashley sighed. "I'm sorry, Harold. I...I'm messed up. My family...they are so dysfunctional. I have no one to talk to..."

"What about the ladies—Claudette, Rachel, Sylvia and Mona? Can't you talk to them?"

"It's been different since I've been out of prison. Claudette has my daughter, Reagan, and now that I'm out, I want her back. It has caused some tension between me and Claudette, and I don't want to hurt her by taking legal action to get my daughter. She's taken care of Reagan the first six years of her life, and Claudette is her legal guardian. And there's my mother and father, who've yet to forgive me for marrying a black man. Mona is entrenched with what's going on with Michael. Everyone has something going on that has them preoccupied, and I don't fit into anyone's schedule."

"You're being too harsh on yourself, Ashley." Harold went to her, held her, and looked down at her. "If you need someone to talk to, I'm here. It might help me."

"I appreciate it, Harold. You've been through a lot, but so have I. Life behind bars was a living hell. It taught me a valuable lesson. I have to find another way to deal with the complexities of life without inflicting physical or mental harm on someone. At the end of the day, all we have are those who love us." Ashley looked up into Harold's concerned eyes. "I only want to be loved."

Harold bit his lip. He brushed the top of Ashley's shoulders with his hand. "You are loved."

Before Ashley could catch her breath, Harold's lips met hers. She met him halfway, and seconds turned into minutes. Passion replaced indifference and the only sounds were moans and groans as they locked each other in a passionate embrace, their lips tasting and exploring, allowing lust to take over.

Harold's arms rolled down Ashley's back until he felt the mound of her buttocks that he squeezed and held. Ashley continued to moan and take deep breaths as she felt the tenderness in Harold's hands as he engaged her body. She unbuttoned his shirt and planted kisses down the middle of his chest, stopping just short of his navel.

"I've got to get back to the office," Harold said, grabbing the front of his shirt.

"Shhh," Ashley said as she took her forefinger and placed it on his lips. "Let's go upstairs and continue where we left off."

"This is wrong. I...I...shouldn't be doing this. Lust is trying to dictate our bodies." Harold was quiet for a second, then spoke again. "Denise is probably turning over in her grave."

"She'd want you to move on, Harold. Let's take one day at a time." Without shame, Ashley reached down and guided her hand over the front of his pants, only to find that Harold was already game. His rock-solid manhood protruded through his pants and pushed upward when Ashley touched him again.

Harold tried to look away but couldn't and immediately pulled her close and kissed her as if it would be the last time. Resisting Ashley was a chore as his body closed the gap between them, thrusting his manhood up against her. Harold leaned on the dining room wall, pulling Ashley's arms up with his. "I've got to go."

"We have time."

"The snow...the..."

"We've got time. The deadline for the document to be in Washington is five o'clock Eastern Standard Time. It's eleven-thirty."

"You win."

"Thank you, Harold. If loving you is wrong, I don't want to be right."

"It's only sex, Ashley. But I'm with you."

"Then you're doing me a favor, and I won't forget."

"Don't say it like that."

"It is what it is."

"Let's stop talking."

"I'm ready, Harold."

61

O vercast skies were not going to dampen Michael Broussard's
spirit. Sitting on the edge of the bed, he lifted his left leg up
and put on one sheer, brown sock, then repeated the ritual
with the other foot. Finally, Michael stood up and went to the
walk-in closet. He lifted the hanger with the mustard-colored
shirt that Mona had picked out for him to wear that hung next to
a brown, lightweight-wool Brooks Brothers suit.

Michael almost collided with Mona, her face covered with cold
cream, as she exited the master bath in a hurry. "I don't want to
be late for my mediation hearing, Mona," Michael said, allowing
a faint smile to grace his face. "But I don't want you to scare
anybody either."

"Baby, get yourself together and then you can worry about what
I'm doing. I'll be ready when I'm supposed to be. Your assignment
is to stay focused on what you've got in front of you today.

"You're going to come out of this sexual harassment suit
victorious. I truly believe in a higher power and the fact that
you've got a good case. You're awfully lucky that Trina was able
to negotiate a mediation hearing instead of taking this to a full-
blown court of law."

"Thanks for believing in me, baby. Trina knows what she's doing.
Plus, she has Peaches' murder to prosecute. All of that said, I
want this nightmare to be over before the new year rolls around.

And I'm praying, Mona, that with the ammunition we have, Madeline Brooks will no longer be on staff at Emory, and her two-faced, lying, sexual harassment ass will be sent packing to Timbuktu or hell. I don't care."

"What if she's sent to prison?"

"That's highly unlikely with mediation. She will pay a stiff penalty if found guilty and will probably be fired from Emory. Baby, fix my tie."

Mona stopped dressing herself and fixed Michael's tie. She ran her hands over his chest, removing any foreign objects that amounted to one small piece of brown thread. "You look handsome, baby."

Michael held Mona in his arms. "Whatever happens today, baby, know that I love you. I'm sure some things will be said that might be tough to hear. Madeline Brooks is my past. You are the love of my life."

Mona smiled and kissed Michael on the lips. "I love you, too, baby. I'll always be by your side—'til death we do part."

"I know you will. " Michael sighed. "Twenty more minutes before we roll out of here. Thank God, the snow melted in time."

"See, God's already got your back. Now I'm going to finish getting ready."

Michael watched as Mona put on her chocolate pantsuit and pulled on her brown leather Cole Haan boots she'd been dying to wear for some time. He was blessed to have her in his life and grateful that his lustful, sinful ways were long before she'd come into his life.

Trina waited inside the lobby of the courthouse for Michael and Mona to arrive. She was hopeful that today's mediation would bring an end to Michael's suffering, as he called it. It made her think about the life she'd snuffed out so long ago and the reason she'd made the choice she did. Her only regret was that she hadn't told Cecil the full story...the truth of it all, and maybe if she had, there might have been children in her household and the feeling of selfishness and deceit someone else's history.

She banished the thought as Marvin, Rachel, and Harold walked toward her. Puzzled, she put on her best smile as they closed in on her space.

"What are you all doing here?" Trina asked.

"I'm surprised you'd ask that question, Trina," Rachel said. "You know we support our friends...our family. At the end of the day, who else do we have to lean on?"

Trina had hoped that this wouldn't be a three-ring circus. This was supposed to be a mediation hearing with the involved parties only. She'd have to break it to them gently when the time arose. "You're right." Trina turned again, and there was Kenny and Sylvia. "Looks like the gang is all here."

"Hey, everybody," Sylvia and Kenny said simultaneously.

"Hey," Rachel, Marvin, Harold and Trina said in response.

"Are Michael and Mona here yet?" Kenny asked like a fight promoter ready to get into the ring and get the show on the road.

"Not yet," Trina said, looking at her watch. "They should be here any moment. We need to proceed to where the proceeding will take place."

"Here they come," Marvin said, pointing in the direction that he spotted them. "Looking good, too."

"They are a cute couple," Sylvia added.

"Lord, here comes Ashley, Claudette and T," Rachel said. "That's what I call support, Trina."

"You've got that right. Cecil couldn't be here because he's hearing a case this morning."

Harold eyed Ashley but stayed close to Marvin and Rachel.

"Hey, everybody," Mona said, her arms intertwined with Michael's. "We're going to win this thing today. Right, Trina?"

"You've got the right attitude, Mona, and we're going to give it our best."

"Do you have some reservations, Trina?" Kenny asked.

"No, I'm very optimistic about the outcome, but I don't want to pull the cart before the horse. Anything can happen, but I've prayed about it, and I feel good that we will be victorious."

"All right," Mona said, breathing in and finally letting it exhale. "I won't lie. I'm a little nervous. Didn't sleep well, but I believe in Michael. And I've got my family to give me the support and strength I need."

"I want to thank all of you for coming out and supporting me," Michael said. "It means the world. I love you guys, no matter what happens."

"Let's go before everyone starts shedding tears," Trina said, briefcase in hand.

"I'm ready," Michael said.

They looked like tourists taking a tour of a museum of fine art. They studied every picture and inscription found on the hallowed walls of the courthouse. Instead of the elevator, Trina took a flight of stairs down to the basement to a room that was designated as the mediation room. Then it was time to pass on the bad news that no one but Michael, Mona, and the opposition would be allowed into the room. This disgusted the ladies and gents, but not wanting to jeopardize Michael's proceedings, they went back upstairs and sat in the back of the courtroom and listened to cases one by one as they came up on the docket.

"Take a deep breath," Trina admonished Michael as they sat around the table waiting for Madeline and her attorney to show up. "Hopefully, it will all be over in a couple of hours, bar any last-minute surprises."

"I have none," Michael said with resignation.

At the top of the hour of ten o'clock, the door to the room where Trina and party sat flew open. In walked Madeline's attorney, Brandeis Walker, Esquire, a slender, six-foot stallion in his stocking feet with a smooth chocolate complexion, who was suited down in a gray pinstripe Versace suit with a touch of mohair. He was followed by Madeline, who wore a conservative Ralph Lauren navy pantsuit, white blouse with a collar that made the suit sizzle as it overlapped the jacket, and navy pumps. Right behind Madeline, Timothy Sosa waltzed in, dressed in his customary off-white linen suit that he wore regardless of the season. Mona's eyes leapt from her face as well as did Michael's, and before Trina could quiet him down, Michael jumped up from his seat.

"What are you doing here, Timothy?" Michael asked, his voice full of concern.

"Who is that?" Trina whispered to Mona.

"My ex and Michael's cousin," she mouthed.

Trina sat up and looked straight at Madeline's attorney. "Brandeis?" Trina said, hoping he would shed light on the matter. The one thing that puzzled Trina was how Madeline Brooks ended up with Brandeis Walker as her attorney, after showing off at the Prime Meridian with another man she'd called her attorney. Brandeis wasn't by any stretch of the imagination a Johnnie Cochran. He operated from a storefront joint in the hood and his practice amounted to helping the junkies and the streetwalkers get their get-out-of jail free card. It took him four tries to pass the

Georgia State Bar, and when he did, he hung a brass sign in front of his rundown building that said BRANDEIS WALKER, ESQ., ATTORNEY AT LAW as if it was worth a million dollars. Brandeis looked good, but whoever gave Madeline his name as a reference, wasn't her friend.

Before Brandeis could speak, Madeline cleared her throat and spoke up with the craziest grin on her face. "He's my witness. He's here to vouch for my character." She twisted her face toward Trina to make sure she understood the answer.

"I object to this, Brandeis."

"Sure you do, Trina."

Trina ignored his snide remark and continued. "In all of our discovery, it was never mentioned that a third person was party to this lawsuit. It is my contention that Mr...."

"Dr. Sosa," Timothy said politely.

"Dr. Sosa has no bearing on this case and should remove himself immediately."

"Not so fast, Trina," Brandeis said. "It may not seem that way on the surface, but Dr. Sosa's testimony is relevant to this case."

Mona and Michael looked between them before staring Timothy down. He sat there with a smug look on his face as if to say, *I've got you now.*

"Shall we start?" Brandeis asked.

Trina was none too happy with this turn of events, but she was surprised that Brandeis had sharpened his skills and stepped up his game. If she could take Brandeis Walker and his party of two and drop them from atop the Coca-Cola building, she would. But she wasn't going to lose this case. They wanted to play hard ball, then hard ball it would be. They had their ace in the hole, too. And if they had to use it, they would. It appeared it might come to that.

62

Trina watched her opponent with a keen eye. Cool as a cucumber, Brandeis Walker picked up a document from the table with his long, slender, and manicured fingers. He was in no hurry, almost calculating in his delivery. He appeared to assess the defendant, taking small glances between Michael and Mona before pronouncing his first word that got the ball to rolling.

"My client, Dr. Madeline Brooks, contends that she was sexually harassed by Dr. Michael Broussard during several brief encounters in Dr. Broussard's office at Emory Hospital. In Dr. Brooks' statement to the EEOC at Emory, she states that while visiting Dr. Broussard at his office, in the course of obtaining medical information regarding cases she was working on, Dr. Broussard was unprofessional—touching her, kissing her, and trying to rub his genitalia against her body."

If looks could kill, it was safe to say that Mona had a knife stuck in Madeline's carotid artery. Her nose flared each time Attorney Walker stated each indiscretion Michael was supposed to have committed. Michael sat stoic in his seat, looking at no one as Walker spat out the lies Madeline had construed to make her case. He flexed his fingers, finally making a fist that he wanted to use but instead forced himself to be still.

"Dr. Brooks tried to resist Dr. Broussard's advances, but she said he was arrogant and wouldn't take no for an answer," Walker continued. "On one occasion, he roughed her up, even to the point of ripping off her blouse. Dr. Brooks is seeking several things: one, an apology; two, a financial settlement—the amount to be disclosed; and three, some form of disciplinary action, i.e., a copy of these proceedings to be entered into Dr. Broussard's personnel file at Emory Hospital.

"To elaborate further, Dr. Broussard and Dr. Brooks were once lovers. It is my understanding that they had a very torrid sexual relationship while in medical school. Dr. Broussard once promised to marry Madeline Brooks."

Mona jerked her head around and searched Michael's face, hoping that what the attorney had said was a lie—a lie because Michael hadn't shared one bit of this information with her. But the stillness of his body only confirmed the words that fell from the mouth of Brandeis Walker.

"Dr. Timothy Sosa is present to attest to the facts in this matter as he was also a medical student at the time, although in Atlanta, but visited his cousin, Michael Broussard, on several occasions in Baltimore where Johns Hopkins is located," Brandeis continued. "Dr. Sosa is also the ex-husband of Dr. Broussard's wife, Mona."

Mona stared Timothy down, then abruptly averted her eyes to a space on the wall behind him.

"Dr. Brooks states that upon seeing Broussard again, she was immediately aroused. And so was he, but she was also aware that he was now married, and that there would be no rekindling of their former relationship. When an offer to transfer to Emory became available, Dr. Brooks took it without reservation. However, Madeline Brooks wasn't prepared for Michael's forwardness and his actions that have led us to this moment."

Bravo, Trina thought. All of this grandstanding wasn't going to help him win the case, if this was all he had to offer.

Brandeis took a moment to regroup. He laid the documents down and held his face up with his hand. "I also submit these photos of my client in which she received several lacerations to the face and arms. Dr. Broussard's actions are deplorable and he should have been charged with sexual assault instead of sexual harassment." With that, Brandeis bowed his head and extended his arm to indicate it was Trina's turn.

Trina sat up tall, the prominent features in her face shining through. "We've listened to your depiction of this case, and we are prepared to refute any and all of it. First, the facts, as you've presented them, are weak in nature because there isn't one shred of evidence to collaborate Dr. Brooks' story. The pictures, ahhh, those were a clever attempt to convict my client of this wrongdoing, but there is nothing on the photos to support or suggest that this is even a photo of Madeline Brooks. Further, there is no evidence of a doctor's statement to collaborate Dr. Brooks' assertion that she was treated for wounds inflicted by a man that meant her no good."

Madeline wanted to protest, but Brandeis held his hand out. Trina glanced at Madeline, who was moving uncomfortably in her seat, throwing a scowling glance at Brandeis, who looked straight ahead.

"For your edification, I have a letter written by Dr. Broussard documenting several incidents of sexual harassment committed by a female colleague…," Trina passed a copy to Brandeis, "that was held in a file should it be necessary to use. It was typed on the computer of Dr. Broussard's secretary as instructed by Dr. Broussard on the date noted at the top of the page. The date the letter was typed is recorded on the computer's memory.

"Dr. Broussard intentionally left off Madeline Brooks' name because he has a heart. He knew that this type of indictment could possibly cost Dr. Brooks her job. However, in the event he needed something to substantiate the things he might have to attest to later, he prepared the letter.

"It is not Dr. Broussard's intention to crucify Dr. Brooks or make her pay restitution for the slanderous, untruthful things she's said about him but to exonerate his name and return to life as it was before this unfortunate incident. Neither do we intend to honor or submit to Dr. Brooks' request for an apology, financial restitution, nor any other item mentioned. Yes, we've come for swift and quick judgment, but I think we can safely say that nothing has been proved here today, and that this matter should be dismissed."

"Not so fast, Miss Attorney," Madeline said, pointing a long finger toward Trina.

"This is not the way to handle this, Madeline," Brandeis warned.

"Don't tell me how to handle anything after the piss-poor way you've handled this case. What kind of lawyer are you anyway?" Madeline asked Brandeis. "If you haven't already cashed my check, I'm going to demand it back."

"Ummm," Trina said.

"Don't you *ummm* me," Madeline said. "You didn't bring anything to the table either. Don't rush me off; I have another bombshell."

Trina looked from Michael to Mona. "Brandeis, I suggest you contain your client. If she thinks she has a chance of proving that my client was the person she described, I'm not so inclined to believe her."

"Trina, Dr. Brooks is evidently very broken up by…"

"Shut up," Madeline said. "You don't know what I am. For all I know, you got your license to practice from one of the local bars on the strip."

"You watch your mouth."

"You shut up. In fact, your services are no longer needed," Madeline screamed. "And as for you, Dr. Michael Broussard, sitting over there all smug next to that witch you call a wife…"

"Witch, who are you calling a witch?" Mona said, her finger pointed at Madeline. "I'll come over there right now and knock you into next week," Mona continued as she got up from her seat, while Michael tried to pull her back down.

"Enough," Trina and Brandeis said simultaneously.

"Well, I still have something to say," Madeline plowed on. "Michael Broussard and I have a teenage daughter for which he has never participated in her upkeep or well-being. He used and abused me those many years ago and left me pregnant to fend for myself." Madeline finally smiled at her grand slam performance.

Fury was in Michael's eyes, and unable to contain himself any longer, he rose to his feet. "I don't know what in the hell you are talking about, Madeline. In all the seventeen years that I've known you, and the twelve years that I haven't seen hide nor hair of you, this is the first time I've heard that you were ever pregnant. In fact, I don't believe a word of it, and you know good and damn well I've never abused you. If nothing else, you were upset because I ended our relationship."

"Very well put, Michael, but the truth is you have a daughter," Madeline countered. "Her name is Michelle."

"I'll take a DNA test first," Michael said very matter-of-factly.

Trina put both hands up to quiet the banter. "This mediation hearing is about the sexual harassment charge that Dr. Brooks filed against my client. This new piece of information has no bearing on this hearing. Again, I say that this matter should be dismissed."

"I'll get a fit attorney and take this to a real court of law," Madeline said, seething.

"I'll bet that you won't," Trina said. "Since it has come to this, we are prepared to back up what Michael Broussard has contended all along...and that is you, Dr. Madeline Brooks, are the sexual harasser."

"That letter is meaningless," Madeline lashed out. "It doesn't prove anything."

"I can't wait to see what you've got," Brandeis said, not offering any more support to Madeline.

"Well, maybe this will," Trina said, as she clicked on her laptop and brought up the video of Madeline trying to seduce Michael.

The room was quiet, except for the video that flashed before everyone's eyes. Mona knew the video existed, but she wasn't ready for the content. Horrified, she got up from her seat and walked out. The others sat transfixed until the video came to an end. Trina looked around the room. "I rest my case."

"Let's file our judgment, and I'm out of here," Brandeis said, not waiting for either Madeline or Timothy to get up. In fact, Timothy was a waste of time.

"You know you obtained that video illegally," Madeline said to Michael. "For all anyone knows, you were using it for your own self-gratification."

"Please, Madeline, don't flatter yourself. I want a DNA test done before I commit to anything. A daughter? Where is she now?"

"None of your damn business."

"You made it my business. It's a shame for you to claim that I fathered a child with you but haven't seen an ounce of evidence that this person really exists. You've been in the city for more than four months, and either you're an unfit mother or have this child tucked away in some boarding school. And what mother doesn't talk about their child?

"And Timothy, you're no longer a family member of mine. I understand why Mona hates your guts. You have no soul or heart."

"Those are tough words from someone who had something to hide. Where's Mona now?" Timothy asked.

"Whatever."

"Shall we go, Michael? The group is probably waiting to hear the verdict."

Michael and Trina moved toward the door and looked back at Madeline and Timothy, where Madeline still sat seething.

"Let's go, Trina." They left the room. "Great job, Trina. I owe you big. I knew you were good and had every confidence in you that this would end in my favor."

"When you have no case to begin with, it doesn't take a rocket scientist to unravel the flaws. I believed in you from the jump, and it was only a matter of time, skill, and that video, before I'd get to the bottom of this and blow the lid off of Dr. Madeline Brooks' lies."

"You were outstanding, counselor. Now I need to find Mona and make things right with her. I tried to prepare her the best I could for what might come, and prayed we didn't have to play that video. I hope that turn of events didn't overshadow the victory."

"I hope not. Well, it's over now. Let's find your wife."

63

A flood of emotions twirled in Mona's head as she exited the mediation room. The graphic video of Madeline seducing Michael was more than she was able to stomach. Yes, Michael advised her of the 'evidence that was going to put the nail in Madeline's coffin,' but he hadn't told her how blatant and in-your-face it was going to be. In fact, it appeared that Michael might have rather enjoyed the slithery seduction. When Madeline flashed her nipples in front of him, it almost seemed that he wanted to take a bite.

Mona hit the wall with her fist, wanting to believe but not knowing what to believe. Michael never mentioned to her that he was banging that witch back in medical school, and then, to hear it out in the open that they conceived a daughter—she didn't care that he had no knowledge of it.

Her head hurt and she wanted to go home. This wasn't the victory she'd expected. In fact, Mona wasn't sure if she and Michael were going to get over the hurdle today's revelation had caused. Their marriage was fractured.

Mona took the steps to the main floor and stood at the top. If she was a smoking woman, she'd light a cigarette, but she hated the smell of cigarette smoke. She shook her head, still unable to unwind the video footage of Madeline and Michael. Mona saw the exit sign and proceeded to follow it.

"Hey, Mona, where are you going?" Sylvia called, walking fast to catch up.

"Damn," Mona said to herself out loud. "Can't even be alone when you want to be."

"Whew," Sylvia said. "Is it all over? Is Michael in the clear?"

Mona turned around, put her hand on her hip, and looked at Sylvia. "Ask Michael when he shows his face. I need a drink."

"Okay," Sylvia said. "Something didn't go right, but you're not going to walk out of here without your sisters. The others are waiting in the courtroom. It has been an interesting day, listening to case after case of bounced checks, food stamp fraud, and you name it."

"Michael has a daughter."

"Michael has a what?"

"You heard me. He and that witch used to be lovers back in the day. Can you believe that crap, Sylvia?"

Sylvia rubbed Mona's back. "It was before your time. Your husband loves you."

Mona covered her face with her hands and began to sob. "What am I going to do?"

"Right now, you're going to dry your face. Michael and Trina are coming toward us and you can't bow out on him now."

"Why not?" Mona said.

"Excuse me, Sylvia," Michael said. "I need to talk to Mona in private."

Sylvia moved out of the way, looked back at her friend, and went back into the courtroom to rejoin the others. Trina followed behind her.

Michael took Mona's face and looked into hers. "It's over, baby. I'm sorry you had to suffer through this, but I had to prove that Madeline was sexually harassing me. I had hoped that the video wouldn't be necessary, but when it was clear that we had to go all the way, there was no other recourse.

"I love you, Mona. I didn't tell you about Madeline, but she was my past. I've had no communication with her since I graduated from medical school until the day I saw her at Harold and Denise's wedding. If for any reason, I should have a daughter that I'm totally unaware of, I will do the honorable thing. I love you and only you, Mona." Mona fell into Michael's arms and they held each other.

Still in each other's embrace, they looked up to see their well-wishers coming toward them. Each person took turns and hugged both Mona and Michael, happy with the news Trina had shared with them.

"Ladies, I hope you don't mind, but the brothers need a man timeout," Kenny said. "Our brother, Michael, needs to let loose. Let's go to Earl's Tavern and let off some steam."

"Letting Michael get loose is what got him into trouble in the first place," Mona said.

Michael smiled at Mona. "I'll be on my best behavior, baby."

"Okay, let's pay Earl a visit," Marvin said. "Congratulations, Michael."

"Well, the girls need a timeout, too," Sylvia said. She hooked her arm in the crook of Mona's elbow. "Let's take it to my house. Our sister, Mona, needs to be loved on." Mona smiled.

"Sounds like a plan," Trina said, followed by the others. "I'll call Cecil and tell him to meet you guys at Earl's," she shouted at the guys.

A defeated Madeline and her sidekick, Timothy, watched as the little gathering vanished from the courthouse. "Michael got off today, but tomorrow is another day," Madeline said. "I'm going to destroy him one way or another."

"Why are you so bitter?" Timothy asked. "You haven't thought about him in years. You see him at your cousin's wedding, and all of a sudden, you think you can rekindle what you had in med school? Please, girl, Michael is so far beyond that time."

"Shut the hell up, Timothy. The only reason you're here is because you want what you can't have. And you thought if I got Michael, you would get Mona. You're a sorry excuse for a man."

"Watch your mouth, Madeline. I'll cut your tongue off with one of my surgical knives and feed it to the vultures."

"And I'm scared of your sorry ass."

"You should be scared of me. Whose bed did you just get out of?"

"That was a mistake."

"Then you ought to make better choices before you lay with strangers. If you thought leeping with me was going to make me sway your little hearing today, it was quite obvious that it wouldn't have done any good. A slut, always a slut. A liar, always a liar. I don't know what the fuss was all about that Michael used to make about you because while you were good, you weren't that good."

"Let me tell you something, island boy; I don't want your ugly ass. And it appears, neither does Mona. If I can't have Michael, then I don't want anyone. I'm Dr. Madeline Brooks and I deserve what Michael has with Mona. I've got to put Plan B into motion."

"Plan A, B, or C...you'll never have Michael. So you might as well get off your high horse and hang with me, or life, as you know it, is done in the ATL."

Madeline took a good look at Timothy. "You're pathetic and disgusting." Madeline took the heel of her four-inch heel and stabbed Timothy's foot. While Timothy nursed and cursed the pain Madeline inflicted on him, Madeline walked out of the courthouse alone.

64

The happy group of men marched into Earl's Tavern to celebrate Michael's defeat over the villain named Madeline. A few liquid spirits would help lift their emotional spirit.

Earl greeted the group heartily and showed them to a table. "Not much going on at this hour," Earl said. "What can I get you?"

"A round of Coronas for my friends," Michael said. "We're celebrating."

"Coke for me," Marvin called out.

"I may need something stronger," Harold said.

"Me, too," Kenny followed up.

"Corona is fine for me," T said, ending the string of requests.

"What are you supposed to be celebrating?" Earl asked with concern in his voice.

"Vindication from the devil," Michael responded. "I was falsely accused of sexual harassment but have been cleared of any wrongdoing."

"Oh," Earl said. "Well, I'm glad that everything came out all right." Michael nodded his head. "Did you all hear about Peaches?"

"We did," Marvin said. "It's a shame. We wanted her off the streets, but by no means dead."

"I hear her lawyer had something to do with it. He and Peaches had something going on undercover. She must have jilted him somehow."

No one saw Cecil enter the tavern. All heads turned when they heard his voice. "How's everybody? Interesting conversation. Please don't stop talking on my account."

"It's about time you got here. Probably parking that new black luxury XJ Jag far away from everybody else so it won't get dented up," Michael said as Cecil joined the others at the table.

Cecil gave the guys the fist bump. "Yeah, an early Christmas present to myself. I took a chance on riding it downtown." The guys laughed. "My license plate is CCatLaw."

"I like that—Cecil Coleman at Law," Kenny said. "Put in your drink order."

"Okay. I'll have a gin and tonic."

"Let me help you to get this celebration started," Earl said and walked away.

"So what did I miss?" Cecil asked. "I did hear that congrats are in order, Michael. My girl came through again."

"Trina is one hell of a lawyer," Michael said. "Couldn't have done it without her. I think she sent Madeline Brooks packing for good."

"Until her next victim," Harold said.

"I don't know what you did to make that woman drop her panties for you," Kenny teased.

Michael gave Kenny a look that could kill, then looked away. The whole table was quiet, waiting for someone to say something. Michael looked away.

"I'm sick to my stomach because I found out I fathered a child with that madwoman. I have a twelve-year-old daughter somewhere in some boarding school that I have no knowledge of."

"It's not the end of the world, Michael," Cecil said, cutting in. "I have a daughter somewhere also, but the mother refused to let me be a part of her life. I've never seen her, never paid child support, and Trina doesn't know."

"Wow," Marvin said. "The only thing I'm guilty of was wanting to give Denise a baby." He swallowed, then looked in Harold's direction. "Sorry about that, Harold; my timing was off."

"No apologies, cuz. You probably owed me that slap."

"Mona knows," Michael began again. "Madeline threw it out there as if she was hurling a spear. She wanted to kick Mona to the ground, and she succeeded. And it didn't help that my sorry-ass cousin, Timothy, was in the room to push the spear all the way through Mona's heart."

"That was your past, Michael," Kenny said. "Lord knows, I didn't deserve a second chance after all the whoring I did in my early young-man years. I dated Sylvia back then and I didn't know how fortunate I was to have the best that God could provide."

"I stand to differ with you," Marvin said. "I have the best."

"No, I do," Cecil said.

"No one's better than my Claudette," T said at the tail end.

"Well, Sylvia is the best thing that ever happened to me. And when I saw her again, I wasn't going to let her get away."

"All men have some whoring in them," T said.

"Not you, man," Michael said, erupting into a laugh, followed by the others.

"Yes, me."

"T, you're a comedian," Marvin said, unable to keep a straight face.

"Yeah, I did bang the hell out of Madeline when we were in med school," Michael interjected.

"Ooooh," Kenny said. "I knew you were a bad boy."

"But I grew up. Becoming a medical doctor was important to me…and to my family. I wanted to make something of myself, so I straightened up and wrapped myself in my studies instead of in Ms. Brooks."

"Enlightening," T said.

The guys looked up and stopped talking when Earl approached the table with their drinks. "Y'all need to get out of this funk," Earl said, placing a glass of liquid in front of each person. "My cook has arrived and I'm going to have her whip you up some of those good ole wings and fries...on the house."

"That sounds good," Michael said, "but I'm going to pay for it all. Six plates of wings and fries."

"Now this sounds like a celebration," Earl said. "All right, I'm going to run over to cook and put your order in. Carry on."

"Thanks, Earl." Michael saluted him. "I feel better already."

Harold took a sip of Hennessy. He looked around the room and raised his glass. "I slept with Ashley." The guys sat stone-faced while Harold held his head back and swallowed the dark liquid until it was gone.

65

The ladies piled into Sylvia's house as if they were attending a ladies auxiliary meeting. They hung their coats up on the brass rack in the foyer and settled into one of the comfortable couches and chairs in the family room.

"Brrrrrrrr, it's cold," Rachel said, crossing her chest with her arms in an attempt to warm up. "I know you didn't turn off the heat with all of this cold weather we've been having. Snow is still on the ground."

"I'll pump it up a notch for you, girl," Sylvia said, thumping Rachel on the head.

"I'm ready for my drink you promised," Mona said, snickering. "I think I'm going to get sloppy drunk today."

"Where is Ashley?" Trina asked, looking around the room.

"She's coming," replied Claudette. "She had to stop at the store first."

"Did anyone notice how quiet Ashley was today or was it just me?" Sylvia asked. "It reminded me of how she retreated from us after she killed William."

"Uhm," Mona groaned. "I hope whatever it is will keep until another time. Today is about me." The ladies laughed.

"I'm going to fix drinks and I've ordered chicken salad sandwiches and wraps from Chick-fil-A. My housekeeper, Marla, is on her way to pick up the order. I set the DVR to tape *The Mo'Nique Show* last night and we're going to watch it. The cast from *The Game* were Mo'Nique's guests." Sylvia turned the TV on and selected *The Mo'Nique Show* and let it run, although no one seemed to be watching it.

"Bloody Mary for me," Mona ordered, ignoring the other stuff Sylvia rattled on about.

"When did you start drinking Bloody Marys?" Rachel asked. "Trying to be bourgeoisie on us today?"

"Rachel, I'll have you know that I've always been bourgeoisie, and Bloody Mary has always been my drink of choice when I'm in this kind of mood."

"Ouch...well, give me a Margarita," Rachel said, "and let Mona have her Bloody Mary."

"Gin and tonic for me," Trina called out. "After today's tension, I might have to get drunk along with my sister, Mona."

"What are you having, Claudette?" Sylvia asked. "Don't say you're not drinking today."

"Give me a pina colada, if you will," Claudette said in sexy tone. "I feel liberated." Everyone laughed.

"Oh, there's the doorbell. Will you get that for me, Rachel?" Sylvia asked.

"Yeah, it's probably Ashley."

"Hey, everybody," Ashley said, as she followed Rachel into the room after hanging up her coat. "Can I use your bathroom, Sylvia?"

"Now Ashley, what kind of question is that? You know where it is. Everyone else has given me their drink order. What do you want?"

"Water for me, thank you. I've been feeling a little under the weather lately."

"Hurry up," Mona hollered after Ashley and Sylvia. "We've got some girl talk to attend to."

Sylvia returned with everyone's drink. "The food should be here any minute."

"I can't believe this has happened to me," Mona began.

"It's not the end of the world," Trina interjected. "Your man was exonerated today. That should count for something."

Sylvia took a swig of her drink and looked at Mona. "You learned some things about your man that happened in the past...in the past, Mona."

"But what you all fail to realize is that Michael should have confided in me. Yeah, maybe I wouldn't have understood, but I wouldn't be where I am now—pissed and confused. And then Timothy had the nerve to try and grandstand on Madeline's behalf. I can't believe I forgave him."

"Maybe he thought with Michael out of the way, he'd have a second chance with you," Rachel remarked.

"I'm going to ignore what you said, Rachel. Now that Malik on the TV show *The Game* sure is fine," Mona said, focusing her attention toward the TV. "He knows how to whip it on those young, crazy, stupid women."

"You know you'd be getting your freak on, if he gave you half a glance," Rachel quipped.

"I have no qualms about being a cougar, if the right young thing hit my path. I can break any young man down..."

"You're still married to Michael," Sylvia interjected. "So what if he found out he had a daughter whose mother just happens to be..."

"Drumroll..." Claudette said.

"Madeline. It doesn't change anything. It was before your time," Sylvia lifted her glass again and took another sip.

"Uhh, it's my life you're talking about." Mona raised her fists in the air. "I can't believe he double-dipped." The girls laughed.

"He's a man, isn't he?" Rachel asked. "I'm sure there was a lot of sticking before he met you. In fact, how many men have you slept with between Timothy and Michael?"

"Too many to count," Mona said, raising the glass to her mouth and emptying the remainder of her Bloody Mary.

"I've made my point. And I've never known you to have a drought between…"

"Damn, Rachel. There's no need to exploit the truth. Anyway, who are you to talk? I have to hold up both hands to count how many husbands you've had."

"You're a lying ho, Mona."

"Okay, okay, okay," Sylvia said, jumping in. "Let's get back to talking about men. Most of you know Kenny's history. He was a bonafide ho back in the day before we reestablished our relationship, but look at us now. We are joined at the hip."

"But Michael dipped his stick in that bitch Madeline's oil well. And damn, they have proof."

"Maybe it would be wise for Michael to get a DNA test," Claudette interjected. "I wouldn't rely on the words of a liar."

"You know what, Claudette? You are a woman of little words, but you come through and make sense when it's needed."

Claudette waved her hand at Mona. "I've always made sense; it's just that you never stopped long enough to listen." The girls laughed again.

"Here is Marla with our food," Sylvia said, getting up to help. "You all can eat in a minute."

"How about another round of drinks," Rachel crooned. "I think all of our glasses are empty."

"Your hands aren't broken, sister. Fix it yourself, if you're in that big of a hurry."

"Ummm," was all that came out of Rachel's mouth.

"I want you all to know that Ms. Trina walked all over Madeline's testimony."

"She didn't have a chance, Mona," Trina said, getting up from her seat to give Mona a high-five. "First of all, she had a ten-cent attorney and he was no match for me."

"You go, attorney," Rachel shouted. She pointed her finger at the TV. "That Mo'Nique is crazy. Now if I should consider becoming a cougar, that hot thing I'm pointing at—Pooch aka Derwin Davis of the fictitious Miami Sabers—is who I'd want," Rachel said, shaking her head with her mouth open like a woman in heat. "Have you seen the six-pack on that brother?"

"Marvin would kick his ass and yours, too," Sylvia said, as she brought in the drinks on a tray, followed by Marla with the food.

"Whatever. But there wouldn't be anything left after I finished sexing that cutie to shreds. Melanie and Janae, move over young sisters, and let an experienced older woman tender that brother." The room exploded with laughter.

"These folks are actors and actresses on a TV show," Claudette began, "who have lives of their own. I'm sure they don't even act like the characters they portray on the show."

"It doesn't matter," Rachel said. "I want that cutie, Derwin Davis, or whatever his real name happens to be."

"You're hopeless, Rachel," Sylvia said. "Drink that Margarita and forget about that fine boy because he's not thinking about you."

"Whatever."

"I was raped by my mother's brother a long time ago," Trina blurted out. Hands flew to everyone's faces, their eyes fixed in place. Sylvia went to Trina and hugged her as tears flowed down her face. "My mother didn't believe me, even though I fought with my uncle, and he had the scars to prove it. Nevertheless, I got pregnant and I had the baby aborted. Cecil doesn't know about the rape. It took me a long time to have a sexual relationship with a man."

"I'm so sorry, Trina," Mona said. "I think I speak for all of us. That's a terrible burden for you to carry."

"It was because I had no one to talk to about it. When I got older, I promised myself I was going to be somebody and I buried myself in my work. I've deprived Cecil of the child he has always wanted, and I feel so selfish because now, after being around you all, I wish I had a child. I got my tubes tied six years ago."

"They are God's precious gift," Sylvia said, still rubbing Trina's back.

"Ashley, why are you in the corner all by yourself with your mute button on?" Mona asked. "I know you have something to contribute to the conversation."

"I'm pregnant," Ashley blurted out. "I'm going to have a baby… got the results a few minutes ago when I was in Sylvia's bathroom." Ashley looked straight ahead while the others looked at her in disbelief.

66

As the day wore on, the needle on the thermometer took a slight nosedive. Trina turned the heat on in her car, shivering as she waited for it to warm up. She honked the horn at the others as they left the warmth of Sylvia's home; each woman caught up in the revelations of the day, especially Ashley's shocking reveal—that didn't-see-it-coming announcement that she was pregnant. Who in the world had Ashley met in such a short time to have fathered the embryo growing inside of her? Trina let the thought roll around in her head. No. It couldn't be Harold.

Trina surprised herself, sharing for the first time the story of how she was sexually abused. And she was glad she'd done it. The ladies...her girlfriends were so understanding and didn't judge her actions. If only her mother had been as nurturing, maybe she'd have a daughter or son that she would've been able to watch grow from childhood to adulthood, go to college, get married and have kids of their own. Trina shrugged her shoulders; she would never have children. In actuality, it was time to forgive her mother and move on.

Trina drove the few blocks to her house. She pulled up to the mailbox, emptied it, and drove into the garage.

"Umph, Cecil isn't home yet," Trina said out loud. "The guys must be having some kind of celebration."

Dragging into the house, Trina laid the mail down on the oak table that stood in the foyer before taking off her coat and scarf. Moving into the family room, she dropped her purse on the couch, kicked off her heels, raised her arms in the air and yawned. It had been a long and exhausting day, but one that she gloated in. It was priceless to see Madeline's face as she viewed her starring role in her first X-rated movie. Well, it may not have been the first. And Brandeis loved every minute of it. He'd gotten his money and was through with Dr. Madeline Brooks after the way she treated him.

Trina turned on the nightly news. Crime, crime, and more crime inundated the news. She was about sick of it until she heard Robert Jordan's name. Her ears perked up like antennae reading a coded message that hit its airwave. Jordan had gotten out on bail, but it appeared that some evidence turned up that was considered more incriminating than what the authorities originally had in their possession. No doubt, it was a crucial piece that would implicate Jordan in Peaches' death.

Trina reached for her purse and pulled out her BlackBerry. She had forgotten to turn it back on after she'd left the courthouse. Once turned on, she noted at least a half-dozen phone calls had come from her office. She paced the floor and after four rings, there was no answer. She hung up, dialed again, and moved from room to room, impatience setting in.

As she walked through the foyer, she picked up the mail that she'd laid on the table earlier. She cocked her head and held the phone to her ear while she thumbed through the pieces of mail until her eyes landed on an envelope with a return address marked "Superior Court, DeKalb County." She sliced the thick envelope open with her fingers, adjusting the BlackBerry between her ear and shoulder. Clumsily, she pulled out the contents and scanned the document with eyes trained to extract essential information.

She balked, then froze completely. The BlackBerry slid from underneath her chin and fell to the floor.

"Back child support payment? Who in the hell is Simone Charise Coleman? This has to be a mistake." Trina turned the envelope over. The summons was addressed to Cecil Coleman.

"Cecil?" Trina asked out loud. "Why would he be getting this notice? He doesn't have a child or does he? All this time he's harassed me about not having a child. I'll be damned, in the shadow of our marriage, he's got a grown-ass baby girl who now wants Daddy to pay up."

Trina went to the bar and fixed herself a gin and tonic. Silence engulfed her thoughts. She held her head, then picked up the glass and tasted her drink, letting the liquid swirl around in her mouth. She forced herself to absorb the contents of the summons while she paced the room. Tears joined the anger that was building inside of Trina's head. Choking on her tears, she slammed the glass down, breaking it into shards.

"He has a damn child. Cecil has a damn child, and all of this time, he has accused me of depriving him of being a father. He has a damn child that he hasn't taken care of. What would Cecil have done, if I had given him the child he wanted?"

With lips stuck together, she willed herself to stop crying. She stuck her fingers in her mouth and bit her fingernails. The hurt, the betrayal she felt was deep because she knew in her heart that Cecil was well aware that he had a child. They shared everything... well, almost everything; well, hell they both had secrets. It was going to take faith and a whole lot of forgiveness to get them through yet another ordeal. She thanked God for her sistahs, who she knew would be there if she needed them.

Tired of the silence, Trina strolled into her bedroom, flopped down on the bed, and waited for Cecil to come home.

67

Woody and Buzz Lightyear, the animated characters of *Toy Story 2*, were entangled in a brawl. Michael Jr. was a captive audience as he sat silent, watching his favorite characters embroil themselves in another mess, only to have to defuse one situation after another. Arms folded, Mona looked in on him as she wandered throughout the house, analyzing and reanalyzing all that had transpired earlier in the day. She loved Michael Sr. with all of her heart and soul, but the realization that he would be forever connected to Madeline Brooks broke her heart.

She jumped at the sound of a door opening. Almost as if Michael Jr. had telepathy, he ran past Mona in the kitchen just as his dad entered. Michael Sr. took off his coat and laid it on the back of a chair, then scooped Michael Jr. up and gave his little man a man kiss.

"Hi, Daddy," Michael Jr. said. "I'm watching *Toy Story 2*."

"Your favorite movie," Michael Sr. said. "How many times have you watched this one?"

"Six, and Woody was stolen by the toy collector."

Michael Sr. hugged his son again, gave him a once over, and let him slide to the floor. He saw Mona observing them silently with a stealthy look on her face. "Son, I love you."

"I love you, too, Daddy."

"Look, buddy, I need to talk to your mother a moment. After I finish talking to her, I promise that I'll sit down and watch the rest of *Toy Story 2* with you."

"Yeah!" Michael Jr. shouted and sauntered off.

"Hey, baby," Michael began.

"Hey," Mona said, barely above a whisper.

Michael crossed the kitchen and stood in front of Mona as she leaned with her back against the granite countertop. He held the countertop with his hands, making Mona a prisoner. Mona unfolded her arms and raised them in an attempt to push Michael back. He gently wrapped his hands around her wrists and brought them back behind her, until they rested on the countertop with their bodies touching.

"I hope you aren't still mad at me," Michael said, his mouth close to hers. "I'm innocent and Trina proved that today. I love you, girl...only you."

Mona untangled her hands from his and folded them across her chest, but allowed her eyes to meet Michael's since he wouldn't let go of his gaze. "You have a daughter with Madeline. She's not going away."

"I don't have a daughter until I take a DNA test that proves such. I won't disagree with the fact that I was intimately linked with Madeline, but that was a long time ago. But give me a break. Wouldn't you think that someone who claims that they're so in to me, would've checked on my whereabouts before now and at least have the decency to let me know that I fathered their child?" Michael released his arms and walked to the refrigerator and took out a bottle of water.

"That's the problem. Madeline isn't a decent woman and you had a...a relationship with her."

Michael swung around to face Mona, at the same time, throwing his hands in the air. "That's beside the point, Mona. What kind of mother puts their child in a boarding school for the better part of their life? I wouldn't have known anything about a Michelle if

Madeline hadn't made a last-ditch effort to pin that sexual harassment suit on me. During the few months she's been in Atlanta,
Madeline hasn't once mentioned that she has a daughter, let alone
that she and I have a daughter."

Mona's arms were still folded and she quite liked the fact that
Michael was standing his ground about his mysterious child. "And
what will you do if this Michelle person turns out to be your child?"

Michael looked at Mona thoughtfully and took a sip of water.
"I'd own up to my responsibilities and possibly establish a
relationship, if she wanted to do so."

Mona walked over to where Michael stood with the bottle of
water to his mouth. She took the bottle out of his hand, set it on
the table, and wrapped her arms around his waist.

"That's what I love about you. You're a man of integrity and
always take care of yours. I wouldn't want you any other way. I'm
going to be honest and say that I hope all of Madeline's theatrics
about you having a daughter is a lie, but should the tests come
back positive, I'll be in your corner."

"Baby, that's all I needed to hear." Michael held Mona by the
back of her head and kissed her passionately.

68

The yellow-and-white Checker Cab rolled into the subdivision with no fanfare. In its own way, the cab was somewhat out-of-place as the upscale neighborhood rarely caught a glimpse of the yellow-painted car with the black-and-white checkerboard running around the perimeter of its body on that side of Atlanta. Usually, sleek limousines ushered the neighborhood passengers to their destinations, but no one seemed to care one way or the other.

Simone sat back and watched as the cab drove past the fancy homes with their wrought-iron gates; full-elevation brick exteriors; and well-kept, manicured, and landscaped yards. Fancy expensive Christmas scenes played out on some of the front lawns. It only meant that the people who resided in the neighborhood had more money than the have-nots, and Simone was unimpressed.

She unfolded the paper with the address written on it in bold black letters—"555 Lake Front Drive." The cabby made a sudden left turn and drove a couple of blocks. Hidden from view and the rest of the subdivision was a huge lake surrounded by brush and tall pine trees in the background. Simone stared in wonderment, then brought her face forward when the cabby jerked the car to a full stop.

"You're here," the cabby said.

Simone pinched her lips together, then let out a soft sigh. She looked to the right and took in the view. Her immediate thoughts were interrupted by the cabby pulling the door open. Although somewhat reluctant to get out, Simone finally emerged. "Brrr," Simone said and wrapped her scarf tight around her neck.

The cabby closed the passenger door and rushed to the trunk of the car. He retrieved Simone's matching red suitcase and overnight bag and placed them on the sidewalk. Simone paid her fare, picked up her suitcases, and proceeded up the walkway without giving the cabby a second glance. She only looked back when she heard the cab speed away.

Her eyes took it all in, and her thoughts ran rampant. Simone had lived sixteen-and-a-half years on this earth in a substandard environment, when she could have been living the good life. All the questions she'd asked her mother over the years about her father, only to be told he was dead, left her infuriated. Now that her mother had found someone she wanted to give all of her attention to, she decided it was time for Simone to become acquainted with a man she thought to be dead, but somehow had risen from the ashes.

Simone hated her mother. How could she ship her off to someone she didn't know? What if she wasn't welcomed? Heck, it was Christmas, a time that she and her mother always shared together.

Simone loved Christmas because she and her mother would go shopping for gifts for her grandma and grandpa, and her mother would always get Simone what she wanted. Christmas Day was always filled with love as they sat down to Grandma's table filled with good food that they ate until they stuffed themselves. Simone remembered how her eyes filled with tears when she opened up the gift from her grandma that contained her first diamond bracelet.

Now her mother wanted to be alone with...with some dude named Ted. He took up all of her mother's time, and Simone resented him for it. She resented the way her mother dismissed her as if she no longer existed in her life, but the day her mother told her they needed to talk and banished her from her life, is the day Simone will never forget.

Her mother said it was time that Simone's father paid his dues. She'd raised Simone, and like any good mother, saw to it that she'd been clothed, fed, had a place to sleep, and got a decent education. *She was done*, Simone remembered her mother's words, and Simone was done with her.

Simone stood in front of the large oak door with the small peephole at eye level. On each side of the door was a panel...a row of two-by-two windows that ran down both sides of the door, draped with a sheer mesh, off-white-colored drapery. Simone was tempted to look through the window panes but thought better of it. She sighed, put her luggage on the porch, and reached up to ring the doorbell.

She couldn't do it; she couldn't ring the bell. Reaching up again, Simone hesitated, but before she could talk herself out of it, she pushed the bell. A deep sigh rolled from within her. Simone waited, but no one came. It had never occurred to her that there was a possibility that no one would be home. "Brrr," she said, as the cold air engulfed her.

There was nowhere for her to go because her mother made it clear that she wasn't to return. Simone had enough money to take a cab back to the city and get a hotel for a night or two, but what would she do after that? She could go to her grandma's house, but she wanted nothing to do with her mother.

Ten minutes, fifteen minutes passed and anger filled Simone's heart. She picked up her suitcases and was about to turn when the door suddenly opened. A woman in her late-thirties or early-forties stared back at her. She was beautiful and had a nice smile. Simone smiled back, although she didn't really want to. But because she needed a place to stay, she relaxed her lips and smiled back.

"Hello," the lady said, eying Simone's suitcases with suspicion. "May I help you?"

"My name is Simone, and I'm looking for my daddy."

Laced with an attitude, Trina looked the young lady up and down who stood on her front porch with luggage in hand as if she was coming for a visit. She looked to be about fifteen or sixteen, medium height, nice-length hair combed around her face, wearing a black-leather coat that covered her clothes, a purple-and-pink knit scarf situated around her neck, and what appeared to be a pair of black leggings clutching bony legs in the dead of winter.

"Sweetie, you must have the wrong house."

"No, I'm positive this is the right house. Your address is 555 Lake Front Drive."

The smile left Trina's face and the letter addressed to Cecil from DeKalb County surfaced in Trina's memory bank. "And who is your daddy?"

Simone looked into Trina's eyes without blinking. "Cecil Coleman is my daddy."

Trina stood on the porch with her hands on her hip. As an attorney, she had prosecuted many cases and had won just as many over the years, making decisions and utilizing her best judgment in matters that would boggle the mind. Standing on her porch was a case she wasn't sure what to do with...well, she knew what she wanted to do with it, but her conscience and the attorney she lived with would not like her ruling.

Trina looked for any trace of Cecil in the girl who called herself Simone, and thought that there might have been a small resemblance in the way she turned up her lips. Trina sighed, unsure of what this meant and how it would affect her life with Cecil. He had a daughter, and she had nothing. And now she wished she hadn't said anything to the ladies about her past, her rape, or her abortion.

"Well, can I come in?" Simone asked with some confidence.

"Not so fast, sister. Your daddy isn't here," Trina shot back.

"Well, can I wait inside for him?" Simone said defiantly.

"What's with your suitcase? We weren't prepared for any visitors."

"I've come to live with my daddy. My mother doesn't want me anymore."

Trina looked at Simone, trying to quiet the animosity that was building up inside of her. Cecil might be her daddy, and 'might' was a pretty strong word, but Trina wasn't ready to play stepmother to some hormone-enraged teenager who threatened to disrupt her life. Simone looked afraid and was in full beg mode for a place to stay. Trina moved back from the door and held it open.

"Come in."

69

Cecil drove south on Interstate 85. He laughed out loud as he recalled the last few minutes of the conversation at Earl's. The guys had let their guard down and were playing the dirty dozens.

Your ex-lover, Madeline, got so much on top, she might be hiding the daughter you haven't seen between each breast, Marvin had said to Michael, slapping the table while the others were doubled over with laughter.

After Peaches blackmailed your behind to the tune of fifty-thousand dollars and put those naked pictures of you and her in your wife's hands, I bet you wished that Rachel had beat you stupid in Steak and Ale for having lunch with your secretary, Michael said in return. *It would've been a whole lot cheaper.*

Cecil slapped the steering wheel at the memory. That was some funny stuff. Earl walked up to them upon hearing Peaches' name too many times, though, and told them the celebration was over, that they had had enough to drink, and it was time for them to go home to their wives. It didn't take them long to get up and scramble to their cars.

Cecil was happiest because he knew that Trina helped the celebration along by defeating Madeline Brooks at her game while giving Michael his life back. His baby deserved an expensive gift from Tiffany's, and he was going shopping tomorrow to make sure that whatever it was he purchased would be wrapped and under the Christmas tree.

Cruising along, Cecil looked down at his BlackBerry as a call came through his Bluetooth. It was Trina, and he hit the Bluetooth button immediately.

"Hey, baby, I'm on my way home."

"That's good because you've got a visitor."

"A visitor? Who is it? I'm not expecting anyone. I left the guys about an hour ago."

"Well, maybe you need to scoot home a little faster because I'm not used to entertaining this type of visitor."

"Trina, why are you being so mysterious? Who in the hell is it? Your momma?"

"Don't talk about my momma, boy, but you're going to die when I tell you who it is."

"It can't be anybody but my country cousins from Alabama that finally sniffed out where I live." Cecil laughed. "It probably took them two years to find me with their compass and outdated world atlas."

"It would've been funny, if it had been them standing on the porch. But I can guarantee that you're not going to laugh when I tell you who it is."

"Well, tell me," Cecil said. "You're ruining my good mood."

"Simone."

"Who in the hell is Simone?"

"Your daughter. She's here with her luggage with plans to stay... not only for one winter, but possibly two."

There was nothing but quiet. No nasty comebacks.

"Cecil, are you there?"

"Ah shhhhhhhhh........."

"Cecil?" Trina called. *Boom, boom, boom* was all she could hear. "Cecil, say something. Cecil, baby, what's going on?"

Trina's breathing became labored. The phone still pinned to her ear, she heard background noises, but Cecil had yet to say anything. "Cecil," Trina called out once more. "Talk to me, baby. Talk to me. Everything is going to be all right."

Trina shot around at the tap on her shoulder. Simone jumped back as the look on Trina's face scared her.

"Is there something wrong with my daddy?" Simone asked.

"Your daddy? That man is my husband...my whole world. And at the end of the day, whether he's your daddy or not, we're the ones who'll grow old together."

"Well, you don't have to be nasty about it. All I did was ask," Simone said, rolling her eyes and shaking her head.

"How old are you?"

"Old enough to want to meet my daddy." Simone's nostrils flared and she turned to walk away.

Trina grabbed Simone's arm. "I'm sorry. Don't go. I don't know what's going on, but I feel like something awful may have happened to your daddy."

"Hey, sweetie," Kenny said, when he heard Sylvia's voice. "You girls have a good time?"

"The guys must've had a better time since you haven't found your way home yet."

"I'm on my way home now, baby. You'll have all of my attention."

"You sound guilty. What did you and the fellas get in to?"

"We drank a lot of liquor and had a lot of laughs. Time got away from us. Lord, Cecil just flew past me in that new Jag he bought."

"I know he was happy that Trina won Michael's case and put that crazy Madeline in her place."

"You know... Oh my God...Jesus. Sylvia!"

"What, Kenny? What's going on?"

"Cecil. Oh, Jesus."

"What, Kenny? What about Cecil?"

"Sylvia, Cecil ran into the back of a Mayflower moving van... and now his car is pinned underneath it. Damn. I've got to stop and help him. I'll call you later."

Southbound Interstate 85 became a strip of horror—a chaotic scene. Traffic was now backed up for a mile or more as the two-car accident became a fifteen-car pile-up. In the far-right lane, a black Jaguar was crushed underneath the back of a large May-flower moving truck. Sirens could be heard in the distance while witnesses to the event pulled to the side to offer help.

Kenny pulled over and parked his car on the shoulder of the interstate along with others. He rushed between the cars of the onlookers who had slowed to a crawl to observe the horrific scene. Sweat poured from Kenny's brow as he made his way to the May-flower truck. He was stopped short as several police cars pulled up and began to block off two lanes of traffic as well as assess the damage. Flares were put out to warn oncoming cars and highway patrolmen directed traffic.

As Kenny crept toward the site of the wreckage, a highway patrolman pushed out both hands to block access.

"Sir, you need to go back to your car and wait for an officer to speak with you."

"I'm not part of the pile-up; that's my good friend's vehicle under this truck."

"Sir, you don't want to see this. The top portion of the car is completely caved in, and until the tow truck gets here, we won't be able to tell if your friend, or whomever is in the car, made it. But I can tell you this; it doesn't look good at all. There's a lot of twisted metal, and the car appears crushed in the worst way."

"You may need my assistance; that's my friend under there," Kenny repeated, pointing at the car.

"Are you sure it's your friend?" the officer asked.

"Yes, that's his license plate number, CCATLAW, which stands for Cecil Coleman at Law."

"All right, move over to the side and don't get in the way. If we need your assistance, we'll let you know."

Kenny stood next to a police car and stared at Cecil's car that was stuffed underneath the truck. There were no signs of life, and Kenny feared the worst. The scene reminded him of how fragile and vulnerable life was and how much he loved his family and friends. Tears began to flow down his face and he shuddered at the thought that he might not see Cecil alive again. Kenny was very much awake now and vowed to not drink and drive again.

Traffic was now a virtual parking lot. A tow truck, fire truck, and a couple of ambulances pushed their way through to the accident site. Kenny watched as a team used the Jaws of Life to pry the car from underneath the truck. Then he saw one of the persons from the wrecking team hold their head down, then turn around and shake it at the others. Kenny shook uncontrollably.

Two patrolmen pulled up a white cloth to obscure the accident site while paramedics moved in to pull the victim from the vehicle. Kenny's shoes wouldn't move and stayed locked in place, waiting to assist if needed. When it was all over, a white sheet covered the remains that were placed inside one of the ambulances. The officer who had spoken to Kenny came over and gave him the news.

"Sorry that the news isn't better; your friend didn't make it. His head was decapitated from his body."

A loud wail came from Kenny's body. He dropped to his knees right in front of the patrolman, placed his head to the ground and cried out loud. Before Kenny knew what was happening, two paramedics picked him up and moved him near the ambulance and took his blood pressure and temp. When given clearance, one of the paramedics stayed with him until he calmed down. There was a line of cars with injured folks that still needed attention.

When Kenny felt up to it, he was escorted to his car with a warning not to drive, if he didn't think it was safe for him to do so, given his state of mind. Kenny was thinking about how lucky he was not to have been given a breathalyzer.

70

A cold chill coursed through Sylvia's body. She waited patiently for Kenny to call, and now she was worried after almost forty-five minutes had passed, and he hadn't called or answered his phone.

With a hand on her hip, Sylvia stood still in the middle of the family room and let her thought processes work. Before she knew it, she reached down and picked her keys off the end table. Next she collected Kenny Jr. from in front of the television and headed outside. She jumped in her car and headed for Trina's a few minutes away.

In three minutes flat, Sylvia was in front of Cecil and Trina's house. All seemed quiet, but she sat still before getting out. She wanted the story Kenny had conjured up in her head to have a happy ending.

"Let's go, Little Kenny, and see what Aunt Trina is doing."

"Can I watch *SpongeBob* at her house?"

"We'll see."

Sylvia grabbed Kenny Jr.'s hand and scrambled up the steps to Trina's house two at a time. Sylvia took a deep breath, pushed the doorbell, and waited.

"I've got to go pee, Mommy," Kenny Jr. said.

"Not now, Kenny. Hold on a moment. We've got to see if Trina is here first."

"I've got to go bad, Mommy."

As Sylvia was about to ring the doorbell again, a young lady answered the door. Sylvia jerked her head back and squinted her eyes as she searched her brain for recognition. The girl looked back at Sylvia, not amused in the slightest.

"Hello, my name is Sylvia. Is Trina home?"

"Yes, she's here. She's pretty upset, though."

Without waiting for the girl to invite her in, Sylvia pushed past her, with Kenny Jr. hanging onto her arm.

"Well, damn," the girl said.

"What did you say, and who are you?" Sylvia asked with a scowl on her face. "If you haven't noticed, there's a child in your presence."

"Well, excuse me. Everyone is so rude around here."

"I didn't catch your name."

"I didn't give it to you."

Sylvia sighed. "I apologize. I need to see Trina."

The girl stepped aside when Trina entered the foyer, Kenny Jr. making *shame on you* motions with his fingers. Tears were in Trina's eyes and she seemed paralyzed with fear.

"Trina, what's wrong?" Sylvia asked. "Are you okay?"

Trina shook her head no and the tears burst forth. She grabbed Sylvia and held on.

"Tell me what's wrong, Trina."

All heads turned when the young girl spoke. "My daddy is dead. He was in an automobile accident."

"Your daddy?" Sylvia asked.

Trina wiped her face with a Kleenex and held her other hand up for the young girl to be quiet. "This is Simone, Cecil's daughter."

"Oh," Sylvia said, taking another look at Simone.

"We met less than two hours ago. I was on the phone talking to Cecil...telling him that Simone was here, when all of a sudden, I heard Cecil yell out and then this terrible noise. I was notified... received the call that he had been killed minutes before you arrived. It's all my fault," Trina wailed. "If I hadn't called to tell him about Simone, he would be alive now."

"I'm so sorry, Trina." Sylvia put her arms around Trina and hugged her.

Trina pulled back and wiped her eyes. "What brings you around?"

Sylvia sighed. "Kenny witnessed the accident. We were on the phone when Kenny saw Cecil drive by. The next thing I knew, Kenny was saying that Cecil hit a truck and he had to help him. I haven't heard from him since then, and I came around to see if you'd heard anything."

Trina sopped up her tears with the Kleenex. "I don't believe it, Sylvia. Cecil can't be gone. I don't know what I'll do without him."

"I can't begin to imagine how you feel, but you know you've got us and your extended family to lean on."

Trina shook her head. "Thanks, Sylvia, but if I hadn't made that call, my husband would be alive."

"Don't beat yourself up, Trina. You couldn't have predicted that Cecil was going to run into that truck."

"I know. Do you know what I really feel bad about, though?"

"What, sweetie?"

"That I may have cheated Simone out of meeting her father."

Sylvia looked from Trina to Simone, who sat sulking on the couch. "Hindsight is twenty-twenty."

Everyone jumped when Sylvia's phone rang. "It's Kenny."

"Hey, baby," Kenny said softly.

"I've been worried about you."

Kenny sighed, and then there was a moment of silence. His voice was faint. "Cecil is dead, baby. He didn't make it. Someone needs to get to Trina."

"I'm with her now; she already knows. I'll call the others."

"How is Trina doing?"

"Not well."

"I'm on my way. I'll see you when I get there."

"Drive safely." Sylvia ended the call, closed her eyes, and prayed.

71

"Rachel, stop screaming and call Claudette and Ashley," Sylvia shouted. "I'll call Mona and Michael. Tell them we're at Trina's."

"I can't believe Cecil is dead. My God, Sylvia, when is all the pain going to stop?"

"I've asked myself the same question."

"Where is Kenny Jr.?"

"He's with Simone."

"Who's Simone?"

"Long story. I'll tell you all about it when I see you. Make the phone calls, Rachel, and get your butt over here. I'm a nervous wreck."

"Okay, okay, okay. Marvin is looking at me with a thousand questions. See you shortly." And the line was dead.

Sylvia beat her hands on the wall. "God help us!"

Sylvia and Kenny, Rachel and Marvin, Mona and Michael, Claudette and Tyrone, Harold, Ashley, and their children were assembled at Trina's. Everyone was numb from the news. Even Mona was at a loss for words.

"Everybody, we're going to pray for Trina and her family," Marvin said, as he held his wife's hand and reached for Trina's with the other. They made a large semi-circle, each family grouped together.

"Trina, I'm so sorry for your loss. Cecil was our brother, and we're going to miss him dearly. In the short time that I've known him, Cecil has been more than a friend and a confidant. I can't believe that we were together only a few hours ago, and now we're here...like we were when...Denise left us a short time ago." Marvin looked in Harold's direction, but Harold was staring at Ashley. "And, it's the friends you cherish the most that you want around at a time like this. Let us pray."

"Excuse me," a young voice interrupted. "My name is Simone; I'm Cecil's daughter."

The grief-stricken group lifted their bowed heads and stared at the young girl who had dared to interrupt Marvin's prayer. If it had been another time, another place, or another set of circumstances, lips would be moving wildly and ferociously, chewing on the piece of gossip that would have made any tabloid front page sizzle. So the group just stared as Simone continued.

"I know you don't know me, but I'm a young lady who wanted to meet her father. Tonight, I lost the chance to do that, but if you'll let me," Simone looked up at Trina and then away, "if you'll let me, I'd like to offer the prayer."

Twisted eyes continued to stare at Simone while their inquiring minds wanted to get at the heart of the story of this newcomer. Their silence, however, thickened the air like a bad pot of lumpy gravy. But it was Trina who spoke up between sniffles, offering a smile to Simone. "Go ahead, Simone."

With every head bowed and eyes closed, Simone began. "Dear God, my whole life I prayed for a mother and father who'd love me. After being told and believing for most of my life that my daddy was dead, I suddenly find out that my father is alive. I wanted to meet him, possibly have a relationship with him. I missed the part of life where daddies cuddle their daughters, go with them to the father/daughter dance, have conversations about becoming a teenager and going out on a first date.

"Today was supposed to have been the day I met my dad for the first time. I wasn't sure if he would like me, but after my mother put me out, and I had nowhere else to go, I was going to do everything in my power to convince my dad I wouldn't be any trouble, and that all I wanted from him was his love and some help to go to college."

The group was getting restless, the children agitated, but no one opened their mouths to complain.

"I was denied the one thing I wanted. All I wanted was for my dad to acknowledge me and say he loved me. He must have been a nice man because everyone seems to love him. I pray that my dad is in a better place."

Simone stopped, and there were collective sighs in the room. And then, Simone broke down and cried. "All I wanted was my daddy...I wanted his love, and now he can't give it to me."

Trina went to Simone and put her arms around her and gave her a big hug. Lifting Simone's face, Trina's wet tears met Simone's. "What a beautiful prayer, Simone, and you are not to blame for Cecil's death. You're welcome here as long as you want, and you've got all of these surrogate aunts, uncles, and cousins who'll support you as well."

Sylvia went to Simone and hugged her, followed by the others. "We'll get through this."

Out of nowhere, Harold blurted out. "I know we're here for Trina...Cecil, but while we're huddled together, I think Ashley and I have something we need to tell you."

"Oh, hell, here we go," Mona said. "I've got to take a seat on this. Children, go into the game room until we call you." Michael Jr., Kenny Jr., Serena and Reagan went into the other room.

Ashley stared straight ahead without saying a word. She didn't react when Harold spoke.

"Ashley is pregnant and having our baby. Please don't stand in judgment. It is what it is—one life for another."

"What a cruel thing to say," Claudette said, throwing a pointed finger at Harold. "I'm sure that Trina would rather have her husband with her."

"Just as Ashley wished her daughter, Reagan, was with her?"

"Oh, so is this what it's all about, Ashley?" Claudette asked, redirecting her anger. "You letting Harold do all the talking for you now? Go on and have your baby because you ain't getting Reagan. Come on, T; let's go."

"It isn't like that, Claudette," Ashley finally spoke up.

"So, you're saying you don't want Reagan back?"

"Don't put words in my mouth, Claudette. I'm not saying that at all. I respect the fact that you and T have adopted Reagan as your own, and I can't think of better people to be her parents. And I would never do anything to take Reagan away from you or compromise our friendship."

"Well, you better put Harold in check and tell him to get the story straight."

"Claudette, Ashley," Sylvia said. "Trina is suffering. This is not the time to hash out your differences."

"Trina is the reason I'm here," Ashley said defiantly, giving Harold a mean look. "I shared with you ladies earlier today that I was pregnant, and now you know who the daddy is. The end." Ashley went to Trina and gave her a hug. "I'm a phone call away, if you need anything."

"Thanks, Ashley," Trina said. "I'll let you know about services for Cecil when I get them arranged."

Ashley nodded her head and was out of the door, followed by Harold.

"That's a darn shame," Claudette continued. "You all said that heifer wanted my baby. Now, I'm really pissed off."

"Calm down, Claudette," T said. "Ashley had nothing to do with Harold's outburst. Harold felt some kind of guilt...used this moment to get sympathy for what he'd done because he talked about it earlier today. Jesus, Denise hasn't been gone that long."

"He's your cousin, Marvin, and he does have history," Mona interjected.

"Leave it alone," Marvin countered. "Harold is a widower and Ashley is single. They didn't do anything wrong except exercise some freedom because they were both needy and lonely. I can't believe y'all have the nerve to sit in judgment. Remember, we all have skeletons."

The mood in the room made an abrupt switch. All of a sudden Trina erupted in laughter, the tears still streaming down her face. "Come here, Simone." Trina put her arms around her. "Welcome to the family. These people love your daddy, but they always have some kind of drama going on." Simone smiled. "But at the end of the day, even with all of their drama, it's these people, my family, who I can count on day or night for friendship and some good sisterly and brotherly love."

"That's right," everyone shouted almost simultaneously.

Trina looked around and smiled. "We are family."

Reagan hugged the back of the wall and began to cry. She couldn't believe grown ups were arguing about her. Did Ashley, her biological mother, really give her up completely? She loved Claudette, but Ashley was going to have another baby who she'd be giving all of her love. All that talk about Simone wanting to know her father made Reagan want to be with her mother, but she didn't know how to say it.

ABOUT THE AUTHOR

Suzetta Perkins is the author of several novels including *Behind the Veil*; *A Love So Deep*; *EX-Terminator: Life After Marriage*; *Déjà Vu*; *Nothing Stays the Same* and *Betrayed*, and a contributing author of *My Soul to His Spirit*. She is also the co-founder of the Sistahs Book Club. Suzetta resides in Fayetteville, North Carolina. Visit her at www.suzettaperkins.com, www.facebook.com/suzetta.perkins, Suzetta Perkins' Fan Page on Facebook, Twitter @authorsue, and nubianqe2@aol.com.